THE BORODINO SACRIFICE

CHASING MERCURY
BOOK ONE

Paul Phillips

I QUATERNI BOOKS

In memory of Peter O'Donnell,
with thanks for the inspiration
& apologies for any imitation.

When you are old and grey and full of sleep,
And nodding by the fire, take down this book,
And slowly read, and dream of the soft look
Your eyes had once, and of their shadows deep;

How many loved your moments of glad grace,
And loved your beauty with love false or true,
But one man loved the pilgrim soul in you,
And loved the sorrows of your changing face;

And bending down beside the glowing bars,
Murmur, a little sadly, how Love fled
And paced upon the mountains overhead
And hid his face amid a crowd of stars.

W. B. Yeats (1865–1939)

PART ONE

BETWEEN THE LINES

CHAPTER ONE

He spotted the girl immediately. Even as the ragtag band of partisans dismounted from the vehicles, he made out the slightness of her wrists and neck and shoulders in the makeshift fatigues.

Bradley lay motionless on the carpet of pine needles and watched the play develop a hundred and fifty yards away. Three cars were hull-down in the long grass – Mr Jones' Citroën sedan to one side, the captured staff car and Kübelwagen on the other. Including the girl, the partisans numbered six, all decked out in a medley of moleskins and corduroys and carrying an assortment of weapons that spanned a century or more.

Facing them across the clearing, Mr Jones looked out of place in his hat and raincoat. Hot too. It was a fine spring morning. Birds and bugs chirped non-stop and sunbeams made a dancehall glitter-ball in the treetops. Beyond the trees where the land fell away, the snow was melting on the mountains. It was one of those scenes that war often surprised you with, when you found it hard to believe anything was wrong in the world, much less everything.

Jones raised his hat in greeting, picked up his suitcase like his train had come in and set off towards the partisans. Limeys, Bradley cursed under his breath for about the zillionth time, though not without admiration. Back where he came from, they called it chutzpah.

But not around here, anymore.

The partisans gave Mr Jones a wave and moved forward

too, but they were carrying their weapons at the ready. The girl stayed in back. He still couldn't see her face under the peaked cap she wore.

Hearty voices, too far off to make out the language. The partisan leader was a big sonofabitch with a wild red beard, a rabbit-fur bonnet right out of the Jersey Barrens and a manner designed to intimidate. Worst luck for him, behind all the jolly japes baloney, Jones was built and balanced like a linebacker.

There was an exchange of smokes of course. It would be a bad deal otherwise. Seeing the blue curls in the shafts of sunshine Bradley sniffed, beguiled by the seeming closeness. But that was his mind playing tricks. At this distance all he could smell was the sap of the pines and the cindery mass of the soil they had annexed. And himself, sweating under all this netting and foliage. He would have loved one of those cigarettes. It was the perfect moment in the perfect morning for a smoke. But he had a job to do.

The partisans had something else to exchange. The girl brought forward a package the size of a picture book. When she handed it to redbeard she barely came up to his chest.

Jones reached out. What followed happened so fast that someone without Bradley's special gift might have missed the half of it, or jumbled up the sequence in their memories, which was what most folks did. Not Sam Bradley though. Ever since he could remember, he'd had the knack of seeing things happen like slow motion movies. It had made him a fair ball player and in a fairer world might have gotten him into college. Once, it had made him a fair soldier too.

The girl lifted her submachine gun and fired a burst in the air. No muzzle flash in the sunlight but Bradley registered five spent cases ejecting. He even noted how she controlled the gun as it too fought for freedom...

Everybody froze. Then a couple more partisans levelled their weapons at the remaining three. One of the pair, a fresh-faced farm boy, held an ancient fowling piece. The other, a haggard, greasy fellow, had a German officer's pistol.

Jones lowered his hand and stepped back. There was a leak of smoke as he exhaled into sunbeams that were really nothing like dancehall illuminations. They were like a searchlight battery probing the cloudbase above a breathless city, insubstantial fingers raised in impotent defence.

Lots of shouting all at once. A thunderclap that must have come from redbeard. A shrill reply from the girl. Everybody looked at everybody else.

Silently, invisibly, Bradley did the same.

The girl made to face up to redbeard, her mouth forming authoritative words. As she moved, her associate swung his pistol towards the scattergun kid. Bradley saw the dust kick up from his jacket before he heard the shot. The girl reacted, turning and ducking a shoulder to bring her weapon to bear, but she was too late. In the instant she diverted her attention from him, redbeard hefted his lever-action carbine and clubbed her down with the stock. Even before the kid sank to his knees and pitched forward, she had vanished into the grass.

Excited faces. An exclamation from one of the men – sunlight catching spit. Wide-eyed crowing from greaseball, full of gypsy blood or moonshine. Then redbeard spun-cocked his rifle like some damn dude show and aimed it one-handed where the girl lay.

The violent crack, so much louder and sharper than the submachine gun or the pistol, split the morning in half.

Pause. The ringing of the shot and the clatter of birds' wings, still rising. Words from redbeard, ending in what had to be a laugh. Jones' upturned hands – well whatcha know, Joe? The package slapped unceremoniously against his chest.

Bradley let out a long-held breath. His heart was thumping on the pine needles and the petrified sinews of their roots. He had a rotten taste in his mouth and a sudden need to pee. Whatever he had just witnessed, there was something new in the air now, a low note humming beneath the sounds of the forest. It made everyone look like the enemy.

He knew what he thought he had seen. When the girl and

her buddies had raised their weapons, it had looked official. Didn't matter that they were lawless people in a lawless land, it had looked like an arrest. And when the dark guy had gunned down his young comrade, that was a betrayal. Far as farmboy and the girl had known, greaseball was on their side. They'd trusted him and they were dead.

And Jones had just stood there. He still held the partisans' cigarette in a steady hand. Now he turned back to his car and Bradley let him go, keeping his attention on the remaining four. He watched them so close he could see the sweat and bugs they mopped off their faces with their sleeves. He watched the set of their shoulders and the angle of their necks and he felt the jumpiness relaxing in them, just as the hairs on the back of his own neck were settling. Even when the Citroën's motor turned over they spared it no glance. Their job was done.

So was his. He hoisted himself on his elbows to inch backwards under the netting but the final impetus eluded him. No way was this over. His heartbeat told him that.

Having carried Jones's suitcase to the staff car, redbeard looked like he might reverse it to load the bodies. Instead, it lurched forwards and crabbed up the slope into the forest. In the clearing, greaseball raised his arms and arched his spine, riding up his undershirt to reveal a thick-haired belly, which he slapped. His two comrades knelt in the grass and came up with the girl's limp dead body. Except she wasn't dead. Her head moved of its own accord as it lolled in and out of the bloody mess at her shoulder. Her cap had gone and her hair was fair and cropped short. Bradley saw a flash of woozy eyes coming back from that precious nothing to a world of pain and fear.

Laughter floated over, audible above the low-geared whine of the Citroën flanking through the scrub. The sounds were slow yet distinct. Seconds took eternities now. Everything was happening in a sinister choreography, like something preordained. The girl was passed from man to man. They were slapping her, tearing at her outsized clothing, catching her each time she fell. Then the guy with the pistol seized her around

4

the back of her head and tried to force the muzzle into her mouth.

Bradley saw his own bullet take part of the gun and the palm of the hand away. Fingers flew like droplets from a water-splash. The girl dropped. That was good.

In slow motion, the crosshairs of his scope moved across three bewildered faces, as they had moved all morning across every aspect of the clearing, but now his finger moved fractionally too – once, twice, three times.

A breeze stirred the long grass around the remaining vehicle. The sun shone through the pines onto a deserted scene.

*   *   *

That ought to have been the end of it but of course it wasn't. Killing had consequences. Wasn't that what this was all about?

At the rally point Jones was hopping mad. He had heard the shots and made Bradley tell the rest. The young American considered lying and thought again. Jones had a way about him, not like an officer but like a bank manager, or like he imagined a bank manager might be.

Stripping off the camouflage hood and smock, he grabbed a jerrican from the trunk and soaked a rag in gasoline to clean the green and brown crud off his face and hands. His hands were shaking. He told himself it was his infuriation with Jones. Maybe it even was. The guy was laying it on pretty thick.

"How exactly did you contrive to misinterpret my orders?"

"War's over, Mister. I wasn't about to sit back, see rape and murder done."

"Murder, he says! What do you suppose they'll call what you just did? You are here to watch my back, not to act as an avenging angel! Good Christ, the hubris, man!"

Jones's moustache twitched with righteous indignation right enough but Bradley had to grin. He wasn't altogether sure what hubris signified, other than it was more than just pride and had something to do with defying the gods. But then you had a guy in a business suit in a Moravian forest, somewhere near the old Silesian border and most likely behind Soviet lines, with any number of bandits and Nazis roaming the woods caring not one damn for the niceties of an armistice – and he had the sass to threaten his only ally in this madness? If that wasn't some kind of hubris Bradley didn't know what it was.

"Least you got what you was after," he growled, an attempted armistice of his own.

"That's not your concern, Private. As far as you are concerned this transaction never took place."

It was a truce then. Cessation of hostilities.

"We should get outta here."

He pulled on the woollen tunic Jones handed him. They called it a *gimnasterka* because it went over your head and sure required gymnastics when that coarse wool snagged on the bristles of your scalp. Standard Red Army issue. The matching side-cap went onto his fresh-shaven head and the brand new M1 sniper into the bracken, experimental spotting ammo and all.

Jones' preparations seemed confined to hiding the non-existent package under the seat and reloading his cigarette case with little cardboard tubes from a pack of Belomors. Bradley hoped there were Russian papers to go with the smokes. He accepted one as he put the car into gear and set off along the trail. The rough, hot tobacco was nothing like the Luckies he had dreamed of back in the woods and did little to calm his pounding heart, but he was gratified to see his hands had stopped shaking.

He exhaled. Blinked. Took another breath.

That was how you did it. Until you didn't.

Russian cigarettes or incriminating American rifle, war or no war, from now on it would be touch and go. Between them and the Third Army at Pilsen lay every shade of Shinola. In the two days since the surrender, the Reds had been pushing south and west to occupy this remnant of Czechoslovakia that the Nazis had called the Protectorate of Bohemia and Moravia. Sure, they hadn't taken time to secure their flanks, nor to do much mopping up, but that in itself was a mixed blessing. He and Jones might slip through only to run slap bang into a band of diehard Nazis, and no *papirosi* or phony movement orders would help them then. Or they might encounter the Vlasov army, those so-called Cossacks who had fought alongside the Nazis before turning on their masters. No prizes for guessing how they would react to what looked like an unmarked vehicle of the Soviet secret police. Even the demobilized Germans might kill them for the car and a better chance to outrun the dreaded Ivans.

While you were at it you could throw in communist and anti-communist guerrillas on the rampage, the Czech National Committee militias springing up in every village, and the self-styled Revolutionary Guards who'd crawled out of the woodwork and found some surplus Afrika Korps uniforms to confuse the heck out of everybody. Plus every other bastard with an axe to grind. Plus at least two air forces overhead.

And if they made it through all that, Patton would probably shoot them coming in.

Bradley opened the window to spit out flakes of the Russian stub.

"You a betting man, sir?"

"Are you giving odds?"

Bradley watched the road awhile. An endless tunnel of pines.

"All I'm saying is You Know What better be worth it."

Jones put out a hand to brace himself as they went over a bump.

"One should never underestimate the boundless possibilities of Chaos. I fully expect us to be swept along in the general flow."

Bradley nodded. Away from the meat grinder of the railroads and highways, the country lanes were clotted with

German-speaking refugees, including all those who had switched their uniforms for civilian clothes. On the way in, heading east, they'd had to contend with fists banged on the hood, fingers drawn across throats in warning or threat, frequent detours to lie up or skirt the crowds. But this time they would be just another log in the jam. The people on the roads watched the sky, the treeline, or the boots in front. They didn't look too closely at their fellow travellers, didn't dare. The bonds of shared experience were breaking down. From now on, that kind of thing could spell a death sentence.

The second ingredient in Jones' hash was the Red Army itself. Before the two of them and their guide had set out, they had already seen plenty of steam blown off, but when news of the surrender reached the approaching Soviets, the rain-laden skies had lit up like Combined Ops. The self-inflicted casualties didn't bear thinking about. The Reds were still advancing, but Bradley doubted there was a sober man among them.

And then there was Prague. The people of the capital had risen up against the last gasp of the Nazi occupation, seizing the radio station and calling for assistance. So far, intel reported, the only help had come from General Vlasov's men, who had switched sides, still wearing their Wehrmacht uniforms. The city had become a magnet for German forces, freedom fighters and the Reds – everyone except the Yanks less than fifty miles to the west, which was tough given they were the ones the Czechs had appealed to in the first place, but it was another bit of Chaos to rely on.

"It's a runaway train, huh?"

The Limey's thoughts must have been elsewhere.

"I beg your pardon?"

"This," Bradley said. "Everything. A runaway train."

Jones gave an ungentlemanly grunt.

"The war you mean. It's not enough to sign a piece of paper to put an end to it."

Bradley blinked and saw three startled faces one after the other. Three different faces yet the same face. The crosshairs

8

made it the same face, same as the faces at the pillbox slots of the Vierville draw, same as the face in the yellow porthole of the iron cylinder that had stood in a forgotten corner of Hell.

He was brought to his senses by a hand on his shoulder. Jones was getting his attention, prodding at the rear-view mirror to tilt it back towards him.

Something bright danced in the blur of dust and trees. A vehicle in their wake, kicking up a dust trail of its own. He pushed his foot down on the gas pedal.

Jones had knelt right around to peer through the small rear window. With the increased speed he had to raise his voice over the clatter of stones.

"It's the Hun jeep thing."

"From the rendezvous?"

"It would seem you didn't get them all."

"We can probably outrun him."

"And come flying out of this plantation straight into a Soviet column? No, we'll have to finish what you started. Shall I...?"

Bradley laid a hand on the Russian burp-gun between them.

"Forget about it. With this thing, on the move like this, you'd be lucky not to blow your own head off. I'll have to get out. Can you slide over?"

"Of course."

"See where we duck into the trees again, after this next bend. I'll go in too fast and brake hard. Oughta be a big cloud of dust. You keep driving."

"Understood."

And don't forget to wait a ways up the road, Bradley thought, too late to voice it. As the Citroën wallowed into the bend, he used his left hand to open the suicide door and his right to grab the gun. He stamped on the brake to slew the car around and kicked out, rolling to make the cover of the bracken and coming up on one knee with the weapon ready. Though it shook him like an electrified fence, it was done in a couple of seconds.

Which was just dandy, except he'd misjudged the dust the manoeuvre would throw up. He heard the Citroën's throttle open again, and the rattle of the approaching Kübelwagen, but it would be a close call whether he'd get a glimpse before it hit the bend.

When it did fall, it didn't fall like dust, it fell like a white sheet whisked off the new year's model at an auto show. The Kübelwagen was bearing down on him. He saw the painted-out German cross on the hood and the wipers flicking at the dust.

And the girl, white-faced behind the wheel.

In that second, he lowered his point of aim and leaned in to help the compensator hold the burp-gun level. He emptied the whole drum into the hood and saw the car drop at the front as something collapsed. Stones flew everywhere but it kept coming at him.

Rear-engined. Those little people-wagons had their motors in back.

There wasn't time to jump aside. He shut his eyes as the vehicle ploughed into the stand of saplings. It skimmed his elbow, showering him with fake glass and foliage, before crunching to a halt against a bigger tree. The motor stalled and a merciful silence descended like that thick white dust, punctuated only by the ticking of hot metal and the birds returning to the treetops.

He had to use the empty burp-gun to get up. His hip and shoulder ached from the roll through the undergrowth, he'd skinned his hands and his head was pounding. He found his side-cap and put it on, feeling shreds of leaves caught in the stubble.

"Gee, lady," he breathed. "Don't you ever give up?"

She lay twisted across the seats with her legs in the crumpled footwell, but nothing looked bent at the wrong angle. Bradley wrenched open the door. Her ankles were pinned by the pedals where they had come forward. He could fix that.

Her leg tautened as she tried to pull herself upright. A groan escaped from the depths of her and Bradley saw the wide-set eyes glaring down at him over bloodstained cheeks and chin. From this foreshortened angle her dazed scowl seemed like the sulk of a petulant child.

Some child. He stood up again as she aimed the Sten-gun at him. It was the one she had fired in the air in the clearing, the one she ought to have emptied into redbeard from the get-go. But its distinctive side-loading magazine was missing. He snatched it from her.

"*Spasibo*," he said, playing the part.

"*Pazhalsta*," came a cracked voice. You're welcome.

Leaning over her, he forced the Sten between the pedals to lever them apart. Her bare feet slid out of her felt boots and she wriggled backwards across the seats. For the moment all pretence of masculinity was gone. She drew her knees to her chin and cradled her useless arm. Her eyes never left his face.

He yearned to speak to her, but knew so little Russian, and no Czech, or whatever she was. He tried to smile but it was beyond him. He just stared back at her.

The front of her field jacket was open and bloody. He saw where she had packed her shoulder with greaseball's gypsy neckerchief. Blood and dirt caked her close-cropped hair and one of those grey-blue eyes was beginning to seal up. Yet she did not appear the least bit pathetic. Even wounded, cornered and knocked half-silly, even looking like a cross between a sulking child and a threatened animal, she radiated something completely unexpected. It was like nothing Bradley had sensed before, and he had been up against some tough customers in his time. Not fatalism, he had seen that, nor fixation. More a sort of determination, against all odds. The power of the impression made him catch his breath. Maybe that was it, maybe she never did give up.

It was all there in those eyes and that poise. He was afraid she had a pistol or a knife, or would go for him with her nails the instant she saw an opening. Although he was pretty sure he could subdue her if he had to, he knew there was nothing he could say or do to stop her trying.

The Sten looked bent. He handed it back.

"*Spasibo.*"

No response, just those roving eyes, sizing him up, searching for weaknesses. He had to get out of there, fast.

Was there a quizzical glint in that bruised gaze as he backed onto the track, covering her with the empty burp-gun? Was there a hint of amusement in the arch of those eyebrows – or had he imagined it? She was hidden by the trees now and all of his certainty had evaporated in the deafening stillness of the morning.

But one thing he was sure of, limping towards the dust-wreathed Citroën that waited in the tunnel of trees. He was through with telling Jones what had happened.

CHAPTER TWO

Mr Smith insisted on taking the Métro to Montmartre that morning, partly because they would have to change lines, which was always exciting, but largely because he knew how much it irritated Mr Jones not to use their driver. His subordinate was a sound chap with a fine record but he needed reminding every now and then that he was a public servant too. Staying at the Ritz could instil an unfortunate self-importance, even if one's suite were among those that had been flood-damaged when Hemingway machine-gunned his water closet. (There was the full case for the dangers of self-regard!)

Few uniforms mottled the platform or the carriage. Despite its penchant for revolutions and the privations of recent years, Paris had remained in the eye of the hurricane. Only the banners on the *Combat, Monde* and *Figaro* gave any indication of the turmoil beyond her banlieue. The French were shelling Damascus. The Chinese had cut off the Japs at Nanning. The assault on Okinawa continued. Closer to home: eyebrows raised at De Gaulle's awarding Monty the *Grande Croix* of the *Legion d'Honeur,* but all united in calling on King Leopold to abdicate for surrendering Belgium to the Nazis while the French had been helping to defend it. Which was bordering on the pot calling the kettle black, in Smith's humble opinion.

He was, he acknowledged self-reproachfully, a man given to opinions, humble or otherwise, and a good many had ended up getting people killed. Yet over the past six years there had been a need for men with opinions and the willingness to take decisions based on minimal information. Alas, those times were passing. Party politics was back and in a little over a month the nation was going to the polls.

Winston might not accept it, even the voters might not expect it, but Smith had made it his business to read people's private thoughts and he knew the bitterness that had dawned with the VE Day hangovers. The old system was forever tainted. It was going to be All Change, he was sure of it, and he would be surplus to requirements again. That didn't bother him, he could take a comfortable early pension and by Jove he was worn out enough. He was content to let the politicians and bureaucrats take up the baton and establish their post-war world without him. But while he still had a measure of influence there were certain things he could not leave unfinished and this was one of them.

They came out into the shocking sunlight of a late May morning. Even the shadier buildings along the Boulevard de Clichy had been scrubbed and the sails of the Moulin Rouge wore a fresh coat of brick red. Business, it appeared, was booming. Having lost their vehicles to the German retreat, the citizens had responded with a most un-Parisian hotchpotch of bicycle-drawn trailers and taxis. But it was the procession of smart GIs and scruffy Tommies that attested to the quartier's liveliest trade as they gravitated, even at this hour, to 'Pig Alley'.

Smith looked up at the *butte* and his knees ached. Perhaps their driver might have been the better idea after all.

"Will he play along, your man?" he demanded of Jones, who was still bristling from the humiliation of the Métro.

"He's no one's man, sir, but he'll do as we ask."

"Can you be certain?"

"You have seen his 201. You and I may place no faith in the mumbo-jumbo of the 'trick cyclists' but it's plain to see he has an intense hatred of violence perpetrated against the fairer sex. Simply won't let it happen."

"Quite so." Smith nodded, his mind elsewhere. "Inexperienced, of course."

"Speaks elementary Hun. Grew up in a largely German-

Jewish neighbourhood, although he is not himself of the persuasion. Then there was the crash course from his people. Even has some pidgin-Russian. In my experience that makes him more qualified than the entire American intelligence community put together. Resourceful too," Jones added.

"Trigger-happy, I believe you said."

"Well, aren't they all? But he's a crack shot all right."

"Shame he has lost his nerve then." Smith caught his colleague's arm with the crook of his umbrella. They waited at the foot of the hill for a pair of First War veterans to hobble past.

"I'm teasing you," Smith said. "Chap has every right to be down in the dumps, from what you showed me."

"I don't think he'll snap, if that's what you're asking. As for being a loose cannon..."

"Well, precisely," Smith said. "And he's up there, we're sure?"

The other man's shoulders tensed under the light mac he wore. Broad shoulders, Smith reflected. They would need to be.

"I was careless to let him slip away after the Czech trip."

"You weren't to know he'd go AWOL the moment you came back across the lines. The logical course would have been to milk our gratitude for all it was worth, rather than high-tailing it here to Paris."

"It's a good place to lose oneself."

Smith smiled amicably.

"But not good enough, eh?" He pointed with his umbrella. "Well then, onwards and upwards!"

Their objective lay at the headwall of a ravine of shuttered apartment buildings, below a steep flight of steps and a cart ramp leading back into the daylight. Parked at an unneighbourly angle in the narrow street, a US Army jeep had attracted a gang of youths dressed like Hollywood gangsters in gaudy shirts, hats and coats several sizes too big for them. One sat on the bonnet, checking the action of a large revolver. They closed ranks around the vehicle, though not well enough to screen the urchins siphoning its petrol.

Their leader drew breath to call out some threat but was silenced by a glare from Jones. The two men sidestepped the gang and entered the apartment building. Jones spoke with the po-faced concierge, who left them in no doubt it was strictly an affair *ricain*. However, she did have advice for anyone ascending to the 5th. Given the capricious nature of the electricity supply, only a complete idiot would use the lift. As if on cue, the lights in the dingy lobby flickered and Smith was moved to wonder if the coincidence had less to do with the mystical link between concierge and building than the presence of a loose connection which might be nudged beneath the level of the *loge* window. Not that such suspicions were of any practical value.

He set off with grim determination up the stairs.

*   *   *

In the one room apartment overlooking the Rue Tholozé, Fabienne Denis sat on the edge of her bed fearing for the safety of her porcelain dogs. The *ricaines* were so big and space so confined it seemed inevitable a wayward piece of kit would sweep one of her precious ornaments to its destruction. Of course it was not a big thing, not with everything else that was passing, but the dogs had been her mother's and her mother was gone.

So was her father. It had been nine months since the fighting on the Île, which was the last time she had seen him. He had joined the police under the occupation, not out of any misguided notion that he was remaining loyal to France but because of Système D. To survive, to put food on the table, one had to *Débrouiller*. One found a way.

When, sensing the day of reckoning drawing nigh, his colleagues had called the strike and barricaded themselves into the Prefecture of Police, Guardian Denis had been home on

16

compassionate leave. *Pauvre papa*. Like everyone in France who had worked under the Germans, he knew he must be seen to be resisting at the last. His life depended on it! Yet there was his wife dying of the cancer for which there were no medicines or hospital beds, nor even sufficient nourishment to fuel the struggle. How dare they judge him, they who had never faced such a decision, those August heroes who clamoured loudest for reprisals, pointing their tainted fingers at anyone whose ill-judged attempts at self-preservation might distract the mob from noticing their own.

Finally, with head hung low, he had gone to the Île and Fabienne's mother had died that same night. It was the eve of the Liberation. In the morning Fabienne had made her way down to the river. The tanks were still burning from the battle in the Tuileries, and one could hear sporadic gunfire through the cheering of the crowds and the pealing of all the bells of Paris, but on the Île de la Cité it was over. If she wanted to see her father, the *fifis* told her, she could visit him at Fresnes prison with the other *collabos*.

But she could not, because of Système D. She had her own battle to fight, her own name to clear, and if she was to live by her wits she could not be seen to be sympathising with the sympathisers. There was no place for sympathy in France. It had vanished as surely as the Germans had vanished, and more completely than certain other spectres.

Regarding the *ricain* slumped, sulking, in the remaining chair, she felt only regret that she had once again chosen an inadequate benefactor. For his predicament, nothing. She had even experienced a moment of relief when the MPs had burst in and seized him. Throughout five flights of clumping army boots she had been convinced they were coming for her. But she was back where she had started and would have to find another way to feed and clothe herself. That was it. There was no court of appeal. There were no rules to Système D. That was the only rule of Système D.

So she did not bother wondering why they hadn't taken

him away, she only worried about her porcelain dogs and wished all these uncomplicated, uncomprehending giants would just hurry up and go. In such a frame of mind she was not even surprised when a very English voice called her name through the door, nor when two equally English gentlemen entered at her command, the elder bright red in the face. With practised indifference she got up to offer him the bed, it being the only place to sit, and went to fetch a glass of water.

But it was insupportable! There were now five men in the apartment and with every movement the floorboards protested. Heaven knew what the neighbours and Madame Valentin made of it! Mercifully, the *ricain* MPs soon excused themselves with the most cursory of salutes. Her own *ricain* seemed not to register their departure. Fabienne's indifference turned to scorn. Hers no longer.

The older gentleman, a dapper man of perhaps fifty years, mopped his face with his handkerchief and found breath to speak.

"Private Bradley, my name is Smith. Mr Jones you already know. We have come to offer you a job of work."

Now her curiosity had been pricked, Fabienne found she could understand the English better than she had understood the American. All the same she put a bored look on her face and affected not to listen.

She was aware of Bradley regarding the newcomers at last. After that strange, flat greeting of his – *How ya do-an* – he too seemed completely disinterested and posed his first question in the manner of clumsy small talk.

"So am I under arrest or what?"

It was Mr Jones who replied.

"We aren't about to throw you back to your military police for being absent without official leave, but it would be advisable to remember we are operating under their indulgence. Is that clear?"

"As mud."

Fabienne looked up from her apparent reverie to find Mr

Smith watching her.

"I thought we might take a stroll." He levered himself off the bed and returned his handkerchief to his breast pocket with a flourish. "Pity to waste such a splendid day."

"Anything you say." Bradley rose too and flashed her a smile, which she mirrored. "Gotta go with these guys, Fab. *Tout à l'heure, chérie.*"

"*D'accord*, Sam."

He was moving towards her to bestow a parting kiss when he noticed the look on her face. Instead, he scooped up his blouson and sack from the foot of the bed and touched two fingers to his temple in a salute of his own.

The door closed and she let out a whistle. She knew she would not see him again.

* * *

"Charming girl," Smith broke the silence halfway down the stairs. "Her father's in Fresnes, of course, with a collaborator's dossier to his name."

Bradley cursed under his breath.

"We've no idea what these people had to do to survive."

"Oh, I'm not judging anyone, Private, simply stating the case. You see, if you give us the slip, the denunciations in the Famille Denis dossier will acquire a more compelling nature. You do know what they'll do to her if she's incriminated?"

Bradley turned to stare. Jones seized his arm and guided him downwards, adding: "Particularly if it were suggested her collaboration had been of the sort they call *horizontale*."

Puffing now, Smith grimaced.

"I'm afraid it is how one conducts this sort of business. There are few people in our line of work who do so voluntarily. Indeed, we would be suspicious of anyone who did. Yet rest assured it is important work, or we shouldn't be asking you."

Bradley sneered.

"And what is it you're *asking* me to do this time?"

"Not here. A little more privacy, if you can suggest somewhere in the vicinity."

"Sure. Know just the place."

He saw the relief on the older man's face as he led them obliquely downhill to an iron-wrought overpass overlooking the cemetery. They descended the dense tiers of family crypts. Here and there a solitary mourner or a group in black lent impressive scale to the avenues and monuments, but on the floor of the necropolis, where the sounds of the city were muted and the dusty light hung in the trees, the sense of solitude was profound.

"Quiet enough for youse?" He went to sit on a slab.

Jones took off his hat and coat, extracted a Thermos flask and passed it over.

"You need to sober up. As I'm sure you've discovered, you can't get a decent cup of coffee in Paris these days, so that's a concoction of my own devising."

Bradley unscrewed the top, struggling to keep the surprise off his face. He had indeed tied one on last night, and the night before, and kept himself topped up in between, but the gritty aroma of the fresh Java was more intoxicating than any local liquor.

He was aware of Jones watching him.

"Sergeant – we've arranged for you to have your other stripes back – your secondment to our service for the duration of this assignment has been approved in principle by SHAEF, but the details are hush-hush and can be reported to no-one without the say-so of myself or Mr Smith. No ifs, no buts."

Smith cleared his throat.

"Jones here gave a glowing report of your conduct on his Czech excursion a couple of weeks ago. It convinced me we did the right thing in borrowing your talents from your people – I mean, they were about to lock you up and throw away the key. Well, now we have something else for you. In recent days Churchill has been talking about an 'iron curtain' descending across Europe. We want you to go and have a bit of a poke about behind it."

Bradley laughed.

"You fellas ain't really called Smith and Jones."

The older man contrived to look offended. "Are you asking for our credentials? Do you suppose impostors could command your MPs to release you into our charge, as you have seen my colleague do on two occasions? My dear chap, we can and will supply you with any amount of authentic documentation, but you really must take us on trust."

Bradley shrugged. In his brief experience of War Department operations he had already discovered nobody introduced themselves properly. It wasn't for fear of capture by the opposition but of being subpoenaed in future Congressional hearings. They were the real enemy. There was no reason to imagine the Limeys went about things differently.

Jones put something in his hand, a photograph of a young woman. Not a mug shot but one of those professional studio jobs with a soft focus and washed-out eyes from the long exposure. He noted the elegantly piled hair, the smart dress collar, and the blank, wistful expression. She could have been any dame in the world.

"Her name is Ludmila Suková. Field name Milena Kristeková. Codename MERCURY. *Nom de guerre* Jana Slavík, or 'Nightingale' – Slavík means nightingale, apparently." Jones sat on the facing grave and Bradley saw that rare smile brighten his puss. Did he like the word, or just the subject? Out came the cigarette case. Bradley shook his head.

"Codename? Field name?"

"Mmm." Smith was sounding glummer all the time. "She is one of ours. I put her in. And now she is missing."

"She has gone native," Jones said, heedless of the shadow that crossed Smith's face. "Until two years ago she was simply a liaison officer co-ordinating matters between ourselves, the Czech Intelligence Service in London and the R3 – their underground movement centred on Velká Bíteš. But then she was given free rein to establish her own network in anticipation of the expected uprisings. Clearly it ought to have disbanded by now, or placed itself under the authority of the Czech National Council. Yet we have reason to believe the MERCURY or 'Nightingale' circuit is still active."

"Doing what?"

Jones' lip curled.

"We suspect they're trafficking in people. It's a lucrative trade. Without anyone to vouch for you on the Continent nowadays, you're a non-person, unless you can come up with at least one document in your name. Six days ago, a refugee escaped from the Soviet zone and presented as proof of identity a *Kennkarte* issued by the Bohemian and Moravian Reichsprotectorate. Unfortunately for him, he was recognised by a former slave labourer in one of the DP camps. Turns out he'd been a Czech collaborator and was wanted by their people. We had a squint at his false ID and confirmed it came from a run of blanks we'd issued to MERCURY. Had a word with the chap before we sent him back. Claimed he bought it on the black market in Brno."

Bradley couldn't see it. What business was it of his, or theirs? Surely it wasn't that they wanted their documents back? They might look like bookkeepers but he had already seen Jones in action and knew it had to be bigger than that.

"Well, I guess if she's knocking up new identities for Nazis, it'd be worth knowing."

"Worth knowing!" Jones almost chuckled. "Sergeant, it would raise the most appalling diplomatic stink. Stalin is already accusing the western allies of co-opting our former adversaries to work against him. It's all paranoia and brinkmanship, but if he could produce actual proof of a former Allied intelligence group aiding and abetting his enemies, behind his lines..."

"I get it."

"He gets it, Brian," Smith said. "Personally, I doubt MERCURY is in it for a share of the Nazis' ill-gotten gains, but something untoward is going on."

Jones nodded, conceding.

"It's possible the *Kennkarte* was traded, not sold for profit. The circuit might have gone free-lance, selling information to the highest bidder. Or it has become a fifth column group sponsored by Moscow. We need someone to find out."

"And bring her home," Smith said.

Bradley stared.

"Ain't that the Czechs' business now?"

"The Czechs may have got most of their territory back but they are losing their independence from Moscow daily," Jones said. "On top of which the whole notion of national boundaries is a trifle redundant at present, and MERCURY had access to materials which would enable it to expand its activities into Germany, Austria, Poland..."

He hesitated before adding: "Also, Ludmila Suková has British nationality."

Smith let out a defeated sigh.

"He needs to know. Sergeant, Mila is my wife. My name *is* Smith, although she has never used it. She escaped from Prague in '39 and presented herself to us soon after. At first, she just lent a hand with the Czech government-in-exile. Translation, mediation, sort of thing. We were married during the Blitz. Then, in October '42, after Heydrich's assassination and the Lidice and Ležáky reprisals, she volunteered to go back."

There was no mistaking the emotion in his voice. Bradley had heard it before, the raw mixture of pain and pride when people spoke of loves and loved ones surrendered to the war effort. Maybe that grim fall evening he had begged her to reconsider or even forbidden her from going. It would not have made any difference in the cold light of day.

"Someone must bring her home," Smith repeated.

"But why me? You got better people..."

"You and Jones here are the only ones who have seen her recently – and even you did not recognise her, did you Brian? It was only when the contents of the package were examined that we were able to put two and two together."

Bradley stared at the photo. Could it be? The sitter's pale gaze might be the camera's best attempt to capture that luminous grey-blue stare, but the eyes were smaller, the face heavy-featured. Might that just be the lights and make-up? Could a boyish haircut and a life outdoors have bleached that thick, wavy hair so fair and fine? It seemed bizarre this woman could have transformed herself into that girl, but he had to admit it was possible. Her face had been swollen and covered with grime and he had seen her too briefly to be certain. He might close his eyes and fancy he pictured her now as he had seen her then, but he could not have described her to a police artist with any hope of a likeness. Yet Smith was right, he would know her if ever he saw her again.

He became conscious of the two men studying him.

"I gather you found a less-than-permanent way to prevent her tailing you," Smith gave his colleague a look. "The report rather skipped over that particular action."

"We had our hands full," Bradley said.

"Oh, quite right. But I am curious. How did she look?"

There was more than curiosity in his voice. Maybe not the unrestrained emotion of a parted lover but definitely that of a concerned husband, and untainted by the usual British vice of embarrassment. Despite everything, Bradley felt for the guy.

"She looked swell. Under the circumstances." He ran a finger inside of his collar, as if flushed from physical exertion. He'd caught a little of that British vice himself.

"Was she conscious – did you speak to her?"

"Barely, on both counts. A few words in Russian."

"Of course, you were in their uniform. Well, that might prove fortuitous, wouldn't you say, Brian?"

The other man continued to examine his cigarette.

"If he finds her, and if we're right about her dealing with the Reds, I can see it could be useful."

"Look," Bradley got to his feet. "I appreciate you getting me out of trouble, and I'm happy your 'Czech excursion' went OK, but you got to be kidding if you think I'm the guy to pull this off. I'm just a soldier, a Ranger. If I was useful to you, it was on account of my sniper training. You want to help the war effort, get me off these charges and let me go kill some Japs."

Smith looked surprised.

"Do you want to go and kill some Japs? Jones here was of the opinion you are, er, 'burned out' in that regard. We understood it was the reason for your transfer to Joint Intelligence Objectives Agency duties. Wasn't that why you were retrained and attached to the OVERCAST operation?"

He had to turn away to hide the shock at how much they knew.

"I'm not at liberty to discuss that, sir."

"Quite so. Well, I'm afraid you are in such bad odour with your own people the question of going to the Pacific theatre is immaterial. You can choose to do this for us, or you can wait for a ship to take you back to a military prison in the United States. Perhaps that's what you really want – the chance to go home?"

"Forget about it." Bradley studied the buildings that towered over the cemetery on the hillside. So many windows. He was feeling trapped. Outflanked. But there was something else. It had been sparked by Jones' words and his matter-of-fact tone. The girl in the photograph, the girl in the woods, and the casual reference to giving her free rein to establish an intelligence network behind enemy lines. The grotesqueness of it all stirred something in him. It made him feel ashamed.

The truth was he had been waiting for something like this. Or he had been drifting, with only the dream of this to keep him going. Picking fights. Picking up girls. Letting them pick him up, in Fabienne's case. Getting smashed. It helped with the nightmares, but never enough. When he wasn't daydreaming of an assignment, he was picturing himself on a rooftop, with a .45 he'd found somewhere and the sun sinking into the city.

"If I say I'll do it, what happens?" he heard himself ask. It was Jones who replied.

"You'll be flown immediately to Scotland for special training. We can only spare two or three weeks but it will have to do. There are people working on your cover as we speak, so that side of it ought to be ready. Then, when you return to Paris, you'll accompany me to the east."

"Behind your iron curtain?"

"There are certain points at which the Russians will be letting certain people in. At least there are presently discussions being held to establish the routes. Naturally we could also enter their zone illegally, but it would be better to have their permission this time."

"And why the hell would they give you that?"

Jones' moustache twitched in a show of umbrage.

"Because we are a legitimate humanitarian agency! Mr Smith and I work for a War Office department tasked with expediting the British contribution to the United Nations Relief and Rehabilitation Administration. As you have seen, Sergeant, the vast majority of the people of Europe are undernourished and ill-served by the most basic amenities. Millions are displaced and many more have no roofs over their heads. The situation in the east is a crisis of Biblical proportions. When winter comes, hundreds of thousands will die without our assistance."

"So you go over there to negotiate with the Russians about accepting relief. And I come with you as, what, some UNRRA liaison guy – and after that I'm on my own?"

"We can discuss that at greater length." Jones retrieved his coat and Bradley saw from the swing of the material that there was a gun in it. "Will you come with us?"

"To the British Embassy?"

The two spies exchanged a look.

"In a manner of speaking," Jones said. "We're at the Ritz. The embassy's still chock-a-block with furniture left in store by British nationals when the Nazis first rolled in."

Bradley studied him, reading nothing. It might be true.

"Is there anything else you need to know for the

moment?" Jones said.

He picked up his own gear from the grave he'd been sitting on. Emile Zola, 1840–1902. Remains later transferred to the Pantheon. Above the slab was an elegant stone arch with that bony look you found on the Métro signs. Within the arch, the bust of a youngish, bearded man regarded him blankly from beneath a shock of hair.

Sorry, bud, can't recall what you're famous for.

"What was in the package?"

Smith gave an unsubtle cough.

"We can't tell you that now," Jones said.

"I shall try to obtain the authority to tell you, if and when you come aboard." Smith rose as well, with a smile. "Anything else?"

"Yeah. That threat you made about Mademoiselle Denis."

"*Forgetaboutit*, as you'd say. Just didn't want you skedaddling as soon as we were in the street. Not sure how wise it would be for you to go back though. Bit of a flap on."

"Ain't so sure she'd want me back," Bradley said. "But you don't get it. I'll do this for you, but not under your goddamn threats. I want you to do something for me."

*　　*　　*

Two weeks later, on a rotten night in the bomb-damaged industrial suburbs south of Paris, Colonel Richard Campbell Smith watched another pale smear detach itself from the stipple of rain on the car windows and come flickering towards them.

The blur became a slot of sickly light, weaving through the barriers that warned motorists away from bomb-craters and caved-in mains. The rattle of the motorcycle penetrated the percussion of rain and windscreen wipers, rekindling Smith's despair. That he was obliged to file a route and timetable whenever he was away from the hotel or the legation he could accept, for the nature of his appointment required him to be accessible. That the despatch riders they sent after him were expected to navigate the backstreets with their headlamp cowls still in place, even though the black-out had been lifted, was a far less comprehensible example of the cloying bureaucracy which prevailed nowadays. A few months ago, the soldiers would have made up their own minds about that sort of 'bull', but now even the old salts lived in fear of transgressing petty regulations and incurring the wrath of the administrators. The risk was too great. Everyone was praying to go home.

"Here comes another one, sir," his driver said. After such a prolonged silence, she could not help yawning.

"You might make an effort to sound less bored, Jenny."

"Not bored sir, bloomin' cream crackered!"

Smith let out an amused snort and sought to make it sound indignant.

"We'll have none of your ATS ribaldry here, thank you, Corporal. For your information, we are all tired," he added in a gentler tone.

"Yes sir, 'course sir, sorry sir."

Tired wasn't the word though. His driver's cockney had come closer. Knackered. As in worn-out and worthless, fit only for the knacker's yard. And like an old, lame workhorse, a part of him welcomed it.

But that was nonsense of the worst sort. The horses had no knowledge of what went on in the knacker's yard. A process like that depended on their ignorance, or rather their inability to comprehend the logic of it. (Ignorance, of course, being the blissful state in which the knacker's neighbours sought to keep themselves.) What was happening to him was so mild as to make an obscenity of the comparison. The only note of tragedy was that he had to watch it unfolding, and too soon. They were going to hold their election. The result, despite appearances, was a foregone conclusion and only the absurdity of holding it at all would delay the inevitable. Half the electorate was overseas, some still fighting in the jungles of Burma and Borneo, others in the hands of the Japanese. The postal ballot was going out to those who could be reached, although Smith doubted many candidates would follow the campaign trail that far. Those who were not dead or dying would cast their votes and it would still be a few weeks before all the results were returned. (There was a war on, after all!) Only then would the purges begin.

The motorcycle had halted alongside. Weighed down by sodden battledress and leather jerkin, a young man was trying to raise his goggles, balance his machine on its kickstand and salute. There was a crash as the motorcycle toppled over.

Across the road, a face flashed white against the brickwork.

Jenny handed him a rather soggy envelope. He gave a nod of acknowledgement through the window, but the rider was busy wrestling with his fallen mount.

Most Secret and Urgent. Inside, a slip of paper bearing seven typed words.

A Nightingale is singing in Hammersmith Grove.

*   *   *

Corporal Simmonds thought the funny noise was the old man stifling a sneeze, until the mirror caught the glint of tears. Poor old bugger. She could hear the thickness in his throat just from his breathing. At once she felt guilty for saying how tired she was. Like Ma always said, there's plenty worse off than you, girl.

The boss had been in an odd mood all night. When she'd picked him up from the Quai d'Orsay, he had spent the first ten minutes venting his spleen against the diplomats he'd been in conference with, and when she had compounded things by getting lost, she had expected him to blow up. Instead, he'd just seemed dejected they would be late for this other matter, and now he was on the verge of breaking down.

"All right back there, sir?"

"Just the old leg giving me a touch of gyp."

Yeah, she thought, I should coco.

"You might turn the engine over though. Getting steamed up in here, aren't we?"

"Right-o, sir."

His reflection was back to staring out the side window at the shadows across the street. One or two figures skulked there, although most had congregated around some kind of brazier further up the road. It was hard to see with the streetlights knocked out and the shadows of the wall around the huge mill or whatever it was that reared above them against the faint glow of the city. Between the cobbles and the wall, a stream had swollen the gutters, churning with sludge from some bombsite around the corner.

At the sound of the starter, the figures stirred again. Jenny saw that one of them, wrapped in scarves and shawls and carrying an umbrella that had seen better days, was a girl not much older than herself. At first glance she'd taken her for a crone. Outside the centre, you got used to seeing the French like that, all old and broken.

No crone ever took off like this one though. She was up and running with her brolly turning inside out. Had they frightened her so bad, like some wild animal? No, Jenny saw what it was. A low iron door had opened in the wall near the light of the brazier. The figure of a man had stumbled out into the street and the girl was running like a mad thing to greet him.

She heard Smith's intake of breath as the figures spun around in a fierce embrace. Was he recalling a similar moment – a wife, a daughter – or was it an old wound reopening with the knowledge no such reunion was possible? No way of telling for certain, with the old man, and no way to ask of course, but she heard the crack in his voice and made up her own mind just the same.

"Pull up to the kerb over there if you can without splashing them, Jenny. I thought we'd offer them a lift back to Montmartre."

CHAPTER THREE

As empires waxed and waned, the old town in the trade pass had been known by many names. Now it had only a grid reference on a military map. The only people within its walls were trying to get somewhere else.

Except for those who had nowhere else to go.

To Karel Sec, clinging to broken earth beneath the matting of the tent, it seemed the ground itself was grating back and forth like that frontier, borne by Dr. Wegener's motions of the planet's crust. As the nameless town crumbled away, he dreamed of all the generations of its dead, crushed and crumbling too.

It had been Habsburg, then Czechoslovak, then German. The Americans had come, then the Soviets. The Soviets said the Americans had not come at all. The German-speaking population that had lately become the majority was fast becoming the minority.

The new inhabitants had nothing in common, save a preponderance of false papers, disbadged tunics and the desire, more desperate than hunger, to leave. Most gazed beyond the hills to the hazy peaks of Bavaria. Others drew hope from the rumours of Americans in the neighbouring districts. Some, especially those in the striped clothing, had no recourse but to throw themselves on the mercy of the Soviets. In many cases this proved a mistake.

Several weeks ago, they had permitted the Swiss Red Cross to establish a depot here. With the Red Army also malnourished, an evolutionary struggle had developed and as the strong had grown stronger they had taken to seducing the nurses, often in groups and sometimes to death. Now the warehouse stood empty and the hospital rang to the cries of soldiers who had distilled antifreeze through their gasmask filters and gone blind on the concoction – the issue of antifreeze in summertime, it was said, being the Red Army's equivalent of the British navy rum ration.

With its market stalls and clotheslines, the town by day resembled an immigrants' rookery from a bygone age, but at night it was transformed into an infernal foundry as engineers toiled to repair the railway and solve the riddle of its all-deciding Sphinx.

Waking to the giant locomotive's impatient whistle, to another dawn of amplified fanfares and slogans, Sec knew he had come as far as he would get, yet the certainty of his imminent extinction was no more remarkable than thirst or a full bladder. It was just something one woke up to. Unlike the other matters there was nothing to be done about it.

He rolled his blankets, tying them round his shoulder. He unwrapped his spectacles and checked his overcoat for knife and mug. No pocket-watch or wallet left but he had yesterday acquired three quarters of a packet of cigarettes for barter. Might he allow himself one as he waited in line for the standpipe? Request noted, he told himself with the memory of a smile. Although not yet thirty, his face was lined and the eyes behind the cracked glasses sallowed with pain.

A phantom among phantoms, he slipped from the tent and vanished in the gloom.

*   *   *

In the camp commandant's office, struggling with blunt fingers to fasten the hooks and eyes of his tunic collar, Major Nikolai Mikhailovich Tsibulkin cursed the moron in the mirror for foiling his endeavours by swaying so.

The worst of it was that the visiting major from Military Intelligence seemed unaffected by their night of vodka and slivovitz. Shortly before dawn, which was when his travelling companion, Comrade Novák, had fallen, Major Korolev had flicked a disparaging glance down at the little man and picked up the files again. Moscow training, Tsibulkin reflected. With talents like that he was destined for the top.

While I dig like the *batrak* I am. Rooting out the weeds. Scraping off the blight.

"*Nichevo!*" He tore loose the collar. "What does anything matter in this cock-stinking bone-yard they have me commanding?"

"Spoken with true revolutionary zeal." Korolev's laugh was brisk, studied, probing. A GRU laugh through and through.

"I do not mean I doubt the importance of this posting."

"Yes, yes. And as I said some hours ago, I'm sure these duties will pass to Czechoslovak State Security very soon." Korolev looked down at Novák over the top of his papers. "Well, soon enough. You and your men will be able to go home."

Tsibulkin's men. There was a subject for proper laughter. His rabble, more like. He couldn't control them. The political officers couldn't control them. Nor in most cases could their excesses be excused by violations of their Motherland. For every Russian, Caucasian or Tatar under his command, he had a former partisan who only understood Polish and at least two Ukrainians, and for every Ukrainian who had fought the fascists, there would be another who had worn the *feldgrau* or thrown in with the anti-Soviet insurgents. There were also Moldavian and Romanian detachments in the area, but who knew whose side those born-through-the-arse bastards were on?

As for going home, his men had a surprise in store for them. Stalin had proposed that all those who'd allowed their lands to be occupied by the fascists might no longer be granted leave to live there. So even if one escaped suspicion, he'd probably return from the Great Patriotic War to find Mrs

Urchenko had packed her bags for Siberia. Not that he'd be able to read the note. Not that there'd be a note. Not that there was any land to return to.

Nichevo. Don't think about it. Just run this pretence of a transit camp as best you can and let the blue-tops run the actual screening camp inside it. Send the fascist prisoners, Red Army deserters and former POWs to the rear. Clothe the rest, somehow. Feed the rest, when possible. Keep them alive until the blue-tops have made their determinations. Then you can get back to the line, the auxiliaries and the Komsomol girls.

"Are you married?" he asked the GRU major.

The younger man's eyes did not leave the page but Tsibulkin saw him wince, inside. You got used to noticing things like that.

"Yes, married. You?"

"Never found the time," Tsibulkin said. "But your wife is well, I trust?"

Meaning not living dead in the Gulag apparatus. Not bombed or shelled round the twist. Not burned alive or nailed to a barn door for target practice.

"She is well, thank you. In Moscow."

"Moscow, no less! And you miss her."

Korolev looked up. There was cold steel in his eyes at last. "Shall we return to this matter?"

Tsibulkin shook his head and nearly swooned.

"I have to inspect the... fucking guard or something."

"Indulge me. The fucking guard will wait." Korolev tapped the file. "This man, Karel Sec, who was known as 'Václav' in the counter-revolutionary underground movement. You interrogated him personally?"

"Let me see – yes, that's right. He was trying to get across to the American Zone."

"Why do you think that was?"

Tsibulkin raised his eyebrows into his hairline.

"It's why they're all here!"

He fought to keep his eyes off the drinks cabinet, the one

that was never used because it was not a drinks cabinet. He would be in deep shit if the GRU turned out to be interested in that, but he didn't think they could be. Surely it would be a matter for the blue-tops – and he knew for a fact the camp's NKVD captain had a very similar cabinet draped in a very similar cloth in his office. Things like that one made a point of knowing.

Korolev gave no sign of noticing his discomfort.

"But this man is different. He's not a displaced person, nor a former combatant. He's a Czech. This is his country, supposedly."

"As I reported, he says his life is threatened in Moravia, even here in Bohemia, if we can call it that again. The details are unclear. It's hard to communicate with the Czechs at the best of times. But I believe Sec was claiming either to have betrayed members of the counter-revolutionary underground to the communist partisans – for the good of the revolution – or to have inadvertently betrayed good communists to the revanchists."

"Either, or? A confusion."

"Certainly." Tsibulkin cringed. What a stupid choice of word, and the GRU prick was going to pick him up on it – you could be certain of that. They might have secrecy drummed into them from the first glimpse of daylight through their mother's crack but deep down they were all bloody lecturers.

"In other words, uncertainly, yes?"

"Of course."

"And yet, whichever it was, he used that word, 'betray'. You're sure he used it?"

"Yes," Tsibulkin's head was spinning. "I remarked upon it myself, in my report."

"But clarify something for me. Even if he accidentally did them harm, if his true loyalties lay with our revolutionary forces, why does he wish to flee to the capitalists?"

"He did not explain satisfactorily, nor did I judge it the right time to compel him, but afterwards I asked around. The word is this 'Václav' was also a fascist informer."

"Intriguing."

Is it, Tsibulkin thought? I'd call it fucking typical. No, what's intriguing is why you've gone back to this file. I've given you collaborators and informers by the dozen: Czechs, Slovaks, Poles, sub-Carpathians. I've given you Ivans who 'escaped' from fascist camps and those fucking *Vlasovsty* too, or those my men have left half-alive. So why this Sec character, and why you, Korolev, matey? Why the Chief Intelligence Directorate not Internal Affairs or State Security? Why is this a GRU matter and not NKVD or NKGB?

He was no intellectual. Perish the thought! He was somewhere between drunk and hung-over. But the realisation came to Tsibulkin in such a sobering flash he couldn't believe he hadn't seen it earlier. Korolev wasn't chasing criminals, he was recruiting them. He wasn't sending people to the Gulag, he was sending them to the West. When Division completed negotiations with the Americans, and those Romanian Pioneers got the train moving, the border would temporarily reopen. The Americans would send over their Czechs, Poles and Cossacks, in exchange for the people who belonged back in the West. With them would go the likes of Sec – poor, persecuted, stateless persons who the cruel communists had rejected – straight into the plump embrace of a boundlessly benevolent and utterly sentimental capitalist dream. And the Americans, the French and the British would stand around with open mouths, catching flying dicks.

It was then that several events coincided to test his newfound mental clarity. There came a knock at the door, rousing the supine Novák to vomit copiously. Amid this excitement the telephone rang. At the other end, the staff captain from Division sounded equally thickheaded.

Moments later Captain Lesnikov, the camp's senior NKVD officer, burst in with Tsibulkin's adjutant flapping in his wake.

"What can I do for you?" Tsibulkin hoped the blue-top

might step in the sick, but the sod noticed just in time, turning up his formidable beak and pointedly ignoring the GRU major who was wiping his boots behind the desk. "Run out of prisoners to shoot?"

"I have to inform you, Comrade Major, that you are about to receive a visit from a lieutenant-colonel of the Main Administration of Counter-Intelligence."

"Division just told me. Or rather, they said a commander from State Security. You have announced he is from the 'Special Department'. Trying to frighten me, were you? Tell me, was he to be travelling incognito?"

Lesnikov opened his mouth to speak and closed it again. The big-nosed prick looked like he was going for the long-distance constipation record. At the desk, Korolev lit a Kazbek and burst out laughing.

Drawing himself up to his full height, Tsibulkin made a show of settling his cap on his head, a crimson-banded infantry commander's cap like the one this lieutenant-colonel would almost certainly be wearing to disguise his true post within the military counter-intelligence branch of the State Security service that Comrade Stalin had named, somewhat ostentatiously in Tsibulkin's innermost opinion, 'Death to Spies'.

"And what does SMERSh want with our holiday camp? Haven't you been sending them enough raw material to work on?"

Lesnikov seemed not to hear. He was staring at Korolev with undisguised hatred. The miserable cock-swallower wasn't cut out for subterfuge. He ought to have stuck to transcribing informers' denunciations or gunning down his own troops from the rear with the rest of those blue-top ulcers.

Tsibulkin cleared his throat.

"Eh, Comrade Captain?"

Lesnikov's glare swept the heaps of files before targeting the commandant again.

"All I know is you better arrange a rollcall. He's coming

for one of the internees."

*   *   *

From his vantage point by the ablution block, Karel Sec had an unrestricted view of the Kommandatura and the only town gate that had been cleared of rubble. After the burst of martial music and the announcement of the rollcall, he had seen the vehicles arrive and the Soviet officers dismount, leaving their escort guarding some sorry specimen. Now he sat finishing his half-loaf of black bread, wondering what he was going to do.

It had been a good morning so far. His cigarettes had yielded the half-loaf, a sliver of lard, a mugful of watery borsch and, from one of the sentries, a scribble of imitation handwriting on a scrap of paper they called a *propusk*, a permit to go foraging beyond the perimeter. He had given half the bread and lard to a skeletal wretch of indeterminate sex and received some Neapolitan blessing in return. Only the jabbering and hair-pulling of a lunatic boy outside the laundry spoiled the torpor of another meaningless day.

It was not so much that he was consciously weighing his options, more as if he were observing himself from afar, like a man watching a spider stalled on the ceiling, vaguely curious as to which direction it would next crawl. The spirit in which he had obtained the *propusk* was that of the watcher, bored, flicking balls of newspaper at the little arachnid to hasten its decision. In truth, of course, he did not care.

When had he attained such equanimity? It must have been recently because he could recall his Bohemian trek being propelled by the urge to escape. Then blabbing to the commandant, pleading for the real, once-in-a-lifetime *propusk*... What had he thought to achieve, by running, and when had he stopped running, and had he stopped running?

"Philosophy, Václav?" he said to himself, in the gently mocking tones of another's voice, from another time.

Yes, Miss Slavík, and no, Miss Slavík, not philosophy, as

well you know. I'm just curious, or not even that. What it is, if you want to know, is that it *is* curiosity, but not *I* – and what's any impulse, robbed of the Self? How can I be curious, how can I care, when I no longer exist? For me, finally, it's as the Russians say: *I* is the last letter of the alphabet.

And another voice, gentler still and full of giggles.

"Such theories! For a schoolmaster, Karel, you don't know much. Here, darling, let me show you..."

Oh, weren't they right, both of these women around whom his life had turned? What use was theory, in a world where only the outcome meant anything?

His eyes filled with tears as he recalled the look on his wife's face the last time he had seen her. The realities of that other late spring morning set his teeth on edge like the lunatic child. The grinding wail of the emergency brakes on the tram cars. Sparks flying. The ear-splitting violence of the grenade. And in its ringing aftermath, dull shots, the Germans shouting, a birdsong of passengers through the blown-out windows.

He had been crossing the road to the stop that would take them to their day's work at the school, striding ahead, not speaking to her. Why had that been? An argument about the occupation or the curriculum? She had hung back at the screech of tyres from the dark Mercedes skidding down the hill between the outbound and inbound trams. Supposing that the German driver had misjudged his speed, he had formulated something scornful to say for when they were speaking again. He had thought he was angry with her and the world, never realising he was experiencing his last moment of peace. Then it had happened – the ambush, the assassination – and they had remained on either side of the bend on the hill, watching one another as the road between filled with busybodies, then Czech police, then Germans. With such pandemonium he might have crossed over to her a dozen times before the Germans came, but he had not. Was it fear of attracting official attention or just fear of being seen as a busybody too? Had he been separated from her in those last minutes by nothing more real than *politeness?*

He had watched her and she had watched him until the Order Police came and crossing was impossible. At first, they had exchanged glances of abbreviated concern, apology and, yes, curiosity. Then the rumours had swept the bystanders – Reichsprotektor Heydrich, the Butcher of Prague, gravely injured – and their looks had begun to linger, until they no longer saw anything else. And the sound of the trucks, the bellowed orders, the field-grey arm that seized Sabina's, tearing the sleeve of her daisy dress. Hadn't that been it, the argument? Schoolboys, sunny day... Her face in that instant, her eyes not on the German but on her husband's. The last message enciphered in a look.

Oh, that look! To say *I* do not care!

And so, on this morning three years later, Karel Sec mopped his eyes and, ever conscious of making a public display, used the rag to wipe his eyeglasses before replacing them. The sun was higher. He saw the lost souls assembling in the square and the Russians advancing towards them. The soldiers and their prisoner had joined the officers.

"They have come for some unlucky chap, I think."

The speaker was the doctor, Wlasnowalski, a gaunt, middle-aged Pole with a homemade eye patch. He had once had a practice in Warsaw, before they moved him into the ghetto. Apparently he was Jewish; it had been news to him as well. At a camp called Auschwitz he had lost his eye to another doctor and on the death march that followed, as the Nazis sought to scatter the evidence of their industry, he had collapsed in the snow, left for dead. But he had not died. By one of those arbitrary miracles that mocked the million unanswered prayers, he had been rescued by Czech farmers and brought to Theresienstadt, where the Red Cross was taking over the German camp. How he had ended up here Sec did not know, only that he had lent assistance to the Red Cross before they left and still helped the Red Army medics, although he was clearly in need of treatment himself.

"*Dzigndobry, doktora*," Sec said in his clumsy Polish. "I believe you're right. The Ivans are looking for one of us."

"A traitor, a deserter, a criminal, do you think?"

"Here, doctor? Surely not!"

Wlasnowalski had to clamp wishbone hands on drumstick knees to laugh.

"Certainly it's an interesting cast we have..." Coughed out, a phrase too Polish or learned to translate; a quotation, perhaps, from a dramatist or a poet whom Sec had never read and now never would. "And our stage, Karel. Bruegel's little people upon Caspar Friedrich's landscape. See how we invade the Germans' fantasy?"

Sec squinted out over the town. If one ignored the haze of brick-dust there was something of a Romantic folly to it. The meticulously shattered towers, the Medieval and Renaissance ruins that had not been ruins a few weeks ago, the frame of impervious mountains. Yet he could not share the old Pole's hope in seeing Bruegel figures, cavorting peasants, blithely unaware of their allegorical meaning. If the Germans' vulgar vision of depopulated landscape had been subverted, he would have cast the new occupiers from Bosch, not Bruegel. The demons and the damned.

But there was no place left for such idle talk. The paintings had been stolen, the books burned. The little people were dying.

"Your invasion force is on its last legs," he said.

Wlasnowalski sighed.

"I must speak to the Russians about the train. We might arrange another transport of the sickest to Linz, if the Americans will have them."

"But you, doctor, why don't you put yourself on the first train home?"

"To Poland? There are no Jews in Poland now my friend. Yes, I know. Before, I was not Jewish but now, believe me, I am. Palestine, that's the place – I can't leave my bones here in Europe. Will you come to the *Appell*, Karel?"

"Soon." Clapping the doctor on his shoulder, he pulled back the blow as one might for a child. It was not squeamishness. So many of these people were so easy to injure by accident. Even a proper meal could kill them.

And there were the Russians, scuttling, shouting, prodding them all into ranks.

He thought about the old Pole. The old Jew, rather. That was what he had said. Before, I was not Jewish. Now I am.

Then, side-stepping the mustering phantoms, he was walking too, in the opposite direction and as fast as he dared. He had recognised the prisoner shuffling forward between the Russian guards.

He ducked into the empty Red Cross warehouse and as he adjusted to the uncompromising stripes of light and dark, he repeated to himself: *I* am. For as long as I remember that look and wonder what was in it. For as long as I can run, and keep running.

"*I* am..."

As his voice rang out in this iron chapel, he jumped to hear that other voice from another time, softer, higher, but not gentle, not now, not here in this world of hard reality.

"Philosophy, Václav?"

* * *

Lieutenant-Colonel Yevgeniy Vasilevich Andreev of the Main Administration of Counter-Intelligence, immaculately if misleadingly attired in infantry service uniform with a crimson cap-band, leaned on his cane and swatted at the local insects with his prized pair of taupe kid gloves.

If anyone had benefitted from the Boss's surprising decision to reintroduce Imperial trappings it was Andreev, who in his broad-crowned commander's cap, braided shoulder-boards, grey tunic and blue breeches looked every inch the Tsarist officer. In the classless uniforms of the Bolshevik age he had felt perversely self-conscious, but there was something about the post-Stalingrad pageantry that suited his lean frame and hooded gaze – suited also the cane, which was no affectation but a hard won trophy to go with the gold stripe above his right breast pocket. The rest was all a deception: *maskirovka*. He was no elitist. Only last year he had commanded a penal battalion and shared the sufferings of his *shtrafniki* in the Debrecen swamps as they blunted the fascist counteroffensive. Yet he enjoyed the impression he made. If his present situation required that he sail under false colours, let them be bright! He had even toyed with the notion of an unnecessary monocle, and it would have amused him to adopt one, had they not been deemed degeneracies.

Much of the pleasure came from the uncertainty with which people appraised him. Was he the privileged son of a lofty apparatchik? He was not, but in his rise through the ranks had acquired powerful sponsors. Was he truly on the staff at Division? Only the most gullible accepted him at face value but few indeed knew how frightened they ought to be. In this case though, someone had let the cat out of the bag, for the degree of deference with which he'd been greeted went far beyond what he might have expected had he genuinely been an officer of infantry or even a puffed-up parasite on the State Security behemoth, which was the misconception he preferred.

He lashed out at another insect and was gratified to see Lesnikov flinch. Andreev suspected the NKVD captain was the one who had let slip that he was SMERSh. Intelligence work, the English called it! Perhaps that was their sense of humour? But the Russian word was better. *Razvedka*. The meaning was broader, more uncertain. It meant doing whatever was necessary. Anything and everything.

Off along the front of the square, in a cosy huddle with the commandant and the little Czechoslovak civilian, the GRU major was more of a concern. The fellow had said nothing so far, not out of disrespect but not out of deference either. It was infuriating not to be able to pin down why he was here or what he was doing keeping company with this Novák, who had the look of a politician, albeit a tad green about the gills this morning. He would have some digging to do when he got back to Front Headquarters at Dresden.

Nemakhov, his aide, re-emerged from the furthermost ranks and headed back across the square, followed by the two SMERSh soldiers and their prisoner. The latter could barely walk, so Nemakhov signalled ahead with a thumbs-down.

"Not here then?" Lesnikov said. Andreev ignored him. He gestured with his gloves to the commandant, who came running.

"Is this everyone? Answer truthfully."

Major Tsibulkin flushed.

"We have swept the town, Comrade Colonel. There are some women and children who are too sick to move but all the men are here."

"Yet you are still, what, six heads short?"

"I regret. Some of my sentries issued permits to leave the camp. The internees are not supposed to roam beyond the town, but..."

The man's voice was shaking and he looked red enough to pop. Andreev noticed how the hooks on his collar did not marry up with the eyes. They had overlapped by one.

He decided to smile. He had learned it was more unnerving.

"Looking at this lot, I'd be surprised if anyone got far. You have the names?"

"Here, Comrade Colonel."

Andreev used the clipboard to beckon the others. He watched Tsibulkin watch the prisoner approach, seeing him anew through Tsibulkin's eyes.

He was a big man, even a giant, had he been capable of standing up straight, which plainly he could not. His long legs ended in bundles of tenderised meat. His huge fingers twisted like gnarled twigs around the black balloons of his hands. He'd once had red hair but scalp and beard had been crudely shorn, leaving matted tufts and raw bald patches. His features were swollen, his eyes slits: one dark, one bright, moist scarlet.

Andreev tried to pin down Tsibulkin's thoughts, using his own, or a simpler version of them. He remembered a Russian bear in a liberated zoo. The fascists had eaten all the other animals and chained prisoners in their pits and cages, but they had kept the bear alive, for some purpose. It had gone quite mad of course.

"These names." He cast an eye down the virtually illegible register. "Can any of them be your 'Václav'?"

Tsibulkin jumped out of his reverie.

"The man you're looking for is called 'Václav'?" In his excitement he snatched the board back. "Yes, this man here, Karel Sec, he is 'Václav'!"

"And how do you know that? There is no record in the NKVD reports."

"I've been conducting my own interrogations, to assist Captain Lesnikov. I interrogated this man myself. In fact, I was discussing the case with Comrade Korolev."

"And why was that?"

"The major... expressed an interest."

Andreev regarded him for several seconds. Having established a mental connection with men like this – it was like locating a carrier wave – he had found he could modulate it not only to read their thoughts but also to transmit his own.

Enough to make the man tremble, at any rate.

Are you playing with me, Tsibulkin? Have you guessed I know about the travel agency you and Lesnikov are running here? Are you offering me your drinking buddy Korolev in a general sense, to distract me from the loot in your safe, or are you truly playing the game, and with the both of us? Does your cabinet contain a contribution from Karel Sec? Did your guards walk him across the border zone, perhaps?

It was at this point Captain Lesnikov chose to clear his throat.

"I wish to state I knew nothing about any of this."

"That's perfectly clear." Andreev raised his voice. "Comrade, would you join us?"

The young major strolled over, smiling, like a virgin after seven abortions. He didn't bat an eyelid when Andreev mentioned Sec's name.

"Yes, I selected that one as worthy of further investigation. Why do you ask?"

Andreev dropped his airs and graces like a stone.

"Don't fuck with me, Korolev, you won't slide up my arse without soap. Do I have to remind you the GRU is prohibited from recruiting double agents?"

"Was he already a spy? I believe the evidence was... inconclusive?"

Andreev pointed his stick at the prisoner.

"Call that inconclusive? Buček can identify Sec as working for both the resistance and the fascists. He has also testified Sec had contact with British spies. That puts him firmly within my jurisdiction and well out of yours. If you know what's good for you."

Korolev shrugged. "I simply chose his name from the files here."

"And your Czech bum-chum?"

"Comrade Novák is observing for the Czechoslovak National Security Corps. As you'll be aware, they are establishing a State Security Service for when we pull out. Novák is a loyal Party member ensuring the new practices will be acceptable to Moscow." He gave a complicit smile and repeated. "I simply chose the name from the files."

"That was a mistake."

"Acknowledged."

Andreev nodded. He wondered what the *zeki* were making of this. The internees, he corrected himself. They were not prisoners, not quite, or not yet, although it was a subtle distinction. Their emaciated ranks were swaying and their eyes, intent upon the Soviet commanders, hollowing as the sun reached its zenith. How many had stood like this in the fascist camps? Several wore the clothing. More would have the numbers beneath their sleeves. He wanted to tell them that what went on here was a different type of selection, for an altogether different fate. But of course he could not. In the first place he would shortly be needing all his authority when he came to question them as to the whereabouts, habits or known associates of this absconder. His authority and their fear. In the second, well, however much he knew it to be true, he doubted they would believe him.

"Now will somebody, anybody, find me this 'Nightingale', Karel Sec!"

CHAPTER FOUR

The truck laboured over country roads, creaking like an ox-wagon. Sec could smell the flammable gas, and beer from a leaking barrel, and an older trace of livestock. Something on the floorboards danced and drummed like hailstones. Gravel? Bullets? He saw nothing through the chink of daylight at his chest. With his hands behind his back it was a struggle to sit upright.

He could smell something else, close, either side. Waxy grease on metal and canvas. It conjured up the meadow in the pre-dawn mist, the paraffin lamps and the drone of the bombers – then parachutes billowing, the exciting weight of the containers, a crackle of greaseproof paper, the musk of the guns. There was something heartrending about it, forever enmeshed in the thrill of the countryside at night, of first, metallic kisses and illicit dreams.

A turn sent him toppling. A boot on his chest righted him again. He shuddered at the casual violence. He was nothing more to them than a sack of coal or a barrel of beer.

In such a manner they had dragged, kicked and carried him from the camp, full of haste and anger, cursing his sloth, which was only weakness. He had not resisted, but neither had he been able to make his legs function as they demanded. He was too afraid of what would happen at the end of their march.

Sec had recognised the sentry patrolling the rear of the warehouse as one of the more prolific writers of the more illiterate *propuski*. The way he turned his back indicated he had been paid off in advance. Soon they had been crossing the fallow ground, using the remaining cover – a blasted tree, a bullet-riddled scarecrow no less convincingly human than the figures they had left behind. Before they skirted the gendarme's post, she had stopped and fixed him with that piercing gaze.

"Are you going to be quiet, Václav?"

"Yes, Miss."

He saw something tug the corner of that broad peasant mouth, some last vestige of good humour. He had always thought of the groove there as a mark of self-awareness, not age. Even now, streaked in dirt, with an old scarf over her hair and a ragged coat draped across her shoulders, with one arm in a sling torn from blackout sheets and the other hand clutching a pistol, she still looked defiantly unblemished.

So they had run on, stumbling in the furrows, until they had come to the crazy barn. Having borne the brunt of a gale or blast without effective bracing, the building had leaned over with its timbers still aligned, as though distorted by a wide-angle lens.

Yet there remained perpendiculars in this unsettling landscape. They were revealed at the front of the barn. It was obvious they were perpendiculars because they hung true as plumblines from the rafters. Not farming folk. The man wore a skiing jacket, the mother and daughter actual stockings, and there were suitcases and decent shoes scattered beneath them, albeit muddy from their trek. Most likely they had come south and west from the Sudeten Reichsgau once it had returned to Czechoslovak jurisdiction. It would have been a hard journey in many ways. Finding the border closed, they had chosen to trek no further.

The two young men had seized Sec by his arms, while a third man, unseen and suddenly present, forced a sack over his head. Ice shot through his veins.

Then the jet-whine and knocking of the wood-gas generator. As he was tossed in and the truck jolted forwards in a noxious vapour, he started using his brain again. They had come all this way for him, *she* had come for him, to snatch him from under the noses of the secret police. They wouldn't have taken such a risk just to drive him out into a field and put a bullet in him. The bag was a blessing, not a condemned man's hood. It meant they were taking him somewhere they didn't want him to see, because they didn't want him to be able to describe it later. Later. The word was all he had to cling to.

*   *   *

She sat facing him across the big steel table, flanked by the older man and the youngster in late teens or early twenties who was obviously his son. Now there was no twist to those Slavonic lips. Her face was blank, her wide-set eyes cold as stone.

"I need you to tell me what happened, Karel. Where the package came from. Why you betrayed me, and to whom."

Despite his experience of interrogations, Sec jumped twice. Once at the use of his real name instead of the underground codename with its undertones of camaraderie and affection. Once again at the harsh reality of that word, betrayal.

"Slečna Slavík – Miss 'Nightingale' – I believe you already know who I conspired with. I think you saw him today as a prisoner of the NKVD, this man Buček."

"Buček," she repeated back to him. She was not asking for confirmation, nor was his answer such. This was a reckoning.

"Yes."

"What I know about Buček is what happened at the handover. He and Kobylka killed Little Jan and tried to kill me."

"I heard something of it, Miss, but I did not know about Little Jan. I'm sorry for that. For everything," he tried to add. But that was not what she wanted from him.

"You were the intermediary who arranged for me to join Buček's group with Kobylka and Little Jan. You urged me to take Kobylka, so I assume you knew he was working for Buček, and that they were waiting for us to show our hand."

"Yes."

"You told them we'd try to stop them passing on the package, that I wanted it myself."

"I told them that was my understanding of your plan."

"And this is Buček...?"

"...and Kobylka, yes."

"No others?"

"Two of Buček's men, Hála and Cermák, but they were foot-soldiers, Kobylka's cohorts. The first approach came from Kobylka, then I met with Buček."

He saw her narrow her eyes at each name, even the last two, Hála and Cermák.

"Why, Karel?"

"Because they had something on me." The burden was constricting his chest, as it had suffocated him when first he took it on. Soon he'd be free of it.

"What was it?"

"That I had worked for the Gestapo."

His eyes did not leave hers, but he heard her two companions suck in their breath and the older one mutter a savage oath. He knew they were cradling their guns under the table and now he had confessed a part of him wished they would put them to use. As calmly as he could, he lifted his hands and removed his spectacles to clean them.

"You were a *Vertrauensmann*?" Her tone was mild, her thoughts unfathomable, as they had often been. Had she known? He guessed not. Suspected? Perhaps afterwards, surely not before. Was she angry? The word was meaningless: everyone was angry now. Disappointed? How could he dare to contemplate such an obsolete peacetime emotion?

"A confidant, that's right, reporting to the Erlan company in Brno. That was just a front for informers. I joined underground groups to obtain information on them. Communist groups, the PRNC and R3, everyone."

"My group?"

He gave his spectacles a last wipe. It was a miracle they

had not been further damaged in the bag. When he replaced them he saw the disbelief in her face. She had trusted him.

"No, Miss. Or rather, I did join your group with a view to exposing it, but circumstances changed. I did not inform on you."

"You'd have been arrested for failing to report."

"I went underground, properly. I became 'Václav' for real. I fought for the resistance. I killed Nazis. Even if I betrayed you too in the end, Miss Slavík, please remember I killed Nazis."

"I know you did. I have seen you do it."

The older man cursed again.

"As I saw the Vlasovs kill the SS in Prague! But are we to forget all those they murdered before, when they were doing their dirty work for them?"

"Hush, Josef," she said. "What circumstances changed?"

"My wife..."

He had thought he was going to tell it, simply and calmly, as he had told her he was a Gestapo informer, but no sooner had he moistened his lips than the words crumbled in the back of his mouth. He shook his head, ashamed. Tears welled again.

Miss Slavík told them to fetch him a drink. The young man, Vojtěch he was called, brought a glass of water. Sec drank like a castaway.

"Your wife?"

"Sabina. She died. When I heard, there was no reason to help them anymore."

"So they had her, as a lever?"

He let out a shrill laugh that made everyone start.

"It was more subtle than that! We must credit them with ingenuity if nothing else."

The anger had risen in him too now, his boundless rage at himself and all those who sat in judgement. He jabbed a finger at the man Josef.

"I'll tell you something, brother. Heydrich died a soldier's death. You won't hear that anywhere but it's true. The Butcher, the Hangman, the biggest Nazi of them all, died a soldier's death. When our martyred heroes pulled out their guns, this psychotic clerk, this preening bureaucrat, this coward and bully drew his pistol and stood up in the car, firing back. When the grenade exploded in his face, he vaulted over the side, covered in blood, uniform in tatters, and ran after them, shooting, until he collapsed from his wounds. Where does that fit in your scheme of things?"

"You were there that day," Miss Slavík said.

He nodded, trying to remember without remembering, to feel without feeling.

"Sabina and I lived in Liben, it was all we could afford. We were teachers at the same school. That morning we were catching the tram into town as usual. I didn't want her to wear that dress – some of the boys were quite uncouth, especially the sons of, you know, the collaborators. Then it happened and the Germans came and rounded everybody up. I was across the road from Sabina. I might have crossed and been with her, but we were taken in separate trucks and I never saw her again." He tried to lift his chin but the strength had deserted him. "In the Pečkárna they told me they were torturing Sabina. Then they told me the deal. If I became a confidant, they would treat her humanely. If I refused, or I failed to provide information, they would shoot her. This was in those dark days after Heydrich when they could do anything. They were going to wind up the underground once and for all and needed informers to do it. What they didn't tell me was they had offered Sabina the same deal. You see their reasoning? Why go to the trouble of imprisoning one, when they could get two willing recruits?"

Josef cursed. Miss Slavík just nodded.

"They placed you in different parts of the country?"

"Sabina, I eventually heard, was in Bohemia. I was in Moravia, as you know. It was easy to join the groups. All those cut-outs, all those underground names we made up for ourselves, calling them codenames. The secrecy was a big, bright badge we wore. Nobody ever asked the right questions. I took the codename Václav but all the time I was Karel Sec, and he betrayed a lot of good Czechs to the Gestapo in '43 and '44. At first, they gathered intelligence, piecing together the networks in their files, investigating the links that we – you – should have investigated yourselves. Then they started the arrests. Many were tortured or took their own lives because of Karel Sec."

"And Sabina?"

"My wife was less successful. The second group she infiltrated exposed her, somehow. Perhaps she took someone into her confidence. She was always a very open person. They beat her to death some time over Christmas '43. Needless to say, my handler at Erlan chose not to tell me."

"And after that you were with the Slavík network."

"You were so earnest, planning for the big finale and the future of Czechoslovakia, but all I wanted to do when I heard about Sabina was to kill Nazis and eventually we did. I'm grateful to you, for giving me that."

"So who told you?"

"Kobylka. He must have heard it from Buček. Buček knew everything. He was going to expose me, before I got my chance. I couldn't let that happen." He marvelled at the twisted logic, but it had made perfect sense at the time. Only since the killing had ended and the desire to kill had faded had everything stopped making sense.

"That Kobylka," he said, remembering. "He's a nasty piece of work!"

"He's dead," she shifted her shoulder under the black sling. "So are Hála and Cermák. And Buček's in the hands of the Russians. That leaves you, Karel."

He jumped as she slammed down her revolver, but it was just the weight of it on the metal and she was only freeing her hand to search for cigarettes. Sec recognised her gold lighter. Having offered them to Josef and his son, she slid the packet and lighter across the table and her sleeve brushed the butt of the pistol, swivelling it towards him.

Smoke caressed the cobwebbed roof-space. The derelict mill was poorly shuttered and dusty beams of late afternoon sun were slinking across the walls. Sec heard an insect trapped somewhere, and the ticking of a watch. He was about to tell her what she wanted to know when he became aware of another sound growing closer, a motorcycle, free-wheeling over rough ground. None of his interrogators showed any alarm. The machine's muted approach must have been a pre-arranged signal.

The rider entered in a cloud of yellow dust. It was the second young man who had sprung him from the transit camp, a tall, fair-haired fellow they called Tomáš. Hooded as he had been, Sec hadn't realised they'd left anyone behind.

"No chance at all," Tomáš was saying. "The Ivans have surrounded the whole area. I was lucky to get out when I did. They must have brought in a motor-rifle brigade!"

"You're a popular man," Vojtěch told Sec, no doubt eager to appear to be taking an active part in the interrogation. In truth he sounded impressed.

His father was less so.

"Idiot! You know what this means? They will call out every man in the district. They arrive before dawn in their black crows, and everyone must report for their *malenki robot*. Just three days, they say. But don't think this 'little work detail' means you'll be repairing roads in your own district, close to home. There is no way home!"

Miss Slavík stubbed out her cigarette. Her arm brushed the revolver.

"We don't know that will happen here. As with the Nazis, what is done freely in the east is done with more discretion in the west."

She regarded Sec again.

"According to the sentries we bribed, those Russians who brought Buček to identify you weren't normal secret police, they were SMERSh. Does that surprise you?"

"I don't understand."

"Soviet military counter-intelligence. Working on special projects, orders from Moscow. Wouldn't you say that was overdoing it, to pick up a Gestapo informer?" Seeing his blank expression – blank bordering on stunned, bordering on terrified in this land of shifting borders – she rapped on the table with small, pointed knuckles.

"The package, Karel. You must know more about it than you let on. More than Buček too, I'd say. We only saw him from a distance, but he didn't look like a man who had managed to hold anything back."

"But it was Kobylka! Kobylka first got hold of the package. It was meant for your group but he gave it to Buček's. Buček gave it to... whoever you saw! I don't know what was in it, only what I told you I'd overheard at the time, something about an electro-magnetic separation process. I don't know what that is. I teach geography!"

"But you know how Kobylka got it. You know who gave it to him, don't you?"

He shook his head. It was the final cursed ballast. Then there would be nothing left to bind him to the rolling, turning earth. He would float away like a balloon, rising higher and higher until the air became too thin to breathe and there could be no more Karel Sec, no more Václav and no more I. Did he dare let go? Would she be waiting for him there?

"Not who, Miss," he said at last. "But I do know where."

*　　*　　*

All that had been some time ago. It had been dusk when they departed. Now it was dark.

Karel Sec sat at the table where he had sat all afternoon and evening. Now he was alone he leaned forwards and placed his face in his hands.

Like a child in delicious terror of monsters, he peeked between his fingers. The moonlight glinted on his spectacles, and Miss Slavík's pistol, lying where she had left it.

"We cannot take you with us," she had said. "We cannot keep you until your story checks out. Everyone is looking for you and someone will find you. So you must swear to me, on your love for Sabina, on her love for you, you have told us the whole truth."

He had sworn. He had seen she believed him.

"Now we are going, Václav." Her voice was lighter, as he had remembered it. If not affection, there remained something tender in the way she said his name. What an unexpected blessing, to hear one last time the tenderness of a woman saying his name.

"I understand, Miss."

The men had already left the room. As she rose, she laid her hand on the gun but did not pick it up.

"I'm sorry for everything that has happened to you. You have been through a lot. More than most of us."

"As the Ivans say, *I* is the last letter of the alphabet."

His heart had leapt when he saw she was going to say it, and with proper affection. It was all he could have asked for.

"Philosophy, Václav?"

And she was gone.

The man who had once been Karel Sec, and was Václav again, had sat back and removed his spectacles. Twilight was descending into darkness. He would not need them now. He picked up the packet she had left and, frowning at its weight, found the gold lighter tucked in with the last three cigarettes. He looked up guiltily, although he had already heard the vehicles disappear over the hill. A mistake? A parting gift?

On an impulse he sniffed the lighter, but it smelled only of gas. He flicked it open and lit it, flicked it shut again. He turned it over and over. On its side there was an undecorated panel for an inscription. Perhaps it had once held an inscription, for it looked indented, repaired and repolished, but if they'd been there the words had been effaced.

He lit one of the cigarettes. There would be no call for

barter again.

Later he lit the second. Later, perhaps, he would light the third. *Later.*

It was tiredness that made him put his face in his hands. There were no tears now. His heart had been buoyed by that last blessing, the tenderness of a woman, even directed at a worm such as he – a traitor, a nothing, a black joke, a geography teacher in a land without place names or frontiers, on a continent with its populations upended, in a world where the maps were redundant. But he no longer minded what he was or what he had been. All that mattered was the look on her face as she had said farewell. The look that said he was a human being in her eyes.

And the other look he carried in his mind. Sabina's look as the Germans parted them forever. Why had he spent so much time and anguish searching for its meaning, when its meaning had been there all along? It hadn't meant sorry, or wait for me, or be true to me. It hadn't been a promise to behave well or an entreaty to him to do the same. Neither had it meant do what they want, nor don't let them use me against you, nor any of those other fanciful notions he had brought to his obsessive cryptanalysis.

Sabina's look meant I love you. In the end, that was what human beings said. Not we love each other, not you love me, not any form of love passive, abstract and ideal but *I*, *I* love you. That was what being human was, it was what defined their existence.

"I love you."

He flung out a hand and fumbled for the gun. Eyes tight shut, he brought it up to his head and fired.

CHAPTER FIVE

"What I am about to disclose is so secret the authorisation had to come from Number 10!"

Bradley frowned and shook his head.

"Downing Street!" Jones yelled. "The War Cabinet!"

They were lying like a pair of helpless beetles on the walkway above the bomb-bay. Restricted by the sheepskins and harnesses, Jones had to wriggle onto his side to check that the wireless operator and navigator were otherwise engaged in their compartments beyond the main wing spar. He even rolled the other way to look aft, although the rear of the airplane was jammed with boxes stamped BENGAL FAMINE MIXTURE (POWDERED), AMIGEN PROTEIN HYDROLYSATE (INTRAVENOUS) or labelled in impenetrable Cyrillic characters. Apparently satisfied, he huddled closer.

"Sergeant, your people – and mine – are working on a weapon with an explosive force a hundred thousand times greater than the kind of bombs this crate carried on this trip."

"Did you say a thousand times?"

"I said a hundred thousand times." Jones brought up two Michelin-man arms as though holding a basketball in his mitts. "A bomb this size could destroy a city. If we were to drop it now, we'd be vaporised."

Bradley peered over the edge of the walkway, where a couple of small inspection windows looked into the bomb-bay. Because the bomb-bay doors had been left ajar to accommodate the huge containers of supplies slung in the bomb-racks, beams of white light shone through the windows, bright ellipses rippling over the boxes like full moons on a harbour swell. He knew they were flying just below 8,000 feet to spare them the oxygen masks, but he needed this illusory view to confirm their altitude to himself.

Not as high as on ops, but still a mile and a half in the sky. Vaporised?

"That would end the Pacific war tomorrow."

Jones had read his lips.

"Unfortunately the weapon won't be ready tomorrow. Nor next week. Nor next month. We've been working on it for years. So were the Germans. That's right, they were working on one. Suffice it to say many of the raids you've heard about over the past two years have been directed at the German project, as well as most of the raids you haven't."

The Englishman clasped him in an urgent embrace.

"I'm telling you this because it has to do with the package we collected, yes? The weapon is an atomic bomb. It releases unimaginable energy by splitting the atoms of an unstable substance, uranium. Uranium atoms exist in different forms, called isotopes, but only the rarest – the purest, if you like – can make the bomb. The great difficulty is in obtaining sufficient quantities of sufficiently pure uranium. Understand?"

Bradley moved his head in acknowledgement. He figured it would make more sense if he kept listening.

"The German boff..." Jones was cut short by a piercing whistle and blast of wind as the airplane banked. For several seconds every surface rattled independently. Then they were bathed in warm sunshine from the forward section. The cacophony diminished. To Bradley's ears even the drone of the motors was muted.

It seemed they had been flying for ages. The engine note and the vibration had become the norm, the bass resonance of the four cruising motors lulling him into a daze, so that even this insane talk of city-vaporising basketballs had a job breaking through. Perhaps they *were* short of oxygen and ought to strap on their masks. Perhaps Jones hadn't told him anything about a bomb made from an atom.

He had been on the move since the previous morning. Perhaps the morning before that. The car to Inverness, the overcrowded sleeper to London, the Anson to Paris... He'd been looking forward to a coffee and shave in Paris, but there was Jones, driving out onto the apron, gesturing towards the white-painted bomber already running up its engines.

No rest for the wicked, they said.

*   *   *

"Czecho?" The training officer raised his eyebrows. "Not sure we've ever prepped a chap for Czecho before, not one of ours anyway."

"And Berlin," Bradley prompted. He knew it was all an act and even suspected the training officers were Czech. This one was a lieutenant and wore the badges of the Royal Engineers. Sanders, he called himself.

"My, my, we are going to be busy! And we've only three weeks? Well, let's see... no time for signals training and suchlike, but you shan't be able to take a W/T set anyway. We'll settle on some code words and free cryptic styles once we know how your comms are to be arranged, get you memorising them. I see you were a Ranger, so I'm sure we can take your armed and unarmed combat skills as read. Demolitions? I'll put you down for the crash course. That's mine, as it happens..."

Beyond the misted windows of the office in the stable block, a persistent rain pattered at the rows of Quonset huts. It sounded like fingernails drumming on a desk. Bradley turned back to face Lieutenant Sanders' unblinking stare.

"Huh?"

"I said 'How's your German?' I used colloquial Berlin dialect. Didn't understand me, did you? How's your Russian? That bad, eh? Czech?"

Bradley shook his head.

"Dear, dear. You do know what I said before was true? It wasn't anything like France or Holland. The Czech Army-in-exile supplied their own volunteers and more often than not Czech Intelligence ran them. We helped out with the commando and parachute courses and a spot of cipher work. The men knew the language, the country and its customs backwards

— and so they ought to have! They had only recently left it."
  "The men."
  "Well, yes. And the woman. But that was a very particular case."

*   *   *

"Sergeant?"

  "Sorry sir. I'm listening."

  "I was saying... the German boffins at the Kaiser-Wilhelm Institute were the leaders in this field before the war. Those we didn't flatten in Berlin will be in Soviet hands, but we have captured a number in southern Germany. Much of the uranium research was transferred there once Berlin and Frankfurt began to reap the whirlwind. And it was not by accident certain US Army units pushed so quickly into Heidelberg and the Black Forest ahead of the designated French occupation forces."

  "You're kidding me." It was like finding out he'd been fighting a different war from everybody else.

  "I rarely kid, Sergeant, and never about this. What we have discovered from the scientists we captured is that our own chaps have overtaken their research in any case. The issue is no longer pure theory but experimental physics and chemistry. If you like, we are no longer so interested in the top men who understand it all. We are after the little men who have been fiddling about with ways to make it work in practice."

  "Sure," Bradley said. He got that bit.

  "Now, despite your protestations to the contrary, I know you were involved in your country's OVERCAST project to obtain the services of the rocket technicians, so you'll appreciate the context. We are eager to get these chaps, and just as eager Stalin does not. Which means cutting out the French as well."

  "But didn't you catch them in, where was it, Heidelberg?"

  "That general region. We discovered only a fraction there. In the first place, the Nazis dispersed their industry when we started in on their cities. In the second, this was nothing like their rocket programme. We're talking about dozens of projects, each experimenting with different methods, each funded by a different ministry or based within a different company, each staffed by its own merry band of secretive, jealous, competitive individuals. I'm sure you can imagine what these scientists are like. All they care about is the funding to carry on with their work and the promise of recognition by their peers. These were men of many nationalities, including a good few who ought not to have been developing weapons for the Nazis, had they ever stopped to think about it. They were spread out across the Reich, in research institutes, universities, country retreats. Many have been scooped up by the Soviets or our own people, but many more have gone to ground, and one of these has caught our attention."

Jones produced a photo-copy of a page from a German scientific journal. Whatever Sanders might think of his conversation, Bradley had been taught a fair bit of technical language before his posting to the Joint Chiefs' OVERCAST project, yet most of the words here were beyond him. In their midst, a grainy picture showed four men in pre-war suits posing beside a piece of apparatus that looked like a cross between a hotel lobby decoration and the kind of thing you hung above a baby's crib.

"The man on the left is the subject of the article. Werner Heisenberg, won the Nobel Prize for Physics. Next to him is Otto Hahn, the chap who first discovered uranium fission. We have both of them, in a charming house near Cambridge, although I'd rather you didn't spread that around. The tall fellow in the middle is of no concern – he has been in the United States since '41 – but the one on the right is our man. He isn't even named in the article. As far as we can tell he was only there to supervise the uranium isotope measurements, but this is the sole picture we have of him. His name is Theodor Lossner. He is a Czech citizen of German extraction and was at that time a Professor at Karl-Ferdinand University in Prague. Got that?"

Bradley grunted. He could hear him fine now. The air no longer howled around the patch where the upper turret ought to have been. Perhaps they'd begun their descent.

He examined the picture. A miserable looking bunch. Professor Lossner was the most sour-faced of the lot – the youngest too. Without the heavy round eyeglasses, he might have been one for the ladies. But no, that was a nasty twist to his lips, you could tell. Not a ladies' man, or not that sort of ladies' man.

Perhaps it was how you were meant to pose for a serious scientific snapshot. Like even if you weren't letting on, you knew deep down what you were going to do to the world and what the world would think of you in return.

"The package has to do with him?"

"Correct. I know it's a bad picture but study it because I am going to burn it." Jones brought out a battered hipflask, took a slug and passed it over. Cognac.

"Thirsty work, all this yelling."

"Yes sir. Thank you sir."

"Right, here's the thing. Lossner is a uranium nut. Always has been. Grew up with the mines at Joachimsthal, which is where the Nazis got all their stocks once they'd annexed the Sudetenland. His speciality is electro-magnetic isotope separation. It's a very efficient way of enriching the uranium, which means increasing the proportion of the rare isotope. As I said, the German atom project was always hampered by the lack of sufficiently pure uranium. They were managing to get around it by using something called 'heavy water' until our cloak-and-dagger boys visited their manufacturing plant in Norway. After that they were forced to explore other processes for enriching the uranium to such a percentage they no longer required this heavy water. The point is that it's here, apparently, atomic research stops being theoretical and the production of a bomb becomes a viable proposition. Professor Lossner's process was a significant step towards it."

"But they never made this bomb, right?"

Jones shook his head.

"From what we can gather they were getting close, but some critical miscalculations set them back, for which we should all be grateful. Even you, Bradley. They were developing a long-range aircraft to carry one to New York."

Maybe he wouldn't have believed that on the ground. Up here, detached from the world, it made him queasy thinking about it. All those skyscrapers. All those atoms.

"So this guy would be useful to have around?"

"Exactly. With the casualties being sustained in the Pacific, our own bomb can't come soon enough. Lossner's process is of enormous interest to your people and mine. Don't worry, Sergeant, they're the same people, it's a joint effort at this level. Anything and everything to speed things along!" He smiled behind the flying cap and its dangling oxygen mask. "It's also imperative he doesn't end up with the Soviets. If they've unearthed any theorists from the Kaiser-Wilhelm Institute, letting them find a chap with one of the practical solutions is absolutely unacceptable. Churchill and Truman are going to have to inform Stalin about our bomb, but let's not tell the blighter how to build one."

"And the package was what?"

"It contained a selection of Lossner's notes. We were tipped off as to their existence by one of our sources in Czechoslovakia. Not the MERCURY group. Provenance is uncertain but we let the chaps in Cambridgeshire have a look and they're convinced it's genuine. Chatted all night about it when they thought we weren't listening and I suppose that's Nobel prize-winners for you. The problem is the notes are incomplete. Mr Smith and I are of the opinion they constitute a proof of identity. Professor Lossner, we believe, is going to come out of hiding to offer someone his services. We would like that to be us."

"You're not asking me...?"

"Heavens no! There are professionals working on this. Your mission remains as briefed. Bring Ludmila Suková home if you can. Failing that, report back on the activities of the MERCURY or 'Nightingale' circuit, so we can take steps to shut it down. I have obtained authorisation to tell you about the package because, as we both saw, the woman is somehow mixed up in this. She tried twice to prevent us from getting the papers. If she is still working against us or pursuing her own agenda, it could jeopardise the efforts of the people who are looking for this charmer." He took back the photo-copy in one glove and tugged at the other with his teeth. "Of course..."

"What's that sir?"

"...if you should happen to get any lead on Lossner, don't keep it to yourself."

Jones' lighter appeared in his hand and he played the flame over the bottom of the photo-copy. It took a while to catch fire, then the grim-faced professors were engulfed. Jones switched it to his gloved hand as the embers blew along the airplane.

"A fitting end, wouldn't you say?"

Bradley nodded. He couldn't figure Jones out. One minute he was all classified-this and top-secret-that, the next sounding off like a maiden aunt.

Some of it he could guess. Even if they wanted to wind up MERCURY, Jones' business behind the iron curtain must involve maintaining other networks. Nor did it take a genius, or a Nobel prize-winner, to see they were hoping his mission would flush Lossner out. But there was something big they weren't telling him and it had to do with the girl. What were they hoping he'd blunder into?

He kept coming back to the handover. Jones had told Smith he hadn't recognised the girl. Even if that was true, it meant he'd met her before, so you had to assume she'd have recognised him. In which case, given what had happened, she was surely working against them now.

So why go to the trouble of pulling her out? Because she was Smith's wife? Bradley had believed the old guy in Montmartre. But it didn't explain Jones acting like it was a big deal too. And none of it explained why they had turned to a burnt-out G.I. who couldn't even read Russian to take care of their business in the east.

Of course, he wasn't just a G.I. and somehow they knew that. They knew he'd been reassigned to OVERCAST and he hoped they understood that all he'd been tasked with was escorting unidentified civilians into Nazi establishments ahead of the main force. However much they knew, he had to assume it included what had happened in the slush and sleet of Bavaria that day in April. Wasn't that how they had got ahold of him?

Was it also *why*?

"Huh?" He'd been miles away, and getting close to a place he had no wish to revisit.

"I said how was Scotland?"

"Scotland was a blast. Literally, on a couple of occasions."

"Glad to hear it. But they've also briefed you thoroughly on our official business?"

"Sure. I'm UNRRA all the way. William Brown, attached to the Berlin mission. Friends call me Bill."

"Well then, you will have passed through the Training Headquarters in Granville. I've stayed at the Hotel Normandie myself."

Bradley smiled.

"Unfortunately, I never visited the *reception billet* at the hotel. As you'll recall, sir, a couple of months ago the Germans launched a last-ditch commando raid on Granville from their base on the Channel Islands. My class was due to arrive at the hotel right before it was hit and instead we had to make do with temporary tented accommodation. I did attend the training school itself in Jullouville, however."

Jones shook his head.

"You were fine with the Granville story. Now, an UNRRA team comprises a director, doctor, welfare officer, cook, and various supply officers, nurses and drivers. Which are you?"

"The Berlin team is concerned with negotiation and planning. It is not active in the normal sense. As for myself, I was given a specific investigative brief back in the States. I'm to conduct a study of the scale of the problem in the Czech Displaced Persons camps and report back via the Berlin mission. This has been cleared with the mission's director, Captain Trushnovich, who is himself a Soviet citizen."

"Why aren't you serving your country in her armed forces?"

"I was. US Rangers, 2nd battalion. I was wounded in Normandy and discharged on the grounds of disability."

"Got the wound?"

"A bunch of shrapnel scars and a gouge out the side of my skull."

"Hmm... saw that before. Give you much gyp? Keep you awake nights?"

"How do you mean?"

"I was told you woke up in a funk every night in Scotland, or on the nights you managed to get to sleep at all. Screaming blue murder, they said. Unhealthy habit."

Bradley stared at him.

"I've had nightmares, since Normandy. More, lately. But I won't yell out anything compromising, if that's what you mean."

"Normandy, yes. Were you Section Eighted?"

"If they want to make that assumption, I can live with it."

The Englishman brushed at his moustache. Thoughtfully. Maybe.

"Goes without saying they'll assume we're spies. Stalin assumes everyone is a spy as a matter of course."

"Must make it difficult to filter out the real ones."

Jones threw him an expression of violent scorn. Disgust almost.

"Make no mistake, Sergeant, the Soviet counter-espionage machine is formidable. It would dwarf most Western armies. And yes, they do know the difference between those they accuse of being spies and those whom they actually suspect. If you treat this lightly, I guarantee within a week you will have been swallowed whole."

* * *

"A one-way trip, it was. That's why we could only ever use Czechs. No way back, you see? We could get a bomber over there – just – on a long winter's night, for a few days either side of the moon, weather permitting. Drop men and supplies. But no pick-ups. They knew they were there for the duration. God and Gestapo willing."

Sanders looked miserable.

"The other reason we'd only use Czechs is their Intelligence here had a direct link with Moscow. We found that useful at times, but I doubt it helped the men we dropped."

"The men."

"Well, yes. And her."

* * *

After his words of warning Jones lost interest in the mock-interrogation. They sat unspeaking until they noticed the upper half of a leather-clad figure observing them from the shallow arch above the wing spar. The RAF crewmember held the oxygen mask to his mouth to speak into the intercom, then let it fall and called out something instead.

"Go and see what he wants."

Bradley got up into a crouch and clambered over the lesser spars and obstacles to the solid bulkhead of the main spar. Although this area between the wings was also jammed with bags and boxes, he spotted a fold-down rest-bed, which he coveted. It was near the heater. It was also covered in bananas.

"What is it?" he mouthed, but the wireless operator just beamed at him through the arch and pointed upwards with a finger. No need for gloves, near that heater outlet.

Above the Limey was a glass dome from which light flooded into the forward compartment. It would be for the navigator to take his star readings. This was a night bomber after all, that was why the paint on the exposed ribs and stringers changed from primer green to matt black forward of this bulkhead, and why there were black curtains around the equipment in those work areas behind the cockpit.

"Come and look!" The guy grinned. Bradley caught the words "...red carpet treatment!"

"How do I get through with all this on?"

"...ruddy parachute off."

He wasn't having that. There were stanchions, cylinders and hoses everywhere but with a superhuman effort he got one leg over the spar and let the Limey pull him through like popping a cork.

"Well done old chap!" They were both panting.

Now he was in the forward compartment, Bradley heard music. A rhythm section, slow, and the creamiest vocal quartet. The wireless operator had one of his sets tuned to an AFRS transcription.

"That the group used to be with Dorsey?"

"Spot on. Pied Pipers. Lovely June Hutton!" He was ginger, with a spiky attempt at an air force moustache. The kind of irrepressible little guy you'd gladly throttle at a party but not up here, in his private domain. He sang along, scampering ahead of the song. "*Dream — when you're feelin' blue...*' Well go on, stick your head up, take a butcher's!"

"A what?" As Bradley stood up in the dome, the words died on his lips. He was outside the airplane. The creaking and juddering had faded away, to be replaced by a cleaner engine note and a rush of air against the glass. The whole world harmonised with the hypnotic rhythm of the song. At first he saw nothing. It was so bright they might have been orbiting the sun like a moth around a lamp. Then, narrowing his eyes, he saw them. Sleek shapes hovered above the giant airscrews on the port side. Red stars on olive green. Russian fighters.

As he watched, they bounced and jostled like magnets, alternately attracted and repelled by the bomber and each other. They were drifting closer, inboard of the great, whitewashed wing. He saw their shadows creep across the ghosts of the RAF markings.

One of them dipped a wingtip and broke upwards into a roll around the bomber. From his bubble he watched it pass overhead, upside down, before it disappeared beneath the wing on the other side. He turned his head and, sure enough, there was the fighter rising up on the port side once more to resume its original station. He had seen something like that before. Dolphins, playing in the bow-wave of the troopship, on another sunny day, a thousand years ago.

The Limey was fussing at him and trying to fit his head inside the dome.

"Did you see? The pilot, old chap, the pilot!"

The fighters were so close he could indeed make out the figures of their pilots through their canopies. Yes, there was a face turned in his direction. A cloth flying cap, with goggles pushed up on the forehead. A broad, rugged face.

"See her?"

Her? He switched to the other fighter floating just behind and above and there she was. Not much doubt about the small, round head, the feminine features and the narrow set of her shoulders as she turned around in her seat. Certainly no mistaking the kiss she blew to him, Hollywood bombshell style.

"See her?"

"Sure do. Yeah, I see you, hon. You're a doll. Lemme give you a wave... Whoah!" All at once the world tilted over, Beautiful Buckette Rogers and her buddy fell out of sight, and he smashed his head against the inside of the dome. The Limey steadied him.

"We're coming in for our approach. I have to get back on the R/T. Give her my love won't you."

"Wait a minute. You mean this is it?"

The guy didn't hear him. The motors roared as the pilot put the airplane into a turn to starboard. Holding on for dear life in the dome, Bradley saw a blur of clouds, land and lakes. The noise subsided, the turn eased off. There it was, spread out ahead, the big city.

He heard the song on the radio, or another like it. Only seconds had passed. But everything was different now.

As the airplane renewed its turn, Berlin lurched upwards and loomed over him. In a never-ending loop came street after street and block after block of yellow-grey dust and empty grey-brown boxes. Not a wall had its four corners, not a building its roof. Not a tree was in leaf nor a public space green. What natural colour remained seemed unnaturally excessive: the weeds grown unchecked across the winter's bombsites, the recent shell-craters like African waterholes. Then, when you thought it could get no worse, there'd be a whole block reduced to ashes.

And there was something else. He hardly believed it, but he could *smell* Berlin from here. The damp of churned-up earth. The reek of busted sewers and flooded basements. The sharp, sour tang of putrefaction.

The city smelled like it looked, like something brought up from the bottom of the ocean. And it looked like that atomic bomb had done its work and broken everything down to atoms too. At intervals a sign of previous human habitation passed beneath – a cart without a horse, a streetcar in a crater, a tank or an artillery piece like a squashed bug on a splash of scorched ground – but there was nothing moving and nobody to be seen. How could there be? Everything was dust.

As they levelled out, Bradley watched the shadow of the bomber, huge and broad-winged, rushing over the ruins like... well, not like any moth, more like the Angel of Death. A second shadow detached itself. He looked up and there was the girl in the fighter keeping pace with them.

Not knowing what to think, he raised a hand. The girl dipped her head, threw him a wink and shot up into the sun.

Bradley came down out of the bubble. It was one hell of a crazy world they were trying to save.

If that was what they were doing.

PART TWO

BEHIND THE CURTAIN

CHAPTER SIX

The hotel had once stood in the middle of a block and was now on the corner. Its address was a backstreet behind Alexanderplatz but now it looked out over the square.

This rise to prominence had nearly been the death of it. At some point it had tried to turn itself inside out. Now, from certain angles, it could be caught displaying its interior décor to prospective customers in the street, just like its more scandalous sisters.

What remained of the stucco facade was splashed with shrapnel and timber-shored like a ship in the stocks. There was no glass in the windows, no steam or water in the exposed pipes, no electricity in the tangles of flex. Every surface inside and out wore a coating of brick dust. Yet there was something majestic about the hotel's continuing existence amid the gutted shells and rubble mounds. However faded, or phony, the glamour of the *Gründerzeit* endured, grander now in this city of ruins than ever in those golden days.

Emerging from the lobby, Bradley blinked in the strange daylight. As a sniper his instinct was to calculate range and elevation, but stripped of cues such as crowds, cars and shopfronts, the fragmented landscape played curious tricks. Where it had been pulverised like this wasteground, everything appeared far away. Where the buildings had been chewed up by machine gun fire, they seemed closer and smaller than they were.

In reality there was nothing small or fancy about Alexanderplatz. In their love of vast, square blocks – in the case of the station, vast glass vaults – the planners might have been Americans. After London and Paris, it came as a shock. The department store opposite, with neon letters on the roof, might have been on Fifth Avenue. JONASS & CO.

Then, as you were convincing yourself the destruction wasn't so bad, that the big stores at least had survived, you took two steps, the sun shone through, and they were skeletons. The building with the neon letters had a diagonal bite out of it, slicing down from that CO. Maybe it hadn't been an abbreviation for Company but a stranger word, now lost. Those red-rusted streetcars weren't waiting at a terminus, they were a sloughed snakeskin, a crumpled memory of shape and mass. The El-train tracks that had once rattled the rooftops now tottered in empty space. Only advertising columns and subway ventilators stood sentinel, ruffling their feather coats of survivors' messages.

Across the square, picking over the debris of the newly vacant lots, were the *Trümmerfrauen*, the rubble-women. They worked in human chains with bare hands and buckets, hunched in headscarves and aprons or overalls sewn from blankets. None would look up, for fear of drawing attention. Many bore evidence in toothless grimaces, black eyes and broken noses of times when this tactic had failed.

Several had tied scarves across their faces. Today it wasn't just flies and mosquitoes. Before he knew it he was back in the Hackensack marshes, choking on the fug from the rendering plants at Secaucus. Summer heat – the dead were making themselves known.

There were children among the rubble-women. It had become his ritual to give one a wave. The little girl checked her mother wasn't watching and waved back with a grin. She was painfully thin, with bony knees in boy's shorts and a boy's haircut, yet for all her mother's efforts her femininity shone out. Feeling guilty for having exposed it, Bradley turned and headed towards the river. What a world, in which innocence must be disguised!

He felt self-conscious in his ODs and UNRRA armband. Armbands nowadays carried more weight than old uniforms. Yet he knew it wasn't either of these that enabled him to pass unmolested through Soviet-occupied Berlin. What kept the soldiers away, or sent them packing when they came up to him demanding his wristwatch – *Uri! Uri!* – was the continual presence ten or twenty yards behind of his very own secret policeman.

He looked for today's shadow and spotted 'Eddie', as in Edward G. Robinson. Little Eddie could be relied upon to stick to him diligently, but always at a distance. Only if Jimmy or Georgie came on later might he strike up a grunt or two of conversation. If it was Bogey, he was screwed.

He was growing accustomed to Russian ways. First came the red tape. Not even your personal Public Enemy could help sidestep that. Partly it was to show you it was their city now, their zone of occupation, their victory. That was why the bomber had spent all afternoon on the Tempelhof taxiway, even with its supplies in urgent need. For hours they'd watched bulldozers making giant toy-boxes of broken transports, while the tower repeated that they had violated Soviet airspace and had no permission to land. But the bureaucracy wasn't all an act. Whatever their official capacity, everybody was afraid of everybody else, and nobody dared take responsibility for anything. The upshot being that when somebody, somewhere, could be persuaded to endorse the requisite paperwork, the Reds were as relieved as you were, and happy to make you feel at home.

Which led to phase two. Liquor. Next to these guys, his army buddies were sissies at a soda fountain. They drank like there was no tomorrow: a likely outcome, given the quality of their hooch. The reception at the airport had run into the reception at the hotel, and that had run on until dawn. Although he, Jones and the RAF crew had started out minding what they said, before long they might have given chapter and verse on the whole op without noticing. But by then their hosts were just as loaded and anyone manning a hidden microphone would have had his nerves shredded by breaking glass and tuneless songs.

That was the third phase. Surveillance and suspicion, interspersed with further bouts of vodka. The abiding, uneasy sensation of being watched, alone, and hung-over. And at every fresh obstacle the phases were repeated. Bradley had begun to despair of ever breaking the cycle and starting his enquiries in earnest.

For the first few days he'd shown up at the UNRRA mission in the north-eastern suburbs. That meant asking for a ride and the only working phone was in the hotel lobby. Possibly it was the only one in the city, save that at the other end – supposedly in an army signals detachment, more likely operated by the NKVD. The set-up didn't leave much elbow-room, not least because his jeep would arrive with a Russian WAC or a Komsomol interpreter at the wheel. At which point, with studied nonchalance, Eddie, Jimmy, Georgie or Bogey would stroll over to the rumble seat.

The UNRRA planners were among the first westerners to be granted a toehold in the conquered city but in true Soviet style they had been dumped far away from the one place they might have been able to function, namely Zhukov's headquarters in Karlshorst. Sweating it out while he waited for his travel orders to be rubber-stamped, Bradley sympathised. Most of his fellow Yanks on the team were 4-Fs looking for a way to live with themselves. None seemed to mind he knew doodly squat about planning an aid effort. They were all picking it up as they went along.

"Just bang on about Jews and calories," Jones had told him on the airplane. "Johnnie Red isn't interested in the former and doesn't understand the latter."

Since then, he had seen Jones at the UNRRA offices only once, for five minutes on the fourth day. Now wearing the service dress uniform of a Guards major, the Englishman had beckoned him out into the street.

"Borrow you for a moment, Brown..."

There was a dark limousine parked outside with a collection of Soviet civilians in it. Jones inclined his head to them and turned Bradley to walk in the other direction.

"Your papers have come through. I've left them with your front desk. All set?"

Bradley grimaced.

"How do I get away from my shadow?"

"You don't. Not until you need to. Preferably not even then."

The area was a modern housing development that had escaped severe damage. Evidently it was a popular billet with Red Army commanders for the concrete maze was scattered with Lend-Lease jeeps. The two men retraced their steps.

"If I were taking the Tube to Hammersmith Grove," Jones said. "I'd look in on the polio doctor. Quite the best ear specialist, is the good doctor."

"I'll remember that."

The crossing points at which the iron curtain might be opened to displaced persons had been given codenames drawn from London subway stations: Oxford Circus, Marlborough Road, King William Street and so on. Bradley was scheduled to inspect camps near each. Hammersmith Grove sat on the lines of demarcation between the US and Soviet forces south of the Pilsen salient. As for the polio doctor who specialised in ears...?

Jones lowered his voice.

"Mention Cracow. He'll mention Warsaw. You mention Spring. One other thing. Good news too." Jones' eyes said otherwise. "An UNRRA mission is being established in Prague to arrange shipments into Czechoslovakia, so it shouldn't be long before you'll have plenty of company. The director looks set to be a Russian."

"I understand, sir."

"Good luck, Brown. See if we can't do something for those DPs, and pronto."

How long ago had that been? Four days, five days? And

he was still stuck here in the big city, stooges on his tail, with his liaison officer telling him daily on the phone and nightly over vodka, *Izvinite*, no transport available.

Well, enough of that. He was through with getting under their feet at the UNRRA mission and going stir crazy in the doll's house hotel. He had his travel papers. He had a King's ransom in gold sovereigns in his waistband. And he'd had his warning. Any further delays and the real UNRRA officials would be there to blow his cover. He'd damn well *buy* some transport on the black market if he had to.

He passed the red shell of a municipal hall, its tower whittled away like a stick of jerky the dogs had got to. Reaching the river and the island, it was impossible not to think of those old sepia photographs of the San Francisco quake and fire. What hadn't burned out or collapsed in the air raids had been shot to pieces by tanks and artillery. Beyond the bridge there was only the blackened carcass of the palace, a whole city block of it.

Statues turned to stalagmites turned to stalactites on the murky Spree. The water, dense with particles, swirled round submerged shapes. Sunken barges. Uprooted trees. A civilian car, blown off the bridge or pushed through the parapet by a tank. Children at the water's edge wielded a pole. He couldn't see what was floating there and didn't want to.

Imperial buildings were one thing. Ravaged palaces he could handle. Apartment blocks brought down on their shelters, collapsed stations like the one on Alexanderplatz, were something else. They didn't make you feel good about mustering a thousand bombers to burn out Hitler's black heart.

Nor did the faint signs of life you glimpsed here and there amid the ruins, ribbons of cloth and smoke, flickering across the monochrome like butterflies in a cemetery. They belonged to the refugees from the east who had no claim to the precious basements.

They lived on the rubble because the Red Army lived on the street. Every block meant negotiating shaggy ponies and sideshow wagons. When you breathed in, fearing bodies, you got horse shit instead, and human shit, and their cooking. In the distance, along the dust-haze of the Unter den Linden, he thought he saw a train of camels.

Crossing the next bridge, an Ivan on a bicycle swerved towards him, stared beyond and swerved away. Bradley stopped to check his map and saw Eddie develop an interest in the Great War tank that sat hog-happy among the carbonized tree-stumps and shell-craters of the museum gardens. It was a crazy way of tailing someone, in plain sight, on your own... only Eddie wasn't on his own now. Fifty yards behind him, sticking to what passed for a sidewalk, strolled another guy in another gangster's fedora, another unnecessary overcoat. And across the road, flanking him, a dusty Volkswagen crawled the curb, motor ticking over, a guy in a Panama and dark glasses behind the wheel.

There was no-one else going his way, no other possible target. It had to be a snatch team. They were going to pick him up.

*   *   *

Andreev noted the flecks of blood on Nemakhov's shirt and wrinkled his nose in disgust. Not with his aide. He knew he took no pleasure in supervising work like this. With himself.

Nemakhov just looked sick. When Andreev had completed his phone call, he reported with a weary shrug: "He is talking, Comrade Colonel."

Andreev nodded. They always did.

"Productively?"

"Can't tell. It may be a lead."

"Then I had better come and see."

He locked the dossiers in his safe and followed Nemakhov through the soundproof door. The captain was rolling down his shirtsleeves. There was the beginning of a spring in his step at the knowledge that for today the work was done.

Nemakhov unlocked the cell door at the end of the block and stood aside.

The prisoner was seated in a metal chair, bent forward, head in his hands. Of course he was. They always were. There was a bucket beside the chair with a sponge in it. The two SMERSh soldiers had been trying to clean him up.

Andreev eased himself into the facing chair and rested his cane across his knees. How many times had he sat thus? Dozens, if you counted the war. Perhaps that was different. At the front, the 'tongues' had been fascist soldiers, grabbed from their lines by his patrols. That didn't make them any less terrified than civilians, but it did mean they were easier to break down. Once the fantasy of honour and self-sacrifice had evaporated, a soldier could be persuaded there might be some reward for spilling his guts. A western-style POW camp, for the gullible ones. Although as a rule one had more time to spend on them, civilians were harder to convince. They grasped intuitively how they had fallen through a crack in the veneer of human civilisation. They knew there was no escape from the machinery on the other side.

And when someone could not be convinced they had a future, the only recourse was to make the present unendurable.

As Nemakhov slammed the cell door, the prisoner's fingers tightened to fists in the matted mane of once-fair hair. He jolted as though electrocuted, which he had not been, Andreev was reasonably sure, and slumped again, waiting.

Andreev took out the gold lighter. He rubbed his thumb across the blank panel where an inscription had been removed. Not an annoyance. Not a challenge. Just another box to be filled in.

His files had many such empty boxes, but many more had been completed. People and places, names and codenames, organisations, objectives, connections. Sec and Slavík. Lossner and Slavík. Berlin and Bohemia. UNRRA and BORODINO.

He let the prisoner see what he was holding.

"Tomáš, Tomáš, Tomáš..." he began.

*   *   *

Bradley quickened his pace along Unter den Linden. The *Trümmerfrauen* had been busy. Two broad trails were clear of rubble either side of the boulevard, winding here and there to skirt the burned-out tanks and half-tracks spilling from the scrapyard of the median strip. Light traffic picked its way around the obstacles, mostly soldiers or civilians on bicycles. The odd Red Army truck or horse-drawn wagon teetered past in clouds of dust, piled high like Okie jalopies with salvage or loot: corrugated iron, stacks of rails and sleepers, a brass bedstead, a rusty boiler cylinder, lavatory bowls, a grandfather clock. And always the old men and women with their handcarts of junk and firewood.

It would be slim pickings for them here. The buildings either side looked long since derelict, stripped of furniture, floorboards and stairs. Even the famous lime trees were shredded and charred.

Ahead, where there ought to have been the Brandenburg Gate, all he could make out through the haze was Stalin's face, bobbing up and down. He squinted, feeling seasick. A monolithic placard was being installed, no doubt to spoil the grand vista of the East-West Axis, which even the bombers had not been able to destroy. Stalin himself seemed awful smug about it. Rising above such devastation and misery, the red-bordered icon was as unnerving as an effigy on an alien shore.

The Volkswagen rattled behind him. For now, there was no option but to keep walking. Duck into a ruin and he'd be cornered. The sidestreets looked impassable and certainly no safer. Soldiers and civilians had clustered there, at field kitchens or de-lousing stations maybe, but maybe not. Plus, he'd make himself seem guilty leaving the boulevard and he still clung to the hope he was being passively followed rather than actively pursued. Taking to the alleys might be the opportunity they were waiting for.

He prepared himself for the snatch if it came. Should the car pull up as though to ask for directions, he'd affect not to notice and veer off, breaking into a run. That way he'd have a head start. If the men on foot caught up it got more complicated. One man might be dealt with – settled on a rubble mound – are you alright? – is it your heart? – let me go for help. The two together would be a bigger problem, especially with the pistols in their coat pockets. Terrain would be critical. He needed cover, or crowds.

Up ahead, on the south side, the boulevard opened out into a rubble-strewn plaza where men and women were hacking meat off something long dead. At the swarm's edge, children stood waiting with prams and carts.

The open space lay beyond the clutter of twisted metal on the median. The car would struggle to find a way through. Off to the left of the road, a German 3-tonner sat on melted hubs. Sunlight fanned through about a thousand bullet holes, but it was solid enough. He had made up his mind.

As he passed the truck he threaded through the median, ducked behind it and ran for the ruins at the western side of the plaza. There was no one to see him except the crowd engaged in the butchering. For several seconds he was shielded from his pursuers: long enough to begin climbing the rubble mound beside the big, crescent-shaped building. The rubble would halt the Volkswagen. With luck it might hold up the men.

He scrambled as fast as he could, knowing a twisted ankle would spell disaster. Passing the far corner of the crescent, still ascending, he knew he must be visible from the road, though hopefully not in the first place they'd look. He ignored the urge to turn and check. He was all instinct now, clawing at the rubble, grunting with the effort, until he reached the top and pitched himself over the other side.

The mound fell away but a bed of something softer broke his fall. Rats, and a damp mulch of charred paper. Burned books. Not the degenerate books from all those years ago but what must have been state-approved books from the library here, turned to charcoal by the incendiaries and shovelled out like so much trash.

Bradley slithered into a crater that passed for street level. All around, the broken buildings pierced the rubble as though they had forced their way up from a world below. To the south, through the holes in the walls, he saw another open space and the shattered eggshells of two cathedrals. A military band was practising, competing with unintelligible announcements over a loudspeaker system. Too public. Too Russian.

To the west lay a major road that had been cleared along the middle. Friedrichstrasse maybe – he could make no sense of the pre-war map. Peering down the gorge to the thoroughfare, he saw pedestrians, riders and trucks moving in both directions. A dented yellow streetcar rattled past. On its side was an advertisement for Zeiss. From its roof flew the hammer and sickle.

He had wasted precious seconds. His only chance was the modern building straight ahead, but he could see no way in. No time to scout for a door beyond the rubble mound. He ran right up it and in through a first floor window.

It must have been an office or a ministry, but now it looked and smelled like the inside of an oven. Every surface of the outsized rooms had been scorched black, then pockmarked with the lighter scars of shrapnel and bullets. They had fought room to room here.

Amid the shreds of desks, cabinets and panelling that littered the floor, he picked out familiar angles of tattered field-grey. An elbow. A knee. Another arm bent across a fleshless face. He saw they had been boys in bigger men's clothes. Even desiccated corpses didn't shrink that much.

He began to uncover the bodies and lever them over, brushing away the flies and maggots, searching for anything he could use to defend himself. But their pockets were already turned inside out and even their boots had gone.

Another experience he had no wish to remember, nor any

hope of forgetting.

But only as long as I live, he told himself. Which may be no time at all.

A further search of the debris turned up a spent *Panzerfaust* anti-tank tube and a stick grenade. Booby-trapped? He lifted the grenade gingerly. Not booby-trapped. Still alive, for the moment. He carried it into the adjoining room, expecting to find more of the same, in other words a whole lot of nothing. He was wrong.

The Russian who was next in turn spun around as glass crunched under his feet. Bradley discovered the muzzle of a burp-gun was just as threatening even with its owner's pants round his ankles.

The other soldier was still heaving away at whatever poor creature lay in the debris. Bradley didn't like that much either but what was he going to do, throw the grenade?

The words popped into his head. *You are not an avenging angel! The hubris, man!* Yes, indeed. And who was he to say the woman was ready to be put out of her misery? As far as he could gather, any women still alive in Berlin today were those with a fierce will to carry on living, at any price.

The submachine gunner swayed back and forth. He hadn't even called to his pal. His addled gaze went down to the grenade. Bradley decided to throw it anyway, unarmed. The soldiers were so drunk it might distract them long enough for him to get into the other room and out the window. A flick of the wrist was all it would take.

He was on the balls of his feet, trying to keep his intention from his eyes, when he heard a scrape in the stairwell off to his right. The Russians heard it too. The gunman turned his head, then his gun. His buddy started clambering off the woman, fumbling in the rubble for his own. Both still had their pants at half-mast.

A .45 automatic appeared through the banisters, then a hand, then an outstretched arm and a Panama hat. A voice, not Russian, barked out something in that language which roughly equated to *Drop it!*

Bradley spun around and headed for the other office. He took two strides before the second hood blocked the doorway, still wearing his fedora and raincoat and carrying a burp-gun of his own. The narrowed eyes above the mean little moustache registered Bradley's decision to continue the charge and he shoulder-checked it without taking his aim off the soldiers. It was like running into a wall.

"Cool it, Ace," he grunted out of the corner of his mouth. In English. In American.

The first hood kept rising from the stairwell with the Colt held out like something ceremonial. The soldiers backed away, lowering their guns, clutching at their pants. Another barked order saw them sling their guns and scuttle past him down the stairs. Their heads were bent as they went, their eyes averted. They looked grateful.

Still inching forwards with that fencer's gait, the man dipped his arm until it was aimed at the woman on the floor. A bedraggled head looked up from the debris and two hands lifted in a gesture of compliance. The wrists and inner arms were horribly bruised. Before Bradley could call out not to shoot, the man's arm relaxed. He tucked the pistol away in a shoulder holster, for the first time registering the other two. He still had on his dark glasses.

"Holy shit, Mike," he said with a nervous laugh. "That was pretty intense!"

"You OK?" Bradley took a couple of seconds to realise Mike was talking to him. He mumbled an affirmative, all he could manage for the moment.

The two Yanks, for such they indubitably were, went over to help the woman. With his hat and coat off and his greying crew-cut and sports jacket visible, the one called Mike looked so much like a high school wrestling coach Bradley couldn't believe he'd ever thought him an NKVD enforcer. Mike's companion – and superior, it seemed – was harder to pin down. In his Panama, seersucker and slacks he might have been vacationing in Florida or, given those Ivy League tones, the Hamptons. He didn't carry himself with the other's military stiffness, yet there was an inner poise that was not to be messed with.

At length, Mike wrapped the German woman in his raincoat and led her downstairs. Bradley laid aside the grenade and accepted a cigarette.

"I'm glad to catch you away from your tail, sport, but I wish you'd picked a different building!" The man held the match rock steady until Bradley's less-than-steady breathing had drawn the smoke, then he offered his hand.

"Walter Sloane – call me Wally. And our Good Samaritan friend down there is Major Mike Murphy. I can't resist saying that."

"Bill Brown," Bradley said. After Sloane's comment it sounded even phonier but if he noticed he chose to let it ride. "Ain't you worried about the major going out that way? If those guys stuck around..."

"Mike can look after himself. And those guys will be long gone, believe me." Sloane took off his sunglasses. Pale eyes sat uneasily in a nest of grey-tinged creases, older than the rest of him. They noted Bradley's expression, flicked to his armband and came up again. It was an unsettling gaze, piercing yet glazed-over, as though there was something boiling away to steam in there, but coolly appraising and quizzical with it. Bradley wouldn't have liked to play cards against the man. He couldn't tell if he was set to pull out his gun or burst into tears.

"You can't save them all, you know," Sloane added. "The Germans, I mean. The women and children. There's a strong body of opinion says most don't deserve saving anyhow, but I can see you don't hold with that."

"We're not here to help them. UNRRA doesn't give relief to German nationals."

"Oh, absolutely right, sport, nor should it. But sometimes one can't stand by."

Bradley didn't know what to say, or what he was dealing

with. A Yank who let Soviet troops think he was from their own State Security. Who would have the sand for that? The thought occurred that Sloane might actually be working with the Reds, in some prototype joint administration. He'd made that provocative comment about catching him away from his tail, but what if it wasn't the overture it seemed? Maybe Sloane had him marked down as an UNRRA do-gooder and thought he'd run into the building to save the woman. He might just be watching Bradley's back as he would any compatriot in the city.

But his next words changed all that.

"Look, Bill, sorry we spooked you back there. We were waiting for a chance to talk to you but this isn't it. NKVD tails may be not too bright and I doubt yours will report your disappearance until he has to, but it'd be safer to pop up again, don't you think?"

"Sure. But I don't get it..."

"Hmm?" Sloane wasn't listening to any more BS. "Tell you what, get back onto the Linden via the rear of the library. Just walk out fussing with your fly. We'll fetch the car if it's still there and meet you this end of the Tiergarten. Ought to be a crowd around the new memorial works. I'm sure we can bump into each other without your fellow taking much notice. How's that, sport?"

"Yeah, OK," was all Bradley could muster. He was taken aback by the assumption he'd want to meet with them again, but Sloane was right, of course. Either his cover story was being checked and he had to keep up appearances or else these two were wild cards who might be able to help. Whichever it was, he had to find out.

"Oh Bill," Delving into his hip pocket, Sloane produced a little pistol and a spare magazine. "You might as well have this. Better for self-defence. I always find grenades so... inflexible."

CHAPTER SEVEN

They were a cosy party in the lounge that evening. The fire was lit and in pride of place among the clothes horses sat the five civilians, all of them smoking like chimneys.

The Russian heavies stuck out in their cheap rayon suits. One had a bald bullet-head. Another's face was as shrapnel-scarred as the hotel. Only the third seemed like he might genuinely be a civilian, although his ready smile and Uncle Joe moustache suggested a career in politics.

By contrast, with their red armbands and horn-rimmed eyeglasses, the Germans were unmistakably political animals – exiled communists who had sat out the war in Moscow and were playing the returning heroes. Better fed than their countrymen, yet still somewhat weasely, they had that peculiar combination of furtiveness and smugness. After so long looking over their shoulders they were going to cash in, big time.

There were six other guests. Bradley and Lieutenant Belkin. Two Red Army infantry captains playing cards. A pair of rather odd ladies. Theatrical was the word that sprung to Bradley's mind, though he wasn't sure why. Maybe it was the pre-war finery of turbans and feathers, or the tilt of the head into profile that accompanied each gesture, even smoking their terrible Russian cigarettes in extravagant holders. They spoke of people or places they had lost – Aschinger, Hertie, Wertheim – and sang along with the gramophone. One was younger than the other, though neither would see fifty again. Mother and daughter? Beneath the similarities of dress and manner, they did not look alike. A grand dowager and her travelling companion, he thought, without understanding the words. Or, since they were clearly Berliners and had probably lived in the hotel for years, call them travellers in time, marvellously exempt from total war.

The twelfth person in the lounge was not a guest. Karl-Heinz, barman, bellhop and night porter, was a German lad of about fifteen with a palsy in his arm and leg. Whether he'd been born like that or had cracked under the bombing Bradley didn't know. The Russians treated him as a simpleton, but from the disappointment in his eyes when he dropped something, you could tell he still had a mind in there.

Getting the Reds to notice anything like that was an uphill struggle. Everything was. The drink, the smoke, the odours from the drying clothes, even the unpredictable momentum of the endless German *schmaltz* on the gramophone made sure of that.

He'd have given anything to listen to the BBC instead. Since arriving in Berlin he'd had no news from the Pacific. The last he'd heard they were mopping up on Okinawa and in the Philippines but the main Japanese islands lay ahead, and if the Japs had fought like that for every two-bit volcanic reef, God only knew how they'd meet landings on their home soil. Three guys from his old neighbourhood were in the Marines.

It was hard to feel part of that now. Here in the ruins of the old world, people acted like the whole war had been fought on the eastern European front. The orient was of no consequence, except as the distant source of the grumbling camels, chintzy wagons and Mongol faces that manifested the Red Army's universal righteousness. As for the west, well, it began and ended at the Elbe. Some Yanks and Britishers had set up camp there. The way the Soviets put it, you'd think the Germans had invited them in.

With selective memories like that, it was no surprise they weren't so hot on the BBC. At the UNRRA mission they'd been encouraged to tune in to the Soviet alternative and the team's director had translated the newscasts that punctuated the anthems. Plenty of Stalin, Zhukov and the victory parade in Moscow. Plenty too on the subject of agricultural recovery and unprecedented productivity in the factories. Even something on those Heroes of the Soviet Union still rooting out and severing the heads of the Fascist Hydra in Germany. About the war with the Japanese, nothing.

It killed him he was in a position to do something useful and couldn't get started. Sure, this MERCURY set-up was a sideline, but if he could pinpoint Lossner for Jones' professionals, maybe he'd have done his bit to bring everybody home.

Karl-Heinz came around the tables clearing ashtrays. The civilians demanded another bottle of *Schnapps*, the generic term for spirit. They were three sheets to the wind and the kid misheard something about the number of glasses. One of the Russians leapt up and smacked him in the chops.

Lev Belkin, his liaison, was no diplomat either.

"These Fritzes – you call them Krauts, yes?"

"We did, before we licked them."

"Licked?"

"Before we defeated them."

"Ah, yes. And now? I wonder what you think of them."

"I think of them as a defeated nation."

"That is a clever answer, Bill. But you have sympathy for them."

Belkin was about his own age, and a soldier too, though he ought to have swapped that khaki cap for a blue-crowned one.

"My job is to help the other peoples of Eastern Europe. The only Germans we're empowered to assist are the Jews."

"Ah, but the Jews are not Germans, surely."

Bradley stared at a paler rectangle on the smoke-grimed wallpaper where a picture had hung.

"I believe certain people hereabouts said the same thing."

Belkin laughed and refilled their glasses.

"You are too clever for me, *Tovarich*. Let us drink to their defeat and our victory!" They knocked back the shots, as they had done a dozen times. Bradley gasped, as he always did. Belkin enjoyed that. Then his grin faded. "Bill, I have been told to issue a reprimand. You must desist from fraternizing with the enemy, or your permission to stay in Berlin shall be revoked."

Bradley felt a kick that wasn't the juice.

"I don't understand."

"You have been observed, half a dozen times..." the slick sonofabitch was proud of his English phrasing. "Signalling to a fascist street worker."

"The kid on the bombsite? Christ almighty, Lev!"

"Bill, this is fraternizing. Your orders are not to acknowledge them, unless you are putting them to work. These are the orders from your zone you must abide by. In our zone, we are not so strict."

Bradley shook his head and something rattled.

"I'll say! What is it you call it? Committing an act of violence against the civil population?" He looked across at Karl-Heinz, but he didn't mean that and Belkin knew it.

"I believe you are speaking of the offence known as an 'immoral event'..."

Bradley snapped.

"Offence? You got to be kidding, it's goddamn R&R out there! You can do that to them, any time you like, but I can't wave to their kids?"

A couple of the fat cats by the fire had turned to glower. No one else was speaking. The two captains were bent over their cards, the ladies turned away in dramatic profile – one of them fanning herself, with a real *fan*, for Chrissakes! – and Karl-Heinz was having kittens. Even Belkin seemed shocked, although Bradley suspected this was for the benefit of the Party members.

"Excuse me," he said, in German, then in Russian. To Belkin he added, in English: "I am sorry, Lev. Guess I better hit the sack."

"You are in a spin, my friend. I understand."

"Yeah, like you say, in a spin."

Up in his room, lighting the oil lamp, negotiating the buckets they had positioned to catch the rain, he congratulated himself on his smart exit. He drank most of the water from the jug on the washstand and splashed the rest on his face. Not as drunk as he'd made out, but he was drunk, damn it, there had been no avoiding it. This habit of toasting everything and knocking drinks back left no chance to tip them into the nearest aspidistra.

He went to the window and leaned his head into the breeze through the boards. No sound came from the benighted city.

After a while he dragged a chair to the wardrobe and retrieved the bundle from on top. He sat on the bed to unwrap the pistol.

It was a Czech .25 with a double action that did not re-cock the hammer, calling for a firm trigger pull every shot. Not a gun for a gunfight but it was small and safe enough to hide in a pocket. He ought to have brought something like this, but there had been one of those going-nowhere British debates about getting searched. Now Sloane had come to the rescue, and provided an extra 8-round mag. Thoughtful man.

He had stripped the weapon to clean it when he heard footsteps on the tortured boards of the landing. There was just time to flick the bedspread over the parts before the knock at the door.

Karl-Heinz held a candle and his other uniform pants. He'd left them by the fire when he'd lurched out of the lounge. So much for not so drunk.

"*Danke schön*, kid."

Karl-Heinz muttered a shy *bitte schön*. The mark of the Russian's hand was still on his face. He made to go, but paused. Did he expect a tip? This wasn't a real hotel anymore and there was no money to speak of in Berlin. Prices had been frozen, ration cards were to be honoured and the Russians had printed an occupation currency, but it was worthless. There was nothing to buy. Barter, that was the currency now. One egg equals four pieces of coal equals three cigarettes.

Bradley reached for his Luckies but Karl-Heinz shook his head. He was struggling with a spasm in his arm and leg. The fair hair flopped aside, revealing the purple crease of a wound on his temple.

It could have been shrapnel. Even a bullet might have been unprovoked. The Russians hadn't picked their targets during the final assault. But like a dog worrying at an infected paw, his thoughts returned to the *Volkssturm* boys in the ministry building. Most kids called up for the city's defence would have run back to their mothers first chance they got. Those dead boys, Karl-Heinz's age and younger, had fought the Red Army room to room, and for a patently lost cause. That took something else. It was the same thing as the Japs on Okinawa and he didn't want to think about it.

He had considered extending a hand or showing off his own wound. Instead, he drew back. He still had sympathy, sure. What was the future Karl-Heinz had fought for? To wait on the Reds and endure their abuse until they got around to interrogating him and packed him off to the salt mines? He had sympathy in spades, as worthless as the currency. Belkin was right. They were the enemy. He had seen what they were capable of.

The tremors had passed. The candle was steady. Bradley closed the door.

*　　*　　*

A few hours earlier it had all seemed much simpler. He'd picked up Eddie on Unter den Linden as Sloane suggested. Sure enough, the NKVD man was stalled by the bullet-riddled truck like a bulldog waiting for the mailman. Bradley led him up the boulevard and past Stalin's face – gazing westwards now – into the Pariser Platz. Here increased activity matched the increased destruction. In front of the pitted columns of the Gate, women MPs in tight skirts and jaunty berets were directing traffic from the south and the East-West Axis: trucks, carts, and those goddamn camel trains, overflowing with booty. Now it was obvious what was happening. The city was soon to be divided into occupation sectors and the Soviets were making sure nothing of value remained in the west.

He headed towards the scene of the other coup they were planning. He saw it rising above the shredded trees and statuary. There were trucks around it, cranes, crowds, but it dwarfed them already. Soldiers and Berliners, forgetting for a moment to hate each other, were caught up in the spectacle. Flashbulbs popped off. A tank motor chugged and spluttered. A cloud of smoke and the din of metal tracks on stone.

A T-34 lurched into view above the crowd and crashed to the horizontal. There was scattered applause as the driver opened the hatch, but rather than waving he promptly launched into an argument with an engineer who had clambered onto the hull. They were joined by an officer with a film director's spyglass. After a heated exchange, the driver dropped inside the tank to emerge once again for the cameras.

The crowd dispersed. Now Bradley could see the film crew and the shape of the monument beyond the plinth. Still under construction, of the same marble blocks, it formed a crescent reminiscent of the library building. The whole structure had a disproportionate blankness to it, like it wasn't built for these worker ants around it but for people twelve feet tall.

At the front of it on the opposite side, once more to a crossfire of flashbulbs and applause, another T-34 mounted a ramp onto its plinth.

Where had the logs come from? Across the Charlottenburger Chausee, what the map called the Tiergarten looked like the Somme. In the distance, above the smog of brick-dust, Bradley made out the upper ramparts of the Zoo flak tower, a concrete castle that had proved more durable than the old Schloss on the island. Closer to hand, a ditched Focke-Wulf was belly-down in the dirt, surrounded by Russians posing for photographs.

In the other direction, brown-clad figures crawled like termites over the black heap of the Reichstag. They were chalking up their names.

He heard Sloane's voice at his side.

"The Russkis claim these were the first tanks into Berlin, although the way they assaulted the place, I'd hazard those are scattered somewhere on the outskirts."

"And this is a monument to their victory?"

"More than that, sport," a long finger indicated the broken ground in front of the structure, between the tanks. "They've buried their dead here. Thousands upon thousands of them. And the joke is, this is going to be the British sector. I guess you have to understand the Russian sense of humour to appreciate that. The marble blocks used to be the walls of Hitler's Reich Chancellery."

There were still sufficient bystanders to make their conversation look casual. Bradley threw him a sideways glance. Same get-up, same sunglasses. Eddie lurking. No sign of Major Mike.

"Bill," Sloane said. "What are you doing here?"

It wasn't an official tone so much as one of amused exasperation, like you might use with a pal who ought to have called a cab by now. But it was plain he didn't mean what are you doing at the Russian memorial, or even what are UNRRA doing here.

"Trying to get out of town." He told him the cover story. He figured UNRRA didn't keep their business secret. And Sloane sure as hell had to be in a position of authority to be wandering the streets of Berlin without a Russian tail.

It seemed he was right about that.

"I may be able to help you there. I know people who know people, as they say. Mike and I have been sent by the State Department to assess security arrangements for TERMINAL.

SHAEF has also asked us to scout out some real estate in what will be the American sector – in case the Russkis honour the agreement and actually let us in."

It all made sense, on the face of it. TERMINAL was the codename for the forthcoming conference in the Berlin area. Stalin, Truman and Churchill, or Churchill's successor, would be deciding how to carve up the rest of the continent. There'd also be a victory parade right in the heart of the former enemy capital. Naturally the security would take advance planning. If the US military had been left cooling their heels at the Elbe, they might deign to ask someone else to reconnoitre their objective for them, especially if that someone had a military man in tow. But Bradley didn't believe Sloane any more than Sloane believed him.

Now the tank motor had been cut, he heard the rumbles of thunder from the east. Above the crooked chariot and the rippling red silk banners on the Gate, darker clouds were looming.

"It's going to rain," Sloane had said.

Bradley had nodded, thinking.

One of them was going to have to show his hand.

*   *   *

It was five minutes to ten when Bradley rose from his bed and crossed silently to the communicating door. The lock had been easy to pick. He eased it open and crept into the next room, to be greeted by the stark light of a bomber's moon.

Not so long ago a moon like this would have sent the people of Berlin scurrying underground. Even now, jaundiced from the ever-present dust, there was something menacing in how it gleamed on the puddles and blackened the ruins of Alexanderplatz.

He could see across the square from here. The room's front and side had fallen away, as had much of the ceiling. Directly below, festooned with the same forlorn messages as the poster columns, stood the remains of an eight-sided iron pissoir. He saw a strangely burdened figure emerge from the shape of the 'Café Achteck' and he shinned down the bricks and plaster to meet it.

Like him, Sloane wore the dark civilian garb they had bought in the black market by the Reichstag. He was wheeling two bicycles. Without a word they set off past the shell of the police headquarters and were soon swallowed by the shadows of the sidestreets to the south. The moon gave enough light to follow the stream of cobbles that meandered through the rubble. At the few remaining junctions where tanks had not demolished the corner buildings, the dim glow of phosphorescent arrows marked the way to long-buried shelters. Here and there through the ruins they saw flashes of campfires. From time to time they heard distant shouting or drunken singing and once a piercing scream, but the streets were deserted.

This was the price of Sloane's assistance – maybe his way of laying his cards on the table. By his own account, he and Murphy had been scouting the suburb of Zehlendorf for suitable US accommodation. During their tour of the district, they had observed intense Soviet activity around what looked like a light industrial site among the parks of Dahlem. Since it was evident the Soviets were systematically stripping west Berlin of its industry, Sloane wanted to find out what had attracted their special attention there. If they were to wait for the zone to become theirs by right, it might be too late to discover what was missing. Such pieces of information were crucial bargaining chips.

That didn't sound much like security planning or army recon but Bradley already suspected Sloane had a flexible brief. The thing about this night-time jaunt, as he called it, was Major Mike would have to stay back at their billet in the centre. Although they weren't always tailed, they were sure the Russians had microphones in their room. Mike would be required to keep up a two-way conversation till midnight, with some snoring thrown in afterwards from Sloane's side of the room.

The jaunt was a little unconventional, but it would be OK. However, it did require two. One to snoop around, one to keep lookout. What did Bradley think?

Bradley thought he needed this man on his side. He was almost certainly working for OSS, the Joint Chiefs' Office of Strategic Services. That didn't just make him useful to know, it made it essential to keep on his good side. A word from Sloane about a Yank high-tailing it around the Soviet zone on behalf of the Limeys and the entire US military and government machine would come down on him like, well, like a ton of bricks, regardless of who had approved his assignment. Even if they didn't throw him to the NKVD, he'd probably never see daylight again.

Or if Sloane was in cahoots with the Reds – Bradley didn't see how, but if the guy was somehow playing both sides – what else could he do but go along with it? The Lubianka or Leavenworth. Either way he was screwed if he didn't.

Berlin was truly the Big City. Having snuck past the drunken sentries beneath the Landwehr Canal footbridge they rode for ages through the ruins. Crawling up mounds to scout ahead, they skirted checkpoints that announced themselves with accordions and folk songs and lay low when a posse went past on the hunt for Gretchens. In theory the curfew had been lifted. Navigating the remains of Kreuzberg, they heard music and voices from the rubble: either a nightclub had reopened in the cellars or the ghosts of old Berlin were entertaining again. In reality the streets were far from safe for all but a handful of privileged civilians. The men were dead or far away. The women knew better than to venture forth for water until the Russians had passed out for the night. There were also special NKVD patrols using dogs to sniff out Wehrmacht deserters and SS diehards, Sloane said, but no one must have informed on any tonight. Mostly they saw rats. In the poorer streets of Schöneberg they retched as the smell of bodies under the collapsed apartment buildings mingled with the lilac in the overgrown sidings.

The hands of Bradley's wristwatch had passed one o'clock before they reached their destination. Judging by the landscaping around its villas and public edifices, Dahlem had been a fashionable suburb, although most of the open spaces were now dug up for victory gardens. At the barbed wire fence that ran along the road, all Bradley could make out on the far side was a row of bushes, but Sloane swore it was the place.

They went under the wire, through the bushes and over an area criss-crossed with gravel paths. Even with the vegetable allotments it was more like a municipal park than the light industrial site Sloane had described. What had the Germans been hiding here? How had they defended it? Had they mined the paths between the hedges? The old nausea from Normandy twisted his guts. He fought to control it, as he had then, with the practicalities of terrain – avenues of approach, fields of fire, cover and concealment.

They were in the grounds of a complex of buildings. Of the faintly moonlit shapes blotting out the stars, at least two were the size of mansions, with steep-pitched roofs full of dormer windows. Each bore the marks of air-raids, especially the one with a spiked turret like a Prussian helmet. The other was dwarfed by a cylindrical extension that resembled the Harrison gas-holder from the murky skyline of his childhood memories. Lights at the windows glinted on trucks parked below. Firelight spilled up the lower walls. The Russians had come in their hundreds and were working through the night.

Looping over the dips and rises, the paths converged on the buildings, yet Sloane made for a wooden barracks structure that was partly hidden by a stand of immature trees. Bradley's relief evaporated when he saw more trucks on the far side. It was just as Sloane had described, but how the hell had he and Murphy spotted anything from the road?

Bradley worked around the perimeter to pinpoint the sentries. They had lit fires to dry their kit, hopefully ruining their night vision. Two at the front. Two near the water tower around back. Any number in the truck park. Every sentry he saw was sitting or sprawled. He smelled *makhorka* tobacco and saw the gleam of a bottle.

"There's a side door," he told Sloane. "If you can get in there, they can't see you. I'll be in those bushes. I can watch front and back from there."

"I'll be quick, sport." He sounded tense, at last. Bradley remembered that slow march up the stairs. It had spooked the two rapists. Even he had been unnerved. The man knew how to get serious when the odds were against him.

"Got no way to warn you if they come sniffing. Never was any good at owl calls."

He saw the flash of Sloane's grin.

"Well, it won't happen, but if it does, make a disturbance and try to draw them away. I'll meet you back by the bikes. If it looks like they've rumbled me and are about to storm the place, fire a shot and get the hell out, don't wait for me."

It was a good forty minutes after forcing the side door that the shadow re-emerged. The sentries hadn't budged. Sloane was clear to head straight back into the bushes.

But Sloane had other ideas. Bradley saw him inch along the side of the building to the front. He reached the corner, knelt and disappeared. The barracks block was set in concrete foundations that formed a trench around it, sitting lower than the surrounding banks and the border of saplings. Maybe it was rudimentary blastproofing or the wooden structure rested on a more substantial bunker. Sloane was making his way across the front, out of sight of the sentry post, but he'd have to show himself as he crossed the ramp at the entrance. Sure enough, the figure broke cover and scuttled past, going on hands and knees again as it vanished into the shadows there. Now he was somewhere between the sentries at the front and the men by the trucks on the far side. What the hell was he doing?

Bradley's heart sank. One of the sentries from the back was on his feet and headed for the front, following the line of the bank, not the shallow trench behind it. There was no urgency about him, but neither was he just going to take a leak. He had his rifle slung and a bottle in his hand: planning to offer a nip to his buddies at the front. He wouldn't be able to see into the trench on the far side of the front doors from there, but if he had enough *Schnapps* or conscience to give the guys in the truck park their share, his route would take him either into the trench or onto the bank above it. Then Sloane was good as dead. The Russians weren't about to stop and question a civilian creeping around their position.

Bradley was up on one knee, pulse racing. The moonlight came and went on the moist grass. He checked the sentry posts front and back, checked the clouds and wind-speed, waited until the man on the move was past the side door – and timed his run to coincide with momentary darkness. When he eased into the trench at the side of the building, the Czech .25 was in his hand.

He had two options. Jump up behind the sentry, drag him into the trench, and hope his buddies at the front weren't looking his way. Or follow the trench in the opposite direction and get Sloane out of sight before the guy made the far corner and spotted him. No time to consider. No appetite, now, for murder. Crouching low to avoid the remaining sentry, he set off around the back.

The trench was an inch deep in rainwater and matted with the black leaves of burned papers. Beneath was broken glass and other crud. He moved as quickly as he dared, all the while covering the remaining sentry with his pistol. The guy was sitting on the ground, leant against and half obscured by a leg of the water tower, but Bradley could still see the back of his head and part of his torso above the line of the bank. If he turned and spotted him, he'd have maybe one good shot with his pop-gun.

Voices sounded as the patrolling sentry reached the first position and he guessed his sentry was going to turn his head to eavesdrop. Going flat under a couple of heavy gauge water pipes and stopcocks, he kept worming through the water.

Now he was nearly past the rear of the building he could see the firelight from the truck park. Shadows moved back and forth. The men there were on their feet. He was going to have to crawl the whole length of the wall on this side, and if the sentry with the bottle wasn't a conversationalist, if he moved off now, they were finished.

Bradley snaked around the corner, straight into the muzzle of Sloane's .45.

They lay gasping like fish, until a look of recognition cracked Sloane's mask of fear. He wriggled around to indicate the front corner he had come from. The meaning was plain. He'd seen the first sentry was on the move.

In their haste, they scrambled over each other to get back around to the rear. It was only a matter of time before the first sentry finished with the guys in the truck park, and odds-on he'd return to his post this way, the short way. Or the sentry here would get lonely and come looking, or get up to relieve himself. The Russians had been drinking, and Bradley knew where he'd aim his pee if he were the sentry.

A conversation in looks and gestures like an old married couple, or how he thought a married couple ought to be. Hide inside, get in through the side door? No, gotta get out of here. Hear the sentry? Did he go over to the trucks? Yeah, that's him talking with them now. OK, out the way we came. Wait – wait – cloud's coming – OK, now!

Back in the bushes Bradley collapsed but Sloane crouched over him, panting.

"Gotta go!"

Bradley checked his watch. They'd have to pedal but they knew the route and there was still time before sunrise. Then he noticed something.

"Where are your bags?"

Sloane's bicycle had carried panniers and for some reason he'd brought them with him when they'd broken in. Cameras, evidence, Bradley had thought, not thinking, having his own job to do. He was thinking now though. Sloane had embarked on his madcap diversion after he'd been into the building. And he hadn't been pinned down in the shadows at the front, as Bradley had assumed, he'd been around the far side, where the trucks were parked. Doing what?

"No time, Bill! Come on!"

"What the hell have you done?"

He received his answer nine or ten minutes later as they cycled back down into the expanse of the ruined city. Without warning the night lit up and flickered for several seconds – long enough for him to turn and see the fireballs spill upwards from the grounds they'd left behind. One, then another and another, shrinking to a dirty orange glow as the first crack and rumble reached their ears.

CHAPTER EIGHT

It was on her fourth visit to Krypta that she spotted the face from her past and knew he was the one she had been seeking.

Such an adolescent name for a basement nightclub – no wonder it had been so popular with the Nazis. With their studied callousness they must have relished the resonance the word held for every Czech in Prague, after what had become of the Heydrich parachutists hiding out in the crypt of the Orthodox church on Resslova Street, flooded, gassed, fighting to the last bullet amid the bones. She had known Josef Valčík of the SILVER team. She had known the men who sent them on their mission.

In fact this former haunt of their killers was nothing more than a medieval cellar, sprawling under the Old Town a short distance from the square. The thick pillars and rib-vaulted ceilings had inspired the club's owners to paint *ersatz* fresco fragments and hang the vaults with blackened candelabras, but as the booths fashioned from huge beer barrels made plain, it was just an old brewery.

If only all such pretences were so obvious. How comforting it would be if false identities were layered like coats of paint or tree rings. How simple, to have been Jana Slavík in the resistance, Milena Kristeková here in Prague, and to slice across them to find Mila Suková underneath.

Perhaps, in London, planning everything on paper, that was how they believed it to be. Perhaps even Richard had believed that. But in practice the identities grew together into something new. The redundant ones withered, leaving hard little remnants. Knots in the wood, like the *Suk* in her name.

Try to slice those neatly and you'd break your saw.

A sequinned figure materialised out of the smoke. Mila's companion in the booth drew breath in anticipation. Ritualistically, the plump, hairless hands left his drink and were laid out on the tabletop, preparing to keep time.

Though it was probably his real name, Zdenko Kovály was as false as she. A minor cog in the machinery of the Housing Authority, he had signatory responsibilities that made him a bigger wheel in the black market. Thanks to the Nazis there were many empty properties in Prague, and many dispossessed people looking for somewhere to live. The most deserving cases stood all day outside the offices of the Housing Authority. Those with something more tangible than desperation to trade came to Krypta instead.

She had been able to instigate contact with Kovály because he too was a hero of the resistance. Wasn't everyone, now the shooting was over? In his case there might be some truth in it. Although he had worked for the Nazis during the occupation, there was talk of his having spared a number of Jews from the transports to Theresienstad. And surely, people said, if he had started the rumours himself he would have taken credit for something better than saving Jews. It was enough to keep him in with all the resisters-turned-profiteers and profiteers-turned-resisters of the new regime. Perhaps they thought he knew where Jewish treasure was hidden. Perhaps he just knew the best apartments.

For Mila, staking out the club in the hope of finding the man from whom Kobylka had received the package, he was an ideal companion. By the end of the night most of Krypta's shadier customers would have paid a visit to their table. This one with his smuggled currency, that one with his Roma girls, swiftly followed, if one were wise, by the man who dealt in ex-*Sanitätsdienst* Prontosil. Ration cards? Jindřich's gang had them freshly stolen with the all-important records altered. Tractors for the harvest? Petr here had access to some fine examples, fixed up for free by the Amis in Rokycany and yes, the farmers could pay in geese. It was as close as the underworld came to a roll call.

The benefits were mutual. As a romantic, Kovály loved the Krypta for the tragic glamour of its singers. As a businessman, it paid to be seen with a woman on his arm. And they had something else in common besides their secret identities. She brought her glass to her lips to mask her smile. They were both wearing quite appalling wigs.

She tried to let the bite of the *borovička* stimulate feelings of satisfaction. The parade of shadowy faces and furtive whispers had thrown up a positive identification. She was back on the trail at last. But her throat remained dry with the tension that had started the moment she recognised Stransky.

With a rhythmic swish of wire brushes and a slow pulse of the double bass, the band picked up the melody of 'Heimweh', as it had done a thousand times before, but now the half-remembered lilacs and the homesickness had been translated into Czech. As the spotlight played onto the singer, the faces at the tables beside the dance floor were illuminated. There he was. Thinner, if that were possible. Thinner at the hairline too, greyer at the temples. But it was him. The same deep-set eyes lurking in their burrows, the same twin pencil-strokes of a moustache, the same manner of observing with his cigarette, as though sighting along the barrel of a gun.

She nudged Kovály.

"Do you know the man at that table, with the bodyguard-type and the two girls?"

"In the leather coat?" As Kovály's well-groomed eyebrows arched, his hairpiece seemed to move contrariwise. "He's the one you're after? How intriguing!"

"Now Zdenko, you know that wasn't part of the arrangement. I'm just curious."

"His name is Stransky. Doctor Eduard Stransky, if I'm not mistaken. He's supposed to be tight with the National Committee. An adviser on industrial regeneration."

"Does that put him in with the communists?"

"My dear, everybody is in with the communists. I myself have been invited to join the Party and I don't care who knows it. But in Stransky's case, I'd say he's more of a professional fence-sitter. Now the Americans are trying to throw money at us, the Russians will be courting the good doctor tenaciously. If he has a flirtatious nature he could do well out of it, although the little tease might end up getting more than he's bargained for. A dangerous game. But do you mind – I so adore this song."

She picked up a matchbook from the table. It would not have occurred to Kovály to light her cigarette for her. As she shook out the match, she noticed a drinker at the bar looking in her direction. A tall, angular man in his mid 30s with hooded eyes and an aquiline nose. He wore a charcoal flannel suit and was leaning on a cane.

A pick up? Possibly. He had that dark, self-confident allure she knew too well. But there was something about the way he was looking at her. Not inviting, not appraising, or not exactly. As though an amusing thought had just occurred to him.

She cursed herself under her breath. A schoolgirl would have shown better tradecraft than to tip Kovály towards Stransky's table like that. Was the barfly one of Stransky's? If so, she had blown her cover.

But as she caught his eye and his gaze drifted away, the man smiled and gave a shake of his head, as if to say... what? She knew what it was meant to signify. At face value it was a cocky acknowledgement and apology in one: yes, I was looking at you because I find you attractive, but of course I wouldn't dream of doing anything so vulgar as to disturb your evening with your friend. Except she couldn't help thinking it hadn't meant that at all, or it meant something else as well.

What she imagined it had meant was don't worry, I'm not one of Stransky's. But for it to mean that he would have to be reading her mind.

She must have let out a squeak of alarm, however infinitesimal. Kovály was regarding her with concern.

She pretended to hiccup and flashed him a woozy smile.

"I've distracted you from your song."

"I hear it every night. Nor shall I forget the favour you did for me with that intriguingly pristine *Kennkarte* that came by chance into your possession."

"Then you'll also remember it isn't to be used... you know."

An aggrieved, slightly insulted look. He'd have practised that a lot, lately.

"Rest assured, no Golden Pheasant's grisly features shall grace that precious item. If you must know I was thinking of keeping it for myself. For a particularly rainy day."

"I'm sorry. Nerves. A lady's prerogative."

"Oh, indeed." His lips pursed. "Now, what was it you wanted to know? Ah yes, the good Doctor Stransky!"

"Don't look across again, please. But tell me, what was he doing during the occupation? Do you know?"

"Only rumours." He rolled his eyes. It was his customary bluff, but whether a double or a triple she could not guess, nor was she meant to. "He ran a munitions factory in Brno. Exploding cannon shells for the Luftwaffe – is that right? – I'm not *au fait* with such things. A quantity of this ammunition was destined for the Eastern Front and the story is Stransky arranged for the explosive ingredient to be replaced."

"Replaced?"

"With rolled-up notes saying 'To Ivan from your good friends in Czechoslovakia' or something to that effect. If I have understood this correctly, the shells could be fired perfectly well, but instead of exploding inside the Russian aircraft they went straight through. Some must have got stuck and been examined later."

"A very dangerous game." It was an impressive tale, if a preposterous one. She wondered whether to believe it. "Then his stock with the Russians is high?"

"I expect so. This is all second-hand."

"And now he is employed in Prague?"

"Apparently, although I gather his work takes him everywhere."

"Yes, I suppose it would." She toyed with the matchbook and glanced towards the bar. The man had his back to her. There was a mirror behind the bar, but she couldn't see his face. "And he's a regular at your beloved Krypta?"

Kovály uttered a gruff affirmative. Now the song had finished and the applause had petered out, one of his 'customers' was weaving between the tables.

Mila picked up her bag.

"Would you excuse me for a moment, Zdenko darling?"

She moved towards the rear alcove where the cloakroom was tucked away. Most of the club's patrons had managed only an approximation of evening dress and many were too ashamed to remove their coats. The chemical odour of mothballs mingled with the cigarettes and damp.

A young couple in oversized raincoats sat at a back table inside the alcove, lingering over two half-litres of watered-down *světlý*. As she passed she winked to them. The girl rose and followed her through the door that was still marked *Damen*.

Marta, Vojtěch's sweetheart, was a village girl of eighteen who looked four years younger. With her huge eyes and delicate jug ears she was a fieldmouse in the unfamiliar terrain of the city. Although only eight years Marta's senior, Mila felt ancient in her presence. Ancient and somehow sullied. The sensation of dirtiness, unresponsive to baths, clean clothes or fresh air, was a constant companion to her, but Marta's unblinking gaze and translucent, almost-transparent, skin always brought it into sharp relief.

"Two men," she told the girl as she reapplied her lipstick. With a few strokes she sketched the angles of bar, dance floor and side tables on the mirror. "This one, with a henchman and two hookers. Very thin, receding hair, forty-to-forty-five, in a leather coat. The other here at the bar, tall, dark – you'd like him, little one – in a good suit, with a cane. Don't know if he needs it."

"I have them, Miss Slavík."

Mila heard the tension in Marta's voice and was overcome by sympathy. She knew what it was to be starting out. But what could she say to console her? The fear never went away, it was only that one learned to live with it, like the dirtiness. More than that, it was the dirtiness that made the fear bearable, that made it seem purer, or somehow more warranted.

She ought not to have brought Marta into this. She told herself she wouldn't have used her before, against the Nazis, that she was only using her now because it was low-risk and Vojtěch's friend Tomáš had gone missing, but she didn't believe it. Deep down, she knew she had used people every bit as vulnerable as this girl, including, by some perverse equation, her younger self. Yet this was different, that was where the confusion crept in. The people she'd used, and the people who had used her, had been driven by the doomed passions of wartime, when selflessness itself became a sort of self-indulgence. Now the war was over and people were acknowledging the possibility of a future once again. That changed everything. One had a different kind of responsibility. Part of it was to provide an honest purpose for people to risk their lives. But how honest was hers?

"You must call me Milena, little one." She used a napkin to wipe the lipstick from the mirror. Meeting her own grim smile, she almost flinched at the stranger's level gaze. It wasn't the dark wig, the make-up or the unfamiliar clothes. She had become someone else entirely, that was why she had no fear of Stransky recognising her.

Sometimes she found it hard to believe that a savage aspect of her character, lying dormant for many years, had not recently and monstrously grown within her like a cancer. Sometimes she really did think of her former self as another of its victims. If it was so, she knew what had caused it to flourish. What shocked her was that its seed had been in her to begin with.

"Of course. I'm sorry." Marta said. "What do you want us

to do?"

"The first thing is to be ready to follow them if they leave. If it's leather-coat, you two go for a lovers' stroll behind his group, for as far as you can without blowing it. If they have a car, use Vojtěch's father in the van. Josef knows not to make it obvious."

"Yes... Milena."

"If good-looking leaves first, let Vojtěch follow him up into the alley, but only as far as the corner. I just want to know what he does when he gets outside. Tell Vojtěch to be very subtle. I think this man might be dangerous." She turned back to the mirror to adjust her wig and drove the image of the fieldmouse from her mind. "As soon as I get back out there, have Vojtěch go to the bar and get close to good-looking. If he can ask him for a light and hear his voice, that's good, but he's to be cautious, as I said. The main thing is to watch him. I'm going to try something. I'll come back in a while and you can tell me what happened."

She returned to the main cellar. The band was playing again, led by a clarinet in the new American style. Kovály was still with his customer. Mila stood swaying to the music, showing herself, surveying the scene. Several hungry faces turned, but they were just being men. They were deciding whether a seemingly unattached woman with an uninviting manner was worth the price of a drink. As one downed a last slug of courage and got to his feet, she froze him with a sneer and went back to the alcove. She saw that Vojtěch had gone to the bar but this time she did not acknowledge Marta. Instead, she approached two older men who were retrieving their coats from the cloakroom attendant.

"Excuse me," she addressed the less sober of the pair. "Would you be an absolute angel?"

There was a glimmer of interest in his drink-heavy eyes.

Mila produced a lace-edged handkerchief.

"My girlfriend who was just here dropped this. She has only left this moment. I thought you might be able..."

The jowls sagged as his inquiring smile turned to disappointment, but he gave a nod and took the little folded triangle.

"At your service, Miss."

She lingered while they negotiated the stairs and then returned to Kovály, now alone in their booth. The urge to glance over to the bar was strong but she resisted it and accepted another drink instead.

"I have been neglecting you, my poor Milena."

"You've been a perfect escort, Zdenko darling. Did you have a productive chat?"

"Now my dear, that isn't part of the arrangement either." He gave a teasing smile. "I have, however, kept a beady eye on the good doctor for you. It might interest you that he too has been in conference, and with a notable purveyor of petrol coupons. Do you suppose he is planning an excursion to the countryside?"

"I suppose his business trips..."

"But he would have coupons supplied for those. Believe me, I have books of the things."

Out of the corner of her eye she saw movement in the area of the bar. If good-looking was what she was afraid he was, he would be hurrying to follow the man she had approached by the stairs, or at least signalling for someone else to do so. But instead of a discreet exit, there came a commotion. A bar stool crashed to the flagstones, a glass shattered. Now she could look. Everybody was.

Good-looking clung to Vojtěch like a swooning damsel in his arms. Vojtěch appeared stunned. They turned about in a stumbling *pas de deux* and now good-looking had his back to her and she saw Vojtěch's face over his shoulder. He was staring at her, eyes wide with alarm.

Her first instinct was he had been stabbed. The cane must be a swordstick. Before she knew it her hand was in her bag and she was craning for a clear shot. Vojtěch's frown stopped her. His eyes went to Stransky's table and back again.

114

Stransky and his party were on their feet. The better to observe the fuss? No, the leather coat was being buttoned, the girls guided by their elbows. They were leaving.

As the party passed across the front of the bar, good-looking regained his balance and brushed at Vojtěch's raincoat. A waiter crouched and came up with the cane. Good-looking took it with a grimace, brandishing it by way of explanation for the accident. Vojtěch's gaze slid from Stransky's party to Mila again. He had seen they were leaving but was powerless to shake off good-looking and his apologies.

Her hand still in her bag, Mila muttered something to Kovály and jumped up. Now she could see Marta was also on her feet in the back of the cellar. She pushed through the crowd, desperate to attract Marta's attention, but the girl's eyes were on Stransky's group. Having seen Vojtěch waylaid, she had taken the snap decision to follow them on her own.

Mila wanted to scream out to her to abort the surveillance, but it would only have given the game away. It was bad enough that she was making such a spectacle of herself as she moved through the crowd, but she had to warn Marta. Everything had become too dangerous. She and Vojtěch were almost definitely blown. If Marta wasn't, she would be the instant she set off after Stransky, and Stransky would be flagged as their target.

No, that wasn't the issue. The issue was the fieldmouse. Right now, nothing else mattered.

She spun around as a hand took her arm.

*   *   *

In the delivery van in the street leading up to the Old Town Square, Josef Voda cursed as the group of men and women emerged from the arched alleyway with Vojtěch's girlfriend close behind. The surviving streetlamps in the square threw enough light for him to see her hand-signal telling him to do nothing. And the petrified look on her face.

He cursed because he knew it was no work for women.

He had always known this. Even when he had discovered his son in the underground had been working for a woman, even when he had seen with his own eyes what Slečna Slavík could do, still he considered the idea of it an obscenity. A woman's purpose was to create life not to take it. A woman's role in war was to be that which the men were fighting for. And Vojtěch's girlfriend was no Slavík. The masculine codename said it all. That one, he acknowledged grudgingly, had real balls on her. But while Marta might be brave – look at her! – she was just a kid. She ought to have been in ballet classes, or home in bed at this late hour.

And he cursed because not even the Nightingale had planned for this contingency. Marta and Vojtěch were supposed to operate as a couple, that was their cover and their only real defence. As a couple, they might be entitled to signal him to stay put, but he was damned if he was going to let Marta follow those people on her own.

The group and their lonely tail had moved on around the curve of the street towards the light. He would not be able to cross the square in the van, not because he cared about traffic regulations but because most of the big paving stones had yet to be replaced. Where the barricades had stood, now piles of stones awaited the labourers. It was an echo of those heady days of the uprising when, having spent most of his life in the city, Voda had felt compelled to return for its greatest hour and Miss Nightingale had not prevented him. He wondered if he would have obeyed her had she tried.

Well, he wasn't going to obey her now. There were Russian soldiers out this time of night, on passes and making the most of it. And there were the thugs they jokingly branded 'Commissars', the simple peasants and mining folk from the east of the country who had been bussed in by the communists to get rid of any German-speaking Czechs, one way or another, and to bully anyone else who got in their way.

Voda advanced the controls and got out to crank the engine. He would use the van to skirt the square. At least he'd be able to keep them in sight. At least he would be there.

The engine caught. As he stood up again, he saw two dark-suited men exit the alley, walking fast. Voda had no way of knowing if they had been outside or inside the club, but it was plain they were after somebody. They got their bearings and set off in pursuit of the others, breaking into a run.

No need for stealth now. Voda leapt into the van and ground the gears. He barely registered the death-rattle of the meshing cogwheels. In his mind he heard instead that terrible metallic grating, the whine of electric motors and the cough and roar of massive engines. In his mind he saw the tank turning into the square beyond the rain-drenched tricolours, and those confounded Vlasovs coming to the rescue with their rockets. Russians in German *feldgrau*, taking aim at their SS colleagues, cheered on by the Czechs on the barricades. It did not fit with how the world should be, even a world at war. Yet neither did the prevailing verdict on the lips of many Czechs: that it had not happened, that the Red Army alone had liberated Prague. Why must everything be so complicated?

He had almost caught up with the running men by the time they reached the junction with the square. His hand on the steering wheel still clasped the cranking handle but that was as far as his instincts had taken him. He could not even remember if there was a gun in the van.

As he burst out into the open, he was disorientated by the space and light. Seconds passed before he appreciated what was happening, seconds during which some unthinking part of him must have taken the decision to turn right, keep driving, look normal...

The running men had indeed pounced, but not upon Marta or the group she was following. He saw the latter figures casting elongated shadows as they continued across the empty square towards the Jan Hus monument. Instead, the pursuers had seized a couple of old gentlemen who had been waiting on the corner for their car. Voda watched in the rear-view mirror as they were prodded, questioned, frisked...

The road ahead was up. He halted, keeping one eye on the mirror, the other on the shadows of Marta's group as they crept across the façade of the Kinský Palace. In the mirror, the streetlamps caught a flash of white. One of the interrogators had removed something from the older man's coat pocket. It was raised, examined, dropped. It fell lightly, like a piece of cloth.

The second interrogator rushed back down the sidestreet. The first just kicked at the cloth and turned away from the two gentlemen. Now he was staring at Voda in the stationary van. He stabbed with a finger – stay where you are – and began to walk over. His other arm was held crooked at the elbow, shoulder raised. Voda knew the pose of old. It was that of a policeman with one hand on his hip-holster.

The rear-view mirror ignored the open spaces of the square, magnifying instead the man and the remains of the Old Town Hall behind him. Without their stained glass, the chapel windows below the decapitated tower were the mouths of caves. Beside them, the mechanical skeleton of Death peered around the corner of the mangled astronomical clock, its hourglass tilted, frozen in its fleshless hand. Was it trembling, as the mechanism struggled to complete its deliberations?

The approaching man moved between the van and the light by the hall, becoming a silhouette with an icy blue halo. Voda took a moment to notice the second figure catching up. Running over the cobbles on bare feet, she made no sound. Her target didn't register her presence until her shadow came into view, which gave him time only to half-turn before she swished by like another piece of falling cloth. Voda knew she had run right past in case the blow glanced off, because the startled man would then continue his turn to see who had attacked him from behind and she might get in another strike.

But it was unnecessary. Even as she spun on her heels the man's shoes scuffed at the ground and he crumpled forwards into a heap.

Slečna Slavík turned again and kept running towards the

van. Voda saw the cosh in her hand. She tore open the door. Her skirt was bunched up around her thighs. The wig had almost come off. She looked wild.

"Where's Marta?"

Voda came to his senses. He pointed beyond the boarded-up monument, but the shadows had gone. Through the sound of her laboured breathing he heard footsteps echoing on cobbles, but not from the right direction.

At his frown she let out a breathless *No!* that was more like an animal's yelp. Her hands shook the door.

Through his self-disgust Voda felt a guilty wave of relief as Vojtěch appeared behind her carrying her shoes. He couldn't meet his son's eye.

"You weren't here," he said to her.

She looked straight through him and shook her head.

"Someone grabbed me in the nightclub. Just a drunk, trying his luck, but it was time we didn't have and we don't have it now. We must get away from here."

Voda didn't like the sound of that any more than she. The precious time they didn't have. Did Marta have any left?

The doors slammed shut and he gunned the engine.

CHAPTER NINE

In some matters, Sloane was as good as his word.

On the second morning after their jaunt he arrived at the hotel in a Russian-marked jeep, accompanied by Major Mike and a woman he introduced as Fraulein Schelkmann.

He took Bradley's arm and led him out onto Alexanderplatz.

"Place looks worse, if that's possible." Sloane indicated the fresh scattering of half-bricks near the rubble mound. "What happened here?"

"Unexploded bomb. The rubble-women found it yesterday."

"Any casualties?"

Bradley couldn't look.

"Some."

"All the more reason to get away." Sloane slapped his shoulder. "Your carriage awaits. What do you think?"

"Who's the girl?"

"Your interpreter. Speaks English, Russian, German obviously. Even some Czech. Don't worry, she's on the Russkis' list, nothing they can do about it. And she's a damn sight better than anyone they'd fix you up with."

"She's happy to come along?" Bradley didn't bother asking who she was working for. He knew he wouldn't believe the answer.

"Ask her, she's her own person. Jeep's legit – transport pool orders in the locker and requisition forms for gas, although there are extra five-gallon cans in the back."

"Gee thanks, Wally. Trying to get rid of me?"

"You're sore about that business the other night. But that's all it was. Business."

"You don't send people into action without telling them what you're planning."

Sloane kicked at a rock, sending it skidding towards the bust-up streetcars.

"Bill, that's exactly what you do. It doesn't matter what was on those trucks. What matters is we delayed their looting operation. Every hour counts. They're saying they'll let us in by Independence Day."

Bradley had to stop and think. That was less than a week away. Sloane was right, it was time to get moving.

"The Russkis think it was German sabotage anyway. A Werewolf attack, according to their radio."

"Any casualties?"

The sunglasses gave nothing away.

"Don't push it, sport."

Back at the jeep, Major Mike ran through the stowage and Bradley took a better look at Fraulein Schelkmann. The weather had turned since the storm and in her faded print dress and cardigan, with gaunt features and sunburned legs planted in shapeless work boots, she looked exposed, like a sapling. Early twenties to thirties: hard to be sure now everyone dressed and acted older. On one side, her wavy chestnut hair was swept back under the headscarf but on the other a curl had been trained downwards, obscuring her face. Bradley saw why. The flesh around her eye socket was swollen, the eye slitted. The injury didn't appear fresh – there was little discolouration. It looked like her cheekbone had been shattered.

He could guess what had happened and saw she knew it. She dropped her gaze, one hand toying with the curl. The grim set of her lips made her manner more shrinking than coy, but the red flush that began to prickle at one cheek showed the skin to be softer than he had imagined. The other side was dead meat.

Just another Gretchen, as the Russians called them.

Another face among millions, each hiding its own half-forgotten biography, each telling the same story instead.

"I'm grateful for your assistance, Fraulein," he told her in his stilted German.

She answered in English. The low voice sounded as broken as her face.

"It is no trouble, Mr Brown."

Sloane grinned.

"Think you'll find that Fraulein Schelkmann, like any Berliner, will be glad to get out in the country for a spell. Chance to pick up some fresh food, *ne*, Fraulein?"

A downcast nod. On a full-grown woman, the sullen child act had begun to look deranged. It seemed the drive to Czechoslovakia would be a drag and Bradley had to remind himself it was still better than being in the company of Belkin, or Sloane.

Her face came up and she gave a skewed smile. Now the pout made sense. Her front tooth had a corner broken off. Her lips would have to be wary of that edge.

"I understand this is no trip to the grocer, Mr Brown."

A leather flying jacket, a parting gift from the hung-over RAF crew, had been brought out and laid across the hood. Bradley picked it up.

"Here, Fraulein – gonna be chilly on the road."

Again the ironic smile, but she shuffled into the jacket. Bradley relaxed. She'd be OK.

Bogey had been leaning on the shoring at the entrance, but when Karl-Heinz carried out the rest of Bradley's kit he vanished into the lobby.

"On the horn to your liaison," Sloane scoffed. "Think you'd better wait for him?"

Bradley looked from Sloane to Murphy to the girl. The men wore amused expressions. The girl's face was blank.

"No," he said. "Fuck 'em."

*   *   *

It seemed moments since his head had hit the pillow but when the telephone rang the major awoke to the shuttered light of mid-morning. As he swung his boots off his cot and grabbed the receiver, he registered the hubbub of typewriters, telephones and voices in the hangar. The day shift would have been on the go since the reveille.

"Korolev," he grunted, nearly gagging. The buzz of the earpiece synchronised with the buzz in his head and for an odd moment he heard himself echoing in space.

"Arkady Ivanovich, did I wake you?"

The gravelly tones were those of his superior, Colonel Dvortsov, calling from GSGV, the new administration for the occupying fronts. Dvortsov knew he had worked all night. They had last spoken just before dawn.

"Of course not, Anton Romanovich." Korolev found his cigarettes and lit one. The buzzing stopped. The nausea increased.

"Bullshit, Arkady, I can hear you snoring. Why don't you ask me how I slept? Well, I didn't. Some prick filed a report that kept me up reading."

Korolev was on his feet in an instant.

"A report?"

"A load of fish-scales from Czechoslovakia. Some sneaky bastard thinks his cock-eyed investigations are more important than my beauty sleep. I've a good mind to give him the rope to hang himself."

Korolev punched the air. His mind was racing.

"There are my responsibilities here..."

The army personnel unit in the airstrip hangar was working night and day to comply with the new directive regarding demobilisation of the older privates and NCOs. These men and women were under military command, outside the Soviet Union, and it was considered advisable to screen them before letting them in again. Exactly who had issued this advice remained uncredited, but a vetting commission designated PFK had been established, under the auspices of SMERSh.

Starshina Zaitsev too unreliable to be left on German soil? Bring him back! But not home. His engineering skills would benefit a certain reconstruction project. Gun-layer Novikov denounced as politically suspect? Straight to the Gulag! Someone else would determine whether his family should join him. It was all perfectly logical if one set aside the fact that these people had fought for their Motherland, while those deciding their fate had not.

Of course, there were plenty of commanders who weren't about to give in without a fight. It was not just a question of loyalty to their troops – they knew they would be next. So the imperative became to choose which file went to which official, at which time of day, with which brand of *Schnapps*. To lose files, doctor files, forge signatures and issue mistaken travel orders. To misassemble troop-trains, alter timetables and miscount wagons.

Dvortsov had volunteered the local GRU administration. Korolev had no problem with that. If the purpose of military intelligence was to assist the army in achieving its objectives, surely that included preventing the army from destroying itself from within.

No, the problem was he wasn't very good at it. He could command men in the field and even order them to lay down their lives, but typists, secretaries, clerks? On the one hand it required great subtlety, for anyone might be a SMERSh informer. On the other, he was forcing them to risk everything for the sake of some brute of an Ivan who'd likely have beaten or violated them for wearing spectacles. Korolev hadn't the ruthlessness for that and Dvortsov knew it.

"I'll send some ramrod to take over, Arkady Ivanovich. I want you doing what you're good at."

It was plain what he meant. He wanted to score one against the Chekists. Dvortsov didn't bother differentiating between NKGB, NKVD or SMERSh. As far as he was concerned, they were all the descendants of Dzerzhinsky's revolutionary secret police, the dreaded *Cheka*. Korolev's report on the manhunt he had witnessed near the Bavarian border had stirred the colonel's interest. If he could catch them in some wrongdoing or throw a spanner in their works, to Dvortsov's way of thinking that was one in the eye for their screening teams. Possibly he had something personal against this Lieutenant-Colonel Andreev. When it came down to it, most intelligence work was driven by internal rivalries. You stabbed the fellow in the back before he stabbed you.

Korolev replaced the telephone on its hook and lit another Kazbek.

Oh, it was personal all right.

*　　*　　*

Getting out of Berlin took forever. South of the *Mitte*, Fraulein Schelkmann's local knowledge was no more use than the pre-war map. By the time they had negotiated the checkpoints at the inner and outer cordons, the black sedan was on their tail.

Beyond Tempelhof, the road ran alongside the railway for a spell. They saw a train rattling into the city, civilians clinging to the carriages. Most were kids.

"*Hamstern*," came the cracked voice. "They go to look for food in the fields and smuggle it back to Berlin. We call them hamsters."

It was the first time she had uttered anything more than an uncertain direction or a curt translation of the Cyrillic road signs that had been posted over the bullet-riddled originals. Bradley glanced down at the sour face half-smothered by the sheepskin.

"Were you in Berlin during the war?"

"Not for the bombing or the battle. My fiancé was a communist. He was in and out of the camps for many years. Eventually we heard the next time he would be arrested it would be very bad. We fled to Moscow before the war in the

---

125

east."

"But you never married?"

"Dieter was arrested anyhow, in Russia. He was two years in a labour camp. Last year he volunteered to come back to Germany, ahead of the spring offensive. I received a letter. I did not see him before he was sent."

"I'm sorry. He was killed?"

"Who knows? Nobody knows anything." She was back to gazing at Hitler's empty *Autobahn* as it unravelled ahead of them. "I told the Russians I would work for them if they let me return. Perhaps one day Dieter will come back. Anything is possible."

And you got back to Berlin to help the Reds, only to have them do that instead, Bradley thought. It was true enough. Anything was possible in this world.

So was she working for Sloane out of spite for the Reds, or was it a double bluff to curry favour with the only people who could really help her? He felt a pang of self-loathing. Now he was at it, casting her as something to be used. Just another Gretchen.

"Fraulein Schelkmann," he found himself saying. "May I call you by your first name?"

Americans, the shrug said. Or it was something else. Europeans. The redundancy of names.

"Renate."

"And you must call me Sam."

"Mr Sloane called you Bill."

"Well, I prefer Sam. Yes, Renate?"

"Yes, Sam." There it was, that wounded half-smile. It was worth it.

Although there proved to be no shaking off the faster sedan, the US-built jeep ate up the miles. South of the ring road and the last Berlin checkpoint both vehicles had to slow down to negotiate a battlefield. There were shell craters in the concrete and burned-out armoured vehicles either side. Even the forest had burned. Work-gangs of prisoners hauled at the wreckage – human oxen, driven by soldiers on horseback. After that there was little traffic. Occasionally they sped past a northbound army truck full of gawping Ivans. Once a Russian ZIS overtook them and vanished. Mostly all they saw were long columns of defeated people trudging the median. A mile of refugees, another mile of grey-clad soldiers and their mounted escorts. Then, often for mile after mile, nothing. Aside from church steeples and hop-kilns, hilltop chalets and stretches of forest canopy, the landscape itself was hidden behind the embankment.

When they stopped to fill up the gas-tank and share Major Mike's spam-and-cabbage hoggies, the black sedan pulled onto the shoulder two hundred yards behind them. Bradley made out two occupants through the windshield. One wore a broad-crowned army cap, the other a fedora. Lev Belkin and one of the stooges? He hoped it was Belkin. The smooth-talking liaison officer had impressed upon him that it would be necessary to follow a designated route and check in at every municipal commandant's office along the way. Now he'd have to earn his keep instead.

A couple of hours further on, surely well over three quarters distance to the Sudetenland, they came upon their first major obstruction. Red Army sappers had dragged torn-up telephone poles across both carriageways. Beyond the second set of barriers, a grey mass of people must have been accumulating for hours. They might just be detonating unexploded ordnance, but Bradley wasn't about to swap questions. He followed the waved flag onto an exit ramp and asked Renate to find a detour on the map. After a few miles they drove through a deserted village and got their bearings. There was a minor road through the woods that would rejoin the highway before it wound into the Elbe valley at the city of Dresden.

All at once he was back on the road in Czechoslovakia, on the day he met a spiky little fledgling who turned out to be a Nightingale. Same overhanging pines, same flickers of sunlight and sand, same dry scent on the air. Although here the road was metalled it was the same impression, also, of driving through a tunnel. But now it was a tunnel with a blockage.

As they rounded a curve, several figures emerged from the undergrowth a hundred yards ahead. Bradley saw the submachine guns but his first thought – another Russian checkpoint – had barely formed before he noted the ragged mixture of civilian clothes and field-grey uniforms and his instincts took over. Armed Germans from the forest. Diehard Nazi guerrillas. Werewolves.

He heard Renate's intake of breath and was aware of her leg flexing as though stamping open an imaginary throttle. But there was no crashing this roadblock. Six men, weapons levelled. They would have no chance.

Bradley dipped the clutch and began to coast to a halt.

*   *   *

"What's that confounded stink?"

Dvortsov had pulled a few strings, or rattled a few cages. Only eight hours since their telephone conversation and already Korolev was showing his replacement around the operation in the hangar.

He took Captain Bel'chenko's ramrod-stiff arm and directed him to a patch where the concrete floor was stained and cratered.

"There were airfield guards holding out when our tanks got here. One of our tankists drove in, turned around on the spot and drove out again. We've hosed it down a dozen times but can't get rid of the smell. Like a poultry market, isn't it?"

No reaction, save impatience. Dvortsov had chosen well.

Korolev introduced Bel'chenko to their PFK cadre – the official one anyway – before throwing his kit together. No one looked up. He would not be missed.

His driver was waiting by the staff car on the hardstand. Neither was a beauty but both would do.

"Take me to Bohemia," he told her. "Prague first, then we'll see."

The first person to talk to was Novák at the Czechoslovak National Security Corps. Then, probably, that idiot Tsibulkin again, assuming he was still in charge of the transit camp near the American lines. An idiot he might be, but if he hadn't done some private digging into the Karel Sec case to find out how to cover his own back, he had no business being a Red Army commander. It was a pity Tsibulkin had witnessed the SMERSh bastard warning him off, but Korolev was confident he could still frighten the camp commandant into playing along. The damn fool had been at such pains to distract him from the camouflaged safe in his office, it was plain to see he had a little moneymaking operation on the side. It wouldn't take much to get him talking.

Korolev put his feet up on the dashboard and tilted his cap over his eyes.

"If I wake up before Wenceslas Square there'll be hell to pay."

*   *   *

"Sam, these are Nazis here..."

"I know," Bradley hissed. "Just play it cool."

He kept his foot on the clutch and forced the jeep into reverse as it rolled up short of the men. The nearest approached on the passenger's side. Wearing a field tunic over farm-worker's overalls, he was bareheaded, unshaven, and cradling a Schmeisser machine pistol on its sling. No doubt he was also surprised his prey had turned out to be a guy in a shitty-looking cross of British battledress and Yank Class Bs, plus a beaten-up girl in an outsized flying jacket. There was a gleam of curiosity in those weatherworn eyes.

Bradley pulled a dumb-ass grin. The .25 nestled out of sight against his left thigh. His right hand was outstretched in a gesture of enquiry – how can I help you fellas?

Their ambusher flashed a look to check his men had his back. Bradley's right hand shot out to seize the muzzle of the machine pistol, jamming its barrel-rest into the hinge of the flattened windshield. As he buried the throttle, he lifted his other foot off the clutch and the jeep lurched backward, tugging the Nazi off balance. Bradley brought up the .25 in his left hand and pulled the trigger, but by then the guy had lost his footing and was being dragged along, slipping lower and lower behind the hood until the sling broke and the Schmeisser came free.

As time crawled, he was aware of a shriek of fright, woven in with the protesting transmission. Still, she snapped out of it pretty quick, grabbing for the gun so he could put his hand on the wheel, rotating the weapon, aiming it back down the road towards the gang that had clustered around their fallen leader. Good girl.

Maybe two seconds had passed. Glancing over his shoulder to straighten up the jeep, Bradley dropped the .25 and mimed how to use the Schmeisser's charging handle. There came the reassuring hammering as Renate opened up at the diminishing bandits. He heard each thud and slide of the bolt, each cartridge chambering and ejecting, each shot tearing the air and rippling its shockwaves across the membranes of his eardrums.

But time could not crawl forever. He knew it would soon break free and hurl itself forward. He twisted around again but it was too late. Their speed was increasing and he had failed to allow for the curve in the road. All he saw was a blur of foliage as the jeep tipped down the drainage ditch and crunched into a pine-log fence.

CHAPTER TEN

The call had come at six that evening, nearly twenty hours since Marta's disappearance.

The telephone was the only virtue of the Žižkov safe house. True, the view of Hradčany was majestic, especially now, with Prague castle and St. Vitus picked out in gold, but no one among the remnants of the MERCURY circuit believed the commanding location would help them much should they be raided. They were fish in a tank.

In the breathless hour following the call, Slečna Slavík had explained the situation. Despite the tale she had to tell, her voice had been level and her manner in marked contrast to that of Vojtěch, who was climbing the walls.

"That's it," she said now. "That's who I'm looking for. I can't expect you to join me. All I ask is you help get Marta back before we go our separate ways."

She stood against the sunset in a long black skirt, short jacket and plain white blouse. The dark wig lay on the windowsill. Although it had grown out in the past weeks her own hair was still conspicuously boyish. Like the citadel behind her, its unruly spikes were traced in fire.

Shading his eyes, Dušan cleared his throat to speak. As usual, Emil got in first.

"Pardon me, but we thought you were putting together another operation, some more people smuggling..."

"P – p – perhaps a heist?" Dušan said.

Late last night she had used the portable wireless telegraph to summon the brothers from the group's former stamping ground in Moravia, where they had kept a listening watch on the original MERCURY set. They had arrived in Prague on the afternoon train and still had the smell of rough living on them.

"If my plan works out, there'll be profit to be made. From the west or the east."

The brothers regarded one another and shrugged. They are satisfied for the moment, she thought. They may turn on me any day now, but they won't just cut and run.

Nothing so complicated from Vojtěch's father.

"Miss Slavík, naturally we will help you get Marta away from these bastards. But this phone call... it is evidently a trap."

"Evidently," she said. "Remind us what they told you, please, Vojtěch."

"Only that she was all right – which of course she is not! – and that you were to fetch her from one of those fancy apartment buildings on Bílkova Street. That you were to come immediately, and alone."

"Why haven't they bothered to make it sound safe?" That was 'Uncle' Ludvík, the last of the group to speak. Not a member of the original MERCURY circuit but a former army buddy of Josef's – and, Mila suspected, his partner in illegal enterprises before the occupation – he was the oldest and the shrewdest of them all. He brushed at a hoary moustache as he answered his own question. "They know you have no choice but to spring the trap."

"I had reached the same conclusion," she said. "Now the communists have shoehorned their own people into high places, we can't rely on our old contacts at Bartolomějská Street to organise a police raid, or to keep the police diverted if we decide to storm the place. We don't even have time to check out the lie of the land."

"We don't know who has got her!" Vojtěch wailed.

"No, we don't. It might be the Russians. It might be Stransky's people. Whoever they are, it's me they want and that's what they'll get. We'll have to play it by ear."

She faced the window to put on the wig, fighting her nerves. She kept returning to the man in Krypta and the impression she'd had that he was reading her mind. Impossible. But there was something else, something real. The way he had taken Vojtěch out of the game, the look on his face as he acted the part, one of utter confidence, and amusement, like a master player who had already worked out all the moves. She had not imagined that.

Lost in her thoughts, she jumped when 'Uncle' Ludvík touched her arm.

"Miss Slavík, with your permission, I have an idea."

*   *   *

Blue sky, brushed with high yellow cloud. Dusty beams as the sun dipped below the treetops. No sound.

That wasn't right. There was sound, but it was muddy, as though heard underwater. Muffled gunfire. Pause. Voices. More shooting.

There above him, with its red star and hand-painted number, was the jeep's hood. Motor still running? The vibrations said yes.

He shook his head. That was better – or worse. Now he could hear something out of one ear. The other was kaput.

His back and neck ached. His shinbones ached. His head ached. When the jeep had hit the fence, they'd been thrown back into the half-seats with a heck of a force. Renate had been loosing off with the Schmeisser and the abrupt halt had brought it up to her chest in the Present position, with the muzzle an inch from his ear.

Renate. He let his head loll sideways.

No Renate.

He slid a leg over the side and fell out. Now he was lying on the slope of the drainage ditch. It was cool and grey in the gloom of the setting sun. He crawled to the top.

An avenue of pines, vanishing into darkness. Slewed across the crown of the road at the end of a figure-8 of tyre-marks, the black sedan. Crouched behind the sedan, two figures. A green uniform and a lumpy grey suit. Belkin and Bogey.

He watched them take turns to rise from the crouch and fire sustained bursts at targets further down the road, Bogey over the hood of the car, Belkin over the trunk. In the drab wash of the impending twilight, the muzzles of their burp-guns flashed purple and orange, like gas-cookers igniting. At their feet were strewn hundreds of cartridge cases and a half-dozen of the 71-round drums.

Both men, he noticed, had lost their hats. That was pretty funny.

A volley of return fire pinged off the sedan and crazed over the side-windows like ice under an ice pick. A fine spray of glass and dust puffed along the roofline.

There was another ping from the sump of the jeep, but the muted sounds made it all too dreamlike to be alarming. The shooting stopped and he heard shouts from the forest beyond the sedan. Bogey and Belkin yelled back, tossing the words from taut throats that gleamed with sweat. He couldn't hear what they were saying.

A battle with submachine guns, at the limits of their range. Without support, it would continue until one side ran out of ammunition. If it was the NKVD men – they were sure burning through it – or if the Nazis found the moxie to outflank them, that would be that. If the Nazis' ammo ran out first, they'd melt into the woods like good little Werewolves. Hence the shouts, perhaps. A bit of bravado before the disengagement.

Best find Renate and get her into the trees. He stood up behind the peculiarly-angled jeep and tiptoed round to the back. There she was, curled up among the jerricans and other stuff that had come loose in the crash.

Jerricans. That was funny too. He sat on one and offered her a cigarette, cupping an ear at her wide-eyed mouthing. Well, one eye wide, anyhow.

A shadow fell across them. Belkin stood at the top of the

slope. He was also mouthing away but all Bradley could hear was the lowing of distant cattle.

"I'm not a lip-reader, Lev!" He had to bellow to hear his own voice.

Belkin cocked his head and beckoned. The scene was as Bradley had left it, except with Bogey, in shirtsleeves, labouring to jack up the sedan. Both had set their guns down to cool.

Bradley teetered past the three-wheeled car, ignored by Bogey. Up ahead in the lengthening shadows was his Nazi. If he was his. If they'd been Werewolves at all and not escaped prisoners living off the land, or forgotten partisans who'd filtered across some redundant border in search of richer pickings, or survivors of the camps and the death-marches, or liberated slave labourers forewarned of the homecoming they could expect in the east, or Red Army deserters on the run from the likes of Belkin, or any of the other desperate wanderers who might have put on the *feldgrau* and picked up the weapons for warmth or safety. He'd never tell his story now.

Around him lay scattered brass and shreds of fern but there was no other sign a skirmish had taken place. Just an old hobo face-up on the roadside, with his boots gone, and some moth-holes from bullet wounds that had not bled because his heart had stopped. He was so dusty, sallow and emaciated he looked like he'd been dead for days.

A hand on his arm. Lev Belkin, red-faced and sooty, leaned close to speak.

"...is she?"

The girl emerging in a daze from the ditch, a beanpole in big boots and jacket.

"Just another Gretchen," he said, or imagined he said. He was shivering, now.

"Bill, I think... bit of a concussion." Belkin gestured towards his ear.

Bradley touched his own and saw the blood on his hand.

Belkin grinned.

"...when we have towed you into Dresden..."

Bradley shook his head.

"What?"

"...think you have woken up in another world!"

*   *   *

It was nearly two months since Josef Voda had visited the quarter that was crammed between the Old Town and the bend in the river – the former ghetto that had once shared his name. The last time, there had been the bodies strung from every lamppost. Not the bodies of the Jews. They had long since been replaced by the Germans, who had taken over the Sezessionist apartment buildings between the fenced-off synagogues. It was the Germans who had hung from the lampposts in those early days of May.

Now the street seemed quietly prosperous again. There were cars along the narrow pavement, mostly Tatra limousines. The communists had moved in.

At his side in the darkened cabin, Miss Slavík had parted her wrap-around skirt and was fastening a miniature holster to her garter. Voda cleared his throat and looked away. It was one thing that they had lived like animals in the woods – that he himself, returning from Prague, had found her that day as she crawled from the Kübelwagen, and had stripped her smock from her to tend to her wound – but now, on public streets, in a seemingly peaceful city, well, there was something indecent about it, wasn't there?

He shook his head, marvelling at his own sense of propriety and reflecting on how meaningless it had become. A glimpse of stocking indecent, here of all places, where he had seen with his own eyes what had happened to the German women and their children? But he knew what that blink of flesh had roused in him. It was the knowledge that Marta had been in there all night and day, and that at any moment he would be allowing another girl, this girl, to go after her. It was not indecent, it was obscene.

They had already dropped the others at their positions. Voda drew up outside a tall apartment building near the Cubist houses of the teachers' cooperative on the corner with Krásnohorská. Several windows were illuminated, revealing ornate ceilings and chandeliers. Between the windows the facade was decorated with plasterwork in the form of vines and harps and feminine faces spilling tangled tresses. The entrance to the lobby was a golden arch in wrought iron, framed by mosaics.

Quite a heap. It was the kind of place he and Ludvík had dreamed of turning over before the war, but unless one chose to make a display of oneself on the rear fire escape, between the curtain-twitching neighbours and the concierge the only way into apartments like these was to go up and knock on the door.

Voda watched gloomily as Miss Slavík prepared to do just that.

*   *   *

Mila closed her eyes and fought to banish the mental image of the fieldmouse. She settled her beret and wig and checked the contents of her handbag. They were sure to search her, but she had nothing to lose by being armed. They would be expecting it. They knew something at least of who she was.

But what did they know? And who were they? Her lack of preparedness terrified her, as did their faceless professionalism. The obvious trick would have been to let Marta make the call, but they had known the girl would contrive to warn her. Either that or Marta was no longer able to speak. It didn't feel like the amateurish approach she'd have expected from Stransky's collection of double-dealing Czechs. It felt expert, ruthless, boundlessly resourceful and impersonal, like the Gestapo had been, like the Russian counter-espionage police and their local equivalents had become. Like the man at the bar, she acknowledged. It felt like SMERSh.

You bloody old woman, she told herself. What use was thinking like that? Even if the secret police were waiting in there, they weren't just going to arrest her. Had that been their intention, they'd have done so at Krypta. Or if their suspicions had not been confirmed until Marta's interrogation, they'd have got the address of the Žižkov house out of her and apprehended the whole group there. Even SMERSh was just a long arm of a vast bureaucracy. They might be capable of kidnapping people, but they didn't go about baiting traps like this. If they suspected you, they picked you up and made you confess.

Assuming that was all they were after.

Voda was eyeing her as if willing her to call it off. She forced a smile and opened the door.

"Wait up the street. You know what to do."

"Yes, Miss Slavík. But let me come in with you, or..."

"It'll be all right Josef," she said.

Her hand was in her bag as she climbed the steps and hurried through the dim-lit lobby, her heels ringing on the marble. There was no concierge, but she had the sensation of being observed by hidden eyes. She took the lift to the second floor and found the door. The name by the bell was Mezník, which meant nothing to her. Before she could ring, the door was opened by a hard-faced woman in her forties with golden braids coiled over in the German style. Not a maid. In her business suit she looked like a secretary.

"*Herein!*" the woman yapped, making no effort to mask her contempt. Not just a secretary then. More like a concentration camp guard.

Easy does it, Helga, she told the woman silently as she removed her hand from her bag and followed the pinstriped haunches along a chequerboard hallway. Don't know why I've decided you're a Helga, but neither do you know how close you came to acquiring another neat hole between those snooty nostrils of yours, *gnädige Frau*.

138

Part of her was relieved. The Russians wouldn't have Helga fronting for them, so these had to be Stransky's people: ethnic-German Czechs from Prague or the Sudetenland, former collaborators or profiteers at best, parasites on the new regime or fugitives from it. But in the same breath she cursed herself for overestimating the opposition. Notwithstanding the unseen sentry in the lobby, if she hadn't imagined it, this was no fortress. They could have rushed the place after all.

The hallway was L-shaped. A door to the left revealed a grand dining room in disarray and apparently empty. Facing it, between elegant tables displaying African carvings, was a cloakroom that must have backed onto the stairwell or the lift-shaft. The next door, in the angle of the L, was also ajar. It would be the main drawing room, most likely adjoining and partitioned from the dining room. She heard men's voices speaking German and a gramophone playing Schubert lieder. Helga gave her a prod.

"In. They're waiting for you."

Instead, Mila peered past the woman's well-tailored bulk along the upright of the L. Doors either side, then a kink, a couple of steps and a passage leading to the rear of the apartment. Marta might be hidden anywhere, as might any number of guards.

But Marta was in the drawing room with the men. As Mila entered, she jumped up from a couch and tore across the room to embrace her. Through the flurry of tears and kisses, Mila heard her whisper:

"They're going to search you. Here, quickly..."

Marta's small hand delved into her bag and then she was drawing back, hugging herself, as though ashamed of her childish performance. Mila felt a surge of affection.

Here in the drawing room, it was clear the previous occupants had abandoned the apartment in haste. Books lay strewn across the herringbone floor beneath shelves swept imperfectly bare. Drawers and cupboards yawned open. Pictures and ornaments had been torn down. The furniture was mismatched and too small for the generous proportions of the room. The new occupants must have brought it in from lesser rooms.

And they had brought other things. One wall was stacked from floor to ceiling with cases of French brandy and champagne. Against another leaned several crated canvases marked with museum or gallery catalogue numbers.

"I'm sorry, Miss Kristeková," Marta babbled. "When I got here there were too many of them. There are six including the woman..."

"Shut up." Stransky said in Czech.

Choked with admiration for the girl, Mila renewed her vow that she would get her out alive at any cost.

There were three men in the room besides Stransky. Mila recognised the bodyguard from Krypta. The others were older and stouter, one positively obese, bursting from a crumpled serge suit with a southern German cut. His colleague, completely bald with a thick moustache, was dressed for the outdoors in tweed jacket and baggy flannels tucked into boots. None were wielding weapons but on the sideboard near the bodyguard lay one of the new German automatic rifles.

She heard Helga go along the hall again. When she returned she had a fifth man with her. Another soldier type. The sentry from the lobby.

Helga came forward to search her. Her bag was handed to the second bodyguard and the cosh placed on the sideboard. The woman's hands ran up and down her body.

"*Nichts.*"

Giving the Milena Kristeková identity papers an unconvinced sniff, Stransky waved towards an upright chair. Perhaps he imagined she would be unsettled by the disproportionate lack of comfort. As the men lowered themselves into the easy chairs around her, Mila could have laughed. All it meant was they would take an extra second to get moving. Physically and emotionally, they had surrendered the advantage.

The only problem was she couldn't see Marta from here. She guessed Helga had taken her back to the sofa. What the hell, these were amateurs; she would look. Yes.

"You needn't concern yourself," Baldy addressed her in booming German-accented Czech. "No one has touched her, at least not in that way. We are not Slavs."

"What we want to know is why you sent her to follow me," Stransky added in that acid voice she remembered. His bony fingers flicked at the identity papers. "Who are you and what do you want with us?"

"All in good time," she said as breezily as she could. "First, release Marta. If she doesn't walk out of here in the next five minutes, my friends will come in, hard."

Baldy coloured but it was Fatty who answered. His high-pitched wheeze sounded almost amused.

"I think not. Your friends – if they are even out there – must know we will kill you both if they attempt anything."

Well, it had been worth a shot. But this was confusing. Who was the boss? For the moment it was Fatty who kept talking. Mila knew what was coming next.

"Fraulein Kristeková – if that is your name – Herr Müller has told you we have not abused your young friend. This is true, we merely frightened her. But I regret our treatment of her will have to change unless you tell us..."

"No, no, no..." Stransky had leant forward and was staring at her. The same piercing gaze from those shrunken eyes, like gun-muzzles in a pillbox. Her heart fluttered.

"What is it, Stransky?" Fatty demanded.

Stransky too switched to German.

"I have seen her before. I know you, Fraulein, don't I?"

She affected not to understand. Unless she had worked for them during the occupation there would have been no obligation to learn their language. The Nazis hadn't believed in any education for the Slavic races, even here in a land they had decreed to be part of the Reich. That was why they had closed the universities, including Stransky's.

141

"*Ja, ja...*" As he racked his brains, she prayed his once formidable intellectual powers did not extend to noticing or remembering women, but she was fooling herself. "*Gott in Himmel* – it is Ludmila isn't it?"

He let out a laugh and grinned at his colleagues.

"She has changed so much I did not recognise her."

"What the devil are you talking about?" Herr Müller cursed.

"This is someone I knew from Charles University in the old days. This is Ludmila Lossner. She is Professor Lossner's wife."

*   *   *

Lev Belkin had been right to say he would think he was in a different world.

There had been no need for the tow-rope once they'd extricated the jeep from the ditch but still the Russians had insisted on leading the way in their official car. Bradley hadn't had the strength to argue. Nor did he have long to wait to discover why.

As soon as they rejoined the main road it was as if they had passed into another country and another time.

Gone were the resinous pines. Now the night air was rancid with the scorched oven odour he recalled from the Berlin ministry. Gone was the comforting solitude of the countryside in darkness, replaced by a plethora of fires and lanterns that spread across the river valley onto the foothills. Gone, also, was his conviction that he had not badly hurt his head in the crash, for what else might explain the landscape beyond the river?

This was no Berlin. There, however shocking, the destruction had a sorry logic to it: roofs missing where incendiaries had fallen, walls dismantled or toppled by high explosive, holes and scars from shrapnel and shells, oases of surviving structures.

142

This was the stuff of folk tales and nightmares.

Wide bridges spanned the river, converging on what reason insisted must be a city. Yet there was nothing resembling a city beyond the burned barges and foundered steamers along the riverbank, only a gangrenous scar in place of a horizon.

Sprouting from the scar, silhouetted beneath the overcast, the few remaining uprights suggested a petrified forest. Charred spines and thorns. Splinters of church spires. A twisted birdcage a hundred feet high from which the bird had flown.

As if unable to relinquish the memory of the firestorm, the sooty clouds above the obliterated city glowed orange and the river was the colour of blood.

They had come to a halt behind the Russian sedan. The road ahead was jammed with figures. In the scant, unnatural light he saw Renate shiver, yet she flung off the RAF jacket. A tear snailed down one cheek. The other cheek, the other eye, showed nothing.

Clouds shifted. Shapes emerged at the roadside. The cannons of dozens of tanks, raised to mock the toppled steeples and chimneystacks of Dresden. Beneath this honour guard, people shuffled either side of the stalled traffic. The men were old or crippled, limping on crutches or clinging to handcarts. But mostly it was women and children, not wrapped in rags but tattered anyhow. Dresses torn at the front and sleeves. Hair dishevelled. Faces, many bruised and swollen as Renate's, held down in fear or shame.

Renate spoke to one, but he did not hear the response and she wasn't going to share. He had to ask.

"...Sudeten Germans. They are being expelled from Czechoslovakia but now there is nowhere for them to go."

Bradley rose in his seat. The stream of people extended into the darkness.

It was not a different world but the same world. The same world that had set itself atop the long slide into this cauldron in the valley and the worst excesses of humankind, seven years before, and over these very people, and over the very land they had now left behind. Nothing had changed.

*   *   *

Josef Voda heard the mob long before it rounded the corner and funnelled into Bílkova street. The sound of breaking bottles and the snatches of Czech anthems echoed through the maze of modern buildings and ancient alleys. The flames of their torches glinted from the polished coachwork on the parked limousines of the apparatchiks.

The crowd took care to avoid the limousines. They were communists, after all, although Voda doubted many could read even Stalin's asinine tracts without moving their lips. A few had dug out armbands of the self-styled Revolutionary Guards or sported the German helmets they'd adopted during the uprising. Most were simply attired in the flat caps and rough clothes that were the uniform of the greatest army in the world.

Voda's lip curled. Workers my arse! To his mind the main thing about a worker was that he worked and had no time to roam the streets looking for trouble. These 'Commissars' knew no more about hard work than they did about Marx or Lenin. For them, joining the Party's bully-boys was a way to hide themselves in unquestioning numbers – and it wasn't only work they were shy of. During the uprising, the atrocities against the German prisoners and civilians had always been committed by those who kept well back from the barricades. And why did they do that? Voda's squad had joked it wasn't just cowardice: they were afraid if they raised their heads into the Germans' line of fire their former colleagues and customers would recognise them and call out *Servus!*

Now he spotted the man who had originated that bitter joke. Leading from the rear, kicking and cajoling them along like the drill sergeant he had been, 'Uncle' Ludvík was shouting loudest and waving his torch highest of all.

Grinning, Voda drove down the ramp into the cobbled alleys of old Josefov.

*   *   *

In the second floor apartment, Mila heard the clamour and tensed. The bodyguard went to peek through the blackout. As the others turned to watch, she sneaked Marta a wink.

The bodyguard drew back as something smashed the window behind the curtain. Mila gave a polite cough to attract their attention and fixed Fatty with a pleasant smile.

"You said my friends would know not to burst in, but the Commissars down there know nothing of the sort."

"What have you told them?" Baldy thrust his scarlet features at her.

"The truth, Herr Müller. That there are Germans here holding two Czech women hostage. There was no need to hide behind lies. We're not Nazis."

Through the broken window the chanting in the street was audible. There came the crash of the lobby doors bursting open under a press of bodies.

"I hope there's a back way?" Mila said.

Baldy nearly hit her. She was ready to ride the blow and to grab for the tiny vest pistol on her thigh, but Stransky stepped between them, pulling the big man aside.

"Hermann, no. We must go, now. The fire escape."

The bodyguard seized the rifle. The others ran for the suitcases which, like everyone else in Prague these past years, they had kept packed and ready by the door.

In the hallway they heard the drumming of hobnailed boots inside the stairwell. Helga led them around the kink in the passage to the back of the apartment, the men cursing as they went. Mila found Marta's hand and held onto it.

By the time they were on the fire escape they heard the first thud at the apartment door and the voices baying for blood. Below her on the steep iron steps, Fatty was falling behind the others and at the first switchback Mila squeezed past, dragging Marta after her. The other Germans were descending rapidly.

"Shoes off," she told Marta at the next landing. "Come on, little one, I'm not leaving you for those bastards either!"

The mouse's eyes were huge in the darkness.

"Miss Slavík – I'm sorry – Milena... I left the gun from your bag on the chair where I was sitting. I hid it under the cushions and could not get it before we left."

"That's all right, honestly. It doesn't matter now."

"But what was it they were saying to you? I did not understand – my German is so bad – but that man, Stransky, called you Frau Lossner?"

"The others will tell you when we get to the bottom. I told them myself this evening. No, don't stop and gawp, we're not out of this yet."

They reached the courtyard to find Marta's captors gathered round two limousines like those out front. All had their hands in the air. Twin shapes emerged from the shadows of the neighbouring building: the brothers, Dušan and Emil, with machine guns levelled. Mila saw the girl spin around at the sound of Josef Voda's van reversing down the arched alleyway with its back doors open. She watched as Vojtěch stepped from the shadows on the other side, white-faced, pistol wavering, and Marta burst into tears.

She slipped a hand under the girl's arm. Over the cursing of the Germans and the clatter of the fat one on the last flight, she called out: "All of you into the van, now!"

The Mann's vest pistol was in her other hand. In the corner of her eye she saw the mouse's startled gaze and added: "You too, little one. Especially you."

She released Marta's arm, but the girl did not move.

"You're not coming?"

"No." Mila turned back to the Germans, lowering the gun. "I'm going with them."

PART THREE

BENEATH THE ASHES

CHAPTER ELEVEN

"I'll say this for her — she's thorough."

Nemakhov tilted back his hat to admire the gutted apartment, adding: "Not sure I'd want to get on her bad side."

Andreev let out a snort. Like his aide, he was taking care to avoid dirtying his civilian clothes on the debris sagging from above. Reaching the far wall, he prodded with his cane at a pile of charcoal.

Charred timbers grated as Nemakhov followed him across.

"All that booze can't have helped matters." The younger man kicked at a broken bottle, which disappeared between the joists. "And the witnesses say they had flaming torches. These will have gone off like Finnish cocktails. We should check the hospital round the corner — some might have burns."

"We already know who they were." Andreev bent awkwardly to examine a bit of fabric that had been soaked by the fire hoses. "After all, we sponsored them."

"What's that?"

Beyond its blackened fringes, the scrap bore the remnants of whirling shapes in vivid colours. The paint had bubbled and pocked.

"A František Kupka," He saw it meant nothing to Nemakhov. Why should it? Like the Nazis, they were supposed to scorn degenerate abstraction in favour of socialist realism. But oafishness wasn't always the answer, as this débâcle made plain. Not only had the Slavík woman been able to rabble-rouse the so-called Commissars into doing her bidding, but the newly purged Prague fire brigade, its ranks swelled by fellows who didn't know one end of a hose from the other, had let the blaze consume all the evidence.

"You're right, of course." He brushed off his hands. "One of her group must have stoked up the mob. Someone can identify him. But the pressing concern is to establish who was living here and what happened to them."

"Surely it was this Stransky character. The neighbours have picked his photo out and that's how we've linked her to the fire."

"Yes, but who else? We didn't spot Stransky as her target at the nightclub until she took off after him when I buttonholed her young henchman, so we have nothing on his associates – we simply weren't observing them. And because Netsvetailo and Krylov fell for that kindergarten counter-surveillance trick with the handkerchief, we don't know what happened outside. Only that Netsvetailo got a cracked skull and twenty-four hours later one of Stransky's known haunts was put to the torch."

"Krylov thinks he remembers a girl following Stransky's party across the square..."

"...before he and Netsvetailo stopped those old farts instead. And Netsvetailo, of course, remembers nothing." Andreev shrugged despairingly and hoped it was convincing. "If we assume the girl was the young henchman's companion, we can also assume the Slavík group followed Stransky back here. But it wasn't Stransky they wanted. They could have picked him up outside. It was something, or someone, in this apartment."

Nemakhov skirted the room, past the broken windows, to what must have been a sideboard. He picked up a piece of debris. It looked like seared flesh but as he toyed with it a stream of sand poured out.

"So what could that something or someone be? We know there was a package relating to..."

"BORODINO," Andreev said. Nemakhov's scandalised look was a picture. He almost dropped the little leathery lump to put his finger to his lips.

"To that, yes. We know it was meant for the Slavík woman's group and intercepted by Buček's partisans instead."

"But then passed to the British."

"Although we don't understand the circumstances of that," Nemakhov sniffed distastefully. "Buček became incoherent during questioning. But he did put us onto Slavík's contact, Sec, and in pursuing Sec we were able to locate a young man from the Slavík group who had been present at her interrogation of Sec, from whom we established Slavík is now tracing the package backwards to its origins."

"To its origins. Very good, Comrade."

"Karel Sec is dead – apparently by his own hand – but the young man, Tomáš Panek, informed us that Sec told Slavík where the handover of the package to a representative of Buček's group occurred."

"The nightclub Krypta." By now, Andreev was fighting back a smile.

"Indeed. Tomáš Panek is dead, also by his own hand, and was unable to shed further light on the contents of the package, or indeed what Slavík wants with it. Our stakeout of the Krypta produced Slavík herself, along with other members of her group, and the decision was taken not to pick her up but to keep her under surveillance."

"Which we have completely bollocksed-up."

"It might help if you told me how we first got the lead on the package." Nemakhov sounded a little petulant but not very hopeful.

"That's still classified."

"Well then, all we have is the rumour of scientific documents relating to..."

"BORODINO."

"...from which we can extrapolate two possible scenarios. One, the presence of a capitalist spy somewhere within..."

"BORODINO."

"Yes. I find this hard to credit."

"Why? One may safely assume we have penetrated *their* operations."

This time Nemakhov nearly covered his ears.

"One may assume it, but hardly safely! I meant such a penetration would rely on better communications than these handovers described by Sec and Buček."

"Things always go wrong," Andreev said. "If they have a spy inside the programme, his handler could have been arrested for something else."

"I had not considered that."

"It's as well to consider everything. He might have walked under a tram. But go on, please."

"Well, the second scenario is the existence of a fascist scientist at large somewhere within our zone, possibly attempting to offer his services to the capitalists, whom Slavík may or may not be representing. I understand we have comprehensive authorisation both to track down any valuable scientific personnel and to wind up counter-revolutionary espionage groups such as hers?"

"Yes, very comprehensive, and from the very top."

Nemakhov snapped out of his officious manner.

"Comrade Colonel, aren't you concerned those two tasks are somewhat conflicting – and we may be exposing ourselves to... certain accusations?"

If you only knew the half of it, Andreev thought. Aloud, he offered his customary words of reassurance, themselves conflicting: it was all above board and anyway he took full responsibility. As was always the way in the world of *Razvedka,* each statement fell short of the truth. That was the corollary of *Razvedka.* When one had to do whatever was necessary, one was permitted anything and everything, except immunity.

"So," he prompted. "Perhaps Slavík's people were after more of these scientific papers. That fits either of your scenarios."

Nemakhov shook his head.

"All this happened fast. There wouldn't have been much

time to toss the place, not with those thugs on the rampage."

It was true. Their preliminary search indicated the fire had surged through the apartment from front to back. Every room had been torched. They were awaiting a police team to conduct a forensic examination but there didn't appear to be much left in the way of personal effects. A few burned notebooks, inventories of war booty, as far as they could tell. The intriguing innards of a device that turned out to have been a gramophone. The skeleton of a Model 22 or 24 pistol, tangled with the springs of a chair. If there was a safe or hidey-hole they had not found it and neither had the raiders.

"A person then. The scientist himself?"

"Surely he wouldn't be hiding out in Prague. Far too many eyes and ears."

Andreev smirked.

"And other appendages. Incidentally, what *is* that bloody thing you're fiddling with? Somebody's scrotum?"

Nemakhov looked, as if noticing it afresh: a miniature leather bag that had been stuffed with sand. His eyes lit up.

"It's a cosh."

"Then let's try it out on Netsvetailo's skull to see if it fits the dent."

"Of course. She came in, stealthily, ahead of the mob."

"Why would she do that if she was going to storm the place anyway?"

"We disrupted their surveillance of Stransky and we think the girl was forced to follow them on her own. As we know, that's almost impossible without getting spotted."

"So?"

"So they spotted her. Seized her."

"And this was a hostage rescue?" Andreev's eyes opened wide. He nodded. "We must get hold of some of these 'Commissars' and find out what they were told. It's preposterous, but do you know, I think you might be right."

It was preposterous because it meant the Slavík woman was prepared to compromise her entire operation to save one of her operatives. Or did it? Might she have been, as the English said, killing two birds with one stone?

Of course she had been.

"I like your hostage theory, I do. It also explains the twenty-four hour delay. But that isn't why she stormed the place. Perhaps she told herself that was the reason, but it wasn't. Whoever was here – Stransky, others – they had gone to ground and she needed to put them to flight. It's the trail she's following, don't you see? It's the chase."

"And who is she chasing?"

"Well," Andreev said. "Isn't that the question?"

As they left the building a trio of civilians blocked their path. The leader raised a palm to stop Andreev. Being short of stature, and a few steps lower, his hand pressed against his stomach not his chest.

"Halt!" he shrieked in Czech. "Tell me where you are in your investigations!"

Andreev smiled.

"You must ask your own police about that."

"So you're Russians," the little man placed both fists on his hips. "Well, I have influence in Moscow. Tell me what you have discovered. Are you going to arrest the swine who did this? Answer me, or I'll have you writing traffic tickets in Siberia!"

Andreev gestured for permission to descend and reduce the height difference. As the man confronted him again on the pavement, he let him see his pale blue identity card. The flutter of the little Party member's heart was almost audible.

Andreev kept his voice low.

"There isn't any traffic in Siberia. Everything is done by hand. Show me yours."

"I don't understand."

"Show me your hands, citizen."

The word struck him like a blow. Only the prisoners of the Gulag were forbidden from addressing people or being addressed as Comrade. He uncurled a pair of trembling hands.

The plump, pink hands of a bourgeois bureaucrat.

Andreev placed a strip of soggy cloth in them. It was a torn and singed armband painted with the RG of the Revolutionary Guard.

"If this is your neighbourhood, find these people. And the concierge for this building. Have them at the Bartolomějská Street precinct by nightfall."

The police vehicles arrived as they were going back to their car: the forensic team in the van, the NKVD liaison officer with the detectives, although Andreev and Nemakhov both knew Major Vitaliev was actually from the Special Department.

"Comrade Colonel, I've received a message from Colonel-General Rodin at GSGV," Vitaliev said. "He wants to talk to you over the high frequency line at the embassy. Apparently there's been an incident at Dresden that will interest you."

*   *   *

Spurred on by Lev Belkin, the Red Army mechanics had the jeep repaired by midday. Bradley wished flesh and blood were so responsive. After a restless night, the slightest movement sent a spasm from the base of his spine into his kidneys. Although his hearing was a little better, it still felt like his skull had played backstop to another 88.

Yet surveying the exit wound of human misery that spilled out across the bowl of hills and crags, he could not imagine feeling any other way.

Renate's mood, too, mirrored Dresden's plight. She was present, yet she was not, and there was no bridging the distance between them. She had spent the morning with the survivors. Now he watched her shiver in her thin dress and cardigan. He knew he couldn't loan her the flying jacket again but thought she might accept his field jacket. Although it was Government Issue, the flashes made it non-military, didn't they?

"U.N.R.R.A." She pronounced it in full. "The United Nations – against Germany."

"Yes."

"Relief and Rehabilitation – but not for Germany."

"No."

"Why would I wear this?"

"Because it's cold."

For a second, he saw the ghost of that half-smile. Not for his benefit. It was for him she wiped it from her face. But it was something.

"This is a reason," she said.

They sat in the jeep and waited for Belkin. She refused a cigarette, gazing out over the ruins.

"Why did this happen? Dresden was not bombed before. There was little war industry. It was full of refugees from the east. Then, on the night of *Aschermittwoch*... until nothing is left. Ash Wednesday. Is this a *joke*?"

"I thought you were a communist."

"*They* are not – and they want to know."

What could he say? He might talk about the excesses he had seen with his own eyes in Bavaria, if he could talk about that, or the complexities of military necessity, but the obliteration of an entire city in one go did not feel like a justifiable response. It was too – grasping for the word – symbolic, as Renate suggested.

He couldn't help thinking about Jones' bomb, the one made from an atom that reduced everything to atoms, and of the dizzy sensation on the flight into Berlin as it had emerged there'd been a different war going on from the one most people thought they were fighting. A war of elemental forces.

Everybody had been out to whup the Nazis but some had also been preparing for war between West and East. Here, after all, was the Red Army camped out in the Elbe valley, not packing up but staying put, with their endless rows of tanks, guns and rockets facing west. Here was Dresden, or here it had stood, in the path of the advancing Soviets.

And there was Jones, telling him President Truman was about to inform Stalin of the existence of the bomb.

Could Dresden have been a demonstration of the awesome power of the west, right before they announced they'd be able to unleash such destruction with a single weapon? A kind of stunt, as Renate said. A sign on the road that said *Stop Here.*

But I didn't drop those bombs, he wanted to yell at her. Nor did I start this war. And I get you're not a Nazi but if it wasn't for your lot trying to change the world order, they might never have come to power and Dresden might still be standing.

He couldn't say that either.

Instead, he watched the Soviet support troops. His instinct was to see himself as one of them, and all of them as a different species than the men on either side who could decide with the stroke of a pen to destroy Dresden or occupy eastern Europe. Yet the sense of commonality wouldn't come. Where they ought to have been bellyaching, sloping off for a smoke, they had that intense look, like they were privileged to know something you didn't and duty bound to repay the privilege without wasting time about it.

He had known plenty of guys who'd bought into the quest to liberate Europe. In the build-up to D-Day he'd even gotten around to believing in it himself. But he'd never met an enlisted man among the Yanks, the Canucks or the Limeys who couldn't see it was all nuts too. These Reds appeared to have swallowed the whole idea. Could they truly believe they were equal partners in a great enterprise? Couldn't they see their own officers on horseback, or emerging well-fed from the follies on the hillside?

Renate had believed it too, once. But what was going through her mind now? It was like the whole performance with the flying jacket. Had her refusal to wear it been a gesture of solidarity with the survivors of Dresden? Or was it the fear of what might happen to anyone wearing such a jacket among such people?

And then there was the other girl, also unfathomable. If he was losing what faith he had left, what the hell was he doing chasing after her?

All he could think of was the sound of her voice in the silence of the plantation that morning, the bright, breathless whisper, cracked and wounded, speaking Russian, saying *Pazhalsta*, please, you're welcome. Everything that was in that voice.

And the desire – his only creed now – to see and hear her again.

Somewhere nearby, a tank motor turned over. It was followed by another and another. The ground trembled. The windshield began to rattle.

He caught Renate's eye and saw her fear of the metal, of the sense of imminence in the air. Although he knew the muted grumble of their motors was nothing compared with the noise the tanks would make when they moved off, Bradley was impressed enough to share her anxiety. By now it sounded like hundreds of tanks. Thousands. Were they about to roll? Had the signpost of Dresden been ignored?

The snarl of rousing giants had settled to a continuous pulse when, with the toot of a horn, the battered sedan drove into the remount area. Bogey sat stone-faced while his boss came over. Belkin had his fingers in his ears, one hand clutching a buff envelope.

"Loud, yes?" His words were almost lost in the din.

"They going somewhere?"

"West. When your forces come into Berlin, we will move west."

"You mean to occupy the parts of Germany that were designated for the Soviet Zone before we got there first – a trade-off?"

"Perhaps."

"And our forces have agreed to pull back?"

Belkin removed his fingers and canted his head, as though savouring *Kalinka* or *Katyusha*. The air was thick with exhaust fumes.

"They will have no choice." In the same, flat tone he went

on: "We have been called back. You are free to continue."

"Without an escort?"

"These papers confirm your travel orders." He handed Bradley the envelope and gave a formal nod to take his leave of them.

"Wait a minute..." Bradley levered himself out of his seat.

Belkin turned, struggling to hide the resentment he must be feeling.

"What else do you want, Mr Brown?"

Bradley put his hand on Belkin's shoulder. The Russian shrugged it off.

"Say, Lev, we've had our disagreements but, you know... thanks."

"For what?"

"For saving our necks on the road back there, damn it!"

From beyond the trucks came a piercing whistle. One of the nearer tank motors stopped with a cough. Others followed suit, until the only sound of motors was from far down the line. Maybe it was just the echoes from the valley to the south, reverberating in their ears.

Belkin stood there without answering. Finally he cursed under his breath.

"I can't protect you anymore. Go home, Bill. You're going to get yourself killed."

CHAPTER TWELVE

The two limousines sped through the night across the north Bohemian plain. There was no traffic – and no moon to pick out the distant mountains, those natural ramparts that in a world of western appeasement and Nazi brinkmanship had provided no defence.

Of course, it was not only that their French and British allies had betrayed them. Mila stole a glance at her fellow passengers in the leading car. The enemy had lain within their borders all along, waiting to open the doors to Hitler's troops.

She recalled that winter, after Munich, when Prague had been divided against itself: the dread that had hung over ordinary Czechs like the impending snow and the reckless predictions, no less ominous, of the German-speakers and German sympathisers. Until then she had counted many as her friends. One she had counted as her husband.

Because even at the university, where Theodor had been a professor and she a student, even there the great theories of geopolitical necessity, historical inevitability and racial determinism had been advanced. And what began as debate in the bars and cafés had ended a year later at the SS barracks at Ruzyně, where the student leaders were shot.

That was the last time she had seen him. She had fled the country soon after. What she had returned to had not been Czechoslovakia but a benighted adjunct to the Reich. The same bars and cafés were closed or full of Germans, their jaunty signs in modernist founts replaced by charmless Gothic characters. Old Europe itself had looked jealously upon the cocky young democracy in its midst and taught it a lesson it would never forget. In the end it was as Karel Sec had said. They had expended so much energy in the resistance planning to resurrect the Czechoslovakian ideal, never realising it was already beyond resurrection. Their time would have been better spent killing Nazis.

So was there nothing to salvage of a future? She would have to see Theodor to know the answer. She had rescued Marta. She had left the Slavík circuit in one piece. Now, after all these years, she could concentrate on her own needs again.

Wedged between Helga and Stransky's bodyguard in the back of the Tatra, she felt herself *letting go* at last and the sensation was exhilarating. Like the speeding cars in the darkness she was rushing towards an unseen destination of her own. The blurs of trees, telegraph poles and villages were fleeting ghosts. She was in *free fall* again, possibly towards the future, certainly into the past – in one becoming whole and flying apart.

Becoming whole because Jana Slavík and her MERCURY network were finished, and the Milena Kristeková identity had burned with the Josefov apartment; because these people knew her as Ludmila Lossner, Theodor's wife, and it was such a simple jump from Frau Lossner to Fraulein Suková, Slečna Suková, Mila.

But flying apart, because none of her contacts or the tricks she had learned would matter now; because she had been holding on so tight for so long and suddenly she had surrendered herself to these people as surely as she had surrendered the little Mann's.

It had been a long time since anyone had spoken. She knew they were furious with her for forcing them out of Prague too early, but after a day's lying low in Kladno, she suspected it was enough she was Frau Lossner. Whatever network they belonged to, whatever its purpose if they had one beyond survival, evidently they deferred to Theodor.

Now Stransky looked over his shoulder and let the other car past.

"We're coming into Karlsbad. Herr Müller has a call to make. If we're stopped, we'll try to bluff it. If that fails, we'll shoot our way out."

At her side the bodyguard cocked the gun under his coat. Stransky's next words were directed at her.

"Make a scene, Franz will shoot you first."

Their caution was understandable. Here in the former Sudetenland, Stransky's official papers would count for little should they be spotted by the 'Commissars'. Expensive cars full of German-speakers would be red rags to the bulls who had moved in to reoccupy the region, even to the local Czechs who had laboured for so long under German landowners. If they kept moving, they might get through with a few caps doffed in their direction. They had been smart to acquire Party cars. If they were stopped...

All day they had spoken of nothing else. It was surely exaggerated for her benefit and showed a staggering lack of perspective, coming from German mouths, but she had no doubt at least some of what they said was true.

Across the Sudetenland a kind of barbarism was at large. Expulsions, internments, beatings, murders. Families forced to wear swastikas or to go about with an N for *Němec* – German – on their backs. It was not systematic, or not yet, but the gendarmes did nothing to prevent it. Those Czechs who did not participate stood by and watched.

She knew it must be so. She had seen its onset in the western borderlands where they had picked up Karel Sec. Now the Soviet forces were thinning out and the self-appointed authorities taking over, the process could only be accelerated. And up here in the foothills of the Erzgebirge, where there had been so much wealth, so many Germans, she had to admit even some of her own network might have been tempted to join in.

As for herself, was she so pure? Once she had thought the name, the face came back to haunt her. She had not shown much Christian forgiveness towards Karel Sec.

It was 2 a.m. The steep streets and sweeping colonnades

of the spa town were deserted. Under the low-pressure lamps the parked vehicles all wore black stars. But it was the same town and she a schoolgirl again, squashed into father's Skoda between her brothers, seeing the grand facades decked out with flags, the brass bands, string quartets and gymnastic displays, the rich young men in boaters, promenading ladies and richer, older men, in extravagant handchaises, with entourages out of the Habsburg age.

It was the family holidays she remembered, but Theodor had also brought her here. That was less pleasant to recall. It had started well and ended badly, as so much did with Theodor. Was he here now? Since Karlsbad was clearly full of Russians it seemed an unlikely hideout and Stransky had said they were just visiting.

Not here, but he was close.

They swept through town to an area of workers' housing that clung to the escarpment on the far side. Herr Müller's car halted by a row of workshops or garages. A single light glinted off his head as he and the fat man whose name she now knew to be Jarsch got out and unlocked the roller shutters. Their armed bodyguard stood by.

"I'll go help," Stransky said. "We don't want to take longer than we need to."

Franz also disembarked to stand guard, leaving Mila alone with Frau Kaindl, as Helga was actually called. The closer they got to their destination, the less of a prisoner or a hostage she felt, but she knew better than to take her safety for granted.

"Provisions?" she asked as the men loaded a crate in the boot of the car ahead.

"We had to leave a lot behind," Frau Kaindl said acidly.

"Is it a long trip we're making?"

"We are going up into the mountains."

Further boxes and bundles were deposited until the limousines sat low to the ground. The last bundles were long and wrapped in blankets. From the point of balance where the men held them, she knew they were rifles.

They headed north across the river and through the fold of hills. She was thrown against Kaindl and Franz as the road began to twist and climb. Now she knew where they were going. She smelled the spruce and marsh pine and the peat bogs through Stransky's half-open window. And although she could not see them, she sensed them rising all around, the Ore Mountains.

Theodor's mountains.

He had come home. Without an escape route, unable to trust strangers, was that so surprising? And what country it was to hide in, a land of deep valleys, dark forests, high plateaux and abandoned mines. An army could vanish here. Only when the snows came would they have to venture down again.

Something tightened in the pit of her stomach. No one knew where she was. No one would be able to find her if things went badly. But there was more to the feeling than that, because it was a memory too, the memory of her first visit to Theodor's home town and her first suspicions she had made a terrible mistake. For her these mountains would always be as they had seemed to her then: fateful, hiding dark secrets.

Over Stransky's shoulder in the funnel of yellow light, she saw the road sign that gave a name to her fear.

Above the old sign was the new name, Jáchymov. But even in their frenzy of tearing down signs and renaming places they had shied away from removing the former name. Joachimsthal. The old mining town that had given the world the silver Thaler or dollar. And something else, a black rock that had sent the silver miners to early graves.

The town was built around a single road leading up to the mines. Before they reached habitation, Stransky turned off onto a dirt track that ascended in a series of hairpin bends through the trees. They were climbing the hill to the east of St Joachim's Valley, putting the forest and the foothills of the Keilberg between themselves and the town. Now there was another, narrower valley falling away on their left and the hillside on their right became a mossy cliff. That the moss had formed on a west-facing slope hinted at the presence of steeper formations on the other side of the valley. It must be almost a ravine, almost permanently in shadow.

Heavy trucks had used this road in the spring and left the imprint of their loads in the mud of the melting snows. Stransky was fighting the wheel as the big car followed the ruts. Even in the darkness Mila sensed the altitude. She swallowed and her ears popped.

They braked hard. In the beams of the headlamps, the track had disappeared.

"The end of the road," Stransky's words were an incantation. He turned to face her. "Get out please."

Frau Kaindl produced a Luger from her bag and dug it into Mila's ribs. On the other side, Franz had unlatched the door and was backing out with his gun trained on her. For a moment, through her shock, Mila considered grabbing for the Luger. They were amateurs and had bracketed her in a crossfire that might well prove fatal to either of them. The problem was it would be equally fatal for her.

"I thought you were taking me to my husband."

"Get out," Stransky repeated. He too had a gun on her, her own little Mann's.

Had Marta not left her other pistol in the apartment, that back-up weapon would still be fixed to her thigh. In leaning forward to slide from the seat she might have palmed it. With Kaindl and Stransky still in the car, she could have shot Franz and taken the Sturmgewehr, and its 30-round magazine would have given her a fighting chance. The headlamps of the second car were just rounding the last bend. With luck, she might have killed the driver and sent it over the edge.

But she did not have the Mann's and as she alighted Franz backed out of reach. Frau Kaindl slid out behind her.

They were bathed in light as the other car drew up. There was only one chance now. If she could get to the far side of the car she could throw herself over the edge. However sheer the drop, there must be trees beneath. She might not fall far enough to shatter her limbs on them.

She took a deep breath and rounded on Kaindl, brushing the Luger aside. The surprise on the woman's face faded to her customary expression of loathing but she did not bring up the pistol. Mila stepped back. Now there was only the Tatra's dorsal fin between her and the abyss. Could she cover it with a standing jump and a roll, in skirt and heels? Would Franz open fire even though she was not leaping towards any of his group?

A sob of regret rose inside her. She had faced death several times over the past years and had grown fatalistic about it. On occasion she had imagined she might welcome it. But this time she had thought she was so close. It broke her heart that she had been deceived and would not see him again.

"Tell Theodor..."

Stransky laughed.

"You can tell him yourself."

He was grinning. They all were. For a moment she did not understand.

"You mean he's dead too?"

"No, Frau Lossner, I mean you will see him soon. We're nearly there."

They lowered their guns and began a discussion among themselves. Mila got the message. It had been a joke, of sorts, as well as a lesson and a repayment for Prague.

Franz gave her a cigarette and left her alone to smoke it. She wandered to the edge and peered down. No sign of trees, just the cold breath of cloud. Her legs nearly gave way, but she couldn't grant the Germans that satisfaction. They had gathered in front of the lead car to examine the great bite that had been taken out of the road. In the headlamps, through the mist, she saw that the road resumed after fifteen metres or so but in between it had fallen away. An avalanche? The trees above were indeed flattened, but in a radiating pattern. A stray bomb, dropped by one of the aircraft that had got lost en route to Dresden? They had even hit Prague by mistake, and if they could target the wrong city in the wrong country, bombing this

166

valley was by no means inconceivable.

Only the ruts in the track disproved the theory. If the trucks had come this way while the ground was thawing, that would have been well after Ash Wednesday. Had one of them fallen prey to a ground-attack aircraft and detonated? Or had those who were hiding out above this blockage dynamited the road to create that impression?

Herr Müller had located a tarpaulin-wrapped object among the fallen trees. His hand made a rapid winding motion – cranking a field telephone. The blasted road was the moat protecting Theodor's mountain eyrie.

She sat on a marker stone and closed her eyes. There had been nothing overt. They had allowed her own fears to work on her. But the suggestion that she had been about to be executed had paralysed her thinking. It took all her self-control to examine her emotions, defuse her fears and banish them once more. Only a little of the anger would she permit herself to hold on to. It might give her an edge she badly needed.

She spent several minutes breathing deeply, thinking nothing, until her pulse slowed. The scent of the trees and the soil began to dissolve the taste that had crept down her throat. The cool air mopped at her forehead with a mother's tireless love. Now she could think again. The trees, the soil, the mountain air, all were quite benign, the familiar sensations of the country at night. She was not lost. She had some bad memories associated with these mountains, that was all. For a moment she had surrendered to superstitions and imagined an omen was coming true, but the moment and its manifestations had passed. Only the practical realities of her mission mattered now.

Sometime later her trance was broken by the sound of a big vehicle beyond the gap. Although Stransky and the others had doused their lamps, there was enough light in the mist in the valley for her to make out a six-wheeled open Mercedes reversing down towards them. She peered in renewed anticipation, but its occupant was a young man. His hair was slicked back with the sides shorn in the characteristic cut of the SS.

The new arrival threw across a coil of rope and Müller fastened it around a stump as a guide rail. As soon as it was in place the young man picked his way over, stopping to point out certain footholds and handholds at the more treacherous sections of the traverse. Müller clucked. He had come this way before.

It took three-quarters of an hour to ferry the supplies across the gap. When it came time for Müller to shepherd Jarsch and Kaindl over, Stransky approached Mila and clicked his heels.

"Auf wiedersehen, gnädige Frau. Sorry to leave you, but I'm due in Joachimsthal this morning. The Russians are eager to complete negotiations to acquire all future production from the mines. Give my best regards to your husband, won't you?"

She watched as he and Franz commenced their precarious descent in the two limousines, then nodded to the waiting SS type.

"Ja, ja, ich komme mit!"

She tiptoed across the gap while the man brought the rope back behind her. They climbed into the Mercedes with the others and the vehicle began to ascend. After two further bends the road snaked away from the valley's edge and opened out onto a plateau. Weathered rocks or piles of fossilised wood rose from an expanse of peat bog bordered by wild blueberry bushes and dense coniferous forest.

Half a kilometre further on, the dirt road made another turn around an incline to the right and as the Mercedes lurched over its crest she saw their destination. It was built onto the southern face of a molar-shaped tor that appeared at first to be the summit of the mountain. In fact, the outcrop formed the horn of a saddle that fell away in all directions before rising again towards a higher, domed cantle to the south. Burning through a screen of trees and outbuildings on the far edge, the first rays of the new sun glinted on the ruined palace of plaster and glass and made it look like a gold filling in that rotten tooth. For as far as the eye could see, the only sign of human presence was the old sanatorium.

It had clearly been built around the turn of the century, in a fairytale mixture of baroque, neoclassical and sezessionist styles made all the more fantastic by its lonely situation. Flattened against the tor in the form of an E, it was a four-storey block with ornate plasterwork facing the three protruding buttresses and many elongated windows between them, each with a fancy iron balcony. Lately the fairy tale had turned sour, as such tales did. The pitched roof must have been flanked by turrets, but it had been bombed or rocketed and one had collapsed, along with a portion of the upper east wing. Its grandest feature had survived, however. A wrought-iron conservatory ran the length of the building to the height of the second floor windows in what was surely an imitation of the great colonnade at Marienbad. Much of the glass was shattered, much of the white-painted iron discoloured, but its echoes of palm courts and *fin de siècle* elegance endured.

As it loomed over her, she was struck both by the scale of the building and the damage it had sustained. Although it had retained its basic shape it was apparently derelict, walls peppered by shrapnel, roof and upper storeys burned. Presenting such a target of opportunity, the miracle was that having been attacked once it had not been attacked again and destroyed. Perhaps from the air it looked much worse, or was too far from the roads to be overflown. She realised that a pilot would have to approach from the south to see it at all.

The gravel driveway around the ornamental fountain in front of the colonnade was littered with the carcases of trucks and Kübelwagens. The figures in the fountain had been chiselled into the traumatised forms of a Giacometti. Protruding from severed limbs and sagging heads, the rusted frames looked too much like real bones.

"It was a convalescent home for our wounded," Herr Jarsch said. "You can see where there was a red cross on the roof, but the Amis did not care."

"No one has been up here since?"

"There used to be a funicular railway but it was destroyed. The only access is the road we have come by. The Radon Sanatorium was already closed long before the war. I don't think the locals knew anyone was up here. When the surviving wounded were moved out, we moved in."

"And who is 'we'?"

"You'll see soon enough."

The Mercedes descended a ramp to a service area that appeared to have been excavated out of the huge granite stack behind the sanatorium to create a Felsenlabyrinth. Mila saw a brick building marked *Pumpenhaus* and another *Luftschutzkeller*. They drew up in a cobbled yard between an intact Kübelwagen with Organisation Todt insignia and a Wehrmacht motorcycle-sidecar combination. Waiting for them by the service entrance were two young men. Like their driver, both sported civilian clothes and SS haircuts. When Herr Müller stood up, they snapped into the Hitler salute and Mila was engulfed by a fresh wave of nausea. She had not thought she would ever see that again.

So Theodor's hideout wasn't just a refuge for ethnic Germans or collaborators on the run. There were Nazis here. Stransky and Jarsch might be the industrialists they seemed but Müller had to be a party bigwig, perhaps an official of the Todt organisation, which had overseen all the Third Reich's construction and engineering projects, or even an officer of the SS or Gestapo. A cornered beast – and she had walked into his lair.

The Radon Sanatorium. She hadn't heard of it but knew of the therapeutic radium baths taken in the spas of Joachimsthal. Presumably the pump room had once raised the waters from the same underground springs that flooded the silver mines. Most likely the establishment was the folly of a single patron, but he had built it too high up; winters would be bitter here. Possibly it had also been intended as, or converted

170

into, an early example of skiing hotel. The descents into the valleys would have presented ideal pistes. But again, its remoteness was impractical. Later ski resorts in the region had been developed on lower slopes. No wonder it had closed long before it had been attacked. No wonder it had been forgotten.

The men were unloading the supplies and carrying them in. Only Frau Kaindl, German pistol clasped against German bosom, paid her any attention.

Very impressive, Helga, but pull the trigger in that position and you'll smash yourself in the face. I could duck the first shot and pick the gun up when you drop it.

The Luger twitched, indicating the path to the service entrance. Mila shrugged. She had come all this way and there was no sense in backing out now.

She straightened her clothes and walked into the sanatorium. Daylight flooded through the glass front of the building, forming quicksilver pools on the linoleum corridor. Theodor was supervising the unpacking of the crates. The look of astonishment on his face was a picture but she wasn't interested in that.

"Where's Pavel?" she said to him. "Where's my son?"

CHAPTER THIRTEEN

Major Tsibulkin studied the couple across the desk from him and wondered if they were sleeping together.

The man wasn't giving much away. His method of speaking through his interpreter – turning towards her rather than directing his words to Tsibulkin himself – suggested unfamiliarity with the technique, which was odd, but it also granted little opportunity to meet his eye. The most obvious thing about him was his physical discomfort, possibly owing to wounds that had ended his military career and seen him transferred to this relief and rehabilitation nonsense, for he also had the look of a fighter.

As for the interpreter, she was of a type Tsibulkin knew well. He had seen enough of them in the camp to last a lifetime. Broken, violated creatures, carrying their tragedies squirrelled away like heirlooms. This one still had a glimmer in her eye, a bit less of Baba Yaga about her, but that battered face was a turn-off wasn't it?

Not sleeping together, he guessed.

He tried to project an image of sympathetic interest stifled by bureaucratic impotence, hoping it might help to moderate the open hostility emanating from Captain Lesnikov. The NKVD officer had even refused to sit in the presence of an American.

"Please explain to Mr Brown that I wish I could assist. Unfortunately – I should say fortunately – this camp is no longer for assembly and transit of civilians. Since May, we have successfully repatriated all refugees. Therefore, no studies can be made."

There it was again, that tension between them as she translated and the American replied. A forced coolness and a refusal to make eye contact, as if they had been arguing on their way here.

Sleeping together after all.

"In that case, Comrade Major, Mr Brown thanks you for your time, on behalf of the United Nations," the woman said in her German-accented Russian. "He only wonders who were all the people we saw when we drove in."

Bloody cheek, Tsibulkin thought. I'm not surprised you didn't want to translate that for him, Gretchen. Behind him, Lesnikov spoke in a dismissive bark.

"This camp is closed. There are no people here."

Through the window, a line of shabby figures could be seen shuffling between the huts. Old men, women and children, with the Roman N painted on their backs.

Tsibulkin made a gesture of arbitration.

"What the Comrade Captain means is our own humanitarian effort has finished and most of the camp has returned to the jurisdiction of local Czech authorities. I believe they have used the secure areas to confine certain criminals, but you would have to speak to them about that."

The thought had crossed his mind that these might be NKVD *agents provocateurs*. Although he'd seen plenty of Gretchens, he had never met an American before. Lesnikov had insisted on handling all cross-border negotiations once the locomotive had been repaired and the exchanges had begun. Perhaps this American was a facsimile, sent to offer him a bribe for information. Or to offer one to Lesnikov. Tsibulkin doubted the ulcer had the wit to be in on it.

But as the awkward interview ran its course, he had been disappointed. No unorthodox request was made, no bribe offered. Odd though it was, it seemed this UNRRA fact-finding mission was genuine. That was a pity. If he'd known it from the start, he would not have suggested Lesnikov join them – and might indeed have elicited a payment from the

American. On the other hand, he would also have welcomed any attempted entrapment as a chance to demonstrate his unswerving loyalty. He'd been feeling nervous on that score ever since the major from military intelligence had reappeared on his doorstep knowing rather too much about the shipping agents and their customs clearances for Austria and all points south.

"That won't be necessary," the Gretchen said. "Mr Brown asks one last thing – a favour, if you will."

Tsibulkin made himself frown. Was this it?

"If it is in no way inappropriate."

She looked at the American and he nodded.

"Our arrival here was delayed by an accident on the road outside Dresden. Mr Brown has injured his back and wonders if he might see a doctor – if you have one?"

Tsibulkin raised his eyebrows.

"That's all?"

"Yes, Comrade Major. We shan't take up any more of your time. We have many other camps to visit, of course."

Tsibulkin called across to his adjutant.

"Is the Polish doctor still here, what's his name?"

"Wlasnowalski? He's helping the Czechs with their... criminals."

"See our guests are directed to him." Tsibulkin rose and the couple did likewise. The American held out a hand. Tsibulkin took it and squeezed. The fierce grip was returned and a flicker of humour lit up the man's face. Below it, the shapeless tunic was almost Russian: rough, horseshit-brown and quite possibly a disguise.

When they had been shown out, he turned to Lesnikov with a look of challenge.

"Friends of yours?"

Lesnikov's habitual sneer froze.

"You think they were provocateurs?"

Hearing the horror in his voice, Tsibulkin fought the urge to laugh.

"You're the Internal Affairs expert. You tell me."

*　　*　　*

The short walk through the remains of the town took them past the hulks of two T-34s planted on low plinths in a downbeat imitation of the memorial in the Tiergarten. Between them, a bronze *soldat* beckoned his comrades to follow him in a bayonet charge. His head was turned to look over his shoulder but his bayonet pointed west.

So this was 'Hammersmith Grove', what was left of it. Here and there among the ruins, work-gangs with the white N on their clothes were clearing rubble, supervised by shifty-looking civilians in short-peaked caps that reminded Bradley of photographs of immigrants in turn-of-the-century New York. The latter had armed themselves with pickaxe handles. A few locals passed by, bringing their meagre produce to market. Unlike the Bowery types, they seemed genuinely rustic, the women in embroidered bodices and headscarves, the men wearing long coats and broad-brimmed hats. Away from the vicinity of the Kommandatura, excepting the bronze soldier with his brace of tanks, there was no sign of the Red Army. Maybe they really were closing down and pulling out.

At a gap in the strand of barbed wire, their escort spoke sharply with a Czech guard who was falling-down drunk. Presumably he was explaining their credentials, but the guard was uninterested. Gesticulating towards a corrugated iron structure, he slumped again on his busted chair and picked up his bottle. The Soviet lieutenant shook his head.

"You will find the doctor in there. I expect you can show yourselves out."

"*Spasibo,*" Bradley said. The lieutenant gave an equivocal shrug and walked away.

Wlasnowalski was a skeletal figure with receding hair and an eye patch. His white coat, fraying at cuffs and collar, was several sizes too big and hung over a blue-grey striped uniform like the ones Bradley remembered from Bavaria. This too was fraying and had been patched with scraps of blanket. On his feet he wore sandals cut from automobile tyres. But he was clean and animated, and he greeted them with a toothless grin.

Bradley shook his hand, gently.

"Doctor Wlasnowalski?" he began, in English. "My name is Bill Brown. I've never been to Poland, but I had a good friend in the States who came from Cracow."

"Warsaw was much more agreeable," the doctor replied.

"So I hear. Especially in the spring." Bradley gave Renate a sideways glance but she had other things on her mind than spotting suspicious exchanges. Of the forty-odd beds, most were occupied. The young women and children stared back in silence.

"They have been... you understand," the doctor said, looking her up and down. "Some have been tortured. Major Tsibulkin has persuaded the local Committee to let me treat the worst of their injuries. I am not permitted to treat the men."

"You haven't any help?" Bradley asked.

"Ah, no. If I treat the social diseases among the guards I am allowed certain medicines, but that is all." Wlasnowalski ran a hand over his balding crown and threw him an expectant look. "Perhaps, your United Nations..."

Bradley sighed. Over the past days, making their way across Bohemia to this region by the line of demarcation, delayed at every turn by Red Army columns heading east, by the interminable niceties of Soviet and Czechoslovak bureaucracy and, once they had entered the former German-speaking lands, by the long lines of refugees and their escorting militias, they had visited more than a dozen supposed DP camps. Only a handful had been inhabited by people whose state of displacement might be attributed to the Nazis. Most were full of stunned-looking men, women and children daubed with painted letters and swastikas. Yet by post-war logic, people now being displaced from their homes and families did not count as genuine DPs. They were something else.

Aberrations.

"These are Sudeten Germans? UNRRA can't help them." He feared Renate's explosion of indignation, but she was regarding the doctor with a strange expression.

"You were in the camps, in Poland?"

"Ah, yes."

"You can't go back?"

"Not while there is all this work to do here."

When she turned to Bradley, he saw moisture on the undamaged side of her face. The ferocity in her look was all the more striking for the supplication of her whisper.

"If he can do this, then you can help. I know it is not why you are here, but you can make your report, can't you? You can arrange for the medical and food supplies. You don't have to say this is no longer a refugee camp. You can do this."

He looked at her, and Wlasnowalski, and the bed cases. He superimposed other faces, those of the creatures they had found that day in the Bavarian sleet. Then they blurred, becoming the one face, as he had known they would. The face in the porthole.

Jones had warned him an UNRRA mission was being established in Prague. His brief was to take notes for his report but not to submit it. Now he saw he could indeed submit it, in Prague. But attempting to do so would expose his own mission to considerable danger. The real UNRRA team would have no knowledge of him. They might write this off to an administrative foul-up, or they might report him immediately. Jones had said the team's leader was to be a Russian. The man might be working for anyone. It was a huge risk to take. And for what? For Nazi sympathisers.

He thought of Fabienne and what he had said to Smith and Jones in Montmartre, when they had accused her of being a collaborator. That was only the half of it.

Women and children, raped and beaten. Like the woman on the floor of the Berlin ministry, they and their husbands and fathers might have been fervent Nazis or they might not. What it boiled down to was whether you were prepared to see them as people.

But even that wasn't it. The truth was inexpressible, yet he carried it with him and it undermined his every resolution. It was the punch in the guts that turned your guts to mush, that broke your heart and spirit and poisoned the faith and goodness in you, because it was the punch of a master, a father, a god, and you were the dog, the son, the creation.

"All right," he said to them, and himself. "I'll try."

"Good enough," Wlasnowalski said. "Now what can I do for you?"

"It's his back," Renate sounded ten years younger. "We were in an auto accident, and he is in agony, aren't you?"

Bradley frowned. "You're busy here. I'll be OK."

"Nonsense!" the girl cut in. "I'm sure you have things to discuss, so I will go sit with your patients, if I may."

"Certainly, Fraulein." Wlasnowalski looked surprised but he spotted Bradley's nod of reassurance. "So, Mr Brown, you will join me in my examination room?"

"She's OK, I reckon," Bradley said when he was face down on a door laid across two crates. "It was my people who put her onto me, not the Russians."

"I'm still surprised you were able to come here without an escort."

"I can't explain that. It's possible there's an American diplomat in Berlin who's pulling strings on my behalf."

"You're leading a charmed existence. There are people here for whom the presence of any American is an acute embarrassment." Fingers probed Bradley's bare shoulders before moving to the base of his spine. "Does that hurt? Ah yes... and here?"

Bradley grunted.

"What do you mean, an embarrassment?"

"You have seen the two tanks in the station square? Not so long ago, those were the wrecks of American tanks, but now it seems it was the Red Army that liberated this region from the

---

Germans. People have learned to excise any false memories that might contradict this. Some have learned it the hard way, as you say."

"That's crazy!"

"That's communism. Another reason I have no wish to return to my own country. First this camp was for screening refugees, then their own troops. God alone knows how many they arrested. And now they have the local population at it… Sit up please. You really should take it easy for a spell, you've given your back quite a wrench. A disc, here, not herniated, but not right. Sleeping on the ground? Keep doing so. Trouble sleeping?"

Bradley laughed.

"Doc, I've had trouble sleeping for longer than I care to remember."

"Yes, so many scars. Well, I have no medicine for that, or for the pain, I'm afraid. You could try the Russians' favourite, but I expect you wish to remain alert."

"Can you do anything? Put anything back into place?"

"We'll see. You want to know about the Nightingale, yes?"

"I gather you passed a message across the border with one of the returning refugees."

"It has been my privilege to have various contacts in the resistance," said Wlasnowalski, the 'ear specialist'. "Also, I enjoy a respectable working relationship with the local Kommandatura. I try to pass on what I learn."

"Why, doc? Don't you do enough already?"

"As I say, I've no wish to return to Poland. Warsaw is no longer more agreeable in the spring, Mr Brown. Warsaw is no more. I want to go to Palestine. I will need British help for that." He cleared his throat. "Now, the man I mentioned in my message was from the Nightingale network. I was able to establish that he had attempted to sell information during his screening interrogation here. Information about Nightingale, perhaps."

"In return for what?"

"For safe passage to the west. But I think the commandant... you say welched? I think this is the major's speciality here. The man's name was Karel Sec. I knew him a little. Another who had suffered much."

"Knew him?"

"He's dead now, I think. Major Tsibulkin takes the Russian medicine in substantial doses – and he talks. His soldiers come to me with their social diseases. They also drink and talk, especially about something as rare and exciting as a manhunt."

"What do they say?"

"They say Karel Sec escaped with an army of SMERSh soldiers on his tail. They say one of the group that assisted his escape was seen returning on a motorcycle, perhaps to assess the scale of the manhunt. The motorcycle and the man were later traced – and they say the man led them to Karel Sec."

"That's all you know?"

"I know one other thing. A SMERSh soldier was in here. He had fallen off his own motorcycle, drunk of course. It was what he had been drinking that threatened his life, not the broken ribs. An organochlorine compound that is used in the bleaching of pulp to make paper. And I know from when I was on the run from Theresienstadt that there is a disused paper-mill in the hills not far from here."

Bradley hid his disappointment. If this was Jones' best lead, it wasn't much. Nor was he thrilled to hear SMERSh were also on the Nightingale's trail, and with a serious head start. He'd have a heck of a job keeping out of their way, even without the promise he had just made to court further dangers in Prague.

"Do you think that will help?"

Wlasnowalski was looking at him eagerly.

"I'm sure it will, doc." He knew what the old Pole was asking. "You can bet I'll put in a good word for you with the British."

If I get back at all, he thought.

*　　*　　*

That night they slept out under the stars. At sundown he turned the jeep across a hard-baked field that would leave no tracks. They drove into a thicket that had grown up around the gully of a stream. With a bit of hatchet-work the jeep was soon hidden.

Bradley laid out tripwires linked to empty ration tins. He knew he'd sleep lightly but after Wlasnowalski's ministrations he wanted at least to try. Remaining in the Soviet camp under the noses of the NKVD, he'd have found it impossible to relax.

And there was another reason for leaving. They had both felt the impulse to get away from those glowering Czechs and what was being done to the Sudeten Germans.

After they had eaten, Renate spread out the groundsheet and blankets while Bradley reloaded the Schmeisser. It was Wlasnowalski's parting gift, a box of captured 9mm, payment from some grateful Russian Lothario.

As she arranged the camp, Renate sang to herself. No one would have called hers a good voice, but the broken melody was all the music Bradley needed. He marvelled at the change that had come over her. There was a spring in her step, even in those clod-hopping boots, and the good half of her face twisted every so often into a sort of smile.

Finally, she knelt in front of him. Enough light remained to show that she wasn't smiling now. Instead she wore an expression of intense seriousness.

"How is your back?"

"Much better, thanks." He laid aside the gun and grabbed his smokes. She rejected the offer with a slow shake of the head and leaned forwards. Her good eye searched his face, before her chin lifted and her nostrils flared.

"God in Heaven, Sam – you stink!"

Her laughter was good-natured but he felt ashamed.

"I haven't had much opportunity to bathe lately."

She was nodding, her mouth open. A comical look.

"You're right. Oh, then I must also stink!"

"Horses stink, men smell, girls... well, I guess they can get a little high."

"Is that what I am, Sam? A girl?"

"Sorry, a woman," he said, thinking *dames...*

"No, girl is good. I want to be a girl." She looked at him for a long time and then grinned, showing the snapped-off tooth. "But not a smelly girl, eh? Let's go for a swim!"

He stripped to his skivvies, eliciting much laughter from Renate. Halfway through unbuttoning her dress, her mood changed again.

"Don't look."

"Why not? I can't see anything." It was true. She was just an ebony carving with triangles of floral print where the afterglow of the sunset shone through her dress.

"Because."

The water in the stream was barely knee-high but there was a little waterfall over the rocks where they could soak themselves. Coming from the mountains, it was fast-flowing and icy cold. Bradley sat first and yelped. Clasping her thin cotton chemise, Renate tiptoed in and joined him.

It was too cold for arousal. This was something else, something cleansing, for which he did not know the word or even if a word existed. Her shoulders were gooseflesh when he took them in his hands. Her lips were shivering when he kissed them. She knelt astride him and put her arms around his neck. He saw the last glint of light in the black slits of her eyes.

"We should wash," she said. "We're here to wash."

His hands went to the buttons on her chemise. The first, fastened through soaked cloth, resisted before surrendering. Then she was fighting him – really fighting him – and squirming to be released.

"I'm sorry."

"It's not that," she said. "It's what was done to me."

With a great sigh she unbuttoned the neck of her chemise.

Even in the monochrome of near-darkness, he recognised the marks of cigarette burns.

His heart was in his mouth as he bent his head and kissed them.

Nothing disturbed them that night. They woke at first light and watched the young rabbits playing beyond the trees. When Renate parted her lips and the tooth was revealed, Bradley was gratified to see he had taken away a little of her self-consciousness.

He could not tell what else, if anything, he had revived in her, nor could he ask. As he watched her making coffee dressed in nothing but the flying jacket and her boots, with her long hair, tangled from the night, falling over her face and the golden hairs on her legs in the early sun, he could only think the thoughts to which all soldiers surrendered at such times: is this the last, is this the image I'll take with me to my grave?

Following the watercourse, they found the paper-mill two hours later. It too was hidden in a grove, well off the beaten track. Bradley left Renate in the jeep and went in through the only door that had not been boarded up. He took the Schmeisser with him.

The sunlight through the deranged shutters broke up the interior like camouflage material. In the moment his eyes adjusted, he nearly jumped out of his skin.

What remained of a man sat upright at the big steel table in the centre of the workspace. His head, at least part of it, lolled forward onto his chest. Cobwebs were strung between the face and the tabletop. His hands lay on the tabletop, one holding a pistol, and there were other objects: a broken pair of eyeglasses, a crumpled pack of cigarettes, a matchbook. The tracks of tiny footprints criss-crossed the dust.

"Karel Sec, I presume," Bradley said.

Something made him go back out. The contrast was as confusing as the fragmented light in the mill. Inside, there was death and ugliness. A man had put a pistol to his head and destroyed himself. Yet out here the leaves rustled in the breeze, the birds sang, the girl was smiling. He stood by the jeep and kissed her.

"Have you found what you're looking for?" she asked.

Back inside, he searched the corpse. It had rotted but vermin had taken most of the meat and the smell wasn't too bad. He brushed away the flies that were crawling over it, feeling the old disgust as they landed again on him, remembering the flies of Berlin, and of that Normandy summer, a year and a century ago. In a pocket of the mildewed jacket he found a scrap of paper marked with a Cyrillic scrawl. In another, a dented enamel mug. No wallet or photographs of loved ones, no papers with names and addresses. But he had known there would be nothing like that. Several pockets had been turned inside-out.

One cigarette remained in the pack on the desktop. Next to it lay the matchbook. It was almost self-reproachfully he looked inside the flap for a handwritten clue. That would have been too much to ask.

He studied the cover of the matchbook. Black, Gothic letters on off-white wartime card, flecked with brown scales of dried blood. He had considered himself a fool for hoping to find a name and an address, and here they were, staring him in the face.

KRYPTA – Eisengasse – Altstädter Ring – PRAG.

The flies were returning in greater numbers. There was nothing else here. Karel Sec had left no further clues. Bradley buttoned the matches into the breast pocket of his battledress jacket and walked back into the light.

*   *   *

When the jeep had vanished over the brow of the hill, Arkady Korolev lowered his field glasses and rested his head on his forearms. The soil was rich-smelling, the air musky with pollen and hops. On a blade of grass six inches from his nose, a ladybird unfolded its wings and took off on the breeze.

He missed Tanya. His Tanyusha. His no longer. The young girl nicknamed Tanyusha, with whom he had lain like this in the fields, was as dead as that husk in the mill. She might still be Tatyana Koroleva, for now, but it was in name only. She would never leave Moscow for the country. And he would never hear her call him her Arkashenka again.

The American had kissed the German girl once more on leaving the mill. A big, open-mouthed kiss that had lasted too long, in Korolev's opinion. Then again, he had already been inside the mill and seen what sat there. He thought he too might have kissed the girl when he came out, if only to prove to himself not everyone in this world had become a dried-up *Koschei*.

But when he had emerged from the mill, late yesterday afternoon, the sole female in the vicinity had been his driver, Sergeant Simonova. Had he seized her as the American had seized the German girl, he suspected not even his unarmed combat training would have enabled him to survive the experience.

And he had plenty of reason to despise the whole idea of pulling rank like that.

Brushing off his uniform, he walked back to the car that was hidden in the bushes below the rise. The driver's door was open and, as he could have predicted, Sergeant Simonova was busy knitting behind the wheel. The shapeless mass of grey wool was a sweater, he had been told in offended tones. Evidently Simonov, whoever and wherever he might be, was even larger than his wife.

"They've gone," he said.

Simonova's tongue protruded from her lips in concentration as she cast off an edge. Wrestling the thing onto the seat behind her, she shaded her eyes against the sun.

"Did he take the matches?"

"Couldn't see. We'll have to go back down to check."

"And then back to the camp?"

Korolev shook his head. There had been more than the

affirmation of life and love in that kiss, there had been a sense of eagerness too.

"No. I think he took them," he said. "I think we're going to Prague again."

CHAPTER FOURTEEN

From deep within a cane chair in the colonnade, Mila watched the SS press the driveway into service as their parade ground. They wore a mixture of military and civilian clothing, carried a mixture of machine-pistols and rifles, yet the drill brought back Prague's darkest days – barrel chests and bellowed orders, brazen faces transformed into *Walpurgisnacht* skulls.

They were in their element here. Were it not for the wrecked vehicles and mismatched kit, the twenty troopers and their officer might have been the stars of a propaganda piece. Above the tiers of statues and balustrades, behind the summerhouse at the top of the gardens, the far end of the saddle swept up to the dome of the Keilberg. On either side, forested crests undulated above clouded valleys. You could practically hear the Wagner.

And like Tannhäuser or Parsifal, like Castorp at the Berghof, she found herself adrift in time and space. How many days had she been here? Four, five, a week?

What did it matter now?

Are we all the same, she thought, watching the SS charade; is this what the absence of war means? Absence of purpose. Absence of hope.

The interior of the colonnade bore witness to the last gasp and death throes of the conflict. Worn-out handchaises draped in dirty bandages. Stacks of mouldering stretchers. Heaps of iron bedsteads and traction apparatus, all rusted pulleys and tangled wires. On a grand oak table where afternoon teas would once have been served, a clutter of mildewed rags and enamel bowls indicated the more recent presence of a makeshift operating theatre. From the final days, she guessed, when the convalescing wounded had been marched back to the front and the new wounded had begun to arrive in ever greater numbers, when every nook and cranny of the uncaring world had been a makeshift operating theatre. Under the table, beneath the dust and splinters, the mosaics were indelibly stained.

Surely, when it had happened, it had not been in so grim a place. The idea tripped her up and sent her tumbling into a chasm at the heart of herself, but that part of her which still dared to face outwards prayed it had not.

The rest was turned inward and backward, to her arrival here so many timeless days and sleepless nights ago. It was imprinted on her mind: the look on Theodor's face in the moment his astonishment at seeing her had turned to something else. To dread. Without articulating the thought, she had sensed instantly the meaning of that look and although he had not even seemed to register her first words to him, her question about Pavel, still she understood his reaction had to do with their son. It had been suddenly, terrifyingly clear to her. Theodor's expression was telling her what he could not.

As the strength drained out of her, she had almost fainted into Frau Kaindl's arms.

"Mila..." The man she had called her husband, whom she had not seen for five and a half years, had offered a reluctant hand. She saw herself shrinking back from him.

"You must come and sit," he had begun to bluster in German. "I cannot believe you are here like this, but I can see you are exhausted. Come into the lounge. Frau Kaindl, a glass of water for our guest, if you'd be so kind."

So he had fussed over her because he could not say what he knew must be said. And she had allowed herself to be ushered into a long room full of wicker chairs that opened out onto the colonnade. Two women, at their breakfast, had eyed her suspiciously. They were well-fed and tight-buttoned in the Helga mould. She now knew them to be Frau Müller and Frau Jarsch. Frau Jarsch had her four children here.

The children. A part of her wished she could be more charitable towards the boys and girls in their lederhosen and dirndl dresses, but she could not. She detested them. That folksy Bavarian rhythm in their voices as they imitated their father and mother. Their whining demands for food and attention. Their stupid indifference to their plight. She detested them because they represented so much that was too painful to dwell on and a tiny part of her pitied them too. They had been blessed with a better childhood than other children their age, in any other country in Europe, but in shielding them from the realities of the war and teaching them only their scorn and Hitler's accent, their parents had created monsters in their own image. The monsters didn't know they were monsters. They had yet to learn that lesson, but they would.

Her mind was playing tricks. The children hadn't been in the lounge on the morning of her arrival. The memory was overlaid with other memories. She forced it into focus...

"My dear." Theodor spoke in Czech, a sure sign he wanted her on his side. "It took me a moment to recognise you. You look so different."

She pulled off the wig and threw it on the chair beside her. "Tell me," she said.

He took her hand, before she pulled it away. He hadn't changed. Same way of pursing his lips. Like a cat's arsehole, her father always said. Same shock of hair, greyer now. Same polka dot bow tie, she noted in despair as the years began to flicker past and vanish like the trees on the night drive to Karlsbad. Behind the thick-rimmed spectacles, his eyes were moist and solicitous. No, pleading.

"Mila... little Pavel has... gone."

She sucked in one deep breath as though willing her heart to keep beating, but when she exhaled the fickle air, her will went with it.

"Gone? Pavlík?" The words like spasms – contractions – or some kind of opposite.

"I'm so sorry."

A vision flickered past her too – a bird surprised in the undergrowth, a streak of light on the car windows, a child in a little duffel coat, tottering away from her, descending the saddle of the mountain. Going. Gone.

Now her tears were coming, not in floods but in hot globules that burned her face.

"Our little boy."

"Yes. Listen, Mila..."

She must have listened. Theodor's lips were moving – that perpetual snarl and sneer. But no words came.

"Did he suffer?"

His eyes swam behind his spectacles. He stared without speaking for a long time, or so it seemed. The understanding was dawning on her that time had stopped.

"No, he did not suffer. It was meningitis. He just slipped away. That was in Berlin when I was transferred there soon after you left. He received the best possible care..."

Theodor went on but the words had lost their sense for her. They were as duplicitous as the air. Meningitis. Berlin. How could they relate to her son?

And he had died – slipped away, Theodor said – soon after she had left? Five years ago, when he had not even been two years old? How could that be, when all this time she had been carrying him alive in her thoughts and in her heart? Over the last few days she had been so sure she would see him again that she had subsisted in a state of terror at the thought she might not recognise him or he her, and she had stilled some of those terrors with the conviction that a mother would know. Now she realised she had been wrong. The mother hadn't known when her child had died.

The knowledge that little Pavel had been dead these long years made the loss unbearable. She had given him those five years of childhood in her mind and although she had not been able to share them with him they had been more real than anything else in her life. His changing clothes and playthings, passing birthdays and feast days, first statements of self-awareness, questions – and his father's answers. Now it was as though they had been stolen from him, and from her. Stolen violently. Bludgeoned out of him. Torn away from her as surely as though the child had been wrenched from her arms.

Dimly too, she glimpsed the loss of her own recent past as all the horrors and the pains she had endured, and all she had inflicted, became meaningless. The war years and much of what had preceded them, her entire adult life. And chief among the events and influences of that life, this man who sat in front of her, trying to take her hand. Theodor was nothing to her now.

So time had passed in a restless nausea. There were none of the customary practicalities of bereavement to give shape to her grief. No arrangements to be made, as there had been with her parents. No informers to be hunted down, as there had been during the war. There was only Theodor, hovering, fussing, and the Germans and their women and the children. She ate with them but spent her days and nights apart from them, sitting in the colonnade or lying awake on the hospital bed in her room.

The utilities had been destroyed with the railway, but there was water from the mountain and they had laid in plenty of rations. By daylight she had explored what was left of the sanatorium, sometimes passing the other occupants in their own, aimless haunting. They drank the French cognac and Bohemian beers and they smoked the Wehrmacht-issue cigarettes – so many cigarettes, until their smoke hung like the cloud in the valleys below – and they drifted.

The front of the ground floor was taken up by the lounge and dining room to one side of the central lobby and the vaulted indoor pool-room to the other, each giving onto the colonnade through multiple mirrored doors and louvred windows. Although still surrounded by statuary, pillars and palms, the several hot and cold pools had been drained of their radioactive waters and filled with hospital junk. From the smell, they had also been used as a mortuary. The Germans elected to live on the opposite side of the building.

To the rear lay the service areas and kitchens, and the entrance to the cellar. Mila had not been permitted to descend the cellar stairs. But she was free to climb the double staircase to the landing in the atrium and to explore the passageways leading off through the arches around the banisters. Her room was on the third floor in the undamaged west wing and was reached by a less ornate staircase at the far end of the corridor. The top floor was roped off and condemned. She knew she ought to have explored it by night but seemed to have lost her courage with her interest. It was a peculiar equation: she no longer cared whether she lived or died and yet was more fearful of her hosts than she had been when she had possessed a purpose and had imagined they possessed one too. Perhaps it was the fatigue playing on her nerves, the constant weight on her chest and buzzing in her head that left her sick and breathless, oversensitive to the draughts that swept the sanatorium by night and the slabs of dusty sunlight that stupefied the days.

Now, through the broken panes, she watched the parade conclude with the inevitable 'Heil Hitler'. Another ghost. She saw the troopers disperse, some to relieve the sentries, others to check the traps in the forest or to tend the kitchen garden. Their officer, whom they still addressed as Hauptsturmführer, was named Schröter. He too had his wife here, as did four of his men, although in their cases the title was more for convenience. He stood motionless, his hands clasped behind his back, his gaze on the mountains. Then he turned and climbed the steps to the colonnade.

"Good morning, Frau Lossner – and a fine one it is."

He wore the tweeds of a gentleman farmer, albeit with a holster. Mila wondered where he and his men had come by their clothes. If they had been in the field at the time of the surrender it was unlikely they would have been carrying their disguises with them.

What they clearly hadn't managed to acquire was

alternative documentation. With a good enough forgery of the type of discharge certificates that Wehrmacht officers had penned for their men in the last days of the war, no one was going to check any of these Nazis for SS tattoos. Without the means of producing them, however, they were trapped up here. A pity, she thought. *I might have been able to help you there.*

Except back then she'd had scruples. Back then, she had cared.

"Herr Schröter." In dismay she watched him pour himself a coffee from the pot on the sideboard and was forced to add: "Will you join me?"

"Thank you. You will have another cup? Quite wise. I don't know what they put in it but it doesn't bear much relation to coffee. Whereas, when we were in France..." He made a lip-smacking noise she found particularly offensive. "A cigarette, perhaps?"

"Thank you." She did not want one but had learned that smoking gave her an excuse to stay silent. Talk had become an ordeal, not just because of Pavel but because, scruples or no scruples, she could not forget these were the enemy. She had spent much of the past winter and spring trying to kill men like this. If they knew that about her they hid it well, although she suspected Theodor had told them an expurgated story.

"I understand you have received bad news. Please accept my condolences. History will one day record the great sacrifice the German race has made to keep the Asiatic barbarians at bay."

Mila could not help herself.

"If you mean the Russians, I have 'bad news' for you. They are in the next valley!"

And all thanks to you, she added, silently. Schröter smiled.

"This is simply an unfortunate phase. It's a matter of time before the British and Americans join the struggle. You'll see. When they have defeated the Japanese, they will turn to us for help in ridding Europe of the Bolsheviks. I understand your husband has a role to play in this – and you, Frau Lossner, have the means to effect a *rapprochement*."

"Excuse me?"

"I mean your links with British Intelligence."

Mila took a long drag and exhaled. So they knew. Of course. Theodor had attempted to send her the package in April as an overture to a conditional surrender. Clearly the rest of his group were in on it. That was why they had agreed to bring her here. She could not believe she represented their only hope of escape. Between Stransky's dealings in Prague and Müller's in Karlsbad they must be investigating other contacts with the west. But she had to accept that this state of limbo on the mountaintop was at least partly of her making. They had been waiting for the right moment to approach her through her grief.

Footsteps on the glass-crusted tiles.

"Herr Professor." The SS captain stubbed out his cigarette and rose from the chair. He excused himself with a sharp nod and a click of his heels.

Theodor looked terrible. He was unshaven, his bow tie and shirt collar missing. When he removed his spectacles to rub the bridge of his nose, his eyes were red-rimmed. Had he been up all night in conference with Müller and Jarsch, planning their next move? Had there been soul-searching involved?

Knowing Theodor, she doubted it.

"How are you, Mila?"

"All right. Just numb, I suppose."

"Yes, this has all brought it back to me too. A terrible thing."

He sounded as though he were speaking about the failure of one of his experiments. Mila gave a derisive snort.

"How much do they know?"

"Less than I do. They know you were part of a resistance network with a transmitter link to the British, and that you still have an illegal group of some kind. Eduard tells me this much is common currency in the Prague underworld."

"And how much more do you know?"

"Well, I know you went to London, so I can guess at the rest. I thought it best to let them suppose you were a naïve Czech patriot rather than a British agent. For your own safety, Mila. They still remember Hitler's orders about how to deal with spies."

"Yes, I went to London. I married a British man there."

He said nothing. She shook her head before continuing.

"I can see how much that means to you, Theodor. Do your friends know we are no more husband and wife than these SS with their tarts? I didn't think so. What would it do to their trust in you as their saviour if they knew that too was a sham?"

"Pavel was not a sham."

His words took her breath away.

"No. I can't even say he was a mistake, I loved him so. You were the mistake."

Theodor was crying now.

"I loved him too."

"I tried hard to believe that. I wanted to believe he was growing up with a loving father. But I couldn't. I couldn't understand why you would take him away from me. I have never understood how you could do that."

"You were on the run. The Gestapo were after you. I couldn't allow Pavel to be exposed..."

"But you were going to come, it was all arranged! Can you imagine what I went through at Bratislava, waiting for you and Pavel, knowing I had to board that train?"

All at once the tension of those times had come back to her. The tip-off from the Prague police. The escape with her student friends to Brno. The frantic telephone calls and arrangements with other friends in Vienna. The messages routed through to Theodor in his office at the university, even as the university was being closed down. So many brave people risking their lives to help. They would all be dead by now.

She saw herself on the platform at Bratislava, one suitcase filled with all that was left of her past and another containing the toddler's clothes, books and toys which she had imagined to be her future. Twenty years old. Scared to death. Naïve, as Theodor said. But not a child, not an innocent, not any more. Her parents were dead. Her relationship with her professor, born in those times of innocence, had gone sour. Her country was occupied, erased from the maps. But there was Pavlík.

But where was Pavlík?

"Momma coming," he would say. "Momma hug Pavel. Pavel hug Momma."

The travel permits were valid only for a particular Vienna train. Their friends in Nazi-controlled Austria would have one chance to get them to Switzerland. And although they were small fry, the Gestapo dragnet was tightening. It was now or never.

Theodor had agreed to bring their son. She thought he had even agreed to come with them now the university had been closed. Certainly he would pick up little Pavel from her neighbour as he had promised. Certainly he would meet her in Bratislava.

But the train was getting ready to depart. Her mind was full of possibilities – an accident, a roadblock, a delay picking up the papers – but in those days she had still had faith. It could only have been a delay. Any second now, even as the locomotive was whistling, the conductor waving, her friends calling, he would appear on the platform stairs with Pavlík in his arms.

But he didn't. She was rooted to the spot, the cases clasped in her fists. The train began to move. Hands seized her, dragging her away.

If, at that moment, Theodor and Pavel had emerged from the stairs, too late to catch the train, she would have torn herself free from her friends' grasp and stepped back onto the platform to meet her fate.

But he hadn't.

And she hadn't.

She would have to live with her decision for the rest of her life.

How had he come to live with his?

"Why, Theodor?" she said.

He took off his spectacles and pinched his nose again.

"The truth is I agreed to come because I could see no future for any of us under the occupation. I was prepared to risk all our lives because there didn't seem any alternative. But that last day at the university Eduard Stransky came to me and offered one."

"To continue your work – for the Nazis."

"But don't you see? I had it in my power to keep Pavel safe! As a father..."

She slammed her fist on the table.

"As a scientist! All you cared about was your work!"

"That's not true. I would have been able to carry on my work in England or America. It wasn't that."

"Then what? Don't tell me you were dedicated to the Nazi cause. I know you, Theodor, or at least I did. You're not political and you're not that sort of idealist."

"I told you. It was to guarantee Pavel's safety, which you could not. God in Heaven, Mila, you were set on going to London with those other exiles. Don't you think I knew what the Nazis were going to do to London?"

"You're lying. Such a caring father doesn't deprive his child of its mother. If you were going to throw in with the Nazis, you could have persuaded them to let me off the hook. I could have stayed with you and Pavel. And you said yourself it could have been America instead. You could have taken all of us out of the firing line."

"Correct," Theodor pulled a face she supposed was meant to signify self-disgust. It was not an expression she had seen before. "Everything I've said is true without being the truth. I was too much of a coward to come after you. I was petrified of what might happen to me – and Pavel – if they caught us."

"But Pavel died!"

"Yes. And I was working for the Nazis on their secret weapon programme. So now I'm in the shit anyway. Hermann

197

Müller oversaw production at the Joachimsthal mine and he worked hundreds of prisoners to death, thousands even. I was often at the research institute there. I had no responsibility for the labourers but I am implicated. If they find me, I'll be executed with the others. I don't expect you to help me for that reason, but you must believe me when I say the process I've been developing will be immensely valuable to the Allied war effort against the Japanese. It could bring an early end to the war and save countless lives. American, Japanese too, in the long run."

"That was quite a speech. Let me get this straight. You want me to forgive you for taking Pavel away from me because it might save Japanese lives?"

"Not forgive. Understand, perhaps. And help me, for everyone's sake. Nobody wants my process to fall into the hands of the Russians, do they?"

"And the others, they're part of the deal?"

"That's the way it must be. Müller and Jarsch want immunity. The others, the SS, I think they just want reassurance they won't be shot out of hand."

She laughed.

"Don't be so sure. Schröter was just telling me how we're all going to unite behind your wonder-weapon and wipe the Russians out."

"That's the Nazis for you. Idealists, as you say."

"Not pragmatists, like some. But what do you suppose I can do for you?"

"We have a transmitter here. We don't use it because of the Russians' direction-finding, but it could be driven away and used in Karlsbad or even further afield."

"To do what?"

The face was that of her old professor again.

"Don't pretend to be stupid, Mila, I know you're not. To contact London and have them arrange our exfiltration. Failing that, there's your group in Prague. They can bring in the British. I don't doubt the frequencies and codes are in your head."

"You want me to go with your people to Karlsbad to call in the cavalry?"

"No. You'll stay here. You'll write out the exact message for our Morse operator to key in. It's safer that way."

"And you know about safety, don't you?"

He ignored her. The breast-baring was over. He was a different person now.

"Nor do we require the cavalry, as you put it. An agent with authority to grant immunity and an escape route, that's all. I can't believe this is too complicated for them."

Mila lit another cigarette to give herself time to think. Even if she agreed, a direct approach to London was out of the question. Signal plans, codes and callsigns would have been changed as soon as SMERSh began to roll up the surviving circuits. On top of which, Theodor was wrong about the modern codes. There was no way to carry them in your head like the old poem codes. You needed one-time-only pads or transposition keys to compose your message, and her silk-printed key had burned with the lining of her bag in Josefov. Yet she might indeed be able to contact the MERCURY network in Prague or Moravia, using a free cryptic word-code they'd understand, if they were still listening out. There were people they could get in touch with.

But did she care enough about the Allied war effort to permit these Nazis to escape justice? More than that, was she prepared to expose her old group to further risk for such an ignoble cause? Wouldn't it be better just to get away and let events take their course?

She looked up through the loops of smoke. Theodor was trying to read her thoughts. Now they had shown their hand, it was unlikely they would ever take their eyes off her. Getting away would not be easy at all.

But neither would be implementing their escape plan. Because if he believed it wasn't complicated, Theodor was wrong. Evidently he also believed she had received the package and forwarded it to London. It would have been disappointing for him to realise she had tracked him down purely to find out what had happened to Pavel and not, as he had no doubt intended, to begin negotiations for his so-called exfiltration. He had coped with that obstacle, or so he thought. But he didn't know the package had been intercepted and he didn't know by whom.

Contacting London was far from uncomplicated. It might prove to be a death sentence for all of them.

CHAPTER FIFTEEN

Impossible!

Even through a haze that brought to mind a sandstorm, the view from the hilltop in the Grunewald was incredible.

He could see the forest and lakes laid out to the south and west, vivid as a stereoscope at RAF Medmenham. Across the Havel, he could see activity at the Gatow aerodrome – sun glinting on the fuselages of the aircraft bringing delegates to the conference of the three great powers, each with an entourage of bureaucrats, journalists and interpreters.

And spies, of course.

To the east, spilling from the earthworks at the foot of the hill and vanishing into a muddy horizon that belied the summer light, he could see Berlin. It too ought to have been a patchwork of colours. Instead, it seemed to have been chiselled from an ashen monolith.

Ferried between Gatow and the lakeside villas of Potsdam in a flurry of protocol and mosquitoes, closeted in the Cecilienhof Palace under watchful eyes, he'd had neither call nor opportunity to observe what had been done to the city, until now. But what was truly shocking was not the vista itself so much as the fact that he ought not to be able to see it. Smith knew Berlin from before the war. There had been no high ground like this in the Grunewald.

A tall hill, grown from nothing, still growing. Already they called it a mountain, the *Teufelsberg*. A Devil's Mountain of ash and broken stone, of flattened cars and trams, of smashed furniture and statues, of corpses. The Berlin he had known, the old Berlin, lay beneath this mountain. The rubble women had piled it here, first by hand and bucket, more lately by conveyor belt and cart. The carts still plied the winding road to the summit. Some were horse-drawn. Many were not.

Standing by the car in her ATS dress uniform, Corporal Simmonds pinched her nose.

"Dust getting to you?"

"Ain't just the dust, sir. This place don't smell too nice."

"It's the smell of victory." As soon as he said the words he was ashamed of them. This hill, of all places, made a poor stage for portentous utterances, however sardonic. Here were all the great speeches, strategies and horrors of war reduced to their natural conclusion, a rubbish heap. The dead were not waiting for an epitaph; they were crushed beneath the rubble like human backfill, mixed up with bedsteads, typewriters, toys and all the other insignificant wreckage of their lives.

"You're right," he said. "There is a rather unpleasant 'pen and ink'."

His driver widened her eyes.

"Blimey, Colonel, we'll make a Londoner of you yet!"

Smith gave a forced smile. He had hoped she might find him funny.

"Matter of fact, while we're waiting, I'd like you to bring some of your London knowledge to bear on a puzzle I have to solve." He retrieved the transcript from his waistcoat pocket. "Home stations received this communication from a transmitter in Czechoslovakia yesterday and it came over in this morning's diplomatic bag. It's in cryptic rather than code. Perhaps you can help me work it out."

This time her surprise looked genuine.

"You sure, sir? I ain't got clearance or nothing."

"Well," Smith chuckled. "I won't tell if you don't."

"Who is it from, sir?"

He unfolded the sheet of paper and handed it to her.

"It's from my wife."

She studied the flimsy, scanning over the War Office this and Most Secret that. He saw her roll her eyes at the list of transmission times, the prefixes of the stations that had picked it up and the string of identifying callsigns. When she began to read out the message itself, he could have recited it along with her.

RE: PARCEL SENT 9/5 TEACHER WISHES TO PROVIDE FURTHER GIFTS IN PERSON. ADVISE ELEMENTARY SCHOOL NO.78 FULL RELAY TEAM TO ARRANGE RECEIPT WITH HEADMASTER Z MARX, LONDON POETRY SCHOOL. HEAD'S REPRESENTATIVE TO MEET AT AUNT MARY'S, 86 OXFORD STREET, EAST END, SEE TO BY END INST. NIGHTBIRD.

"Ninth of May," he heard her say, to herself as much as anyone; then, looking up: "Day after VE-Day that was. Remember wondering why you had a face like thunder."

"An operation... could have gone better."

"This 'Teacher' sent you something then. Now he wants to meet – to come out of Czechoslovakia?"

Smith beamed.

"And I am the Headmaster. This was transmitted on one of our W/T sets, to one of our signal plans – that's the scheduled timetable and frequency – and in one of our old ciphers, which we have decrypted. But our monitoring stations also detected it being transmitted, unencrypted and off-sked, a day earlier. Although the later version was encrypted and our signals girls had a brief formal exchange with the operator – effectively saying hello and stand by to receive – the messages are substantially identical."

"I see sir."

"Do you? That's very good. The thing is, whichever message one chooses, there appears to be a secondary, even more cryptic message hidden inside the wording of it."

"Like the sender knew they was being checked up on?"

"Exactly. Or, since I'm told every wireless operator has a

unique signature to the way they use their Morse key and we do not know the first operator, rather as though it was designed to be transmitted by an unknown and untrusted third party."

"So 'Nightbird', that's Mrs Smith?"

"Yes."

"So Mrs Smith wrote the message in a way they wouldn't understand."

"Or in a way they wouldn't think suspicious."

"But she sort of tucked away a few clues for you, personally."

"I think so. Briefly – and between the two of us – we were responsible for dropping teams into occupied Czechoslovakia during the war, working alongside Czech Intelligence. I'm sure you guessed that much. Their codenames were chemical elements: BARIUM, CALCIUM, PLATINUM, ZINC, MERCURY and so on. Seventy-eight is the Atomic Number of Platinum, so this message is first and foremost a request – presumably to someone inside the MERCURY circuit, which was the one my wife was a part of – to forward the entire message to London via the PLATINUM circuit's transmitter. Elementary School No. 78 gives the clue, you see. She couldn't send this first transmission in cipher because the first recipient wouldn't have had the key, so she used free cryptic, *en clair*. It's in English – and she specifically requests a 'full relay' of the message – because it is the original message that contains the hidden text."

"Blimey," Jenny threw him a goofy look.

"Blimey indeed. But now the mystery deepens."

"I'll say! If this Teacher needs you to get him out of Czechoslovakia, what's he doing arranging a meeting on Oxford Street and how come he don't know it's in the West End not the East End?"

"The rendezvous isn't in London at all. 'Aunt Mary's' is a safe house in Prague. The rest of the address is unnecessary, although the people who were looking over Mila's shoulder while she composed this wouldn't know that."

"That's her name is it? Mila?"

Helped along by the warm, rank breeze, Smith blushed.

"Yes. Short for Ludmila, you see."

"It's nice." Jenny turned away to flatten out the paper on the car's bonnet. "So, whatever's at number 86 Oxford Street might be a clue..."

"I don't think it's that. You see, she ought to have signed off with a number 80 in cryptic fashion. That's the Atomic Number of Mercury. The fact she didn't suggests it's a pointer to another Atomic Number in the text. Since we know 78 is the PLATINUM transmitter, that leaves 86, which I'm told is Radon. It's not a codename we ever used."

"And who's this Z Marx if he ain't you?"

"Don't know. Nor why it is followed by the reference to the London Poetry School, which, I'm reliably informed, does not exist. Might be a bit of padding to keep up the pretence of an academic message, but I wondered if London Poetry meant cockney rhyming slang and that's why I thought of you."

"No offence, sir, but your wife is Czech, ain't she? Would she be using cockney?"

"When she first came over, her English was good but not fluent. She was fascinated by colloquialisms of all kinds, as she was by any unusual accents or strange pronunciations."

"Thanks a bundle! But I can't see nothing obvious there... 'Marx' might be something, but I don't know it." She frowned as she re-read the transcript. "Hang on a tick. Oxford. Oxford Scholar. Dollar. That's where the other School reference fits in! Could that be 86 dollars? Oh no, you said 86 was this, what's it, Radon. Well, it could still be dollar, couldn't it? Or a crown – five bob?"

"It could be dollar. It could very well be dollar."

Should he tell her? Unlike war secrets that were as superannuated as he, this might be information pertaining to a live operation. But he liked the girl, he trusted her, and she had earned it.

"Dollar could mean Joachimsthaler, from the place where the original dollars, or 'thalers', were mined and minted. It's in the mountains in north-western Czechoslovakia, near the German border. Fits for other reasons too, which I won't go into."

"So she's giving you another location, apart from the rendezvous. Do you think she's telling you where she is?"

"'East End' suggests a place east of Joachimsthal. And I suppose 'see to' by the end of this month could mean 'circa two' – miles perhaps?"

"So all we're missing is whatever this Radon stuff is all about, and this Z Marx bloke who ain't you."

"Well, it's possible Radon is another clue to Joachimsthal. I believe they mine it there." His heart went out to her when he saw her purse her lips and shake her head.

"Begging your pardon but I don't get the feeling you need telling twice, nor that Mrs Smith would think you did. I reckon it all comes down to this Z Marx."

"I have someone searching the works of Karl Marx for any significant Zeds."

She was still thinking. Smith reproached himself for failing to notice her intuitive mind. His office had been crying out for raw talent and he had spent the past year using her as his driver, as though that were opportunity enough for a working class volunteer, and a girl.

Perhaps it was no bad thing the other side were getting in at last.

"I don't reckon it's him, nor Marks & Spencers neither. It's that Z, see? I got a feeling I've seen that, at the pictures. Marx Brothers. That funny one with the moustache and glasses always plays some geezer with a weird name, and it always has a middle initial like that."

Good God, she was right. It had come back to him. He had taken Mila to the cinema the second time they'd met, during the Blitz. A matinée. The Marx Brothers had been playing.

He even recalled her asking about the pronunciation of that middle initial, because it wasn't an English Zed at all but an American Zee. She had found that charming. But what did the clue mean? What had the film been called? What, if anything, had it been about? He knew he had not shared her amusement. Aside from admitting a grudging admiration for Groucho's verbal dexterity, he had found the slapstick antics of the other two infantile and the musical interludes interminable. He had not been able to reconcile the madcap comedy with the bombs falling outside. Mila had. And she had remembered.

Another car was climbing the hill. Smith took the flimsy and replaced it in his pocket.

"Thank you, Jenny." Feeling suddenly protective, he decided he had done the right thing in not recruiting her. Look what had happened the last time!

"Happy to carry on, after your meeting." She tugged her cap down again. With a quick smile, she added: "Tell the truth, I'm too intrigued not to, now, sir."

All chrome and exhaust note, a big, convertible Chrysler pulled up next to their drab-painted staff car. Two Americans got out.

"This is a bloody rum place for a meeting, Sloane," Smith said.

The man's eyes were hidden behind dark glasses, but he was grinning.

"Sightseeing, Colonel. More natural than sneaking around in back-alleyways." He touched the brim of his Panama and inclined his head to Jenny. "Ma'am."

To Smith, he added: "Get through the Teltow checkpoint OK?"

"We do have a measure of authority here ourselves," Smith replied stuffily. "What is it you want?"

Sloane's smile lingered for a moment as he introduced his companion.

"This is Major Mike Murphy. I can't resist saying that. Let me have it, Mike."

A small, buff envelope was passed to Smith. He tore it

open and read the slip inside. There were only three words and no signature.

Babies satisfactorily born.

Sloane offered around cigarettes. There were no takers.

"Potus could have given it to your guy himself, at the conference, but there are too many eyes and ears down there. Can you deliver it verbally?"

Smith nodded and handed back the paper and envelope. Making a point of not looking, Sloane set both alight. He and Major Murphy joined Smith in marvelling at the view.

*   *   *

Head in hands, Josef Voda sat on a long, wooden bench in the room the people of Prague called the 'cinema'. He was thinking about Karel Sec, and he was crying.

He was crying because of what he had said to Sec when he had heard him confess to being a Gestapo informer. And because of the self-righteousness he remembered feeling when Sec had told them how the Gestapo had used his wife against him.

And because, right now, right here in the Petschek Palace, the same building in which they had forced Sec to betray his cause, he was about to do the same.

After his hours in the detention cells, Voda had lost track of time. When they had brought him up, he had thought it would be dark outside, but a grey afternoon filtered through the wire-reinforced windows giving onto Bredovská street. It had been called Bredauer Gasse in Sec's day, and he would have been unlikely to see the blurred legs of Czech civilians saunter past those basement windows, a stone's throw from the National Museum and Wenceslas Square. But he had been here. He had faced this.

They called it the cinema because apart from those high-up windows and two solid doors, the walls were perfectly blank, like screens. Throughout the occupation, thousands of

Czechs had sat on these benches in silence, awaiting their turn to be interrogated, hearing the muffled screams of those who had been called for ahead of them, and projecting their terrors onto those walls. The huge building, remarkable only for its steel shutters and ugly, rusticated stone, had been the headquarters of the Prague Gestapo.

It was supposed to be empty, a place of ghosts. The smashed, paint-daubed windows and shredded blinds, the toppled benches, the black drifts of paper from the burning of the files, all recalled the uprising and suggested no one had set foot in here since. Who, after all, would wish to associate themselves with what had happened here?

Now Voda knew the answer to that question. Although it was not that they associated themselves with the Gestapo, more that they did not care what anyone thought.

And down in the lower basement, in the same cells that had held Karel and Sabina Sec, behind the same soundproof doors of varnished oak, were Vojtěch and Ludvík, his only son and his last true friend.

So he was crying, because he had made the one decision he could make and at last he understood what Sec had done. The utter obscenity of it was baffling. One made the decision for the sake of others, to save their lives. In any other place such self-sacrifice would be noble. Yet here it was the opposite. There was no honourable choice among the two alternatives, that was what he could not force himself to comprehend. He had always supposed if one were prepared to die for one's cause, there would be an honourable way out. Now he saw he had been wrong about that.

Funny, he thought, to learn such a basic life lesson, so close to its end. Because he had no illusions about saving his own skin in saving theirs. He understood that whatever else happened it would end for him as it had done for Karel Sec. It was like an unwritten clause in the contract he had signed. The last footnote. What was the word?

Atonement. He would have to atone for this.

The door scraped across grit or ash. The Russian officer entered with his aide.

"So, citizen," he said in Czech, leaning on his cane. "Is it a 'yes'?"

Without raising his eyes, Voda gave a nod. That wasn't good enough for the Russian. The brass tip of the cane rapped twice on the tiled floor. Amid the debris at the back of the room, something with sharp claws scuttled for cover.

"I will do it."

*   *   *

Colonel Smith came back over to the car. Jenny couldn't read his expression but the excitement of before had evaporated. If anything, he just looked sad.

She bit her lip and fought to hide her concern. She wasn't stupid. The boss was in a bad way, what with the election and all. She knew he reckoned he'd be getting the boot any day now, even though the results weren't supposed to be announced for another week. She had seen him deep in gloomy conference with Winston in the gardens at Potsdam and – Ma would never believe it! – she'd even had a chinwag about it with Mary Churchill, who might be every bit the Lady but was also just another girl in uniform, driving her dad to and fro. It looked a dead cert the PM would be kicked out too. That was why Attlee and those Labour sorts were here, being introduced to Stalin. They were getting ready to take over, and weren't too keen on Intelligence officers who had investigated them in the past.

And now, not only had he broken the Official Secrets Act by taking lowly Corporal Jenny Simmonds into his confidence, but he'd made his first ever reference to his personal life, which as far as lowly Corporal Jenny Simmonds was concerned had always been the Officialest Secret of them all. Not that it was hard to see why he'd been so cagey, if his missus was in Czechoslovakia of all places. What the bloody hell was she doing there?

And who the bloody hell were these Yanks? Who or what was this new funny codename passing messages?

"Potus, sir?" she said.

"President of the United States. Harry S. Truman."

They caught each other's eye and smiled as one.

"Sloane, old boy," Colonel Smith gave her a wink as he called out. "Are you a devotee of the, er, the movies...?"

Five minutes later they were negotiating the track that wound down the Teufelsberg, leaving two confused American agents behind them.

"Well sir?" She was bursting to know.

"Please keep your eye on the road, Corporal."

"Oh, go on, sir. I know you want to tell me!"

Smith laughed.

"Groucho Marx played a character named Doctor Hugo Z. Hackenbush in *A Day at the Races*."

"That's right!" she tooted the horn in satisfaction. "He was a quack. It took place in one of them posh private rest-homes for rich people."

"A sanatorium, yes."

"So, we have a doctor or a sanatorium, and your Radon stuff. Or it's a name. Doctor Radon? What do you think, Colonel?"

"I think you should slow down, Jenny, please."

Yeah, she thought, but that ain't all, is it?

You think you've found her.

*   *   *

The map had been pinned to the blank wall. Andreev used his cane to tap it as he took Josef Voda through the plans one final time.

"I cannot enter the Žižkov house. If Slavík is there in person, she would suspect all three of us. So I will accompany you, but you go in on your own, with the American, and you establish his bona fides with whoever is there. You do it effectively, citizen. This is how you mitigate the charges against your accomplices downstairs."

"And remember," Nemakhov prompted. "When you have gone with the American to the end of the pipeline, you use the transmitter or get to a phone."

"Thank you, I was coming to that." Andreev smiled. He was laughing inside because in all the excitement he had forgotten that part. Unlike Nemakhov, and certainly unlike poor Voda here, who clearly considered himself Anna Karenina, he knew it was irrelevant except as a bit of smokescreen. *Razvedka.*

He felt sorry for the old Czech fighter, of course he did. But really – how long had it taken them to pick up the apartment-torching 'Commissars', two days? And how much longer to identify 'Uncle' Ludvík and the others? Another week at most. With security like that it was astonishing they had not ended up in here years ago.

"Well then," he said. "There's no time like the present."

*   *   *

A few hundred yards away, across the spread of tracks and sidings converging on the main station, Bradley emerged from the train shed that had become the UNRRA warehouse. He saw the girl waiting in the jeep by the police post. As he negotiated the trucks and boxcars in the marshalling yards, his face wore a fixed smile but his spirits were in turmoil.

Renate's features twisted into her own skewed grin.

"You see it all? And they have just started here!"

"It's the American way. We're trying to buy the country."

"Did it not go well?"

"Oh, they're glad enough to see anyone who isn't some kind of panhandler."

"Panhandler?"

His gesture swept the people lurking in the depot and

outside the cordon.

"Half the country's here to explain why they should be the first to get a hand-out, only it doesn't look like the half that needs it."

"But you were able to arrange for the supplies for Doctor Wlasnowalski?"

"Sure." He meant it, the nod, but then he pulled that phony smile again and hated himself for it. "Say, hon, I'm gonna have to leave you here a while."

She bit at her lower lip. The broken tooth made a red mark.

"For how long?"

"The UNRRA folks have promised to look after you and the jeep. They need an interpreter. Or if you don't want to stay, they reckon they can get you back to Berlin."

"But what do you mean, Sam? Are you coming back?"

"I don't know. I'm going someplace and I don't know where that is. The guy I found in that nightclub is coming to meet me. I have to go with him, it's my mission."

He caught himself wondering if what really panicked her was losing touch with the man she was meant to be spying on. Then he saw the look on her face and detested himself even more. He might not be the love of her life, that role might already have been taken by who knew what species of phantom, but he had entered her lonely existence for a time and brought her out of herself a little. That much was precious to both of them. What profaned it was to be leaving her more vulnerable than when he had found her.

Or not. Already her expression was hardening, the pout and the protective shell returning. He watched her weighing up the pros and cons. The stuff in the jeep. The stuff in the depot. The chance of a job.

Maybe, despite everything that had happened, she had her own report to make.

When it came down to it, how much could you know about somebody you met in a place like this? By definition, they

213

were the survivors, and they'd had years to perfect their act. Goddamn it, what could you expect on a continent where it had been compulsory to carry a mask with you everywhere you went?

"I understand," she said.

Bradley shook out a last Lucky and gave her the pack. He would have given a lot more to kiss her goodbye but he couldn't. She knew it too. As he bent his head she turned hers, not all the way but enough. His lips brushed the good side of her face.

"So long, Renate."

He grabbed his bag, passed the police post and pushed his way out. Down the street, the lights flashed on an old delivery van. He raised a hand.

The guy from Krypta was another one, another man in a mask. Bradley had gone straight to the nightclub yesterday, his first evening in Prague. He had worried he would stand out in his battledress but there were three other UNRRA officers at the bar and four or five nurses. Two for one, he'd thought.

The band had hardly got going before the man approached him, waggling an unlit cigarette.

"You have fire, please?" Thickly accented English.

Bradley had taken out Karel Sec's matches and attempted to strike one but the abrasive panel was worn and bloodstained and the match hadn't wanted to ignite.

He could have used the slow-burning fuse in the man's hooded eyes.

"So, you get message." He tucked his cane under an arm, took the matchbook and studied it. "One cannot find these. During war, yes. Now we have peace, is nothing. One must know who to pay."

Bradley had scanned the cellar, nodding. Everyone in the joint looked shady. Spivs, they would have been called in London. Spivs and whores. And UNRRA people. And this guy with the lazy predator's eyes.

"That's capitalism," he had said.

So he had paid. At a secluded table he had removed the tapes from his waistband and counted out twenty gold sovereigns, the going rate for a second date. He had arranged to meet the guy the following afternoon outside the UNRRA depot, and then he had arranged to meet UNRRA themselves. In an hour he was back at the flophouse with Renate. The room was small and the glass hadn't been replaced since the uprising but it didn't matter. It was a hot summer's night and they had slept together under a single sheet on the narrow bed. In the morning they'd crept down the hall and bathed together too.

The van pulled up to the curb. Through the windshield he saw the man from Krypta and, behind the wheel, an older, grey-stubbled guy in a flat cap.

"Come." The man who had called himself Císař in the nightclub slid over to let him in. "Is not far. We may walk, but..." He tapped his cane.

"Sure."

"This one is Josef, another of Slavík, er, net-work." The old boy doing the driving gave him a look. The nervous type.

"Pleased to meet you, Josef."

"Josef is like me," Císař grimaced. "English not good, but..."

"No problem," Bradley said. "Where are we going?"

"Is not far," Císař repeated. "Is this neighbourhood, Žižkov."

Bradley settled back and tilted his head until he could see in the rear-view mirror on his side of the van. The broad switchbacks ascending the hillside were empty of traffic, their cobbles gleaming in the late afternoon light. Two hundred yards back, a sedan was following them. They had it buttoned up tight.

His hand slipped into the top of his army holdall and located the little automatic.

Since finding the matches in the mill he'd known something was up, but he couldn't figure what it might be. The matches had been suspiciously neat, the approach in the nightclub neater. He was being led forwards, he was sure of that. Trouble was, it was the only game in town. It had to be connected to his tail being withdrawn but he couldn't see how or why. If the Reds wanted to pick him up, they hardly had to go to this trouble. If they wanted him to lead them to the Nightingale, why had they quit following him back at Dresden? Renate might have been the answer to that, but he did not or could not quite believe it. It was all too fancy. And if these guys in the van weren't resistance fighters but NKVD or SMERSh, it was their rendezvous they were heading towards, not his. They already knew where they were going and who would be there, they didn't need him.

The likely explanation was the MERCURY circuit had learned of his presence in Czechoslovakia, maybe through Wlasnowalski, maybe Jones. They had planted the matches to draw him here and were going to set out their stall. Maybe they were trying to come back in. Or if it was as bad as Smith and Jones had feared, maybe they wanted to find out what he knew about their activities before disposing of him. He'd have to wing it. Not least because, as Smith and Jones had pointed out, the Nightingale had seen him before, wearing Red Army uniform, speaking his few words of Russian.

But one way or another, he'd have found her.

The sinking sun had turned the windows of the terraced tenements to molten ingots. They pulled up at a steep flight of steps that ascended to a boxy modern building wedged against the hillside. Císař leaned across to unlatch Josef's door for him. When the older man got out, he slid behind the wheel.

"You're not coming?"

"Excuse me, no. Josef goes with you." The man flashed him a handsome smile. "Is OK. These people inside, they want to meet someone from London. This is you, yes? You go with them. They take you where you want to go."

"OK, Císař," Bradley took his hand and shook it.

He had come too far to back out now.

216

*　　*　　*

Driving back down the hill, shielding his eyes from the explosions of sunlight through the railway gantries, Andreev had to admit he was disappointed. The American was an amateur: unalert, unsuspecting. If this was the best London could send over, there was nothing to worry about. But would the fellow have the wit to play his role in the whole scheme – the stratagem, as Andreev liked to think of it?

Representing the Special Department, playing white, he had instigated a variation on the King's gambit. Call it the BORODINO gambit. Unlike in chess, however, in real life it was necessary for the pieces to act the part, and because they themselves had to be innocent of the stratagem for it to be effective, to do so unwittingly. So far, it seemed, black had shown no sign of declining the gambit, but it was important to keep selling it to them. If they recognised he was playing for position they might be able to turn the tables on him and develop into a Berlin defence.

For a second his confidence wavered and he shuddered at the enormity of the risk. Like the real battle of Borodino and, as History repeated itself, like the progress of the Great Patriotic War, his stratagem depended on snatching victory from beneath the ashes of defeat. Tactical withdrawal and the sacrifice of a prize. For Kutuzov against the French, it had been Moscow itself, for Comrade Stalin against the Fascists, so much territory, so many lives. It was essential to persuade an adversary to commit himself, as Napoleon had, as Hitler had.

But this game they were playing now was more like chess than war. There were no armies in the field to count. There was no 'General January' to turn the tide. Strength, and weakness, were in the players' heads, invisible, incalculable, until the endgame.

What if black had its own hidden stratagem? What if the American was himself a sacrificial pawn?

CHAPTER SIXTEEN

Outsized cobbles, slick in the moonlight, formed the tail of a silver rattlesnake that had flung its coils around the town and castle upon the crag. With no windows illuminated, the walls and towers sprouted seamlessly from the trees down in the valley.

From the parapet overlooking the crag, Bradley could see the broad sweep of river that encircled it. The head of the snake. Moonlight pooled on the meadows but there was no sign of livestock, nor of boats along the riverbank. The town, the crag, the whole valley might have been deserted. The only sound was the breeze in the overhanging birch.

And Josef Voda's cursing, of course. Bradley knew that stripe of blasphemy when he heard it. The old guy had kept up the muttered tirade for the half hour they'd been waiting, yet Bradley suspected it was directed not at the guide who had dropped them here, nor at the one who had yet to arrive, but rather at Voda himself.

An odd character. Pretty short on charm, though he must have had something for the Nightingale to trust him. A kind of straightforwardness, Bradley reasoned. There was an aspect to the chunky simplicity of those features, like the stones on the road, which suggested uncompromising solidity. That would be precious to her.

On the wall behind the curb where Voda sat, white letters ran off in a string of angry capitals, clumsily painted but legible in the moonlight. The word NEMCI Bradley knew. He'd have known it anyway from the swastikas either side.

"Josef," he hissed. "What's it say – about Germans?"

Voda hawked and spat behind the suitcases he had brought from Prague. "Er... good riddance."

"The Nazis?"

"People from this town. Good riddance to them. Maybe they were Nazis."

"Maybe?"

"It is enough."

Whatever it signified, the painted slogan made a good marker for a rendezvous, and the deserted bend on the hillside road an ideal cut-out. If they'd been followed, there was nowhere for the followers to hide or loiter.

They were somewhere southwest of Karlsbad, Voda said. He must have recognised the place. Or he had a good nose for the breweries they'd passed. They had been blindfold in the back of the limousine.

Two men had been waiting in the house on Žižkov hill, a German-speaking Czech and his nervy boyfriend, a Hungarian, Bradley thought. There were no introductions. The school-marmish Czech spoke to Voda and went into the next room to make a phone call. The boyfriend just gazed out the picture window.

"If these are the Nightingale network," Bradley scoffed. "I'm Marlene Dietrich."

"Please?" Voda's face gave nothing away.

"What the hell – it's your party."

When the Czech returned he was already donning coat and hat. A shriek of dismay from the boyfriend had kicked off a proper drama of parting and abandonment. Well, who could blame him?

Then the black limousine into the sunset, back down past the depot where not an hour before Bradley had played out his own parting scene. It might have been a year ago.

Craning his neck, he'd spotted the jeep, now with a Russian staff car alongside. No sign of her. Just a big-bosomed brute of a uniformed driver propped against the wing of the staff car, knitting.

They'd turned north across the river to skirt the fortress and soon Prague and Renate were far behind. Somewhere past the remains of the jet fighter base at Ruzyně, as the fireball of the sun obliterated the road ahead, the Czech had pulled over and handed them the blindfolds.

From now on there would be little traffic on the roads and no one about in the villages. Even if they were spotted by some night owl, it would have taken an act of suicidal curiosity to look twice at a Party car with prisoners in the back.

When, an hour or so later, the Czech had stopped again, they had stayed put, hearing gasoline rushing from a jerrican into the tank. Bradley's bag was on his lap and his hand on the pistol. He could have pulled down the blindfold in a second. But this was the bed he had made.

Josef Voda's leg had knocked against his.

"American. These people we go to, they expect you, yes?"

At first he hadn't understood it wasn't a question.

"I don't know anything about them. Císař said they'd introduce themselves."

"No, they expect you. Understand? You must... be like you know this. Like you come from London to meet them, special. If not, they kill us."

He tried to ask why. Only the weight on the seat gave any sign his companion was still there.

He switched to a despondent tone that matched Voda's.

"But how can I fake what I don't know? What is it they want from me?"

"You will see. Slečna Slavík is there, where we go. She tell you why."

"Miss Nightingale."

"Yes."

The ring of finality in that word, uncompromising indeed, certainly infuriating, had halted their whispers long before the Czech climbed back in.

Driving blind again, more ways than one, Bradley couldn't shake off the suspicion these were the enemy. The hiding-out and creeping-about felt amateurish, like they had only recently gone underground. Surely the Nightingale network would be better prepared. Even with Josef vouching for him, surely they'd have questioned him before ferrying him along their pipeline. And the other things that niggled and didn't fit. The matches leading him to Krypta. Císař's self-satisfied air. The spiky German of the queers' tiff. Josef's unease – and now his words of caution, briefing him on the part he must play.

After another hour the car had turned sharp left. Soon it was swooping round curves, plunging into depressions, labouring up rises. The tyres thundered on irregular cobbles. The exhaust note picked up a brushing rhythm that suggested trees, then echoed from walls either side.

If Voda had told the truth and the Nightingale was at the end of the pipeline, either she was trafficking in renegade Nazis and their loot, as Jones suspected, or else she had wound up in the hands of such people. But why bring him to meet her? Who was this guy from London he was supposed to be? And why the hell was Voda saying they'd both be killed if he failed to convince these people? Wasn't he part of their schemes?

The car had stopped. A creak of the emergency brake. A lurch forward. Silence.

Something in Czech. Voda's hand on his face. You may remove your blindfolds.

The minute Bradley and Voda hauled the cases from the trunk, the driver had begun shunting back and forth to turn around. Frosty moonlight gleamed on dark coachwork. Yellow headlamps flashed on white-painted words. The car rumbled away.

Now Voda was at his side, cocking his head. Sure enough, from lower down the road towards the town came the sound of at least two horses, the slow thud of wagon-wheels on the uneven cobbles, and the chink of metal. Bradley leaned out over the wall. Nowhere to hide. They exchanged looks. Voda shrugged.

The dark shape of a cart came around the bend, a single

driver up front. The moonlight glinted on milk-churns behind him, but from the ease with which the horses made the ascent towards them, and the hollow clangour, the churns were empty.

The horses drew up, snorting. The broad features of a peasant lad looked down on them. With a flick of his head he indicated the back of the cart.

Voda nudged Bradley but wouldn't meet his eye.

"Taking me for a ride, are you buddy?" Bradley said.

*   *   *

Mila was lying awake on the narrow bed in her room when the knock came at the door. It was Theodor, and drunk. Even from up here she had heard the partying downstairs.

The night was too hot and close to lie under the covers. She composed the borrowed nightdress around her knees and shook her head.

"Don't you ever sleep?"

Theodor examined her features.

"Don't you?" Swaying, he indicated the chair by the bed. "May I? I saw the light of your candle and knew you were awake."

"I have set the blackout."

"Oh, naturally. I simply wanted to tell you, Mila, and to thank you. We have had news. Your contact from London is coming."

"You've had news?"

"On the wireless, from Prague."

"But I thought you didn't use it here."

"Not to transmit, but to receive. We must know what is going on in the world."

"Hence the party."

"We have little to celebrate. Your man is coming to help us. It is enough, I think."

Yes, my man. But which one? She took cigarettes and

matches from the bedside table and laid the ashtray in her lap. It was a café ashtray in heavy ceramic. Cinzano.

She squinted through the smoke she blew between them.

"The message was from your people at my old safe house?"

"Stransky's people, but yes. The gentleman from London has made his rendezvous and is on his way."

"Did they describe him at all – or get a name?"

Theodor gave one of his condescending smiles. A smile for a child, she thought with a shudder.

"As you must know, it was a matter of a few pre-arranged code-words, nothing more. But I'm sure whomever they chose for this task is highly capable. Anyway, we shall soon find out."

There it was, the unspoken threat, superfluous in this Nazi world. If he is not capable of helping us, both he and you will be in trouble. To disappoint us is to betray us.

Then his mood changed again and he laid a hand on her knee. They both stared at it as if it were a creature that had crept into the room from the forest.

"If you cannot sleep, you should come down, Mila. It can't be doing you any good to stay up here."

She tapped ash into the ashtray, nudging it towards his hand so that he withdrew it. Tap, tap, tap. The way the ashtray moved on her thigh seemed a kind of nakedness.

"I'm not keen on the company you keep, Theodor."

She thought he might be offended. He took the slightest criticism so seriously. Instead he gave a snorting laugh.

"In truth? Me neither! So I shall stay up here. We can have our own celebration."

Before she could reply he had gone to the door again. With a poor mime of naughtiness that clashed with his usual demeanour, he opened it and reached through. When his hand drew back inside the room it held a champagne bottle and two glasses. Mila tensed.

"You had that ready out there."

Now the look on his face was familiar to her. A stranger

223

might take it for a scowl, as she had done for several weeks in the corridors and common rooms of the university. Actually it was his attempt to make himself appealing to the opposite sex. The half-frown, the sucked in cheeks, the cold, appraising eyes behind the heavy spectacles were Theodor's expression of seduction.

*   *   *

As they retraced their path to the main road and turned off onto another country lane, Bradley saw from the stars that they had swung east again. The old trepidation quickened: there had been comfort in heading west. Nor was it reassuring that the guides had spoilt their own cut-out. Going back the same way would enable any pursuers to reacquire them. It was another hint they were in the hands of amateurs.

The old walls and outbuildings by the lane gave way to patchy forest and steep embankments. From time to time they passed beneath timber chalets ornamented in the gingerbread style he remembered from southern Germany. Once, passing a collection of A-frame huts that might have been holiday cottages, they heard a goat, but not a soul stirred nor a dog barked. Propped between Voda and the churns, he let the rocking of the cart lull him into an uneasy slumber.

When he came to, a dull light had seeped into the sky, revealing steep wooded hills that rose from the mist to vanish in cloud.

The driver had dismounted and the horses had on nosebags. Knocking on a churn to rouse his passengers, he pointed out where a firebreak cut through the spruce on the slopes. He said something to Voda and held out two short ropes and a sack.

They took it in turns to tie the suitcases on each other's backs. Bradley looped his bag over his shoulder. Voda took the sack of provisions and the hand-drawn map.

The climb was easy to begin with. Over the first hillside,

the terrain flattened out again in a natural terrace several hundred yards wide. Surprisingly, given the surrounding hills, the Germans had laid out an airstrip here. A tattered windsock still hung from a pole and the broken wings of an observation plane protruded from the overgrown grass like a cat's offering of a half-eaten bird. Maybe it was a satellite to a larger field, an alternate landing site if there was fog in the valley. A dirt road followed the contour west before falling away into the trees.

Above the airstrip the grade grew steeper. The path led through thick coniferous forest where the night lingered. They began to slip in the loose soil and were soon sweating. Bradley let go the pistol in his bag and unbuttoned his jacket.

Finally they reached a pile of logs that was marked on the map. They would be met here, Voda said. Today, perhaps tomorrow. They examined the contents of the sack. A cheese, rye bread, an army water bottle. Pre-war Czechoslovak army, Voda told him.

"You were a soldier?"

"I am in Czechoslovak Legion. We are told to fight for Austria against Russians. There is no Czechoslovakia then. But we fight with Russians, against Austria, for independence. Then come Bolsheviks in Russia. They fight us, we fight them, all way to Siberia. Me and Ludvík, fight them all. War is over, still we fight. Now we fight to come home. You – America – you make Czechoslovakia nation. Woodrow Wilson, yes? Two years more we fight to come back to this nation. Long way. Long fight. Me and Ludvík."

It was the most the man had said. Bradley gave him a sympathetic look but in truth he was envious. There was something bitter to his memories of his friend, but you could tell how special it had been, to have a comrade, an ally.

"And Ludvík, what happened to him?"

Voda might not have heard him.

"So Nazis come. We fight them. Now war is over again. Bolsheviks come. Commissars come. This time I think is no more fighting – is no more Czechoslovakia. What will you do then, America? Where is Woodrow Wilson?"

It was Bradley's turn not to reply. He knew where Wilson's successors were. They were at Potsdam. But they weren't busy telling Stalin to back off.

They jumped as a hare bolted from the slope above them and something metal clattered down through the ferns. An iron chain, rust-brown, twitched back and forth as someone used it to descend.

It happened in the slowest of slow motion. The boot, sock and trouser leg coming into view below the lower branches of the cover. The variegated flecks and dots of the woodland camouflage jacket: a spatter of lichen, mould and moss on fallen leaves.

The last time he had seen those uniforms they had been stacked like sandbags along the wall behind the barracks and the sound of the machine guns had been ringing in his ears. He could hear them now, but it was the drumbeat of blood in his brain.

The old soldier's hand clamped onto his arm like an armoured gauntlet, preventing him from grabbing for the pistol or the Schmeisser that lay folded at the bottom of his bag. Voda shook his head and grunted the familiar, suspicious refrain: "Is OK."

But how could it be, to stand defenceless as the SS trooper sauntered over, to see the field glasses and understand he had been watching from above, and to know from his easy manner that they were still being watched; to endure the contemptuous glare as he circled them like a policeman, poking into their bags with the muzzle of his machine-pistol?

The man had something wrong with the lower part of his face. The meat of his chin was waxen, his mouth twisted into a mixture of idiot pout and animal snarl. When he spoke though wired-up jaws, Bradley couldn't decipher the sounds.

"He wants for us to go first," Voda said.

The Nazi watched while they re-slung their bags. When they had done, Voda went ahead, boots scrabbling at ashy soil and roots that protruded from the hillside like disinterred bones. Bradley hoisted himself up behind him and heard the Nazi following. The heavy chain bore their weight without the slightest give and he wondered what it was fixed to. It was impossible to see where they were going through the ferns.

Then they were out of the ferns and the canopy, ascending the final, grassy incline to high ground where day had already broken. Bradley saw Voda flex aching hands, framed against a huge sky massed with cumulus. Other figures came into view as he climbed the last yards, men like their rearguard, in a mixture of civilian clothes and SS smocks, all armed. Letting go the chain he saw it was bolted into a moss- and ivy-cloaked block that formed part of a larger structure poised on the edge of the escarpment to the right. The upper station of a cablecar or railway, he supposed. A fold of the hillside and the tops of the trees hid his view of the slope beneath it.

He took a deep breath of mountain air. Beyond the trees, distant ranges were emerging from shadow. Forested hilltops shone green and yellow as the sun made its own ascent.

Behind the Nazis, a bright diagonal slid down the tooth-shaped summit and illuminated the building. For a few seconds before the remaining windows burst into dazzling light, he saw it clearly and knew it was his journey's end.

*   *   *

Mila watched the figures come down the path from the funicular. Her hand, protruding from Theodor's old sweater, held the inevitable cigarette but instead of smoking it she was biting at her thumbnail as she squinted through the sun-streaked colonnade windows.

It wasn't cold enough to warrant the sweater, although after what had happened in her room she hoped it might deflect Theodor's passion toward a safer sort of affection. The real reason for borrowing the sweater was hidden in the waistband of her skirt. If things went well in the next minutes, she would excuse herself and return it to Frau Kaindl's room before it was missed. If not, she would be needing it, one way or another.

Everything depended on the men, by now halfway across the parterre gardens. She strained tired eyes and sucked in her breath as she recognised the older man. Why Josef, she thought – and why should it shock me so to see him here?

There wasn't time to ponder it. They were coming up the steps and she was losing her view of them. She made one last attempt to focus on the other man, the one in the brown battledress, but his face was turned away.

Theodor's voice made her jump.

"Are you coming?"

She read his look. She had been wrong about the sweater. There was no affection.

"Of course," she said.

*   *   *

Bradley spotted her the moment he walked into the lounge and at once he was struck by how small and slight she seemed among the Germans and their women. Fragile, almost. Childlike in that outsized sweater. Helpless, maybe. Without knowing how, he understood she was no commander here but a prisoner, like himself.

He was behind his telescopic sights again. The Nazis, Voda, all the others in the room might not have existed, so focused was he on the girl. He saw her in the act of lifting one foot to come towards him, saw her pause and twist to stub out her cigarette, saw her thinking, saw the flash of recognition in the instant she wiped it away. And he saw how the stubbing of the cigarette had been a feint, an excuse to turn aside and get her hand moving – plucking at the rucked-up hem of the sweater as though adjusting her waistband. Lost in the rumples of sleeve and hem, the hand did not reappear, as he had known it would not, just as his own hand remained buried in the bag.

Then, like time rushing forward after slowing to a crawl, she was in front of him. Seizing his arm, leading him to the windows before anyone could object or accompany them, she spoke urgently under her breath, in English.

"Who sent you?"

"Colonel Smith."

"For what purpose?"

"To bring you home."

"When were you sent in?"

"A month ago."

His reply made her frown. It was almost a wince. She nodded, as though acknowledging something to herself.

"Did you make contact with Josef Voda or someone else?"

"A man calling himself Císař put me with Josef and drove us to the rendezvous."

"Smile. We are renewing an old acquaintance. Describe Císař."

Bradley did his best. Tall, dark, with hooded eyes that gave an impression of easy confidence. And how he was plainly dressed yet carried a gentleman's cane.

The girl led him along the windows. Bradley saw the fierce energy in her and felt a stab of anguish. Everything was so rushed. It was not how he had imagined it.

Then, miraculously, she paused. Maybe she too had balked at the ferocity of the rush. More likely she needed time to think — and to make up her mind about him. He watched her eyes move left and right, up and down, across his face and chest and shoulders. He sensed the thoughts behind them, spinning, meshing, clicking into place and progressing, like the wheels of a cipher machine.

But the cipher machine would not work without the correct initial settings. Did she have them? Did she have the basic data she needed?

It was as if a bulb flashed on the machine to indicate readiness, although the flash was the reflected light on the dilated pupils and a certain softening of her features. She had it.

"The man you describe is a SMERSh agent I think. This means Josef Voda is also working for SMERSh. Has he said anything about why you have been brought here?"

"He told me to play up to everybody like I was the contact they were expecting from London. He told me I'd see you at the other end and you'd explain everything."

Above the smile she wore for show, her eyes still probed back and forth.

"And this was enough for you to agree to come?"

"Well, it's what I'm here for – to find you."

He couldn't see exactly how, whether it was moisture or the way her lashes fanned out in a kind of starburst, but her eyes sparkled.

She asked his name. He told her. She smiled for real.

"OK, Sergeant Bradley under the alias William Brown, you have found me. You may wish you hadn't. SMERSh have been ahead of us all along. They have brought you here, I don't know why. But this is what you need to know right now. That man with the black eye is Theodor Lossner. You know who that is? He normally wears thick spectacles but he had an accident last night." For a moment, the fluid voice faltered. "The rest is as Josef says. For your own safety you must pretend to have come from London in response to a wireless message I sent. You must pretend you are here to arrange safe passage to the west for Lossner and these Nazis. Do you have a transmitter with you?"

"Josef has two suitcases. He said they were the MERCURY set and its generator."

"Yes of course. He will use it to call in SMERSh. We must remove the crystals, first chance we get. Then you must stall for time, Sergeant Bradley. They may take you away to transmit another message on another machine. Can you do that? No – then you must pretend. Or if they are watching, you will find a fault with the set. We need to buy time because we need to decide on the best thing to do."

"Sure. Can I ask you a question?"

She had been watching over his shoulder. Her look told him someone was coming.

"Quickly."

"Why trust me with all this?"

Lossner was at her side. There was no time for an answer. But as she turned to address the other man, her gaze snagged on his and one eye flickered shut.

It was pure starlet, that wink, even with the boy's haircut and the floppy sweater. Lana Turner couldn't have done it better.

She switched to Czech. Bradley took the opportunity to marshal his thoughts. It wasn't easy. His mind did not work like hers, could not assemble the data like that. Why had he been so determined to sound so confident?

To reassure her. To earn that wink.

He looked up to find she had left him with Lossner.

"So," began the scientist. The small eyes beneath the beetle-brows were devoid of warmth, though one was colouring nicely. "You have met my wife."

"What?"

"I'm Professor Lossner. Ludmila is my wife. And you are?"

Bradley stared. Whoever had given him that shiner would have been better off using a Louisville Slugger. Had it been her?

But no, she was his wife. That had shaken him, more than Voda and Císař being likely SMERSh agents. What the hell was wrong with him – and everything else besides?

And how the hell could she have two husbands?

It was time to remember what he was here for, not this foolish, self-imposed quest but his real mission. He dropped his bag and extended a hand.

"Call me William Brown."

Lossner nodded, as though he had already used his prize intellect to deduce such trivial matters. He shook Bradley's hand and produced a pack of Wehrmacht-issue cigarettes.

Bradley took one. Lossner leant in to light it.

He normally wears thick spectacles.

Weak or not, wounded or not, the eyes were shrewd. Once again, Bradley felt himself being appraised in meticulous detail.

"Your, er, comrade is from the Nightingale group in Prague?"

"Uh-huh."

"And you?"

"New York." Or near enough. Or never near enough.

He might as well have said Jerusalem. He sensed Lossner's dizzy nausea at the world he was descending into.

"Why does British Intelligence send us an American?"

Bradley blew smoke. Literally too.

"You need someone to get you over the Bavarian border. Know of any British forces round those parts?"

There was the dizziness again. He wasn't used to being spoken to like that.

"You have the co-operation of the Americans?"

"Like you say, I'm here on behalf of the British. If it's what you want, that's who I'll put you in touch with. My people on the border will help you through, regardless."

The guy's English was pretty good. He'd got that.

"So, hypothetically speaking, if we decided instead to talk to the Americans...?"

Bradley glanced over at the others, then clapped Lossner on the arm.

"Thanks for the smoke. Now, we've been travelling all night and need to freshen up. Guess it couldn't hurt to grab some Zees. Maybe you could direct us...?"

Oh, but those poor eyes were pleading. As they rejoined the main group, Bradley picked his moment.

"Regarding your *hypothesis,* Professor, let's say I won't insist your wife is present when we next discuss this."

*　　*　　*

Seated in the far corner of the lounge, Josef Voda was shaking and sweating. He tried to tell himself it was the climb in his heavy coat, and his bad lungs, and his old bones. Deep in those bones where the shaking began, he knew it wasn't so.

These fucking Nazis gave him the shits. Patrolling the woods, giving orders, lighting cigarettes for their fancy women and drinking champagne for breakfast. Acting like they still owned the place!

But it wasn't them either. What was a bunch of Nazis on the run after the Russian secret police?

It was Slečna Slavík. It was this.

And it was a different morning, five months ago, before Prague. The snow still lay on the ground that day, and was piled in drifts in the forest. Only on the Brno highway had it melted away to ridges of grey sludge. The pissy headlamps of the trucks reflected on the highway in the reluctant light. The air was frosty. They were all of them chilled from the night's vigil.

Shivering, like this, but not like this.

Slečna Slavík's hand on his arm. His finger on the double trigger of the Spandau. He felt her shiver. He hoped his bloody finger would work when it came time to crook it.

"Not yet," she kept on saying. "Not the trucks."

The Germans were on their way to the Front. Or the Front was on its way to meet them. Their trucks were mostly furniture vans or farm trucks, running on wood-gas and potato alcohol. One or two were horse-drawn. Better vehicles streamed west on the opposite carriageway. Escaping Nazis and their possessions. Golden Pheasants.

But Slečna Slavík wasn't interested in them.

"Let's fight the war," she had told them. "We are not policemen."

"But they are all Nazis!" Vojtěch, full of anger, had protested as they set up the ambush that night. Anger, and innocence.

"You are new to this group so I will permit you to question my orders this once," she had said, adding in softer tones:

233

"Before, we had a man who thought like that. He wanted to kill them all – any German, all Germans. I have sent him to work with another group. In this group, we exercise judgement. That is how we stay alive."

"What was this man's name, Slečna Slavík?" Voda remembered asking.

"You do not know him. He is a good man, but full of a bitterness that will kill him, I think. His name is Václav."

Jesus and Mary, he thought now. I will go mad!

But he remembered her then, on that grey morning, squeezing his arm as the Kübelwagen came into view with the two officers in the back, saying: "This one, Josef."

And the Spandau kicking on its bipod, with Slečna Slavík feeding the belt. The snow cascading from the branches above, so that he saw everything through blotches of fire and snow. The Kübelwagen skidding, its driver falling sideways, the officers dancing like puppets in the back.

And the truck coming sideways from nowhere, already spilling soldiers.

Making the soldiers jerk like puppets too.

Then the machine gun stopping, the belts exhausted, and the shouting from the trees to one side. The terror of understanding that some of the soldiers had managed to outflank them, and that his gun was empty.

The two Germans by the tree, raising their rifles.

Vojtěch dropping the Panzerfaust as he turned to run in a blind panic.

The first shots going wide. Slečna Slavík rolling over, retrieving the Panzerfaust from the snow – no time to tuck it properly under her arm.

The hot gases of the weapon. The smoke and whoosh of the projectile.

The tree exploding in a shower of splinters and needles and snow.

Slečna Slavík's long hair smouldering.

The slivers of meat on the snow.

And the shivering. This shivering, different from the cold.

He opened his eyes and it was the same girl in front of him. But not the same girl. In her big jumper, with her eyes full of wonder, this one looked fourteen years old, like Marta.

"Hello, Josef."

We exercise judgement. That is how we stay alive.

And the eyes, he thought. She knows.

PART FOUR

UPON THE MOUNTAINS

CHAPTER SEVENTEEN

He was in a passage with cells either side. From the far end came an echo of dripping water and the distant gunfire of a failing lamp.

He passed the open doors, not looking. He knew because he had been here before that each cell contained horrors.

A blink of light revealed the water tanks in the room beyond. These he had also seen before. Collapsible pools made of metal hoops and rubberized canvas, like the skirts of the DD Shermans that hadn't made the beach at Omaha. And like the waterline at Omaha, they were full of bodies.

But these did not resemble the corpses of Omaha. With chalky limbs floating free of the striped cuffs and eyes half-open in dark sockets as though struggling to rouse from a fever dream, they had the gaunt look of invalids and incurables. In the fated light they were restless. In the corner of his eye, he saw them watching. Each time the light went out he heard them whisper *so you're here at last — too late to save us — still in time to join us.*

Behind the tanks stood two autopsy tables. On one was something he could not look at. The drain between them was blocked and the leaking tanks had flooded the floor.

Across the room stood the iron cylinder with the porthole.

The porthole had a weird light of its own, like a radar tube. Any moment now, the face would appear in the thick, yellow glass.

Pfc Gaccione, looking sick, was at his side.

"Go fetch the Kraut officers," he told him.

Alone again with the dead men, he removed his helmet

and propped his weapon against the wall. He knelt in the water and put his face in his hands.

Cry, damn you!

He glanced up at the porthole, looking for the face that matched his own.

Then he knew that one of the dead men had climbed out of the tank behind him, because he felt its hand on his shoulder. The child in him, the child that could not cry, kept his eyes tight shut. If he could not see it, it might not be real. But the grip grew more forceful.

Before he knew it his forearm was pressed against a grey-stubbled throat. As he focused, he saw the shock in the old man's eyes – Josef Voda's eyes.

He leapt backwards off the bed.

"You cry." Josef rubbed his throat, scowling.

"No."

"You, er, call. You shout,"

"Sorry. Bad dreams."

"Is OK. Understand. I have message for you."

"What time is it?"

"Is late. You sleep well."

"No," Bradley said. "I don't."

*   *   *

A long passage, doors either side. Light flooding from the open doors, painting the floorboards in stripes.

Something came flashing through the sunlight. Two boys, in embroidered shirts, shorts and suspenders, their shoes clattering on the bare boards, innocent of stealth or guile.

He followed them to the landing. A gramophone was playing a cha-cha-cha. Through the arches around the atrium, he saw two women dancing. They would step, spin and disappear behind the arches, then reappear in the next space turned about, the other girl leading. They had slicked their hair back in a Latin style and wore too much make-up for the morning. Perhaps they had danced all night.

Downstairs, the other Germans were at breakfast. The room was fusty with the ersatz coffee they had brewed overnight, when the smoke from the kitchen chimney would not be seen. Someone had laid out smoked meats and cheeses, tomatoes from the kitchen garden and that shredded cabbage they kept fermenting in barrels out back. There were champagne glasses on every table. Water was scarce.

Bradley walked out through the open doors of the colonnade and descended the marble steps. The girl was perched on the rim of the fountain. She wore a dark skirt and a white blouse and her spiky hair looked very fair in the morning sun.

She shaded her eyes as he approached.

"Josef gave me your message," he said. "Guess it's time to talk."

"Guess it is." The high-pitched voice he remembered from that day held a hint of affectionate mockery.

Bradley felt himself colour, as he had in the cemetery when he'd reported on that previous encounter to her husband, or one of them. He glanced either side.

"They seem to be leaving us to our own devices."

"Our own devices, yes. But it may not be for long. We should take a stroll."

She set off for the ruin at the top of the rise a couple of hundred yards to the east. Bradley fell into step, ducking under trellises overgrown with blue and yellow flowers. He could not have said exactly why but he was still in awe of her. Maybe it was just that for so long she had been the unattainable object of his quest. Maybe having seen her so distantly through his scope, and then so briefly in the woods that day, he had parlayed her into a mythical creation which not even her physical presence could dispel. But there was something else about her, something real and strangely potent.

They circled the derelict top station of the Incline – it reminded him of the old wagon elevator that had scaled the

Palisades in Hoboken.

"When I walked in the other day, I think you recognised me," he said, recalling her performance with the hidden pistol. "But when you saw me before I was in Red Army uniform, speaking Russian. How did you know I wasn't a Soviet agent?"

A chuckle, almost.

"Your accent is not so good, Sergeant Bradley, but it wasn't that. I heard you, as I lay in that car. Before you spoke to me in Russian you said something under your breath. I wasn't sure – I had hit my head and been shot before that – but I thought I heard it."

"I can't remember. What did I say?"

She deepened her voice and lengthened her vowels.

"*Gee lady, don't you ever give up.* Somehow, after everything that had happened, it was like an encouragement. It gave me the strength to go on."

She caught her lip between her teeth. Bradley looked away. He had heard from the Germans about her son, but he could think of nothing encouraging to say now.

When her voice came back it was dry and quizzical.

"What is it you are doing, Sergeant Bradley?"

He remembered Sloane at the monument, asking the same question, in the same tone.

"What do you mean?"

A sigh, as though she was both reluctant and resigned to press her point, even at the expense of spoiling everything:

"When I come down yesterday, and the day before, I find you talking to Theodor and the others. I enter, everyone falls silent. I leave, discussion resumes."

"Yeah."

"Are you betraying me too?"

It was almost in incredulity that he shook his head.

"I figured if they thought I could put them in touch with my people instead, it would buy us time. They've been arguing the deal ever since, and now, if I've understood them, they want to bring in some new guy of theirs to cast his vote."

"Stransky?"

"That's him. Whoever he is, he seems to have a say in it."

"But this is real – you are working for the Americans?"

"No. Well, there's one I could approach. If we made it out of here," he added. "But hey, if you want to nix it – if you feel it's betraying your... other husband..."

She rolled her eyes. Nicely though. Relief swept through him.

"What must you think of me?"

He couldn't answer that. He only wished she could see the logic of it. Her plan had terrified him. How could you fake a radio transmission? This, if they went for it, gave him an excuse not to use the radio, and just maybe it would throw up a way for them to get to the border. If nothing else, it had given him a good look at the divisions in the group. That would be crucial, when it came time to act.

What he had learned was that for all their grand speeches these people had no cause beyond individual comfort and survival. Lossner, the scientist and husband – not their leader, but their ace in the hole – had communicated his veiled offer to the others but was waiting to see which way the wind blew. Why? Because he deferred to the two big cheeses. Müller the tough-guy politician-type to whom the rank and file appeared to owe their allegiance. Jarsch, the good-living businessman who must have influence over them also, most likely dirt or contacts.

Those three, and the one who moved about the country with impunity, the one they called the doctor. They were the danger-men. The rest had obeyed too many orders to quit now. Likewise the women, even the secretary-type who somehow lorded it over the others and was allowed to join the men's discussions. She would side with Müller or Jarsch. He wasn't sure which yet, but he knew it would be to the death.

There were two problems, of course. In the first place, there was the danger he'd split them too far. Maybe Müller or Jarsch had too many skeletons in the closet to turn themselves over to the Americans. If it came to the crunch, they might elect to dispose of Lossner and any other dissenters. Bradley had no illusions that he and the Nightingale would last long under those circumstances.

In the second place, there was Voda. They had disabled the MERCURY transmitter but even so, surely it was only a matter of time before SMERSh came down on them. Hours, days at best. That made action imperative.

He nodded as he accepted what he had always known. It was all going to depend on her.

*   *   *

Standing with folded arms at the top of the railway, Mila watched the young American out of the corner of her eye. He was probably her own age but she thought of him as young. Why, because he had not seen what she had seen? No, there was a hardness in the set of his jaw, in the creases around his eyes and the furrows on his brow. Not innocence. It was more a wholesomeness, a kind of vigour that robbed the sly look of any meanness. She thought it might be peculiarly American, this quality. Behind the fatigue and the nerves there was an unspoilt honesty about him. To many people nowadays that would be judged a weakness. To Mila, it seemed a source of strength.

Strength was something she badly needed and she yearned to turn to him for support. She suspected he was her guardian angel, the sniper who had saved her from Kobylka and his thugs. If so, given the events of that day, she could only presume he had acted on his own initiative too.

She considered her words carefully.

"I think you have done well with this offer. I hope you will forgive my rudeness."

"Guess I can live with the pain."

"Yes," she said, sensing the gentleness of the irony but not quite understanding. "We must always do that."

She stood close to him as they looked down the slope.

"Could one get away down there, Sergeant Bradley?"

"Sam, please."

"Sam. So you must call me Mila." She shrugged. "I have so many other names, it gets too complicated."

"I know what you mean."

Something unspoken passed between them, or sought to. Mila had the impression of a garbled message that neither could make out.

She thought she saw him blush as he stepped forward.

"Looks an easy climb down what's left of the tracks, but the cover hasn't grown back enough. They could pick us off from above."

"I thought so."

"They brought us up over yonder," he indicated the trees. "Better cover but heavy going. No way to move fast. I need to take a look at the road back there. Is that what you want to do, get away?"

"I guess," she said, amused by her imitation. "Even if they must wait for Stransky, if Josef is working for SMERSh – if he might still summon them – it's the only way."

Her smile faded as she remembered Theodor's visit to her room. Josef's betrayal might not be complete, SMERSh might not come and Sam might buy all the time in the world, but it would not be enough to keep her safe from that. The next time, her training might not help her. The next time, he might not come alone.

That was what had alarmed her about Sam's plan: the ease with which he adapted the parameters of his mission. She was terrified he would leave without her.

And equally terrified at her own helplessness, in thinking that.

And something else. His helplessness. Because he was treating the American option as just that, an option. Because he didn't know.

"They might not choose your alternative," she said.

"Stransky might veto it. Theodor might prefer the original plan because he dislikes variables of any kind."

"I can see that. It's a possibility."

"So, may I ask you what your intentions were, for if and when you found me?"

"I was going to see if you wanted to come back."

"And if I didn't?"

He shook his head as though amazed by his own thinking.

"Maybe I was going to tell them I couldn't find you."

"But if I did want to come back?"

"There's a guy I can contact, through the UNRRA mission in Berlin. Well, you know him. Calls himself Jones. It was him at the handover, that first time I saw you."

My guardian angel, she thought. Precious indeed, in a world of demons.

"Rastislav Zajíček," she said. "That's his real name, at least I think so. He's a Czech emigré and he is Richard's... Colonel Smith's assistant."

From his expression she could identify the English word that nearly fizzled to his lips, but the exclamation he chose instead was mostly alien to her.

"A Limey who knew a good goddam about a cup of Joe, I mighta known! He's somewhere over here, looking for your husband, I mean the professor."

"I don't doubt it. I think he is also working with SMERSh."

That word pulled again at his face. She saw the pattern of his thoughts.

"Because of what happened at the rendezvous?"

"Buček was a good communist. I knew he was trying to pass the package to the Russians. Whoever made the rendezvous would be working for them."

"And it was Jones."

"That took me by surprise but there wasn't time to think. Later I realised it made sense. Someone on the British side always had the Russians' interests at heart. Someone arranged for Moravec of Czechoslovak Intelligence to establish a signals link with Moscow, and then someone advised Churchill to suspend all Richard's activities supporting the resistance: weapons drops, agents. I was the last to be sent. From mid-'44 it was agreed any partisan operations had to be sponsored by Moscow. They were preparing for the post-war power struggle, you see? That same person probably passed on everything he heard about the intentions of the government-in-exile. Certainly the Russians managed to clip its wings once it returned to Czechoslovakia. My guess is it was Zajíček."

"But he must have taken the package back to London or he'd have come under suspicion. I know he did, Smith told me they'd seen the documents."

"And the Russians would have received a copy. A more complete copy."

"They did say the documents were incomplete."

"Then that is why the Russians have been one step ahead."

"But Jones must have recognised you at the rendezvous."

"I think he told Buček to kill me. I think I have you to thank for what happened."

Sam stepped away from her then, as she had known he would. He moved a few paces along the ridge and gazed at the wreckage of the railway.

"Jones put me in to find you," he said at last. "He must have been expecting me to lead him to Lossner. Did he know you were...?"

"Lovers," she said, to complete the distance between them. "You understand, Theodor and I, we were never married. The war came too soon, and other problems. We only let people assume we were married. But we had a child."

"I know about that now. I'm sorry."

For a moment she nearly lost herself in brooding. Something about his openness pulled her up in time. A guardian, yes, but a child too, in his way. He needed her now.

"I never told Richard why I wanted to get back, and certainly not Zajíček. He might have worked it out from

247

whatever message Theodor left for me in the papers. Or someone here told the Russians."

Stransky, she thought. Playing both sides, as always.

"OK, say Jones knew what you were looking for and that's why he put me on your tail. Then it's also why I've had help along the way, from the Reds. They were hoping I'd contact Jones when I found the two of you. Voda is the back-up in case I don't."

"It looks like it. I don't know what has happened to Josef. He was a good man."

"But you sent a message to London. Surely you suspected Jones would intercept it and pass it to SMERSh."

She saw his puzzlement and realised how suspicious her actions must seem. So many names, and so-called husbands. Such twisted allegiances, strange decisions... Then she read what was behind his look. Something burst in her as she grasped that despite everything, he trusted her. She wrapped her arms around herself, tears welling.

"Oh, Sam, I don't know why I did it. I am so angry with Theodor and I could not make myself responsible for these Nazis. I thought if I sent the message the decision would be taken away from me. London would send someone to take charge. Or the Russians would come. If it was the Russians, Theodor and the others would get what they deserve. If it was the west, it would be their own good fortune that spared them. Now I see I have hurt people again. Something has been done to Josef and my group. And you, I have put you in danger too."

She had gone over to a stone bench-seat that looked out to the sea of hills in the east. She heard Sam's footsteps on the twigs and pine needles and then he was sitting beside her and had his arm around her. She turned her face to his chest.

"Poor Mila," she heard her name catch in his throat as he stroked her hair. "Poor nightingale."

His battledress jacket was warm and coarse and musty, like an old familiar blanket. She saw one of her tears clinging to its fibres.

It was so crazy, this letting go. It was a craziness that only happened in wartime, and then seldom, and often incompletely. It was the kind of craziness that had seen her throw herself on Richard's mercy, when the world was on fire and she had felt dead inside. But she had been a girl then. Things were different now. Time then had been measured by a perverse certainty of uncertainties: a siren, a whistling, a shriek. Now, their captors might come for them any minute, but there was so much to resolve before they came.

That was why it was crazy. And necessary.

Because she could not even plan to save herself unless she cut away the layers and saw herself, or what remained of her, in the only way she had left. Through his eyes.

After a long time, it seemed to her, he spoke again in a toneless voice.

"I get what you say about sparing them. It's something I've had to deal with."

"What happened, Sam?"

A grunt of exertion. She pressed her face against him.

"I was detailed to escort a team of scientists into one of the camps in Bavaria. It was part of an operation called OVERCAST, to snap up the Nazis' best brains." At the last word, he shuddered. She heard his heartbeat and knew he had never spoken of this.

"Like Theodor."

"Sure. Only these were Luftwaffe doctors who'd been conducting research into high altitudes and hypothermia, for their jet planes or rockets. They'd been experimenting on live test subjects. I think they were political prisoners or Russian POWs. We found the remains of their experiments in one of the sub-camps and we captured two of their officers. I was supposed to hand them over to the OVERCAST team, but I didn't."

Although his tone was matter-of-fact, his arm was crushing her.

"There was a pressure chamber they'd used to simulate

high altitudes, before they hauled the subjects out and drowned them in freezing water and cut off the tops of their heads. At least, I think they drowned them first. I figured I'd give these doctors a taste of their own medicine."

"In this pressure chamber?"

"Yeah. Only we couldn't make it work, so I put the two guys in there and threw in an AT grenade we'd fused as a bunker-buster. Slammed the door and dogged it down. There was a porthole, built to take real high pressures, so we could watch. They had maybe five seconds. One tried to defuse the grenade. The other guy came to the porthole. He was screaming but we couldn't hear. Four seconds then we ducked. That's plenty of time to get to know yourself as well as you'd ever want to. It wasn't the only summary execution carried out that day, but the OVERCAST guys were pissed. They called a drumhead court-martial in the main camp, at a place named Dachau."

After a while she sat up. He removed his arm and turned to face her.

"Is that what you want to do with Theodor?" she asked.

"I'm through with judging people."

Did he mean her? How much had he heard about her past? Not enough, if he could say what he had said to her. Her scalp still tingled from the ruffling of his fingers. The words, awkward, embarrassed, wonderful, still hung in the air like the pollen. *Poor nightingale...*

"I abandoned my child," she said, and she told him the story of that. Like his own, it was a story she had never told anyone, but where his had been told as a kindness, to persuade her his motives, his *morals*, were as corrupted as her own, her story – her confession – was a warning.

It wasn't really such a big story. Living it had taken forever. Telling it took less than five minutes. When she had finished, she lit a cigarette and let out a long whistle of smoke as if to say there, that's what's left of me, inside, nothing. Her tears had dried. She had not cried as she uttered Pavel's name.

His response surprised her.

"And your parents, what happened to them?"

"They were killed in a car crash, soon after the occupation of Prague. The Nazis announced that as part of the Reich the people of the Protectorate must drive on the right, not the left. Before the petrol ran out there were many accidents. On that day, my mother and father were coming to collect me and the baby. We were going to take a trip to the country. On the telephone mother had sounded excited. She thought this marked an important turning-point for my father, accepting the baby, and perhaps Theodor. I did not want to listen. I was young and stupid. It seemed to me my father should not need congratulating for accepting his grandson. But... *Suk*, you know, in Czech it means a stubborn man. Suková too of course. A stubborn woman."

Or a knot in wood – the saw-breaker.

"It was on a blind turning in the embassy district beneath the castle. A German truck came round the corner and father's little Skoda must have been on the wrong side of the road. Later I wrote a letter to the newspapers attacking the scheme. In those days there were still editors who would publish something like that. Then came the Gestapo."

"And your brothers?"

"They got out, before me. The last I heard they were fighting in the Free Czech forces. Perhaps they are back now, if they... you know."

His downcast gaze was unfocused. He had been thinking, hard, and when at last he spoke she found she had been holding her breath.

"Look, I know my opinion doesn't count for anything, but it seems to me what happened to deprive your child of his mother and what happened to deprive you of yours are pretty much the same thing. If it's anyone's fault it's the Nazis'."

She watched him through the curls of smoke.

"What can I say to turn you against me?" When he did not reply she looked down to stub out the cigarette. "Is that something you know about, being deprived of a mother?"

"A little."

She waited, but he had nothing to add.

"You're wrong, you know. Your opinion counts for a lot, with me."

"Then here's what I think. You got to get away from these people. Doesn't have to be back to London, that's none of my business, but you got to quit beating yourself up about it all. Your war's over, Mila, and that's official."

Despite everything, she almost giggled.

He grinned too, although in his intense mood he clearly didn't understand her amusement, if she did herself.

"I figure I was briefed more recently and my orders countermand yours. So I'm going to get us both out of here, like I promised Colonel Smith, and after that you can do what you want."

"And Theodor?"

"I got my orders there also, even if they did come via Jones. Can't leave him for the Reds, not if getting him to my people can pull something out of this. The upside is we can do both at once. We just got to get to the Allied lines and give them a run-down of this place."

"But even if we manage that, you still can't risk contacting Jones. Even telling Richard might be dangerous."

From the look of him, intense mood and all, he'd thought about choosing this moment to return her scandalous wink. He'd decided not to, but he had thought about it.

"Like I said, there's someone else I can talk to."

*   *   *

They retraced their steps to the path that led onto the upper terraces. Since this was the only property on the hilltop, no wall marked the edge of the gardens, only the rusted ironwork of the summerhouse and what must once have been a lawn. Soon they were wading through overgrown grass sown with brambles and white plumes of goatsbeard. Bradley led, stamping down thorns. It felt odd to consider such things again, yet far from seeming an impediment, Mila's skirt and bare legs were like a promise of peacetime.

He turned to look at her. She was watching her footing, but then she raised her head and gave a goofy smile. With that hillbilly haircut and the tint of sun in her cheeks it was hard to believe she had been a mother, a wife, a fighter, a leader. She looked like a girl on a picnic outing, somebody's high school sweetheart, one of his buddies' maybe. Not his own, of course, she could not be that, but just sometimes, in the right group, on the right day − way back when − your buddy's girlfriend could be the most precious company of all.

The girl thought she made everything complicated but really she made it so simple. He had an ally at last. More than that, he had taken responsibility for her, in a way he could never have done with Renate. That was what mattered. Sure, the future was unknowable. He couldn't look into that any more than he could see into the next valley and the one beyond. But you could tell from here the hills and valleys went on and on without end, turning from green to blue, until they merged with the sky.

"Sam," she was squinting over his shoulder. "I think there are sentries up there."

He had already seen them. Two troopers beyond the crown of the hill, wearing the camouflage smocks he remembered from the SS barracks at Dachau. They were lying still in the grass but they could not lie as still as the men who had lined that wall like sandbags.

"Yeah. We'll stop here."

Facing the sanatorium, they were almost level with the granite stack behind its broken roofline. From the valley beyond rose a steep hillside of dark forest sliced by grassy firebreaks. Some looked more like ski-runs. Perhaps they had been.

"That's Germany, over that ridge," Mila said. "To the

north and around to the west. At first, Theodor's people thought they might get across to the Allied lines that way, but now they say the Red Army has pushed forward into that region."

Bradley remembered the tanks running up their motors at Dresden. The signpost, the symbol, had been ignored.

"So the only way is south-west, to Patton's army." He turned the gesture into one of frustration. "I know he got somewhere close to here, but they've pulled back since."

"Schröter says the Americans are mostly on the pre-Munich border, except for a bulge around Pilsen and Budweis, but nobody seems to have the whole picture. Now the Sudetenland is back to being Czechoslovakia, there are supposed to be our own forces protecting the frontiers again, but people say the Russians are there as well."

"A lot have withdrawn, but they're still there all right, I've seen them."

"This man Stransky is in with the National Committee, don't ask me how or why. He told me some members made a secret appeal to the Americans, that they would not completely withdraw from Czechoslovakia until the Red Army had gone."

"Guess they're worried the Reds might decide to stay."

"A *fait accompli*, yes. Most of the Committee is already communist, so these members are in the minority, but Stransky said they are going to invite American troops to stay here – and come on leave here – to the spas, and Prague, for... what do you call it?"

"Uh-huh," he said. "R&R."

She was looking at him, eyes sparkling.

"Say that again."

"R&R? What's so funny?"

She punched his arm.

"It's a strange language you speak, Sergeant Bradley!"

"OK..." he ran a finger under his collar. The impressions of her small, pointed knuckles were singing on his arm. "So maybe there's a way to make contact with my people where the lines are confused. Marienbad, Falkenau? That's a short hop to Eger and the old German border. Patton's got to be there at least. But it's still, what, thirty-forty miles? All assuming we can get off of this mountain."

"And around Joachimsthal. I know the Russians are there." Seeing his frown, she added: "The uranium mines, under these hills. Stransky told me the Russians are taking over production. It has become their priority since they lost all the stocks of uranium oxide in a Werewolf attack on the Virus House in Berlin. Theodor guessed what happened from the news broadcasts. He used to work there."

Bradley felt sick.

"When was the attack?"

"About three weeks ago, just before I arrived here. What is it, Sam?"

"What's this Virus House?"

"Nothing to do with viruses, that was a cover name to scare people away. Theodor said it was just a big hut in the grounds of the Kaiser-Wilhelm Institute, but he is very proud he worked there with Heisenberg. He says they developed an atomic pile in a pit under this building and any other time he would have won a Nobel prize for his advances in producing the enriched uranium fuel. I know we said we wouldn't judge people but..."

"Jesus Christ," he doubled up as though he'd taken a shot to the solar plexus. "That wasn't a Werewolf attack, that was me."

So, Sloane had been another soldier in Jones' secret war. He had co-opted Bradley into the ranks.

The girl sat beside him.

"What's an atomic pile?"

That helpless look again. This time it meant she knew he wouldn't understand.

"It's a machine, in which to control a uranium chain reaction. That was always the theory. According to Theodor they achieved it."

255

"And it produces a bomb?"

"No, energy. If the reaction is controlled. If it went out of control it might be as dangerous as a bomb." She shook her head. "I was amazed when Theodor told me they had created it in a Berlin suburb. Except I wasn't amazed at all."

And Sloane and I blew it up, Bradley thought. Or we blew up the stuff that had been in it, before the Reds could cart it off to Moscow. What madness was that?

Atomic madness.

It's a joint effort at this level, Jones had told him on the airplane, the day he'd also told him about Lossner, Heisenberg and the Kaiser-Wilhelm Institute. We're the same people, he'd said. Anything and everything to speed things along.

Not an hour ago, he'd been congratulating himself on stalling the Nazis with a double bluff that might sidetrack the Limeys and get Lossner to the Americans where he was needed. Half an hour ago he'd told the girl he knew someone else who stood outside of Smith and Jones' lousy labyrinth. He had thought it would be simple. Yet now the likelihood was Sloane and Jones, as sworn atomic allies, had been working together. Sloane would have picked him up in Berlin on Jones' instructions. One handler passing over his agent to another. He may not be playing a double-cross like Jones, but anything said to him might get back to Jones, and through Jones to SMERSh.

They'd got it so you couldn't trust anybody, even yourself.

Chain reactions. The secret war was being fought by people who thought it possible to control them. They believed they could take an explosion to the brink and keep it in a pit, in a barrack-hut. They thought they could walk the same tightrope with people and their intentions. But they were wrong.

He stretched out a hand, flattening the grass. Soon they'd be blasting under here again. He imagined the hill shaking from concussions far below. And he imagined all that uranium, all those atoms, just waiting.

"To hell with it," he said. "We'll go. Tonight."

CHAPTER EIGHTEEN

Their reconnaissance came to a premature end as they approached the ridge where the road curved down to the plateau. Sentries straddled the deep ruts of the track, their rifles scything out the instruction to turn back. Schröter stalked from the sanatorium in tweeds and Alpine cap, a shotgun broken in the crook of his arm.

"We must go no further, for our own protection" the girl translated. "Past this turning we may be seen by people on the other hillsides."

"Never mind. You can describe it for me later."

They spotted Lossner in the colonnade, a pair of binoculars in one hand. Behind the dusty windowpane and the patched-up glasses, his eyes were stones.

"I can," she said. "But don't forget, I'm coming with you."

Later that morning, while Mila rested, the big three buttonholed him again. They took the easy chairs in the colonnade and Frau Kaindl brought coffee. Jarsch produced a hipflask from the folds of his suit, tipping a slug of 'Göring-Schnapps' into each cup.

"Better, ja?" he said to Bradley. To the others he added something ironic, ending with the word *Gemütlichkeit.*

Comforts of the good old days. You could see he missed them. He'd have filled out that costume back then.

Bradley's smirk faded as Müller turned to face him. No *Gemütlichkeit* for him. No English either. Lossner translated in his clinical tones.

"Herr Müller enquires as to the *method* by which you would alert your authorities to our forthcoming exfiltration. Also the

---

257

timing."

Though he'd been expecting the question, still the abruptness of it threw him. Had they made their decision? Müller was right. Timing was everything.

"There's a dead-letter-box in Prague where I can leave a message." So far so good. But the lie had been designed to get him back there to contact Jones. If they called his bluff now, his potential escape route would become a blind alley.

Listening to the reply, Müller used a fist to brush at his moustache as though wiping away a faceful of grease.

"Can the location of this letter-box be described, or must you go in person?"

Time to change the bluff.

"It would be better if I went myself."

"But if it was unsafe for you to make this trip?"

Bradley met Müller's stare.

"Then I guess I could describe it to someone."

"Good," Lossner said. "You will describe it to Doctor Stransky, if this is our decision. He comes tonight. And how long for the Americans to receive the message?"

Pick a number, Bradley thought. My fictional contact passes it to my imaginary UNRRA truck-driver who passes it to some Nazi vision of an intelligence service in the land of the free and the home of the brave.

"Three days," he said.

"And if we choose instead the British, you send a wireless message?"

On the MERCURY transmitter with no crystals. He nodded.

"And then?"

"Same as with my people. Only difference is who meets us. You get us to the lines and I take you across. Maybe two days. They'll let us know."

Meeting Lossner's eye, he hoped Jones had been right about the savvy of Nobel prizewinners.

*   *   *

"You'd have thought they were planning a vacation when Jarsch raised the subject of their luggage," he told her. He had gone straight to her room, two doors along from his own. "But that's not the point..."

She lay on her bed. A headache, she said.

"I thought Stransky was the point."

"Uh-huh, we need to figure out what to do about that. Do we wait until he arrives, to act as our diversion, or is that too risky?"

"We don't know when he is coming. If we go before, along the road, we might run into them."

"And if we wait, he might want to talk to me. Maybe we should leave it another day."

The hand came off her face. He saw the pain and sorrow and wished he had it in his power to help.

"We can't, Sam. Once Eduard is here, it's too dangerous."

"OK, but get this..."

He told her what he had heard. About Jarsch and his loot. Money, art treasures, family heirlooms, he didn't know, but there were crates that would need ferrying across the missing section of road. About Müller's impatience and concern for the practicalities. Well, no surprise there. And about the question the bald brute had asked of Lossner.

"My German stinks, and the refresher-course from the DoD was mostly technical. But that's how I worked out what they were discussing. I recognised the words."

"What words?"

"Files. Archives. Records. And something else they called the apparatus."

"He has it here," she said. "It must be in the cellar."

"The whole thing?"

"Not the magnets or the tank, I shouldn't think. But the emitters and collectors could be dismantled and boxed up."

"Well, we can't carry machinery, but we've got to check

out the papers. Sure, there could be truckloads, but my guess is Lossner will have an escape-kit standing by, a suitcase he can grab and go with in an emergency. That's got to have the best dope in it."

Mila sat up on the bed.

"We'll never know for sure. If your German stinks, my Physics is not much better for understanding Theodor's work. But you are right, we must take this chance."

"You never found a way of getting down to the cellar?"

"I was too busy feeling sorry for myself."

"I reckon you were entitled."

Her face went dead with self-disgust and she shook her head as though to clear it.

"The door in the passage is always guarded. I was too lazy to try this, but it occurred to me the best way might be through the air-raid shelter out the back. Obviously when the sanatorium was built there was no such place, so I wondered if they had blocked off half of the cellar to make it. Perhaps not, if they used part of the pump room, but there might be a way through..."

"And getting out to the courtyard?"

"Up instead of down. Up to the condemned floor, then down the service stairs at the back, what's left of them."

"I like it. We'll try it. We just need an excuse to disappear for a couple of hours."

They looked at each other.

"Don't blush, Sam. You're already here in my room. It's a good idea."

"Seems a little rushed."

She smiled.

"They have seen us walking together. In wartime, you know, that was enough."

"Won't Lossner go crazy and bust the door down?"

"Theodor will go crazy, yes, but inside. He would not try to come in. He became Czech by an accident of geography, but really he's all German." She gave a dismissive shrug. Bradley was glad to see there was no regret in it.

So, no lock or latch on the door. They'd have to wedge the chair under the handle. The Nazis had left an empty room between them to prevent them communicating. They could climb across the balconies and go out that way when the coast was clear.

"I'll go take a peek next door," he said. "And I'll make sure someone sees me sneak back here looking amorous."

She fluttered an eyelid at him.

"I'll be waiting for you."

*   *   *

The oil-lamp threw huge shadows on the vaulted brickwork of the air-raid shelter. Sparks and zigzags of its warm light danced on the cold black water around their feet.

One could not think about that water, except to hope it had collected here from the rain and mist, instead of rising up the borehole in the adjoining pump room.

Resting against a bank of rusty cages that had once been bunks, Mila watched the American struggle to force the door to the cellar. It was as they had feared during the afternoon recce. The padlocks this side had been easy enough to break but there was a heavier bolt or padlock on the other side. Using the ice pick from the tool rack of the Kübelwagen in the courtyard, it had taken him twenty minutes to prise the door an inch.

She brought her wrist under the light. Past midnight.

"Sam." Although they were alone in the shelter, and underground, she could not resist the impulse to whisper. This place had dark, cobwebbed spaces that were full of childhood terrors. "We're going to have to go."

"Give it another minute. I can get the blade through now and it's shifting. Feels like the hasp is sunk into wood not stone."

"OK Sam." She shook her head in wonder. She had heard

herself use that phrase a dozen times already.

Over three hours now since Stransky's arrival. Two since the moonlit conference in the colonnade from which she had been banished. Fifty minutes since the American had come again to her room.

"They're sleeping on it," he'd said.

She had already collected her things, such as they were. Theodor would have to get by without his sweater.

Bradley had handed her a muddy pair of walking shoes.

"Kaindl left them outside her room like this was the goddamn Waldorf. I figure if she comes out again she'll think one of the SS has taken them to clean them."

"So we're going now?"

"You were right. Stransky's a snake. I kept thinking he could see right through me."

"But you told him about the dead-letter-box."

"Like you described it. The grave along from Smetana, in the Vyšehrad. A chalk mark inside one of the fortress gates to indicate when it has been filled."

"And he believed you? He bought it?"

The smile again.

"He bought it."

OK Sam.

Now she heard the other lock tearing apart.

"We're in," he said, adding with relief: "It's pitch black in there. And dry."

The first thing she saw when she brought the oil-lamp was the rack of Panzerfausts with the red warning stencilled on the tube: *Achtung! Feuerstrahl!*

She ran a hand through her hair. She knew all about the fire-jet out of those.

"These have been unpacked and made ready," Sam said. "Looks like they're prepared for a siege."

"Even Nazis fight when the Russians come."

The cellar was much bigger than she'd expected, with many interconnecting vaults and supporting columns that reminded her of the nightclub Krypta. Every alcove was crammed with shelves and boxes. Her heart sank. It would be getting light in five hours.

Sam called out what he saw. Crates of grenades, ammunition, machine gun parts. Despite herself, Mila sneered. What was it the English said, like a child in a sweet shop? That was men for you. Even with the undoubted evils of the Nazi regime, she could not help but wonder whether this war would still have happened without that deep-seated masculine conviction that it was somehow exciting, somehow honourable, somehow a game – that all this matériel was as utilitarian as the tools on the Kübelwagen, rather than the incontrovertible evidence of institutionalised and premeditated murder.

Or was that an adolescent conceit of her own, finding evil in the tools and thereby diminishing her own responsibility for using them?

All she could cling to was her relief that it was over. Whatever the next phase of her life might bring, this one was so nearly finished. A quick search in here, a walk in the woods, a crossing out of Czechoslovakia and it would be done.

There was even method in the American's manner, she saw. He had established all the military crates were marked. They just had to look for those that weren't.

Spotting a hurricane lamp hooked to the wall, Sam got out his matches. With two sources of light they could cover the cellar twice as quickly. At first, whenever she located a likely-looking crate, she had to call him over to prise it open with his pick. Then she discovered the crowbar. Soon they were on opposite sides of the cellar, kicking, levering, muttering at their finds. Alcohol. Emergency rations. Dress uniforms of the SS and SA. Dresden figurines packed in straw; they would be valuable now.

And finally, bearing the Reichsmarschall's personal seal, the records. Carbons of typed orders and reports. Handwritten notes. More carbons, box after box of them.

She sifted through tables and diagrams, hoping to find a digest. It was only dimly she was aware of Sam moving away to continue searching for the escape-kit.

"Mila."

She was so engrossed it took a while for her to register his urgent whisper.

Lit by the lamp at his feet, his face was mostly in shadow, save the glint in his eyes. The intensity of that look and the thought processes behind it terrified her. What could he have found that would make him look at her like that?

It seemed an age they stared at one another. Mila heard the hiss of the paraffin in the hurricane lamp and her own lamp, guttering, made the shadows flit around the vaults. When at last he spoke, Sam's voice trembled too.

"Mila, I need you to promise me something. I need you to swear to it."

Her heart was beating so hard she could not hear herself. But her lips had moved, she must have asked...

"That you will come with me now, out of that door, away from this place."

"What is it you've found?"

"Do you *swear*?"

OK Sam.

When he stood up he was holding a briefcase, but strangely, like something dangerous.

"Is it to do with Theodor's experiments?"

"Yeah," he said through gritted teeth. "I mean no, Mila, it's not."

She was afraid he had found something that had been concocted by the Nazis to turn him against her, something horrible which could not be true yet was perhaps based on sufficient truth...

And then she realised it had to do with her son.

She snatched the briefcase from him. On it lay an irregular stack of brightly coloured, water-warped papers.

Children's drawings and paintings.

Sam held up the light. She saw blue skies and yellow suns, fluffy clouds and rolling fields with giant flowers, sheep and cows. There were castles and knights in armour, mounted on awkward chargers. She imagined the child's frown as he rendered the legs of the galloping horses, his tongue protruding in concentration.

But it was a fantasy and she knew it. These were the work of Jarsch's children. This was Jarsch's briefcase. Yet if so, what had spooked Sam? She saw him indicate, against his better instincts, that she should carry on.

No painted fields and finery now. War had come to this simplified world. Tanks, fighter-bombers and marching soldiers, two-dimensional in thick crayon, streamed past like a design for a triumphal frieze. The child's frustration was written in the muddy attempts to blend the diminishing colours on the coarse wartime paper.

"That one," Sam said.

The colours had gone. The whole drawing was in scribbled blue wax on smudged grey card. But the castles had returned, or at least a version of castles. A pitched-roofed building with a turret like a giant Prussian helmet. Flanking it another many-windowed mansion, with a round tower, out-of-scale, alongside. Fanciful surely, yet obsessively realised, the two buildings loomed against a furiously crosshatched storm.

"That's the Kaiser-Wilhelm Institute. It's the view from the Virus House."

It was as though someone were beating her about the head, like Müller had wanted to, in Prague. Every time a thought began to form there was another thud and it fell apart again. She had to voice the words to think them.

"Theodor said Pavel was with him in Berlin, in the beginning."

"Yeah, in the beginning. But these ain't scribbles. I'd say the kid who drew these was six or seven, minimum."

"Six," she said. "If this is Berlin at the end, not the beginning, then he was six."

"Guess Lossner lied to you."

She thought about the way Sam had called her just now, the way he had said her name and the fear it had stirred in her. *Mila...* It was the way Theodor had said it on the morning of her arrival here, that morning he had told her about Pavel, when he had told her *little Pavel has gone*. And she remembered the way he had looked at her when she had asked him whether Pavel had suffered.

God damn him. He had seen the opening then to tell her the lie.

But why? It hadn't spared her any pain, nor could it have spared him her grief or her anger. Surely even Theodor would see she'd have preferred to have known the truth: that her son had experienced those extra years of life.

What was he hiding?

Oh Christ, was it that he had somehow caused the child's sickness, by bringing him, as he evidently had, to this Virus House? Or if the death were even more recent, if Pavel had died after he and his father had fled Berlin for the mountains of their homeland, had it been Theodor's fault?

She clutched the drawings and shut her eyes to the blows. She tried to get her brain working again and when it did, she realised what she had been thinking ever since Sam had identified this scrap of paper as having passed through her boy's precious fingers.

Pavel had been here. That was why Theodor had told her he had gone. Not because he was trying to tell her he had died but because he was still alive.

There was something boiling in her. Fierce heat radiated from her cheeks and tears scalded the corners of her eyes. In the depths of her body, it was almost unbearable.

She saw Sam regarding her with apprehension.

"Now you see why I made you promise you'd come with me, whatever happened. I made you swear to it."

The plea meant nothing to her. Photographs, not words, she was thinking. There must be photographs of Pavel, aged

---

266

nearly seven, aged six, and five, four, three. All those years she had come to think of as having been stolen from them.

She scrabbled through the briefcase and up-ended it. Nothing. But where had Sam found it, what else had been there? She pushed him aside, sank to her knees, pulled at the bags and boxes around her like... like a mother, gathering her children to her in a storm.

But nothing. If Theodor had kept a likeness, it hadn't been with the drawings. Of course it hadn't. They weren't the same at all. A photograph was scientific fact, a drawing childish whimsy. One was evidence, the other an embarrassment. If you were Theodor.

"I'll kill him. I'll make him tell me what happened to Pavel and then I'll kill him."

"Mila, you're not thinking. If your son is alive, that's a reason to go on living. That's why we got to get out of here. When we're out, we can send in Sloane's people to fetch Lossner. They'll get him out, and then he can tell you..."

She forgot to whisper. Perhaps she was shrieking.

"Sloane? Only this morning you were afraid he'd spill any secrets to Zajíček and SMERSh, and now you think he can snatch Theodor from under their noses? I'm staying. I'm going to stick a gun in Theodor's face and make him tell me. You go without me. Just leave me your pistol."

"How can I leave you? You're right, of course. If I make it, if I talk to Sloane, that could bring the Russians down on top of you."

"The Russians are coming anyway. Once you're gone and all hell breaks loose, Josef will see to that. He'll get new parts for the transmitter, or use the Germans' one, or he'll get away too and raise the alarm. He won't care about being sneaky anymore."

"Then I'll go up and kill Josef and we'll find another way out of this."

She sighed. Now the blows had stopped, her anger was diminishing and with it her resolve. It wouldn't be long before she started agreeing with his plan.

"I'm not killing Josef. Neither are you, Sam. You must go, right now. You must convince Sloane to send a rescue party and not to tell Zajíček. Because I must stay and talk to Theodor. I must find out about Pavel."

He was studying her. She knew he was running through the options, but what options did he have? Even if he knocked her over the head and carried her away, he must know she'd fight back at some point, and get free, and return here.

"You won't get to him tonight. Their wing is guarded, remember."

"Then I'll have to find the right moment to talk to him tomorrow, or the day after, or the day after that."

"It'll get nasty, with me jumping ship."

She pulled a face.

"Whatever happens, all they can do is wait. It's just a matter of finding a way for them to rationalise it to themselves. I'll tell them you got fed up waiting for a decision and went to trigger the American option anyway. That's not so far from the truth."

"But there's Josef, and SMERSh."

"Yes. I'm going to be counting on you, Sergeant Bradley."

Laying the artworks down, she took the empty briefcase and began to fill it with the documents she had set aside. When it was done, she moved towards him and put her arms around him. She placed her face against the side of his in a French-style embrace. Except, for a moment, she kept it there. Her lips brushed his skin.

"Now you must go."

"I'll..." He shook his head helplessly.

"I know you will," she said, and then, like an admission of something terrible with which neither could burden the other: "I know you'll try."

*　　*　　*

Climbing over the ridge to avoid the sentries, Bradley found he was composing a running report for her in his head. The fact he'd probably never see her again to deliver it only made him more determined to re-establish a mental link. It was a kind of prayer. She would need every break she could get in the hours and days to come. So would he.

Past the bend now, Mila, so I can get down onto the road, no sweat. No sign of trick sentries beyond their perimeter, and I'm keeping an eye out for tripwires, like we discussed. Won't be stumbling in the dark for much longer anyhow. Be daybreak soon.

Here's the plateau, like you described. Boggy, but OK on the road. And now the crossing where the road's gone. What did you call it? Lossner's moat and drawbridge. Good description.

There, ditched all my kit except the briefcase and the Schmeisser. Got to move fast now I'm on the road.

Sky's getting lighter. I can see something through the trees across the valley: lamps, iron towers, headgear. Must be the uranium mines above Joachimsthal. Looks like the Russians are getting set to start production again.

It's Joachimsthal sure enough. I can see the spire of the church at the top of the street, and those steep-pitched roofs and onion-domes of the old buildings running off down the hill. Looks a ghost town. No lights, no vehicles, just tatty frontages where all the ornamental paint flaked off years ago. The Nazis kept everyone away. Guess the Russians will too, except the poor bastards they bring in to work the mines.

Over an hour since I left you. Hope you made it back and remembered to return that dragon's shoes, though that hardly matters now. It's gonna hit the fan soon after dawn when they come calling for me. Maybe three hours. Gotta get off these mountains where they daren't come looking for me before then.

Eventually the words dried and there was only the track, running parallel with St. Joachim's Valley, sometimes rising to breast a ridge, sometimes switching back, but mostly descending into the defile of darkened trees. Above, the stars were pinpricks in a camouflage of lime green and bruised purple. Soon the birds would begin to sing.

He ran through the pain of his exertions, the briefcase hung over his shoulder with the sling from the Schmeisser, doubling as a holster. The time for bluffing was past. Whoever he met, Russian guard, Czech gendarme or civilian woodcutter, he'd have to silence them and keep running. It wasn't any kind of game anymore.

Sporadic thoughts, one or two a mile. If I run into somebody, let them not have dogs. And why did I show you those pictures? Why did I let you stay?

Before he knew it he had reached the bottom of the valley and burst out onto the blacktop below Joachimsthal. He came to a halt and clasped his knees. A deserted road ran straight in each direction but there were trees and rushes along the riverbed if he needed to go to ground.

Down here, however, it was not yet light. He would carry on for as long as he could. He needed a target distance and settled on the main road at Ostrov, where he would turn west towards Karlsbad.

Walking fast now, Mila, he told her. Running is too conspicuous. Passed houses as I came out of the mountains, but now it's sawmills and workshops and dirt-poor settlements broken up by vacant lots. A rooster just now. So far, no people.

After a couple of miles he heard a vehicle coming from the south and hid out in the undergrowth. He glimpsed a beat-up truck as it passed. No telling if it was civilian or military. A quarter mile further on, an old woman lay dead in the road. Hit by the truck, fallen from it? Her shawl hid her face. Bradley let go her wrist and stood over her for precious seconds, deliberating.

I'm sorry, he told the girl as he walked on. On another occasion I might have raised the alarm somehow, at least treated her with some dignity, but there wasn't time and I couldn't leave her, with me walking away like the prime suspect. She'll be better off by the riverbed anyway. At least she's out of the road.

Who was she? Some poor Sudeten woman, I guess. A widow, or else her husband's lying up the road a ways. No, never did see her face.

By the time he reached the crossroads another ninety minutes had passed and a summer's day was breaking. Only the dusty road and tumbledown walls clung on to the monotone of the night. Everything else, the trees and bushes and the hillsides beyond, even the fingers of mist that splayed from the hills, caught the light. After so long in the mountains and the forest, he felt desperately exposed on this rolling plain. His shadow bestrode the westbound road like he was the tallest landmark in the world.

Squinting east towards what the freshly painted sign told him was Chomutov, he saw the glint of vehicles rounding a bend half a mile away, headed in his direction.

His legs failed. Briefcase and Schmeisser fell at his side.

Too much, Mila. All out of bluff. You understand.

He said the words to himself but he did not transmit them. How could he? What was this mess compared with the shit-storm he'd left her to face?

I'm going to be counting on you, Sergeant Bradley.

"Yeah, yeah..."

He levered himself back to his feet. Three vehicles, a few hundred yards apart. They passed behind a row of poplars that flung their shadows towards him like the Japanese flag. A command car of some kind, followed in a strung-out convoy by two covered trucks.

Options? Find somewhere at this godforsaken crossroads to hide, right now, or stick up a vehicle and force it to head for the border.

All assuming it isn't the Red Army.

What do I do, Mila?

Half a minute maximum before they came into view. The

stream that had snaked back and forth beneath the road was now little more than a drainage ditch. A culvert ran under the actual intersection, but it was too full of crud to squeeze in there. The only cover was a rusted oil-drum in the ditch on the other side of the road. It would have to do.

Scooching behind the drum, he peered through the rust holes at the approaching vehicles. The first was a pre-war jeep contraption with an armoured radiator tank and outrigger headlamps. Fireman helmets showed above the windshield. Czech army or militia, he thought.

Coming into view behind it was the first of two Studebaker deuce-and-a-halfs, the kind of trucks the Reds used everywhere nowadays, courtesy of the Lend-Lease programme. Olive drab. They might as well have been broadcasting the Internationale.

The jeep downshifted and his heart sank. They were going to turn off onto the road to Joachimsthal, which meant they'd be slowing to a crawl, right about here.

He eased back the cocking lever, recalling another ambush, when he had mimed the same action for Renate. But she was long gone and probably a double agent and he had too many women in his head.

The jeep was on top of him. As it cut the corner onto the Joachimsthal road he heard its occupants singing along like eagle scouts around a fire.

And his feet were still poking out into the sunlight! Play dead. What was another corpse at the roadside? Now the Studie was next to him, double-clutching and turning too. No songs from the back of this one but frightened faces framed in scarves and furs. More Sudeten Germans, hugging everything they owned, off to the mines or an unknown fate.

He let out a long sigh. One to go. The second truck must have been hanging back. Would it also slow down to make the turn? Were the other vehicles far enough up the road to give him the chance? Was he going to take it?

Well, it's a lovely morning for it... that was what Jones had said, setting off for the rendezvous in the clearing. Back then, thinking him a Limey, Bradley had sneered. Now, saying the words in his head, it seemed less of a joke and more like a battle cry.

He heaved at the drum and struggled to his feet. He was about to aim the weapon when he saw the truck properly for the first time, and the driver behind the wheel, and then – because what the hell else was he going to do – he was laughing.

He let the Schmeisser drop. Muttering a word under his breath, the word he'd avoided saying in front of Mila, he climbed out of the ditch and raised his hands.

CHAPTER NINETEEN

In the days following the American's disappearance, the mountain society fell increasingly under the sway of Herr Müller. Even Stransky, bidding *Lebewohl*, seemed content to bequeath the remnants of the order. Those left behind knew it meant farewell. The doctor, they mused darkly, must have other fish to fry. Like Himmler, Schröter cursed, naming his own fallen idol and the vacuum at the centre of their faith, he had abandoned them in their hour of destiny to make a separate peace.

Once Stransky had departed, Müller summoned Mila again. She was frogmarched into the lounge between Frau Kaindl and one of the SS 'wives', a hatchet-faced peroxide blonde known, for some ponderous reason, as Olga. But if finding herself pinioned by two women gave her hope of favourable treatment it was soon dispelled. In front of Theodor, the Jarsches, even his own wife, Müller raised a hand and slapped her across each side of her face. The first blow exploded in her head with a flash of light and nearly snapped her neck. With the second, his Organisation Todt signet ring opened a gash on her cheek. Raising her head again to stare at him, she felt the blood dripping.

And Theodor had said nothing, done nothing. The faces around the room were incurious or smirking. Only Josef Voda, alone in his corner, looked horrified.

Was it the careless brutality of those slaps or the presence of Josef that impelled her to react – to be seen to react, for nothing might be gained but the probability of further pain? She raised the splintered heel of her shoe, stamped it down

Olga's shin and put all her remaining force into twisting from the waist, knowing the woman's grip would be broken. Sure enough, Olga let go and Mila pivoted sharply, catching Kaindl off balance. As the latter, still clinging to her arm, ducked forwards, she completed the overburdened pirouette and launched from her other foot to butt her on the nose with all the energy of a sprinter rising from the blocks.

It had taken seconds. Both women were curled up in agony.

She returned her gaze to Müller.

"The next one to touch me loses an eye."

Was that a glimmer of respect, of amusement, even? He chewed at his moustache, then frowned at the wailing of the women and the children.

"Take them out of here, please, Frau Jarsch. And somebody shut those two up."

"You keep them away from me from now on," Mila said. "And that one's man."

Although she was starting to feel very small again, she supposed she still looked fierce. They might carry guns and keep their paramilitary uniforms in the cellar but none of these men were proper fighters. Those who had killed would have done so at a distance, with bullets at best, or signatures. In a perverse way they would be scandalised by what they had seen, and by the sight of her now, with a mixture of her own blood and Frau Kaindl's on her blouse and the flesh from Olga's shin on the sole of her shoe. The speed of it, the appalling suddenness of action and its consequences, would have shocked them too, she hoped. Müller aside, these were all dreamers here.

"Where has he gone?" he asked her when it was quiet.

"To the Amis, to arrange for your rescue."

"I wonder. What were you looking for in the cellar?"

"Evidence of Theodor's experiments, to convince them."

"And what did you find?"

She looked at Theodor.

"Evidence of something else."

But Müller wasn't interested in that. Nor was Schröter.

"Let me shoot her. She's lying. She's a spy, a saboteur."

Müller rolled his eyes.

"A saboteur of what, for whom? We know she's a spy, it's why we brought her here."

Jarsch had returned from calming his wife and children. Red-faced, he paced across her field of vision.

"I don't believe her, Müller. She has another trick up her sleeve. The American must have got what he wanted."

"The professor tells us little of import is missing."

"Then he simply fled. They are all cowards, are they not? No rescue is coming."

At last Müller stepped back from her and lit a cigarette, stirring the air with one of those hands.

"I think perhaps you are right. Perhaps we ought to make our own way to the American lines, but with Frau Lossner here as a hostage. She can yet be our ticket across."

"It will take time to organise," Schröter said. "Who is to say that in this time Stransky will not sell us out to the Bolsheviks?"

Müller exhaled contemptuously.

"I think the doctor knows better than to make an enemy of me in that way."

"Then the American..."

"The American was not a Russian spy. Neither is this one. But you may order your men to double their patrols. Break out the reserve weapons, if that will make you happier. And this time we will keep Frau Lossner safely locked away. Her fellow partisan too."

Throughout this exchange Mila had continued to stare at Theodor. She had seen his eyes shift back and forth inside the safety screen of his patched-up spectacles and she had seen his special weakness too. It was written all over him, in his silence and submission. Behind the self-regard, despite the visions of Nobel prizes and named elements, he was a lab technician. The precision of his thinking, his greatest strength and failing, depended on following instructions. Take those away and he was lost.

"Before you lock me up, I want to speak to my husband."

Müller saw the panic on Theodor's face and laughed.

"I'd appreciate it if you didn't kill him."

Mila looked at the man who had struck her so viciously and now found everything funny. He had known about Theodor's lie to her. They had all known.

"I won't kill anyone," she said. "Not yet."

*   *   *

As the little aircraft made a circuit of the Ruzyně airbase to approach from the direction of Prague, Korolev leaned back into the staff car to address Sergeant Simonova.

"Stay with the prisoner. Lock the doors and don't hear any orders to open them."

The impassive slab of face and side-cap that protruded above the knitting told him the car would be as impregnable as a KV heavy tank.

He watched the aircraft float charily onto the runway. Not a type he knew. Whether it came to the Soviet Union on the Arctic convoys or through the dust and double-dealing of the Persian Corridor, the great influx of matériel under the dead American President's Lend-Lease arrangement was not something Korolev could claim to understand. No money had changed hands, as he had been taught to expect of every aspect of capitalist life, nor would the goods be returned. What did the Americans get out of it?

The aircraft turned off the jet fighter runway after less than a sixth of its length, taxiing back past the skeletons of the Messerschmitts. It halted fifty meters away and Korolev saw the bulky figure of his boss climb out. As usual, Colonel Dvortsov was travelling with his junior aide, a striking Komsomol twenty years younger and a head taller than he who was also, everyone said, his 'campaign wife'. Korolev had met her three times now but had never been introduced. He tipped his hat anyway in the western style.

"Good to see you again, Anton Romanovich. Did you have a pleasant flight from GSGV?"

"I'm not here to shake pears from the trees with my prick," the older man's grin contradicted his tone. "Not bad, eh? The plane I mean, you little rodent. Pilot's a Chekist informer, but it gets me around. I dare say Anya here is one of Beria's tongues too, for that matter."

The Caucasian beauty threw them a thin smile and marched off towards the administration buildings to complete what would no doubt be a mountain of paperwork. Both men watched her go.

"That was tactless, mentioning Beria's women," Dvortsov said. "I apologise, Arkady Ivanovich."

"It's nothing."

"Have you heard from her at all?"

"Not directly. Her bloody mother wrote me. Tatyana wants a divorce."

"A bad business. Will you contest it?"

"What's the point? She has the Party on her side. And the Lubianka."

"She was lost to you the moment that Chekist bastard took a fancy to her. Do you know which one of Beria's henchmen it is?"

"Does it make any difference?"

"No, you're right. Bad as each other. Apart from that shit-sucker Beria, but mark my words, one day he'll choke on it!" Dvortsov swung an arm at Korolev's shoulder, nearly knocking him over. "I came as soon as I heard of your new source. What's the latest?"

Korolev squinted in the direction of the staff car and accepted the proffered Kazbek. There was aviation spirit and unexploded ordnance lying everywhere, but what the hell, they were Revolutionaries weren't they?

278

"I'm calling the source TANYUSHA." He met the older man's concerned gaze. "I'm not cracking up, but if we win and one day the facts come out, maybe I'd like that in the file, as a kind of farewell message to her."

"And what does TANYUSHA tell us?"

"The target of the SMERSh operation, who was also the object of this American's recent mission. A fascist scientist named Theodor Lossner. His knowledge would be valuable to the Revolution."

"For BORODINO, of course."

"Yes," Korolev said. "For BORODINO."

Dvortsov laughed bitterly.

"I don't know how the *Generalissimo* managed to act surprised at Potsdam when President Truman told him about this secret weapon of theirs. If they only knew our own programme was well under way, and ably assisted by their files!"

Korolev wondered how many vodkas Dvortsov had consumed to be mentioning that material, even outside. It was one thing to heap abuse on Beria and his security apparatus, quite another to acknowledge the existence of its most secret asset.

"A great pity such triumphs of the GRU can never be spoken of."

"Balls. We've both worked at Khodinka. We know what was being handled there before the Chekists muscled in and transferred our best people to the Front." Dvortsov frowned. "I confess I'm disappointed. I hoped for something we could use to trip them up, but this falls well within their jurisdiction. Comrade Stalin has tasked SMERSh with finding the fascist atom scientists. This explains what Andreev was doing."

"It doesn't explain why he led the American to Lossner." Korolev recounted how, with Tsibulkin's help, he had finally tracked down Karel Sec and found the matchbook Andreev had planted. "I don't see how that can be furthering the cause of BORODINO, or the Revolution."

"Surely Andreev will claim he was using the American to get to Lossner."

"I considered that. Perhaps he was, after a fashion. But it doesn't explain why he let the American escape, nor does it account for his continued inactivity."

"Meaning what?"

"I have been keeping an eye on his progress with the help of our Czechoslovak friends. Andreev has an army in the hills around Joachimsthal – a company of SMERSh soldiers, backed up by at least a battalion of NKVD border troops he has co-opted for the purpose – a thousand men or more. Yet he has not moved on Lossner and his gang."

"This is good. We can hang the bastard with this!" Dvortsov moved away, keeping his back turned. "You really think he's betraying the Revolution?"

Korolev stared at that bullet-neck and felt a surge of emotion he decided to call affection, though he supposed it was envy.

"Does it matter?"

The shoulders heaved in a silent chuckle. Korolev ground out his cigarette on the scorched concrete and waited for more, but it was not forthcoming.

"I do have a hunch about what Andreev is up to," he went on. "If I'm right, it could jeopardise the progress of the BORODINO programme instead of helping it. In fact, it could jeopardise everything we've been fighting for."

A grunt and a puff of smoke. Better than a shrug, he supposed.

"Comrade Colonel, if I'm to pursue this matter I should like your permission to request assistance. As I've reported, Andreev has upwards of a thousand men at his disposal. I have Sergeant Simonova."

"You want to get help from the Czechs again? This Novák?"

"Yes. And not only from the Czechs."

"Take big strides like that and you'll rip your trousers,

Arkady Ivanovich. Your sack will be ripe for the sickle."

"Is that a 'yes' by any chance?"

When the boss turned around again, Korolev saw he wasn't drunk at all.

"Must be all these aircraft – unless I'm going deaf in my old age. I haven't heard a word you've said."

* * *

You were right, Sam.

You were right, she said to herself, to him. Right about the reason to go on living. Pavlík is still alive, and I'm scared I won't make it out of here to look for him.

Where had her strength gone? Her ankles wobbled on her heavy heels as she was escorted along the corridor. She longed to crawl into one of those dark spaces between the open doors. Curl up and give up. Surrender.

The men were following her. Theodor and the SS with the jaw. She inclined her head to listen for their footsteps and the corridor tilted. She put out a hand to fend off the wall. Not the hand holding the sticking plaster and bandages. She would be needing those.

Catching her breath, she squinted at her shoulder. The fresh bloodstain on her blouse had grown no bigger than a small rose but she did not like its brownish colour, nor its musty smell. Silly Mila: she ought to have been changing the dressing at least every day but lately she had been preoccupied. Struggling with the women had torn open Josef Voda's old stitches. But she did not think the dizziness was a fever, any more than she imagined she had been concussed by Müller's blows. What had knocked her for six this time, as Richard would have said, was hearing about her son and what his father had done.

She turned to face him.

"I'll fetch my things and get changed out of this. Are you intending to *watch?*"

His eyes were ice, but it was a far cry now from his ill-judged seduction. Mila understood his contempt. To Theodor's mind, his betrayal had been more than cancelled out by hers. She had rifled through his papers and assisted an enemy in escaping with them. More than that, she had forced him to confess again, this time for real, to his failings, his weakness and his crime. What was that, from a woman, if not another betrayal?

"I think not," he said. The two men stood back to let her enter her room.

"I have to fix this dressing," she called out. "I'll be a moment."

She dared not close the door. Using her body as a shield, she eased open the drawer in the bedside table. Sam's pistol had left an oilstain on a yellowed sheet of lies from the *Volkische Beobachter*.

She recalled how Theodor had answered her last question about Pavel.

"Photographs? I don't think there are any left. You can thank the British 'terror flyers' for that."

She pictured herself striding to the door, cocking the pistol. Instead, she palmed it and tore off a strip of plaster with her teeth. Lifting a leg onto the bed, she fastened the gun to the inside of her thigh and added a few twists of bandage for camouflage.

One way or another, Sam, I'm getting out of here.

Having dealt with the real reason for requesting the dressings, she lingered over re-bandaging her wound. When it was done, she replaced her bloodied blouse. Would Theodor notice she had not changed it? She took his sweater and tied it defiantly over her shoulders. She picked up her cigarettes and matches. She had nothing else.

A last glance around the room. She wouldn't miss it. An unpleasant room, a sickroom. Only at the end had she felt anything but miserable in here.

When you came, Sam. To rescue me.

282

She shook her head at her own stupidity. The young American had been right. The way to find Pavel was to stay alive long enough to do so. But she'd had to know and Theodor was the only one who could have told her.

I might die now, she reasoned with him, her guardian angel. I probably will die, without ever finding my boy. But how would I have felt if I'd come away with you only to hear the rescue mission had been aborted or betrayed, or the Russians had taken Theodor, or he'd been killed in the assault? How would I have gone on living then?

He couldn't answer her, of course, which was useful when one was trying to argue for a cause in which one did not altogether believe. He would have answered though, and quite possibly argued her out of it. Uniquely among the men she had known and however briefly or incompletely she had known him, he had that power over her.

And would I have given myself to you here, in this bed, if you had argued for that?

I don't know, but I know you would never have presumed to ask the question.

She left the room, closing the door behind her. Theodor and the Nazi were waiting.

"OK," she said to neither of them. Without looking, she switched back to German. "Now, beloved husband, you can lock me up."

*   *   *

For an hour the car had forced its way through the lines of people like an icebreaker. The whole world was an ocean of field-grey and sallow faces. Slumped in the back seat, wary of meeting those sunken eyes, Bradley marvelled at their numbers. If these had fought, if they'd obeyed the Führer's final orders and fought to the death...

Like ants in a nest, the Germans were following an unknown design, the lines flowing both ways. Some were being released to salvage their country's agriculture. Most would be bound for the vast prison compounds that had been filling for several months now. From their demeanour, there was no telling which group was which.

Beyond the soldiers stretched the same ragged procession he had seen in Bavaria and Brandenburg, Saxony and the Sudetenland. Women, children, old men and cripples, hunched under their burdens or collapsed at the roadside. And rising from the meandering riverbed of the freshly cleared road, the rubble, the ruins. He hadn't appreciated it before, in Berlin and Dresden. It was only the scale of what had been destroyed that marked those as scenes of absolute catastrophe. But everywhere in Germany looked the same.

Somewhere amid the ruins, unheeded by the multitude, church bells were pealing. Sunday morning, already ripe with a fetid August heat. It was over a week since that morning on the road at Ostrov, when he'd thought his fortunes had changed.

If he'd been looking for a sign, it had been painted across those olive drab tarpaulins, white letters passing like a slowed-down flip book: U – N – R – R – A. Mouthing a curse, Bradley had burst out laughing. With the papers in his pockets, and the one remaining shirt on his back, the westbound relief truck was about the only mode of transport in all of Czechoslovakia in which he stood a chance of getting out. But what tickled him was it was the same truck he'd invented in his phony story for the Nazis, without ever believing in it himself. Finally, Lady Luck had quit schmoozing with the enemy and sashayed over to his side of the street like the whore she was.

It had lasted until the demarcation line, which they came upon soon after Karlsbad. Gradually progress had slowed. Relief trucks crept in each direction, carried like twigs upon a swarm of civilians. At the railhead, an array of mismatched boxcars disgorged a further cargo of refugees, bearing the inevitable N on their coats and cases. Fights were breaking out along the line. Fights, or simple beatings. Everyone, it seemed, had thrown themselves into the mêlée. All except the guards who stood apart in their green-crowned caps, cradling their burp-guns and their clipboards.

"Rooskie border troops," the driver had said. He was a heavy-set guy from the north of England, too old for military service. "N-K-V-bloody-D. They screen everyone coming in from the Yank zone. That is, everyone the Czech border controls have already let through. They arrest half of 'em on behalf of the Rooskies anyway."

"What for?"

"Being Soviet citizens who got themselves taken as slave labour by the Jerries. Being Czechs who fought for the West instead of magically finding themselves with Svoboda's army in the east. Or just being Poles."

"Yet they're letting all these Sudeten Germans out?"

"Haven't you heard? It's one of the last great triumphs at Potsdam, after selling Poor Bloody Poland down the river. Come next Thursday, when the conference ends, all Czechs of German and Hungarian blood are stripped of citizenship."

"What will happen to them?"

"Who knows? Who cares, eh? Tell you summat else. These poor baskets aren't out at all, yet. Other side of the checkpoint here, *your* side, that's still Czechoslovakia, see? There's more fun and games waiting for them there."

"In the American zone? What sort of thing?"

"Luggage inspections. An' that's for the lucky ones, like."

As the truck inched towards the zonal checkpoint, Bradley had heard about recent events. About Potsdam, and Churchill losing the election, and the Pacific. MacArthur had taken back the Philippines. The US was carpet-bombing the Japanese home islands in preparation for the final assault.

And he heard about the relief effort of course. How the Russian UNRRA chief in Prague had arranged for all future shipments to come via Constanza on the Black Sea, with the Soviets taking sole credit for the US-funded aid programme, as well as a good half of the supplies. How badly they were needed throughout the Soviet-liberated nations now, since the Red

Army lived as it always had done, off the land.

"Getting nasty it is. That's why we're doing this, driving in from the west instead. Rooskies don't like it. To top it all they think we're smuggling people out."

He elbowed Bradley's arm.

"As if, eh?"

Bradley had forced a smile. He was keeping his eye on the guards ahead. Would his luck hold out? Wasn't this supposed to be Churchill's Iron Curtain? What if the 'Rooskies' picked their truck for an inspection?

When an NKVD guard climbed up on the truck in front, Bradley's heart leapt into his throat. The Schmeisser, its barrel poking from the briefcase on the floor! For personal defence it was useless, under the glare of so many guns, but if the cabin was searched it would incriminate them both. UNRRA personnel didn't carry sidearms. He was set to toss it out the window when the driver gave an approving grunt.

"Smart lad. Always on the lookout for another trophy, they are. Can't have picked up many of their own, hiding from Jerry in the shitter!" With a wink, he brought out a fistful of wristwatches from beneath the dashboard. As he drew level with the guards he added: "Easier to get in, when we've a load in back, but these buggers like something for letting us out an' all. Aye, don't even look at our papers, you illiterate basket..."

Keeping up his friendly-sounding stream of invective, he grabbed the Schmeisser and passed it through the window. The Russian grinned and waved them through.

In the mirrors Bradley saw the guard pretend to spray the crowd with an inexpert mime of chattering recoil. Too many gangster movies, like his old stooges in Berlin. The watching NKVD officer and a family of Sudetenlanders hit the deck.

"I 'ope that weren't loaded," the driver said. When Bradley did not reply he screwed up his eyes in a mixture of mock dread and genuine anxiety. "Bloody 'ell! Best make ourselves scarce!"

But it was as they approached the barrier at the US side of the checkpoint that Bradley had made his big mistake. Looking back, he ought to have stuck with the truck all the way to the UNRRA depot and planned his next move from there. At the very least he should have let it take him to the Eger border control and out of Czechoslovakia. Instead, with a word or two of heartfelt thanks, he dismounted from the cabin and reported to the MPs at the barrier. It proved to be the first of many similar exchanges. He asked to see their C.O. and they arrested him for having no travel orders.

After hours in the guardroom, he was transferred to a reception-delivery point in a nearby farm, where he spent the rest of the day and all night in the company of a terrified Vlasovite. Next morning, he was marched back to the guardroom and interrogated by a succession of notables including a Third Army XXII Corps top sergeant and a resident counter-intelligence expert from the Eastern Military District Frontier Security team. None seemed interested in helping him establish his bona fides. When he mentioned Walter Sloane and the State Department they just laughed. When he demanded to be put in touch with someone, anyone, at SHAEF, they threw him back in the stockade to sober up. Apparently SHAEF had been disbanded weeks ago. The expedition was over and the allies weren't allied any more.

By the third day he had decided to risk naming Smith and Jones. The MPs would still think him crazy, requesting some five-and-dime Limey liaison office after two days screaming for Ike Almighty, but eventually they'd have to make the call and maybe it would be Smith who answered. However much his instincts told him to first get past the Czech border controls, however much he dreaded Jones' involvement, he could no longer watch the hours tick by, wondering how she was coping on her own.

But the MPs had arrived that morning in no mood for questions. Instead they threw him in the back of a jeep and drove him to Germany proper. At the reinstated border crossing – Czechs on one side, Yanks on both, Russians nowhere to be seen – the Sudeten refugees lined up for the

Czech militia and he got to witness the final 'luggage inspections' for himself. By mid-afternoon they had reached the district headquarters at Bad Tölz, south of Munich. The spa town had been the site of an SS officer cadet school, as well as a sub-camp of Dachau. He was back where he'd started.

The Nazi eagle above the doorway to the Provost Marshall's office in the *Junkerschule* had been attacked with a chisel to deface the swastika but otherwise the building was intact. The officers' pinks-and-greens and the polished helmet liners of the MPs did little to dispel the impression of an unbroken authoritarian tradition. Back when he had left, everyone save Patton himself had been wearing combat fatigues and the roads had been marked with ironic signs scrawled on bits of crate – *This way to Berlin* – *Stop here to kiss your ass goodbye*. Now neat, bilingual boards announced *You are entering... You are leaving... German citizens are forbidden to pass.* Clearly times had changed.

He was shown into a storeroom piled high with confiscated mail. The army had been sending Germany home in parcels. Major Mike Murphy was seated at a green baize card table and rose to meet him. He had Bradley's briefcase and the scientific documents.

"Oh, thank God," Bradley had said.

Now he sat staring at the back of Major Mike's buzz-cut while the staff car nosed through the same crowds, past the same officious notices. They were climbing out of the ruins of Frankfurt towards a parkland complex dominated by a vast yellow-white building seven storeys high and the length of a city block. As they reached the first perimeter checkpoint, Bradley saw it was constructed in a curve with six radiating wings, any of which would have made a sizeable office block in its own right. The biggest surprise was that it looked undamaged.

At the next roadblock he saw the sign.

"What the hell's USFET?"

Major Mike half-turned in his seat.

"I forgot. You've been away. This is the I.G. Farben building. Supposed to be the biggest office building in Europe. Ike moved SHAEF here and it's basically the centre of the continent. USFET means US Forces European Theatre."

"We didn't bomb it?"

"Krauts say we left it intact 'cause we'd earmarked it as Ike's HQ. I reckon we just missed it."

Dodging jeeps and staff cars in the driveway, they approached a heavy-pillared entrance topped by a cut-off rotunda like the bridge of a battleship. Workmen were laying red carpet down the steps. On either side, men and women in many different uniforms filed in and out of the atrium, putting Bradley in mind of those earnest Red Army types at Dresden. No Sundays here either, judging by the crowds. In their midst, with hands in pockets at the top of the steps, stood a man who looked like he owned the place.

Bradley had to laugh. His debriefing by Major Mike and various other OSS or CIC characters had been exhaustive. With breaks while they reported back to their superiors, it had taken four days and most of five nights. Then the drive to Frankfurt and through the ruins: another day of delays and diversions, all unpredictable. As far as Bradley had seen, none of the checkpoint guards had phoned ahead. And yet here, waiting nonchalantly, was Sloane. He sure had a knack for being in the right place at the right time.

"I'm glad you made it, Bill, truly I am." He pumped Bradley's hand. "Or should I call you Sergeant Bradley? Sam?"

"Bradley is fine. Good to see you too, Sloane."

Sloane clapped Major Mike on the shoulder and led them into a high-ceilinged lobby where more workmen were erecting a display of interlocked US and Soviet flags.

"Hope you didn't think all this was for you, Bradley, though I expect you're a more deserving case. We're playing host to dignitaries from the Soviet Repatriation Administration. Seems we're not sending back enough of their citizens and they've come to help us out. Of course they'll all be GRU or NKGB in ghastly disguises."

"Without the 'N' though," Major Mike followed them to the reception desk. An MP was studying Sloane's paperwork and another issuing passes.

"Oh that's right Mike, they're not going to be a People's Commissariat any more. Too warlike, do you think? Or too socialist-idealist? All about presentation nowadays."

Sloane led them across the lobby to a bank of paternoster elevators where MPs were checking visitors' passes and helping them into the moving compartments. A group of glamorous WACs awaited their turn. With a broad grin, Sloane pulled his hands out of his flannels and grabbed the other men's shoulders.

"Look at us. The return of the Tiergarten Musketeers!"

"Been back long?" Bradley asked.

"I come and go." Sloane nodded towards the elevator. "Your turn, sport. Hop off on the sixth floor. Gentlemen's dress-wear, Haberdashery, Cloaks and Daggers."

The human traffic on the sixth floor was noticeably thinner, the mood quieter, the light subdued. They set off after Sloane along a corridor that obviously ran the length of the building. With the imposing scale of the windows and doorways, and the corridor's shallow curve, Bradley had the impression they were following the circumference of a gigantic wheel. The outer circle of the inner sanctum of the holy of holies.

The name on the office door was not Sloane but the man entered like it was his personal domain. In the cavernous anteroom a civilian secretary in horn-rimmed glasses looked up without a flicker of recognition or interest. Two men were seated on a bench against the wall, one reading from a buff-covered file, the other smoking and staring into space. They wore plain ODs and had Airborne-style Mohawk haircuts.

"You may clock out for the day if you wish, Miss Pagett," Sloane said.

Once the three of them had settled in the large, panelled

office, Bradley could no longer restrain himself.

"Look, I don't mind making social calls but the clock is ticking on this one. If we're going to mount an operation, we've got to do it now."

Before speaking, Sloane flicked a look at Major Mike and received a nod.

"The clock is indeed ticking – and how! But don't think we've been sitting on our hands. I know your debriefing has taken an age but the planning for the operation has been running concurrently and we're nearly ready to go."

Bradley raised his eyebrows in amazement.

"In a moment," Sloane went on. "I'm going to introduce you to the officers in charge of the mission. They'll fill you in and I'm sure they'll have a thousand questions for you. But I've called you in here first to clear up a couple of questions of my own."

"Shoot," Bradley said. He was impressed.

"Number one is why you've been telling Mike not to get in touch with your own handler, this Mr Jones."

"Because Rastislav Zajíček is most likely a double agent working with SMERSh. I know it sounds crazy, but if you could let me talk to Colonel Smith, his superior..."

Sloane was shaking his head.

"I know the fellow. Met him at Potsdam. He's out, I'm afraid. Flew home with Churchill for the election recess, never came back with Attlee's party. Night of the long knives by all accounts."

Bradley let out a sigh.

"Then you're going to have to trust me."

Sloane smiled.

"Fortunately I don't have to. This operation isn't anything to do with State. As it relates to Project OVERCAST, it falls under the Joint Chiefs. OSS Special Operations Branch are running things. I just called you in to shoot the breeze. Which brings me to my second point." With an air of embarrassment he looked at the papers on his desk. "Would you, er, leave us for a minute, Mike?"

When Murphy had closed the door behind him, Sloane stood up and stared out over the reflecting pool at the rear of the building. For the first time Bradley could recall, his manner was unsure, his voice hesitant.

"I'm going out on a limb here. The officers you're about to meet will tell you they can launch a mission in the next couple of days. That falls within the window you suggest for the period of inactivity at the Radon Sanatorium while these Nazis set up an alternate escape route. As far as the SO branch knows, it's plenty quick enough."

"And isn't it?"

"To capture Lossner and his associates, sure, hopefully. But to rescue the girl..."

He turned again and gripped the back of his chair. Bradley felt something rise from the pit of his stomach.

"What is it, Sloane?"

"Damn it, I shouldn't be saying anything, but I don't like to leave people hanging out to dry. I don't like to sacrifice people, is what I mean."

"Tell me!" Bradley was on his feet now, hands splayed on the desk, his face inches from Sloane's.

"I can't. What I can say is I strongly suspect the situation at the sanatorium is about to become volatile – possibly tomorrow, almost certainly by Tuesday morning at the latest. I think the girl's life will be in danger."

"It already is."

"No, sport, I mean I think they'll kill her."

Bradley slumped back into his chair. The fear and anger growing in him made it difficult to think. What was it Sloane knew? Did he have a lead into Lossner's group? Or had he heard something from the Russians?

He began to ask who and what, receiving only pained shakes of the head.

"Then why?" he pleaded. "Why tell me this?"

Sloane met his gaze and for a long time said nothing.

Bradley heard the clocks on the wall. Washington. British Double Summer. Central European Time. Moscow. Zebra. Not so long ago everything would have been set to Zebra or military zone time, but the world was changing. Even here at the nerve centre you could sense the desynchronisation and fragmentation of viewpoints. Below the clocks a map of the former Reich was strung with coloured wool. Chalk-marks round a corpse. A calendar read Sunday August 5th.

"When you've finished with your SO briefing, why don't you drop by again?" Sloane said at last. "Doesn't matter how late, I'll still be here."

Bradley tore his eyes from the clocks and stared at him.

"What game are you playing, Sloane?"

*   *   *

For Mila, imprisoned in the pump room, time was measured not in seconds and minutes but by bricks and shifts. Its passing was marked not by the tick of a movement or the beat of a heart but by calloused fingers and endless scratching, like rats gnawing into her skull.

A curse from Josef Voda. The tinkle of metal dropped on stone. A hiss of breath as he flexed aching fingers. Familiar sounds now; more familiar, mercifully, than speech.

She opened her eyes. The only light came from a grille above the door. Since the area to the rear of the sanatorium was almost perpetually in shade, this was usually a dim, grey glow, but as the sun dipped around the side of the building, the glow would brighten, once a day, like this. Late afternoon, it must be.

With no other source of light, escape had seemed impossible. The door, at the top of several rough-hewn steps, was solid and flush-fitting, bolted from the outside. The room itself was practically bare, excavated from the rock to shoulder-height, with a brick barrel vault built over the resulting pit. A thick copper pipe ran in an indentation across the floor, cemented almost flush with the bare rock, and in one corner there was a concrete dais from which some machinery had been removed. The rest of the workings must have been hidden behind the iron hatch set into the rockface opposite the entrance, at the foot of another short flight of steps, now flooded. They had waded down there to try the hatch, but it was bolted or rusted solid. Mila had suggested using the niche for other purposes before Josef pointed out the water was all they had to drink.

Since then, the guards had come every second day with tins of rations and a bucket. One man unbolted the door and threw them down the steps while the other stood by with his submachine gun, ready to turn the stone chamber into a hornet's nest. When ordered, they were permitted to reach up and place the old bucket by the door, but never to mount the steps. It was Josef who was scandalised by this indelicate regime. Mila was just annoyed the troopers had been briefed to take such effective precautions. Müller, she thought, definitely Müller. He would derive no particular pleasure from the enforced indignity, he'd simply fail to consider it degrading.

Locking her up with another man, on the other hand, he would find amusing for other reasons. Müller's compulsion to humiliate Theodor had always been there beneath the surface. Since Bradley's escape he had made no effort to hide it.

On their second day in the pump room, still convinced it was escape-proof, Josef Voda had told her the story of his betrayal. He found it so hard to summon the words it had taken him hours to get it all out. When he'd finished, she'd been so relieved for both their sakes she'd forgiven him immediately.

"Truly, Slečna Slavík? You would have done the same in my position?"

"Truly, Josef, I would."

It was a lie, of course. The real truth was SMERSh had been lucky to find someone so gullible in Voda. Who else would have believed they would ever release Vojtěch and Ludvík, even if he complied with their instructions? But how could she tell him that? He had clung to a slender hope and she wasn't about to tear it from him.

"But Josef, what do you think will happen now they haven't heard from you? Will they find us anyway – do you think they are searching these hills?"

The voice from the shadows had come thick with regret.

"Excuse me, Miss Nightingale. You do not understand. I have sent the message."

"But the American and I removed the crystals."

"On the second day. I sent it the day we arrived. They kept the set separate from the generator and I worried the batteries might run flat." She heard him swear and imagined him raising his eyes to the vault. "I thought you had guessed, that first day."

I had. I just didn't act in time. I should have killed you as soon as Sam told me how you had brought him to me.

But she had not said that.

"You told them everything?"

"I gave this location, as best I could, and the name of your husband." Incredibly, in the midst of his mortification he had managed to squeeze a hint of accusation into that word. Mila considered whether to revisit her own sense of shame, or to decide once and for all that she was through with these self-righteous, self-pitying bloody *men*.

"So," she'd said, keeping all emotion from her voice. "We must assume they will be here any day. I wonder why it has taken them so long."

Back then, she had not told him about Bradley's pistol, which was still stuck to her thigh. He may have been unlikely to betray its presence to the Nazis but if and when the door opened and a SMERSh officer appeared at the top of the steps she didn't want Josef playing teacher's pet. At that moment it might be all that stood between her and the Gulag, or a bullet in the back of her neck beneath the Lubianka.

Later though, they'd had no secrets left. The strange intimacy of the disembodied voice from the darkness had convinced her of Josef's enduring loyalty. His uncomplicated nature, she realised, permitted him to consider betrayal as a singular act, an infection from which it was possible to recover, newly immunized, or a sin committed, confessed and absolved. Now she had told him she'd forgiven him, he could perceive his own deeds as somehow honourable. If Miss Nightingale said it was OK, then surely all he had done was to save his son and his friend. That left him free to look after himself again. And her. It didn't seem to have occurred to him that he was *theirs*.

So she had told him of the gun and they had discussed using it. Too dangerous, he said. No chance of a clear shot at the second guard, and great risk of a lethal fusillade in return. Mila had nodded, disappointed but also relieved. She did not want to take chances, not with Pavel somewhere out there, nor with Sam, hopefully, briefing her rescuers.

"We must think of our sons, Josef. Tell me about him again, when he was little..."

But as the minutes became hours, as days and nights ran into one another, the difference between stories and memories began to blur. The Americans did not arrive. The Russians surely would. Sam had been killed or arrested. Theodor and his cronies had already fled. Perhaps their rescuers, Russians or Americans, would find only two shrivelled corpses in a dungeon. Perhaps they would never be found.

So they had turned their minds again to escape. A night of rain had confirmed the dripping water came not from natural seepage or condensation but a second ventilation channel. With blind fingers and upturned faces they found it, buried in the crown of the vault, and with a metal bracket worked loose from the dais they started scratching at the mortar of the surrounding brickwork. So the shifts began, and one by one the bricks came loose, to be hidden beneath the black water of the well.

By now they had removed two layers of brick to make a hole big enough for Josef. Beyond lay rubble and rotten concrete, pierced by the ventilation shaft. Mila worried they were about to bring the vault down on top of them but there was nothing to do except continue. If they were ready for it, and it was dark, a cave-in might be their best way out.

She clambered to her feet and went to help Josef pick up the fallen bracket. If his fingers were numb it would be the natural end of his shift.

And then – in the absence of scratching, in the pause between breaths – the muffled gunshots, the stamping feet on the floorboards above the cellar, the sound of a bottle breaking on the cobbles outside the door.

The bolt rattling. The burst of light that screeched in a parody of Theodor's voice:

"You sow! All this time you knew! You put me in this trap!"

He was coming down the steps, swaying, a finger jabbing in professorial fury. They shielded their eyes, craned their necks, but could see no accompanying guards.

"What are you talking about, Theodor? What were those shots?"

He sank down on the middle step.

"The shots? I think one of the SS has killed his woman and himself. I suppose you're happy your plan has worked!"

"What plan? What has happened?" Mila was tearing bandages to free the pistol.

"It was on the wireless. Truman has just announced it to the world. Sixteen hours ago, an American plane dropped one bomb on Japan, one bomb with more power than twenty thousand tons of TNT. He said it was an atomic bomb, Mila, and he even said how everyone must thank Providence they have succeeded where we in Germany failed! Do you know what this means?"

Yes, I know what it means. She racked the slide to feed a bullet into the chamber. Theodor looked up blindly.

"My God, it explains why the American ran away – they don't need me! Truman says they have had hundreds of thousands of people working in secret on these weapons."

"They might still need you. If they're going to produce these bombs, they might welcome a faster process."

"Müller doesn't think so. Nor does Schröter. I think he wants to kill me now before the Russians get their hands on me. Oh dear God, the Russians!"

She stuck the gun under his nose. Behind the broken spectacles his eyes widened.

"Snap out of it! Believe me or not, Brown was here because the Americans do want you. They had this bomb and they still wanted you. They're coming to get you."

"If that's even true it will be too late. Müller, Jarsch and Schröter are against me now. They seem to think I've tricked them into staying here, but it was you. You and the American, you tricked us all!"

"You're drunk, you're not thinking and you're not listening," Mila pressed the muzzle against the tape on his spectacles where they crossed the bridge of his nose. "We're leaving, understand? God knows why, but I don't want to kill you, Theodor. You're nothing to me but you're Pavel's father. So you sit tight here while we go..."

There was a blur in the corner of her eye and Theodor's head leaped away from the gun. His body seemed to hesitate before collapsing sideways off the steps. Mila rounded on Josef and his clenched fist.

"Simpler that way," he said.

They ran up the steps and out into the artificial canyon formed by the rear of the sanatorium and the rocky tor behind it. Drawn towards the inviting glare of the sinking sun, Mila took a second to spot the movement at the service entrance dead in front.

Jarsch and Schröter, only yards away. Jarsch was fussing with the holster he'd belted over his Bavarian suit. Schröter had his shotgun levelled.

CHAPTER TWENTY

She must have frozen in mid-stride as she ran out onto the cobbles. She was aware of Josef Voda overtaking her. Then she was falling sideways.

The impact with the cobbles knocked the breath out of her. She registered Schröter drop before the echoes separated into a pistol shot and the crash of the shotgun.

There was a thud as Josef landed beside her. Before she dared look at him she scrambled up and put two bullets into the centre of Jarsch.

She turned Josef over, expecting the worst, but his grey-bearded face wore a vicious grin. He examined his coat sleeve, which was oozing blood. A single buckshot had caught him as he lurched across to shield her. The rest of the spread had been diverted just in time. Mila threw him a quizzical look and he flexed his muscles. OK, his eyes said. She gave a squeak of relief.

Not alone.

Her head was ringing from the shots in the confined space and the odour of the gunsmoke wormed into her half-starved stomach and made her retch. They crouched, watching the service entrance and the ramp that led up into the sunlight. Incredibly, it seemed no one was rushing to investigate.

Josef went over to the two Germans. He drew a finger across his throat to indicate Schröter was dead and bent to recover his shotgun and bandolier. Having unbuckled Jarsch's holster, he set to beating the fat man's face with the shotgun.

"This one is still alive. The other you got through the heart."

She laid a hand on his arm.

"Enough, Josef. We'll lock them in the pump room. If he lives or dies now, it's his business."

It took another minute to drag both bodies to the doorway and pitch them down the steps. Mila had no inclination to check on Theodor. While Josef bolted the door she fastened on the holster and examined Jarsch's pistol. It was a Walther 9mm with eight rounds in the magazine. A good enough weapon at close quarters if, unlike Jarsch, you were ready to use it, but she doubted they would enjoy such favourable odds next time.

"Are we going?" Josef nodded towards the sunlight.

"Not that way, there are always sentries posted at the front and on the track."

She turned on the spot, eyes narrowed. Beyond the brick cube where the entrance to the air-raid shelter had been built onto the cellar, a flight of steps was cut into the rock, leading up to the far side of the tor and the belvedere that ran around the hilltop towards the funicular. Below the belvedere, she knew, the slopes were steep and sparsely vegetated, but if they could get further along the promenade, past the railway, they would be able to make their descent through the forest, the way Sam had come up.

But not like this.

"I'm not running unless we can cover our retreat," she said. "We need firepower of our own."

"But they have heard the shots..."

Something important was nagging through her headache. She grasped at it.

"We have some time. Schröter was coming to kill us, and probably get rid of Theodor. Jarsch – perhaps he was coming to watch. You see? If they heard the shots they'll think it was those two tidying up loose ends."

Silencing Josef's curses with a finger, she led him towards the shelter. The latch was still held in place with the padlock Sam had broken open.

No such luck with the door from shelter to cellar. They must have replaced the lock on the other side. Ankle-deep in the water, Mila kicked about for the crowbar they had left there. The new lock yielded with Josef's added leverage.

The first shock was that the cellar was illuminated. Someone had strung lamps on a line that spanned the vaults. The next came a moment later. At the top of the staircase leading up into the main building the door crashed open and an SS man started down the steps, remonstrating with someone behind him.

Ducking behind a bank of tea chests, they listened breathlessly as two pairs of boots left the stairs and scuffed on the cellar floor. There was the sound of a heavy box being dragged back up the steps.

"They're getting ready to clear out. Quickly, Josef, before they come back."

But what to take? Mila berated herself for scorning Sam's inventory. He would have known where everything was.

"Do you see any rifles?" she hissed.

"I think they already use what they have for the sentries."

He was right of course. It was the less versatile weaponry they kept in the cellar. Grenades — but everything was boxed and there was no time to mess about with fuse assemblies. Anyway, they'd be no use fighting a battle from lower ground.

It would have to be the bloody Panzerfausts again. She went to the nearest rack of the disposable anti-tank weapons and hefted one by its sling. Rock-heavy and unbalanced by the warhead. She slipped it over her good shoulder and tried another.

With relief she saw Josef had found his favourite machine gun, the so-called Spandau. It was the lighter, bipod version, equipped with 50-round belt drums. A man of Josef's strength could carry it on the sling and even fire it from the hip if he had to. She watched him lift the feed cover and fit a drum in place.

"Good," he said.

For her own part she had discovered she could not carry three Panzerfausts. She passed one to Josef and took the shotgun.

"Can you cope with all that, Josef?"

He kicked at a crate of 250-round belts.

"You can put two of these over my shoulder as well."

She looked him up and down, shaking her head.

"I'll have to take one."

"Thank you, Miss. It is as you say – we will need firepower when they catch us."

Mila bent to pick up the belts.

"If they catch us," she muttered.

"That is what I meant to say."

*   *   *

The setting sun had swung around the side of the sanatorium as it sank into the neighbouring hills and now it blazed through the gap between building and rockface, turning the courtyard slick with pools of light.

Josef squinted at the Nightingale, pride swelling his chest. This astonishing girl, standing here with that dirty-white shirt open at the neck, the shotgun in her arms and the rockets and bullets across her shoulders, who had only fifteen minutes ago accounted for two Nazis with the toy pistol she had hidden beneath her skirt. What a piece of work she was! With the scandalous haircut he himself had administered when her hair had burned from the back-blast... and now, in this late sun, in this evening breeze, no longer pale and haggard but shining brightly, eyes full of anticipation, never fright, never surrender... that he should be sharing this with such a girl, and that such a girl had pardoned him and trusted him anew! Here he stood on the roof of the ruined world, ready to do battle again with Slečna Slavík at his side.

Together they set off up the steps to the belvedere.

Hermann Müller was not a man to indulge in wishful thinking. In the world he inhabited, one selected a course of action and stuck to it, regardless. But as he saw Lossner being half-carried along the hall by the redoubtable Frau Kaindl, he couldn't help wondering if he might not have done better to strike out for Switzerland with the other mine managers instead of throwing in his lot with this *beschissen* professor.

Sidestepping the men carrying boxes from the cellar, he strode down the corridor to cut the distance between them.

"Yes?"

Beneath the discoloured nose and eyes, Kaindl's mouth was another laceration.

"Herr Direktor... Schröter and Jarsch are lying dead out there!"

Müller fished for something in his top pocket.

"And?"

She manoeuvred the wilting Lossner onto a chaise longue, beside an SS woman who was alternately clinging to her man and getting slapped across the face for it.

"As you requested, I went with Bock and Dettmer to discover whether Schröter was disobeying orders and executing the prisoners. We found the professor locked in the pump room with the two bodies. In point of fact, Herr Jarsch was still alive, just, but he passed on as we examined him. I suppose I must tell Christa and Brigitte."

"When you have told me."

"Of course, Herr Direktor. They had been shot, and the professor bludgeoned. It is the Czech woman, and her accomplice. They have escaped."

"Where are Bock and Dettmer now?"

"I sent the two SS to pick up their trail. Bock around the driveway to the front, Dettmer up onto the belvedere."

Müller had found what he was looking for. He clasped it in his fist.

"Is each man on his own? Don't frown like that, Frau Kaindl, it is not a philosophical question."

"You think they are in danger, still?"

"I think Bock or Dettmer is dead by now."

Turning on his heel, he began to blow the whistle in strident blasts.

*   *   *

Mila looked down at the SS trooper and tried to feel something nobler than relief. Jarsch and Schröter had been dangerous men coming to kill her, criminals too by most people's reckoning. This one was different. They had heard him hurrying after them and hidden on the other side of the parapet. She had wrapped Theodor's sweater around Sam's pistol and shot him in the head as he passed. Even so she recognised the dead man as one of the younger, less arrogant of the troopers.

She was relieved he had approached them so loudly and gratified he had a Mauser rifle. That was all there was to it. If she could no longer feel pity for Josef Voda, or remorse about what had happened to Ludvík and Vojtěch, it was no use pretending she cared about the SS man. Pretence would have made it worse.

Josef opened his hand to show her a spare clip for the Mauser.

"All he had on him. With the five in the rifle that makes ten."

"It's enough to keep their heads down if we have to."

They heaved the body over the parapet and retrieved their equipment from behind the marble bench-seat. Meanwhile Mila did some addition of her own.

There had been twenty-six troopers, plus Schröter, Jarsch, Müller and Theodor. Counting Frau Schröter, there were five SS 'wives', along with Fraus Jarsch, Müller and of course Kaindl. She did not include the four Jarsch children.

Subtracting Schröter, Jarsch, and now this one, left twenty-seven men and eight women. But she had already crippled Olga, and Theodor had said one of the SS had killed his woman and committed suicide. She really did not think Theodor would fight, nor Frau Jarsch and the SS tarts, but Kaindl and Müller's wife might and Schröter's widow too.

So, twenty-seven or twenty-eight. Enough to continue with their evacuation plans and send out search parties. The Nazis had rifles, submachine guns and anything else they wanted from the cellar. What they didn't have was much more than an hour's light.

A noise made concentration impossible. A whistle, from the front of the sanatorium. Someone was rallying the troops there.

At once the building above them became threatening. The east wing here was in ruins but it had windows nonetheless and the remnants of the balcony around the collapsed turret would be an ideal lookout post now the alarm had been raised. They had to make it to the cover of the funicular top-station before Müller got organised.

Was it Müller? Who else would take charge of the SS with Schröter gone?

On top of which, she thought as she staggered onward – and do pardon my unladylike language, Sam – but wouldn't the bastard just love that bloody whistle?

For the next fifty metres they were shielded by the wall of the kitchen garden and the trellises of overgrown laburnum and wisteria lining the pathway. But between there and the top-station lay another fifty-metre dash across the parterre gardens, virtually in the open, and uphill. They paused for breath and Josef adjusted his equipment so he could bring the machine gun to bear. Mila left Schröter's shotgun and took the rifle.

They were halfway across when two men darted out into the clear ground between the sanatorium and the first tier of the terraces. Still running with a crab-like gait, Josef opened fire. Mila saw the men scramble back behind the fountain and the wrecks in front of the colonnade. A pity. It would have been nice to get one of them.

Not much of the station remained. The winch-gear and the back of the building had tumbled down the incline when it had been blown up. But the remaining walls formed a gun emplacement with a field of fire across the parterre gardens to the sanatorium, a good two hundred metres away. Josef set up his Spandau in the doorway, where the marble facing from the concrete walls had left a pile of rubble. Mila laid down the Panzerfausts and went to the window with the rifle.

"They know we are here now," Josef said.

"We might be able to hold them off until the sun goes down, and in the dark they'll have a hell of a job chasing us down the mountain."

The old man was silent for a minute.

"They will also know this, Miss."

Yes Josef, they'll know it, and they'll have to try something while there's still light. I just didn't want to admit it, she told herself.

"They can't risk a frontal attack," she said aloud. "They know we have the Spandau. So they'll try to outflank us. To get around to our left, on the terraces, they must show themselves, even if it's on the far side. That's still in range for you."

"But the other way, the way we came."

"Yes I know. I can cover the belvedere but if they climb over the edge they can work their way around underneath us. That will be my job."

She moved to the back of the building and edged out on the crumbling floor. If she lay flat on the last wafer of concrete she could see around the wall to the fold in the hillside below the parapet, perhaps a hundred and fifty metres away. But this side of the mountain was already in shadow and it was impossible to judge the depth of cover without highlights. She'd have to keep her eyes peeled.

Another five minutes passed. Mila lost her focus over the rifle's sights and blinked, cursing inwardly.

I've been fooling myself, haven't I, Sam? It won't be properly dark for ages. They aren't going to sneak up on us, giving us time to pick them off. They'll position machine guns at the windows, bring up a mortar if they have one, and when they come it will be under covering fire. I think we're out of range for a Panzerfaust but what if they try to use them indirectly, could they reach us like that? Oh God, I wish you were here beside me.

No I don't, she told herself. What a stupid thing to wish for. If Sam had made it across the lines he was safe at last. He might not have persuaded them to mount a rescue mission, but he was safe and she would do far better to savour that crumb of comfort.

As she thought the words there was a crack in the air, followed a split second later by the sound of a shot from the direction of the sanatorium. She turned to Josef and saw his perplexed expression.

"Josef, down!"

Not a machine gun but a sniper at one of the windows. The bullet had come through the doorway and gone straight out the back, a few centimetres above and to the right of her. Before she could wriggle sideways to press herself against the wall, a second bullet blew a chunk out of the doorframe where Josef's head had been and ricocheted across the station. Ducked down behind the rubble, Josef was firing blind. The spent cartridges danced on the floor and continued dancing as the whole structure vibrated. With every burst, dust filled the station. Mila forced herself to sight on the fold in the hillside again, seeing nothing.

"It's too late!" Her voice leapt all over like the cartridge cases. "They could already be out and across the front. If they get a gun on the high ground, they can cut us to pieces in here. We must go now – out the back – and take our chances."

Josef snatched up the Spandau and rolled into the cover of the wall between door and window. As he did so another bullet hit the rubble where he had been lying. Mila found she had curled into a ball, ignoring the hillside. She peered up at the old man and saw him shaking his head back and forth, his eyes gazing ahead. She wondered if he had been wounded again, until she noticed the fury in that look.

"No, Josef."

He stared at her, almost through her.

"Yes, Slečna Slavík. You go, now. They will not get to the high ground." Discarding the drum, he separated a manageable length of belt and fed it into the gun. The remaining sections he draped around his neck.

Without further word he stood up and ran out of the door.

*   *   *

"There! Take him!"

Crouched behind a truck in the driveway, Müller saw the Czech partisan dart from the station and come zigzagging down the slope towards them, firing short bursts. He heard the glass shatter in the colonnade behind him. Through his spyhole, he even saw their own machine gun rounds pecking dirt at the Czech's heels. That idiot at the second floor window was chasing his target instead of leading him.

What Müller didn't see or hear was any activity from the SS trooper beside him. He rounded on him and repeated his order in a screech.

As the man, looking grim, rose to take aim through the burned-out cabin, his head jerked back and he toppled like a falling tree. Müller let out a gasp as though he too had been struck and felt the backwash of vomit in his throat.

He had never been in action. The noise of the guns and one's own heartbeat was stupefying. Every second seemed to snag and stick as though laden with doom, as though it were one's last. Even worse than the fear of the bullets, which was almost impossible to contain, was the conviction that the great welling of constricted energy in his chest was a heart attack, that his senses, so far off the scale as to be incomprehensible to him, were experiencing the trauma of his dying moment. Yet worst of all it was not climactic but went on and on, the rising screech of a stricken aircraft plummeting to earth.

That sow was laying down covering fire with a rifle. She might be targeting him now! Müller fought the urge to cower and shuffled around to peek at the running man. He had veered off from his suicidal charge and was skirting one of the low, dead hedges of the ornamental gardens, heading for the terraces. The machine gunner and riflemen upstairs still hadn't drawn a bead on him.

As the Czech's bullets disintegrated the fountain, Müller realised the man's path was raising his elevation and bringing him around the corner of the truck. Fresh panic shot through him. He forced his legs to move and scuttled back to the sanatorium steps, where several troopers were huddled.

He noticed the Luger in his hand and pointed it at them.

"Get up! Shoot at him!"

"Shoot yourself," the one called Schiebert said.

Without intending to, Müller shot him in the face. For a moment he expected the others to retaliate and was torn by conflicting sensations of fear and pride. Perhaps the men recognised his growing boldness, for after a few choice words over their comrade they got up and ran past him towards the front of the truck.

In an instant a terrible carelessness had overtaken him. Before he knew it he too was standing upright, insensible of the danger, to watch the three soldiers firing at the Czech. The thought occurred that he had suffered a mental breakdown. There was a certain comfort in the notion.

The Czech had climbed a flight of steps to the upper terrace and gone to ground near the summerhouse. Waiting for a target, the soldiers inched back towards Müller. It seemed to him Lossner's wife must have changed her position too, or else he would surely be dead. The only fire came from the machine gun upstairs as it chiselled rust and slate from the summerhouse, apparently without a clear shot.

Then a scream from the colonnade... The woman Lossner's wife had crippled came hobbling onto the verandah. Of course, she was Schiebert's woman, the one known as Olga. Müller was contemplating shooting her as well when a tap-tap-tap from the summerhouse knocked her back through the shattered windows.

Satisfied with the symmetry of this, he walked up the steps into the sanatorium.

*　　*　　*

Josef Voda finished reloading and peered through the long grass at the building opposite. Although it must have been a hundred metres away it seemed to tower over him.

So many windows to watch. Such a broad killing-ground in front. He knew it was a matter of time now. He only had two hundred and fifty rounds left.

But she would be proud of him. Vojtěch and Ludvík too, if they were still alive. It was easier to think about the Nightingale, to thank her silently for the covering fire he had not even requested, and to imagine her sneaking into the gloom of the valley while he kept the Nazis bottled up. She would be listening to the battle. He hoped she would agree his debt to her was paid.

Yes, she would be listening and probably worrying that the shooting had stopped. He considered firing a burst into one of the windows where the Nazis' machine gun might next pop up but the ammunition was too valuable to squander and so was his new position in the grass, a few metres away from the flimsy and indefensible summerhouse. She would be proud of that thinking too; it was the kind he had learned from her. But she would tell him off for burning his hand on the barrel of the Spandau when he moved it. Why didn't you use the sling, Josef, she'd say. Are you a glutton for punishment?

He gave a grunt and felt the icy sickness from the bullet in his guts. He knew he was bleeding to death, inside and out, but it was a proper, God-given blessing there was so little pain or lack of movement from the wound. Anyway, he thought, you're not going to see her again for her to scold you. All that matters is staying awake for long enough to repel the next break-out when it comes.

What was it Karel Sec had said? Even if I betrayed you, please remember I killed Nazis. Yes.

Perhaps he slept, or what time was left now flowed in fits and starts like the blood. When he roused at the sound of the car, the long shadows were gone and the hilltop had descended into twilight. The big Mercedes was inching up the ramp to the left of the sanatorium, shielding a squad behind it. They had wedged metal plate across the windscreen.

Fuck it – he couldn't let them advance far enough to scatter into the gloom. He aimed at the front of the car and fired a sustained burst, dazzling himself. Through the flare he saw the sparks of the bullets hitting metal. It was too much to hope he could hit the fuel tank but he kept firing until he thought the motor had seized.

Then, of course, came the answering fire from the sanatorium. This time they had seen his muzzle-flash and switched their aim from the summerhouse. He felt the bullets thudding into the bank. But he had seen their muzzle-flash too.

Rolling away from the Spandau, he retrieved the Panzerfaust and knelt up with the tube clamped under his arm. He sighted on the window and depressed the firing lever, dazzling himself again as the propellant detonated and the projectile whooshed away. Even as he fell back he saw that at this extreme range he had missed the window, but the feeble impact of the anti-tank warhead against the stucco facade was followed by an intense glare from the rooms on each side as the hollow charge shot a jet stream of explosive gases into the building. He saw something not quite man-sized and not exactly man-shaped topple from the window to lie smouldering on the roof of the colonnade.

But they had him in their sights now from ramp and

driveway. He saw the flashes along the dark bulk of the sanatorium, like the lights below Hradčany twinkling across the Vltava on a warm summer's evening. Bullets cracked the air. Before he could reach the Spandau he was spun around into the grass.

That must have been before the war, he thought, struggling to remember. There were precious few lights nowadays and there had been none under the Germans. Sometimes, the lights weren't across the river but on pleasure boats returning from the sunset cruise. He had always wondered what it must be like to do something like that.

Lying on his back in the long grass, Josef Voda saw the stars coming out and knew that by now it was dark enough for the Nightingale to fly away.

CHAPTER TWENTY-ONE

By the time she reached the foot of the first descent, her hands were raw from clinging to the roots and her face and legs were all scratches. She had heard the explosion and the volley of small arms fire. Now she listened to the silence.

Good-bye Josef. And thank you.

She adjusted the shoulder strap of the only Panzerfaust she had been able to carry. Cradling the rifle, she tried to get her bearings. She was in a narrow clearing from which, each way around the hillside, ran the overgrown traces of a woodcutter's trail. About sixty metres to the south, she made out the pile of logs Sam had described. In the other direction, she knew, the path would emerge onto the open ground around the funicular. Downhill, the treeline was a swath of darkness.

It was not just the damp air that made her shiver. These trees, these mountains, Theodor's mountains, had always filled her with dread.

She decided to head to the log pile and cut downhill from there, the way Sam said he had come, but she had taken barely ten steps when she spotted movement behind the outline of the logs. She lay flat in the grass and ferns. There it was again. The shadow not of an animal but of something like a man, covered in a pelt of spiky fur.

Another man-creature appeared to rise from the ground. This time Mila made out its rifle, even heard its growl to its comrade. She could scarcely see them against the logs and the treeline beyond, but she had no doubt that with her white shirt and fair hair, they had seen her.

She primed the Panzerfaust and clasped it, aiming for the centre of the pile where the wood might be solid enough to detonate the warhead. As the missile left the tube she was rising, grabbing the rifle, plunging into the trees below. But again she froze.

In the instant of the explosion, bleached by its flash, she saw the woods ahead. Ranks of trees and ferns trembled against their own fluid shadows as the fireball bloomed behind her. Scattered all about them were the scarecrow figures of camouflaged soldiers.

She began to function automatically – aiming, firing, re-cocking – while her instincts searched for a way out. She understood the continued flickering of the forest came from the flash and streak of tracer rounds being fired by a machine gun, but did not pause to consider the consequences of being struck by one of the glowing dashes, nor the invisible bullets between them. In her feral state she did not even grasp what it meant to be retreating up the ladder of roots and branches. All that mattered was to get away from the woods.

*   *   *

"How can you see a thing?" Bradley peered into what seemed a very cramped cockpit equipped with the minimum of instrumentation. "You got ground-looking radar?"

The pilot cackled over the intercom as he flung the tiny airplane into another turn. Strapped into one of two rickety seats in the back, Bradley saw the horizon tilt forty-five degrees and vanish behind the glowing abrasions on the plexiglass as they were drawn in a stomach-churning swoop toward the last embers of the sun.

According to Sloane, Pilot Officer 'Pete' Piotrovski had fought the Battle of Britain in the RAF's Kosciuszko squadron before transferring to special night-flying duties. The inference was he had flown secret missions to pick up and drop off agents behind enemy lines. Not that Sloane was in the habit of stating anything so clearly.

"I wouldn't dream of suggesting it," he'd said yesterday evening when Bradley had returned to his office. "I can't suggest it, sport. But if you were looking for a way back in, on your own, ahead of the assault, there might be someone you could talk to."

"Here?"

"I took the precaution of inviting him to afternoon tea in the mess."

"He's not from USFET?"

"Royal Air Force liaison, but most likely working with their intelligence people. Don't worry, I mean their MI6 department, not Smith's little offshoot. Probably here to spy on us Yanks. I mention him because I rather suspect he has spirited one or two people from behind the Curtain since it went up."

You would not have thought it from meeting the man. With watery blue eyes in a ruddy-jowled face and a stack of hair that was impressively resistant to Brylcreem, he looked like a farmer in town for market day. Bradley had warmed to him the minute he saw that broad grin and heard his laugh. There they were, talking about violating Soviet airspace in an unarmed airplane and making a landing in hostile territory on an unmarked airstrip, in near-darkness, yet the man's humour was so lacking in cynicism it sounded like it had burst through the years from the world before the war.

That same laughter was ringing in his headphones now as they began to descend.

"Pete, buddy, tell me you got some black magic up there!"

Seemingly unconcerned that they were heading for the dark mass of the mountain, Piotrovski turned around in his seat. He was waving something.

"Special night vision device from boffins." He handed over the object and put a finger to his lips. "Sssh! Top hush-hush old boy!"

It was a carrot. Probably carried it on all his missions to

crack the same joke, in the same, crazy accent, every time.

What was crazier was it seemed to work. Looking down through the window in the fabric, Bradley couldn't distinguish a single feature of the blacked-out terrain, yet he reckoned from the shape of the treeline and hills that they were lined up on the old German airstrip. The mountain rose above them on the right. The sanatorium would be up there. Mila would be there.

He saw the tracer a second before Piotrovski opened the throttle again. Then there was only the orange, yellow and blue-banded sky as the airplane made a steep banking turn away from the mountain. He clung to the frame and strained to hear the pilot's voice above the engine.

"Shooting, down there."

"At us?"

"No, something on ground, but..."

Bradley breathed a silent curse. Too risky. Whoever they were, and whoever was shooting at them, someone was catching hell.

*   *   *

Moving as quickly as his leg allowed, it took Andreev ten minutes to climb up through the forest to the path around the hillside and the pile of logs.

Rather, it had once been a pile of logs. Now it was a smouldering circle of splinters. Not all the splinters were wooden.

The NKVD officer's torch played over something in a patch of ferns. It looked like a quarter of beef.

"Give me your report," Andreev was so angry he could hardly speak.

Too unintelligent to realise how worried he ought to be, the man gesticulated along the path and towards the summit.

"Someone came down and surprised two of my men in their *zemlyanka* – that's what we call these camouflaged dug-outs."

Andreev stared at the shape of the man's head and wished he could see his eyes.

"Now I know how to describe those shitholes I nearly drowned in with my *shtraf* battalion at Debrecen." He prodded the officer's chest with his cane. "That's what we call these punishment units. Perhaps you'd like to make a note for your own memoirs."

At his side, Nemakhov cleared his throat.

"It was the girl, Comrade Colonel. These idiots opened fire instead of grabbing her. She must have been sneaking away from the Fritzes."

"And now?"

"Disappeared back towards the top. She could alert them to our presence."

The NKVD officer said meekly: "Pardon me, but I do not think she will get a chance to warn them. Before she surprised my men, we heard gunfire from the summit. If she had to shoot her way out, surely she'll get shot going back."

Andreev grunted.

"You'd better be right. I've spent too many sleepless nights on this for a couple of bonehead border police to screw it up."

"The two boneheads are dead. Another three of my men are wounded."

"Good." Andreev bit his lip and limped along the trail.

"We aren't going in." Nemakhov's tone was resigned.

"Not for the moment. Very soon, but not yet."

"Even though the girl might warn Lossner."

"Try not to sound so sulky, Captain. Even if she warns him, where can they go? As she recently found out herself, we have the whole summit surrounded."

Nemakhov paused. When he next spoke a bolder note had entered his voice.

"What if she fights them and wins? We have seen before how resourceful she is. What if she kills the professor?"

"It's a calculated risk."

"A risk? After all this?" Nemakhov's gesture swept the forest where the men were hiding. "If she kills him now, we'll be in the Lubianka before our feet touch the ground!"

"There is always that possibility. There has always been that possibility."

"When are you going to tell me what's going on, Comrade Colonel?"

Andreev pretended not to have heard. He squinted at the sunset's ochre afterglow where it was cut off by the diagonal of the mountain.

"Did you see that plane, round about when the shooting started?"

"Yes. It circled a few times then flew away. I assumed you would know who it was."

"Now you're getting precious, Captain, and it doesn't suit you. I don't know who it was, but I saw the red stars under the wings when it turned into the sun, and the unusual shape of it. I have a feeling I've seen that plane before."

*   *   *

Back in the top-station, Mila finished counting bullets and reloaded the rifle. Four left. Two in Sam's pistol – not worth keeping now – and eight in Jarsch's. Fortunately, the last Panzerfaust was where she'd left it. They couldn't have searched here yet.

Even more reason to get moving again, but where to go? The Nazis would be patrolling the hilltop, and down below...

Down below, she could admit to herself now, was what looked like half the Red Army. Surely it would be only minutes before they followed her. And to seal her fate when they did, she had probably killed or injured some of them.

She leaned her aching head against the wall, fighting back tears of exhaustion. When she opened her eyes, she was aware of a reddish light flooding through the window and the doorway.

It wasn't the last trace of sunset. Peering over the windowsill, she saw that the sanatorium was ablaze. She was unable to tear her gaze from the oblongs of fire at the upper storey windows and the orange glow on the smoke billowing from the rafters of the derelict east wing. The timbers there had been open to the snows and rains of spring. Would they be dry enough to burn, or would the fire run out of fuel? The Germans couldn't be fighting it without water.

That was why they hadn't come looking for her. They were too busy ferrying their loot out of the building. If they were all working at it, she might be able to sneak past to the far side of the summit and the road.

She slammed a numb fist against the concrete. The Russians would have the road covered. She'd never be able to sneak through their lines in the dark, they were too well camouflaged and she'd end up right on top of them. But she could play them at their own game. Let *them* walk in right over *her*.

It wasn't much of a plan anyway. It was no plan at all without somewhere to hide. The waterlogged stairwell in the pump room? The Russians were sure to check it and it wouldn't be much fun if the munitions in the cellar ignited. Somewhere up on the tor behind the sanatorium? No, the smoke was blowing that way and she'd choke to death before they found her. The long grass around the summerhouse above the gardens? Possibly, although she couldn't help thinking the Russians might choose to come up that way: while it was a tough climb to cut out the last dog-leg of the road, it would bring them out on the saddle facing the sanatorium and frontal assault had always been their stock-in-trade. It was also where Josef Voda must have died.

The best place would be beneath the belvedere. The slopes there were so steep not even the Russians would waste the effort climbing them, and the sparse cover would not invite a search party. If she could secrete herself somewhere, it might be ideal.

Listen to me, she thought. Ideal!

She had no strength left for the Panzerfaust. With a twinge of regret, she left it beside Sam's pistol.

It was horribly bright in the firelight. She told herself to move stealthily through the long shadows of hedges and plinths but none were more than a few centimetres deep and it was all she could do to put one foot in front of the other. She heard shouting. Every few seconds the fire mimicked a shot, and now and then a skirmish. Sowing such confusion, the sounds ought to have pleased her but instead they played on her nerves.

When she gained the cover of the trellised pathway she slung the rifle and drew Jarsch's pistol. She needed to save the Mauser ammunition and anybody she came upon now would inevitably be at close quarters. She checked there was a round in the chamber and let off the safety catch, taking the weight of the gun in both hands. There was nothing she could do about her breathing. For a long time now her heart had been beating so fast and her body shaking with such fatigue she was only able to take in air by panting.

Perhaps it was the sound of her breathing that drowned out their approach, or her heavy shoes dragging through the gravel. She was confronted with the fire-lit figures of Frau Schröter and the SS man with the jaw, both carrying submachine guns. They were yards away and would see her any second.

She took aim at the man and squeezed the trigger. The trigger budged, but nothing else.

Check the safety. Again, nothing. She let out a squeal of exasperation and pulled back the slide. The round ejected. Point – pull the trigger – nothing.

That fat fool must never have stripped and checked his pistol. Perhaps he had dropped it and broken something in the trigger group. Keeping it for show, he would not have noticed.

And because of her own stupidity in not checking it herself, she was dead.

The disfigured trooper spotted her and raised his submachine gun. Beside him, gawping, Frau Schröter jabbed uselessly with her own, which she appeared not to have cocked.

"Shoot her!" she screamed at the SS man.

Mila flung the pistol. As the man ducked she took two strides to close the distance and launched herself at him, clawing for his throat, but his head was down and instead her hands clasped his ears. She tore at them and drove her ragged thumbnails into his eyes.

A shriek, but not from the man. Unable to make her weapon fire, Frau Schröter had run at them and lashed out with it. Mila felt the blow from its wire stock on her back, partly shielded by the rifle she had slung. She clung on and wrapped her legs round the man, working at his eyes, knowing any moment now the strength in his constricted arms would throw her off. He was still holding the submachine gun in one hand, trying to bring it to bear, but as he staggered forward into her, his other hand wormed free and searched for her neck. She tucked her chin in and sank her teeth into a knuckle.

Locked together, both grunting, they spun around towards the parapet. The man managed to punch her head away with his injured fist and she felt her grip failing as he found a better angle to tear her off him. She thudded backwards into the parapet, the impact knocking the remaining breath out of her and digging the rifle in so hard she thought her spine had snapped. But nothing mattered now except to prevent him from straightening up and using the gun on her. Her fingers locked into the straps on his chest and her every muscle contracted, pulling him down on her. She tried to raise her knee to hit him between the legs but instead of responding her muscles exploded with pain.

His stare met hers. One eyeball was inflamed, the other hidden behind a grotesque swelling. His breath leaked from his nose in a hiss. Clamped like a horse's bit between what was left of his jaws was some kind of false palate.

Although it could only have been seconds, it seemed they

had grappled against the parapet for ages. Mila's ribs creaked as he pushed at her with fist and gun to break free. There was no strength left in her and she felt the horrible seductiveness of surrender. Another thing to struggle against.

She had to keep trying, for Pavel, for Sam, and for Josef Voda. Even though the fight was lost, even though the man was about to kill her, or Frau Schröter about to remember how to cock her gun, she would not *let go*.

And then she saw what must be done. She let go. The man lurched upright and would have staggered backwards but for the feet she had locked around his ankles. Instead he toppled.

The instant she was free of him, she summoned the last life in her muscles and rolled on top of the parapet. As she pushed herself out into space there came a burst of fire from one of the submachine guns.

*   *   *

Strange, skeletal figures, dancing in the flames. You could see they had once been women – the curve of a hip or breast, the angle of a neck, an ankle – but most of the flesh had gone and fire spilled through the holes. Their shadows reached towards him. The air around them rippled.

This was what it must have been like in that Japanese city, the name of which he could not remember. The flash would have turned everyone to shadows. The air itself would have caught fire.

It was inconceivable they had done it, without Heisenberg and Hahn, without him. It was ours, he wanted to yell at them. It was to have been born here, out of the forest, out of the German soul. It was our discovery, the fruit of our genius and the price of our salvation.

And I, Theodor Lossner, was destined to be a part of it.

That was the worst of it. The Americans had not only meddled with the atom, they had meddled with scientific destiny.

He gazed at the burning building through the machine-gunned statues in the fountain. The others were rushing back and forth, in and out of the smoke. They were carrying the boxes of his papers. Perhaps they supposed they might yet be able to bargain with them for their lives. But what did it matter now? He would never publish.

Müller joined him by the growing heap of records and munitions in the driveway. He thrust a pistol into Lossner's hands.

"Shooting again at the back – she must still be up here."

"Whom?"

"Your wife, that's whom! Use that, if she comes this way. Not on yourself, mind. You still have a job to do for me. You're going to pay for my ticket yet, damn you."

"What are you going to do?"

Müller ran a hand over his gleaming pate.

"We, Professor. Us. There's no resigning from this enterprise. We're going to load up the Kübelwagen and the Mercedes – flat tyres but it hardly matters. We'll try to drive down through the trees. But first I'm going to do for that sow of yours, once and for all."

Lossner gave a dreamy nod.

"Yes, I understand."

Müller shook his head.

"What a shitting genius," he said.

*   *   *

She was draped over the parapet, unmoving.

"Mila! Are you hit?"

He saw her react to his voice, but as though she did not recognise it, or truly believe it. She kept her eyes tight shut and when he laid a hand on her, she whimpered.

He lifted her bodily and set her down against the parapet.

"Look at me. It's OK."

She stared at him like he was some monster from the

forest. He remembered his face was coated in camouflage paint.

"Mila it's me, Bradley."

"Sam?"

"Sure, baby. Jesus Christ, what have they done to you?"

She tried to rise but her head was lolling drunkenly.

"There isn't time... they'll have heard this..."

"We have a moment."

She seized the proffered canteen in clawed hands. While she gulped, he examined her by the light of the fire. Her eyes were blood-red, set in dark, tear-tracked hollows. She was also a lot skinnier than he'd last seen her, and although the cuts and bruises on her face, arms and legs appeared superficial, the unhealthy tinge around her lips and the bloodstain over her old shoulder wound were more worrying. She looked like someone who'd been pulled from a train wreck and was now going down with shock.

When she had finished drinking, he stowed the canteen and rearranged his webbing, hanging the Thompson over one shoulder and the M1 over the other. He picked up her rifle.

"Any bullets left in this?"

"Four," she said. The precision was encouraging.

"Good girl."

She had spotted the two bundles on the promenade. Reluctantly, he followed her gaze and saw that the woman had been Frau Schröter.

Mila took the rifle from him.

"OK – over the side and down."

"Sam, we can't. The Russians are there."

He tried not to sound disappointed.

"I figured it was them, but only above the airstrip. Think we can fight our way through?"

"I saw dozens," she said. "They were lying in wait. I think there are hundreds, all around. I was going to climb over here and hide until they came past."

He rubbed his chin.

"It's an idea. But we're blown here now. Like you say, the Germans will be coming." He pointed along the wall of the kitchen garden. "I came that way, and round the back of the summerhouse. We'll make for there and check out the lie of the land."

"OK Sam."

Somehow, despite her hobbled state, they made it through the ornamental gardens and across the open ground onto the terraces. Bradley had to lift her up the steps between each tier and lean her against the plinths while he scouted ahead. From the top, crawling through the long grass where once they had sat and talked, they saw the activity in front of the sanatorium. It would have been easy to pick off another couple of SS before they took cover behind the boxes but they decided to wait for trouble to come to them. A little way past the summerhouse they found Josef Voda.

"Looks kinda peaceful," Bradley told her. "Happier than I ever saw him, poor bastard."

Mila wouldn't look.

"At least we have his machine gun now," she said.

"Yeah, we're pretty well set up here."

Behind his swagger, Bradley was alarmed. She seemed drained, emotionally. It was apparent in her dazed manner and lack of curiosity. Having accepted the fact of his return she hadn't even asked him how or why.

He shrugged out of his webbing and took off his sweater. Big though it was for her, she still needed his help to pull it on. Having fought too many battles, her body and her mind were shutting down. He had brought her a D ration bar to help with the former. But it was the latter he would have to work on.

"That was some fight," he told her with admiration. "You were stronger than him."

Chewing listlessly at the candy, she shook her head.

"Sure, stronger." He tapped his temple. "Up here. You were up against a bigger opponent and you gave it everything. He didn't. You had him beat."

No response, but no self-pity either. She was still with him, just.

"Did you find out anything from Lossner, about your boy?"

The voice was like a child's.

"He told me... that Pavel is still alive. Or he was, last autumn." She raised a hand to her forehead and rubbed at the grime there. "No, that's right – last autumn. When Theodor came back to Joachimsthal from Berlin, he no longer wanted Pavel with him. He says it was because of the uranium, but he's lying. He didn't want the responsibility for saving two skins and decided his was more important. He thinks he is a great man."

Bradley was still wondering whether to probe deeper when she went on.

"So Theodor asked Eduard Stransky to find a place for Pavel in the *Lebensborn* programme. You know what this is? Before the war it was a Nazi organisation to foster children of unmarried mothers. Then, when they moved into the east, they took Aryan-looking children for 'Germanization' and farmed them out to childless couples in the SS. I suppose the other children's parents will have been murdered. Pavlik's father just gave him away."

Bradley held her while she wept. He tried to offer words of comfort – her son would be alive, there would be records kept of where he had been sent, the Nazis were big on records, look there in the driveway – but half of them stuck in his throat. What hope remained? The child might be alive but his father had abandoned him and his mother would not live to continue her quest. In the end, that was why she was crying. He could not change what she knew to be true.

As it had been for Josef Voda, this hilltop would be their Alamo.

He wasn't bitter. The pity and affection he felt for this girl more than balanced out his instincts for self-preservation and he was happy to have returned in time to share her story's end, to spare her from facing it alone. Just as Mila had sworn that she could not have lived with herself had she fled with him and never discovered the truth, so he had known he had to come back. Even the thought of his arriving too late and finding her dead made him break out in a cold sweat. How lucky he was, to have timed it so well, to be here now, with her in his arms.

It could so easily have been different. With any pilot other than Piotrovski it would have been. When they'd climbed out of the valley and started circling, it had been all too obvious they'd missed their chance. The light was gone, the airstrip in the hands of an unknown enemy, the fuel gauge running low. Crazy enough to consider flying through mountains in such circumstances, let alone landing on one.

But then as they climbed they had seen the burning sanatorium in its pool of light. Piotrovski said it gave him enough of a bearing to risk a low pass over the peat bogs on the plateau. He had dived and throttled back until the little craft was virtually gliding – and there was the pale ribbon in the dusk. If Bradley could see it, Piotrovski must have thought it a proper flare-path. Without a word, he plonked the wheels down on the rutted surface of the dirt road and drew up in a matter of yards. Bradley wouldn't have believed it possible if he hadn't been clinging to the airplane as it bounced to a halt.

"Is piece of cake," the Pole smirked self-mockingly.

Bradley quit tossing gear out the door long enough to clasp the man's hand.

"Pete, you're a miracle-worker. Now scoot!"

"You want carrot? No, OK, bye."

Without bidding, he told the girl some of it. Maybe in the end, like a child or an animal, it was the tone of his voice she found soothing. Whatever the reason, the tears dried and she clung to him in silence.

Finally she jerked upright.

"Off to the left."

Bradley had been watching the sanatorium. He shifted to the far edge of the hillock. At first he could distinguish nothing. The fire had ruined his night vision. Then he spotted movement in the shorter grass and scrub a hundred and twenty-five yards away.

"I see him." He raised the M1.

"I think another is behind him," Mila said. "Shall I shoot as well?"

"Save your ammo and keep a watch on the house and gardens – in case it's a pincer movement."

He adjusted the scope.

"Get ready to change position straightaway," he told the girl. Although the Nazis had lost any vantage points at the upper storey windows it was still possible this was a feint to draw their fire. "We'll move to the far side of the summerhouse, soon as I give the word. Keep dead low. You take your rifle, I'll bring the machine gun."

"OK Sam."

The blur of a face rose above the bushes. Bradley didn't see him drop. The moment he hit him, the other guy made a leap for the superior cover of the long grass and the second bullet caught him in mid-air.

"Go!" Bradley slung the rifle, seized the machine gun and scrambled after her. There was no return fire, only the screaming of the second man, now out of sight on the middle tier of the gardens beyond the summerhouse. That wasn't pleasant but it would be more unsettling for the Nazis and might act as a deterrent. They certainly wouldn't be rushing to his aid.

"Sam..." Mila's gaze looked feverish. He pressed his canteen on her but she waved it away. "If they found the SS man and Frau... the woman you shot."

Bradley cursed under his breath.

"It was Frau Schröter, remember?"

"If the others found them and came looking for us they would have tracked us past the kitchen garden, not that way. Those two..."

"Those two thought they were sneaking up in back of us." He began setting up the machine gun again. "You're right.

Must be an attack coming from this side."

"You see? Not so dumb after all."

"Not so dumb, Mila."

"Then say what you said before."

"Good girl."

"No, what did you say? Sure baby. You called me baby, like in the movies. It made things... more exciting."

There wasn't time to muster the irony for a reply. Out of the corner of his eye he saw something fly towards them, seemingly defying gravity. With a whoosh the Panzerfaust projectile passed over their heads and hit the frame of the summerhouse in a shower of sparks, bouncing off and tumbling end over end into the night. The Nazis opened fire from the dark ridge of a dead hedge in the parterre gardens. Bradley and Mila ducked beneath the initial volley and when they raised their heads again there were more objects spinning through the air.

Bradley dove for the girl and flung out an arm, forcing her head to the ground. He'd seen three or four stick grenades and guessed each trooper behind the hedge had pulled the cord and thrown in unison. *Ein, zwei, drei...*

The explosions were ear-splitting and the shrapnel clattered off the summerhouse, but they had fallen short onto the terraces and the blast had been deflected. Bradley seized the machine gun and swept the hedge. He thought he saw one or two figures thrown back in the act of rising. The shooting from the hedge stopped. His belt was exhausted. He unslung his tommy-gun and knelt up, firing half-blind at one of the fleeing men and tripping him before he made cover. He switched his aim to the other but missed.

"Not so bad." He searched for Mila in the darkness and caught her grim smile of reassurance. "Two, maybe three down and they'll think twice about trying another assault."

They don't know we're nearly out of ammo, he thought.

* * *

It was as they moved position again that they discovered a way out. Following Bradley towards the top of the hillock, Mila saw him stumble and disappear. Limping over, she found him in a pit surrounded by iron railings that had been hidden by the overgrown grass. At first she thought it was an old grave or shrine, but closer inspection revealed a circular grille of rusted bars, one and a half metres wide, set into the rock beneath. Around it were the stone foundations of what must once have been a turret. These had been covered with rotten planks, through which Bradley had crashed.

"Sam, this is a ventilation shaft! There must be a gallery of the Joachimsthal mine that runs under here."

They were well hidden by the crest of the hillock. Bradley produced a torch.

"Can't see any rungs but it's roughly cut, there might be hand-holds." He dropped a pebble between the bars. They waited and heard nothing.

Mila felt herself coming alive again.

"Can you get it open?"

He patted the pouches on his webbing.

"With a bit of luck. I brought plastic explosive and detonators for busting doors open. Figured maybe they'd have locked you up somewhere."

Mila smiled. "They did."

She saw his excitement. He knew it was their best chance. But he was frowning too.

"It's a uranium mine. You said that was evil stuff."

"Better than the salt mines."

"Well, I can rig it to blow next time there's shooting. But if we go, they can charge over here and drop grenades on us. One of us will have to stay behind."

It was as though he had slapped her across the face, as Müller had done. But it wasn't him, it was life, again. And no, she thought, not after Josef, no.

"Then I will stay," she said. "Look at me. I couldn't climb

down anyway. You leave me your rifle and some ammunition and you go."

"Forget about it. We've been down this road before." He took her by the shoulders. "You got to get away to find your son. That's the only good can come from this now. It'll be OK, you'll have my flashlight and a spare battery. Even if you can't find another exit it's a killer hide-out."

The fire staged another phantom gunfight. Some cavity in the building sucked in air and groaned like the approach of an underground train. A woman screamed.

Mila saw him tense his muscles. Remembering their conversation here that day, she knew – and knew this was her last chance to ask.

"Because your father used to beat her?"

He was standing in the pit, his eyes switching back and forth along the line of the hillock, his rifle at the ready. But his mind was elsewhere.

"Because she used to take it."

"I'm sorry," she said, but he wasn't listening.

"That's a joke, huh. She took it but I couldn't. I was chicken, not her. When he put her in hospital the last time, I ought to have stayed home until she got out. Instead I enlisted. Ran away. Well."

Not again, she heard. Now they had both said it.

He turned his back. Woven into the breath of the fire were the sounds of wounded Germans, moaning and babbling in their own solitary darkness. One was crying for his mother too.

"OK Sam," she said.

She meant it's OK, I understand, *not again*; but he misunderstood, or chose to.

"Then you'll go? Good. Now watch the hill."

He began packing the explosive underneath the corroded lock and hinges, muttering partly to himself, partly to her:

"A det in each and I'll link them with the cordtex, should leave enough to run out a fuse. Soon as I've blown it, you get down there and I'll change position – can't cover the terraces or driveway from back here anyhow – they may be sneaking up again."

"Sam," she said.

He stood, holding the coil of detonating cord.

"No goodbyes this time, baby. But don't worry, I won't be on my own. A force of paratroopers is coming in by air."

"What?"

He stared back. She could see the repercussions as they struck him.

"The assault we planned. A company from the 82nd Airborne, coming in at first light. I have to mark the landing field down in the peat bog. Jesus Christ, they'll run smack into the Russians! I wasn't thinking!"

"You've had a lot on your mind," she said. "What's the extraction plan?"

"An UNRRA-registered C-47 on its way back from Berlin is going to stray out of the air corridor and make an emergency landing on the old German airstrip. The crew will effect repairs and take off again for the American zone at Marienbad. But it won't go to plan, it'll end up in a battle. Mila, you've got to get out, now."

She laid a hand on his sleeve and made a fist in the cloth. "Listen to me."

He was staring at the fuse. When he met her gaze again, the eyes in that blacked-out face looked lost.

"Don't you see, Sam, that's *why* the Russians are dug in – to ambush your paratroopers. It's a trap. Theodor is the bait. We were the decoys. It's all been a trap."

CHAPTER TWENTY-TWO

They had crawled forward to the upper terrace, bringing the fuse with them. From here they could look down through the balustrades onto the tiers of paths and beds. The silhouettes of figures made them jump, but it was only the statues.

No activity around the sanatorium or the boxes out front. By now the flames had engulfed the upper storey. Every now and then they heard another timber groan and fall, another pane shatter in the colonnade, another false exchange of gunfire. Even here, the heat was uncomfortable.

"They'll have to try another attack soon," the girl said. Although they were lying several feet apart, the fire would drown out any noise they made.

Bradley grunted. He doubted they had the stomach for it. They had lost too many. One dead or dying beyond the summerhouse, with his buddy still crying for help from the terraces beneath it. Another behind the hedge in the gardens, also moaning, plus the one he had wounded, at least, as they retreated from that assault. The trooper at the rear. The woman. Those were the ones he had accounted for. The girl had taken out another four, she said, among them Jarsch and their officer, Schröter. With the machine gun Voda must have added to that total.

More than a third of their force. Possibly nearer to half. Even with the fire at their backs they would be hard pressed to regroup after that and if they did launch another attack they would have to sustain further losses, whichever way they came.

He quit worrying about their stomachs and considered his own. Repelling an attack was one thing. Deliberately seeking out targets was something else. It had a name, and a face. The same face he'd seen through his sniper sights in Normandy and in the porthole of the pressure chamber. Back in Normandy, cracking up, he'd thought it was his father's face. Only later, in that sub-camp of Dachau, had he recognised it as his own.

He glanced back at the coil of cordtex he'd been unwinding. Like a ball of string, he thought, because here they were, on the brink of an even more tortuous labyrinth. In the end, that was the reason you went on. It was never simple enough to give up.

"I don't get it." He rolled to look at her. "Everything we've been through, and now hundreds of Reds down there, just to ambush a company of American paratroopers?"

She raised her head from the stock of the Mauser. It was too dark to see her expression but he knew she'd be frowning, her gaze a little distant.

"The Russians have had to promise to withdraw from Czechoslovakia, as the Americans have promised. This has been agreed, yes, at these conferences?"

"So they say."

"If they can show that the Americans have come across from their zone again..."

Bradley thought of the map of Europe as it had been redrawn at Yalta and Potsdam. The chalk-marks round the corpse. Now the Reds had pushed up to occupy half of Germany, now they had half of Austria and Piotrovski's poor bloody countrymen had been sold down the river in a last-gasp sop to Uncle Joe, that left Czechoslovakia as an ugly bulge in the Curtain. A weak spot, pulled each way, neither one thing nor the other.

"Might be an excuse to re-occupy the whole country," he said, knowing she had thought it too. "Newsreel of our guys getting taken... couple of tame Czech politicians to make a phony request for Soviet assistance... even Patton's reputation for Chrissakes!"

A change in the light drew his attention back to the

sanatorium. With mesmerising inevitability, the incandescent structure of the east wing folded into itself.

Half-closing his eyes to restore his night vision, he ducked into the cradle of the M1's cheekpad and scope. If they were burning in there, they might burst out any moment.

"Then the Reds have misjudged everything," he said to himself as much as her. "Patton won't stand for it. He's been looking for an excuse to storm across the demarcation line and this is all he needs. Doubt he'd even bother clearing it with USFET."

"It might be worse. Theodor told me he was scared the Americans didn't want him anymore, because they already have the bomb. Well, if the Russians are prepared to risk him as bait, perhaps they have it too."

Bradley let out a bitter laugh. It hadn't ended at all. This was just a time-out while the combatants forged new allegiances and equipped themselves with atomic weapons.

"But will they still come, your people, if they don't need Theodor?"

"I was briefing them yesterday," he said. "Sloane must have known about the bomb but he couldn't breathe a whisper. He found a way to get me back here ahead of the mission, in case they tried to kill you, but that was all he could do. He knows it'll go ahead regardless, either because they still want Lossner or because everything's so bound up in secrecy. It's how the War Department works. It'll be too late to stop them."

"Then we have to."

It was the fork in the labyrinth he'd been refusing to acknowledge. Again he found himself staring at the small, dark shape with its fiery crown of feathers. The indomitable Nightingale.

"How?"

"You said you had to mark the landing field. Did they give you a Eureka beacon? We could interrupt the beam and send a Morse signal along it. A message to abort."

Bradley threw her a pained look.

"Guess they figured I'd screw it up without training."

"Not even an S-Phone to talk to the aircraft – what do you call it, a walkie-talkie?"

"I got a flashlight and a bunch of flares. All I'm supposed to do is mark out the corners of the field, stand upwind and flash a signal. By then it'll be too late."

She lowered her head onto the wood of her rifle as though it were a church pew.

"The Nazis' transmitter," she said. "If we can get to that we can send a warning."

"I don't have a frequency for the assault team."

"But you must know the codename?" Seeing him nod, she went on, stumbling over her words. He recognised the secondary burst of adrenalin her body was producing as she came out of the worst of her shock. It was like the pills they'd been given before D-Day, the ones every poor schmo had thrown up into the Channel within minutes of leaving the shores of southern England. But with no fuel left in her the effect would be to burn up her last reserves of strength, and fast.

He listened, wincing inwardly. No time to contact London via Prague – if anyone was still alive there. But the codename coupled to a warning of the trap, transmitted *en clair* on a variety of frequencies including the old MERCURY settings, the former Heer, Luftwaffe and Kriegsmarine frequencies and one reserved even during the past years for international distress calls... The intercept stations could not miss all of those. The question was whether the message would be relayed to the right people in time.

"And where their transmitter is," he said. "And how to get to it."

"I know where it is. In the Mercedes, it must be. When they took it away from here to send my message, they used the car to ferry it down to the gap. It's probably why they turn over the engine from time to time, to charge the accumulators."

Bradley allowed himself the briefest nip of hope. It was

better than he'd thought. He had supposed their transmitter would be kept in the guarded wing where they slept.

He used the scope to survey the shadows of the westernmost corner of the building and the top of the ramp that led down to the rear. The car had been there when he had first arrived. At some point since, the Nazis had moved it back out of sight.

He checked his wristwatch. Something like five hours to daybreak. The aircraft would still be on the ground. There was time.

"What's the codename?" Mila asked.

He told her. For a moment she gave no sign of hearing him. Then there came that squeak of a sigh.

"What's the matter?"

"Nothing," she said. "It's a good name. A codename ought to give no hint of what it represents. I expect they employ the services of an elderly gentleman in a book-lined study to come up with these words. An old, grey man with a rug across his legs."

"Uh-huh."

Again the loaded silence. Again the sigh.

"I'm sure it's nothing..." When he didn't respond she went on, almost shyly. "It's just that this word is in my poem. It's the word I loved more than any other in my poem."

"What do you mean?" He allowed himself to shut his eyes. The relief was terrifying.

"The poem I was issued with during my training. In those days everyone had to memorise a poem to use for coding messages. Then, in the field, you were supposed to select five words from your poem at random and turn them into numbers to mix up your text. You sent an indicator group to tell your Home Station which words you had chosen, and as long as they knew your poem they could decipher your message. By the time I came over here they had introduced different codes, but no agent would ever forget their poem, believe me. Richard gave me mine."

"I'm no great shakes on poetry. What was it?"

"It's by the Irish poet, Yeats," she said, and she recited it to him there in the dark.

When you are old...

*   *   *

After she had finished, she wiped away an acrid tear.

"*One man loved the pilgrim soul in you,*" Sam said.

"Yes."

"Guess he knew he was saying good-bye."

She stared at him and almost couldn't speak. Her throat was swollen.

"Perhaps."

"And now?"

She pressed her head against the rifle, trying to knock some sense into it. I am old, she thought, older than I ever dreamed possible. Old and grey and full of sleep and nodding by the fire. And pacing upon the mountains overhead.

"Now your mission is codenamed PILGRIM. It's a coincidence, that's all."

Or a message, she thought. A message sent, as hers had been, through uncomprehending others. Saying what?

That everything would be all right?

Or good-bye?

*   *   *

Müller ran his gaze over the breakout group on the ramp and was relieved that in the deep shadows of the west wing their faces were obscured.

Professor Lossner sat beside the SS driver in the Mercedes, grimly silent. Behind them were three wounded SS men, two capable of using weapons, one burned and blinded from the explosion upstairs that had started the fire. In the back, Frau Jarsch was trying to comfort her children and

Müller's wife was trying to comfort her.

At the rear of the Mercedes squatted the Kübelwagen from the Joachimsthal mine, Bock at the wheel, with Dettmer's widow and the other two SS women behind him.

Around the vehicles, ready to jump onto the running boards or keep pace beside them, stood a further eight troopers. Those who had not been wounded were for the most part drunk and trying to hide it. They did not want to be left behind with the rearguard.

The rearguard! Müller had to swallow his shame as Frau Kaindl reported on its make-up. Three wounded and three volunteers at the front of the building to give covering fire for the breakout. The three volunteers would follow later on the motorcycle combination if they could. Everyone else was either dead or dying around the grounds.

One woman had done this. One Slav woman with her Slav accomplice. It was inconceivable.

The pragmatist in him knew it was time to go. Already the sanatorium had turned from a refuge into a beacon advertising their presence. Only the part of him that still felt anything yearned to stay, to mount an assault on her position with all his remaining men and wipe that *verdammt* sow off the face of this mountain. It was the same small part of him at which the shame was gnawing. But it could be ignored. His fury was spent.

"And the documents," he demanded. "The apparatus?"

Frau Kaindl's battered features were impassive.

"We have managed to retrieve certain samples, Herr Direktor. As for the bulk of the material, we must accept that it is inaccessible at present."

Müller searched her face for any hint of accusation. It was he who had ordered the treasure to be taken out front with the munitions.

"We must accept that much is inaccessible at present."

With a stiff nod, the woman who had been his most loyal comrade went to take her place beside Bock. Müller stood up at the passenger door of the Mercedes and cleared his throat.

"We are going out down the road and across the plateau. We will try to crash the vehicles through the forest and down the hill on the far side of there. All being well, we link up with the road above Joachimsthal and drive out southwards. Our objective is the American lines somewhere this side of Eger. When we get close, we will attempt to cross on foot, but any encounter before that, we shoot our way through. That is all."

He did not ask whether there were any questions. He did not dare.

The shadowy faces were turned up to him expectantly. He raised an arm that weighed several dozen kilogrammes.

"Heil Hitler."

*   *   *

They were still working their way through the terraces when the motors started on the ramp. Bradley pulled Mila behind one of the plinths at the top of the last flight of steps. The girl's eyes were wide in the firelight.

"Sam, they're getting away. The transmitter..."

He fed the barrel of his rifle through the balustrade.

"Keep down," he told her. "There's going to be covering fire. Lots of it."

"Yes."

"You know where we left the fuse, if you need to get away."

Before he could stop her, the girl scuttled across the steps to take up a mirror-image position at the opposite plinth. As she crossed the open space a single shot rang out.

"Mila!"

She lay face down in the shadow of the plinth. With relief he saw she was threading the Mauser between the ivy-cloaked balusters.

"OK Sam," he heard her say.

His heart was pounding. He couldn't find the words.

"That was – very bad."

A giggle. Unbelievably.

A funny voice – amused at herself. A mock American drawl.

"When I'm good, I'm very good, but when I'm bad I'm better!"

For a second before it began, they heard the engine note change and knew the vehicles were coming. Then their mirror-image idyll shattered all around them.

Bradley was roaring like a savage on the charge. But he wasn't charging, he wasn't even returning fire, he was ducking down, turning to Jell-O. The Nazis had a machine gun after all, firing through a loophole in the barricade of boxes. The statues and balusters around them disintegrated. The stone splinters were hammer blows.

One by one he pulled the pins from his fragmentation grenades and tried to toss them over his head without presenting a target. One by one they detonated somewhere in the driveway, shy of the boxes. Gravel hailed down. The shooting continued.

But the girl... he looked for her and saw her lying as she had been, with her rifle through the balustrade, aiming, firing, re-cocking...

Bradley unloaded the clip from his rifle and pulled out another. He held up the bullets to check the jackets were a different colour. He needed to be a different colour himself.

OK. Up on his knees, elbows on the coping. The marked boxes through the scope. One, two, three, four... all the way to eight and the sound of the clip ejecting. Reload – one, two, three...

The world exploded.

*   *   *

"This is what you've been waiting for," Andreev told the NKVD officer. "Stand by."

He glanced at Nemakhov's horrified face, illuminated by

the mushroom-shaped fireball that rose above the mountain.

"Makes you think, eh, Comrade?"

Nemakhov sounded as if the blast that had rattled the blueberry bushes had knocked the wind out of him.

"I don't know what to think."

"No indeed," Andreev said. "A common failing nowadays."

He turned back to the officer of border troops.

"Hold your positions – but prepare to mop up survivors."

*   *   *

The voice was far away, the sounds of gunfire further. Her ears were hissing, her head splitting. She let out an agonised cough, flipping onto her side, retching.

"Mila?"

Opening an eye, she saw only a pink blur. Gradually she made out angles and shapes. The stone pathway. The face beyond in its mask of black and white. The snow.

A hand extended past the face, through the snow. The hand blood-red. The water bottle in the hand.

There was a hole torn in the water bottle. The water dripped and pooled on the thick white powder. Next to the water, another oasis. Blood.

An intense pain pierced her jaw and ear. She tried to move and got the same pain in her arm, but deader, sicker – broken. Every other part of her trembled with the effort.

"Mila..."

The voice calling to her was weaker now and the simple mathematics of that shook her to her senses. Somehow, she rolled over again and propped herself up on her good arm. Because her sleeve had gone, she could see it too wore a fresh pattern of blood and powder.

Sam. He was crumpled against the wall beneath the next terrace, caked in white, one arm reaching out. As she watched, his head fell onto the path and the bloody hand twisted over, pouring the water into the powder.

"Sam!"

Her cry, at first distant, lanced into her skull. She felt her ears bleeding. She began to crawl towards him, using her backside and good arm, leaving a trail in the snow.

Not snow. Dust, and something else – hot ashes, raining down, burning flakes, embers.

Again the gunfire, far, far away. A battle. Not theirs any more.

"Sam?"

Here was her battle, now. As she grasped it, the scale of it horrified her. He was badly wounded – scorched and bleeding to death. His other arm seemed to be missing, the shoulder a jagged mess. And she was injured too, with only one good arm, and alone.

Now she was leaning over him she saw his arm was still there, but wrenched from its socket and bent behind him in a tangle of ivy that had turned to a wreath of white marble. What she had thought was bone was a stone spearhead protruding from the flesh. She plucked it free of the muscle fibres and blood gushed.

A magic trick: something had removed his shirt without unfastening the harness of webbing. Red seeped from a hundred lacerations on his torso. But wasn't that good, for the blood still to be pumping so? Not with the deep shoulder wound, she told herself as she searched the remaining pouches for a field dressing.

Unbuckling the unyielding canvas straps took an age. Even after she had found his medic's kit it was a laborious process tearing open the packages with her fingers and teeth, swabbing clean the wound with the last drops from the canteen and applying the dressing and bandages. By the time she had finished, the dressing was red again in the middle. Forcing his arm back into place was beyond her.

He had made no sound and she thought he must be unconscious. She got him sitting upright against the wall. From

343

the angle of his boots, he had broken or dislocated something in his leg. When she enlarged one of the rips in his trousers, she saw his knee was swollen and discoloured.

She allowed herself a minute to weep in sheer frustration. Then she set herself to finding splints. Thankfully there were broken strips of wood everywhere. It was just a matter of choosing a pair that weren't too splintered.

She got a long strap of webbing unbuckled from the rest. Shuffling back, she fell against him and began to wrap the strap around the splints either side of his knee. There was one thing she wished for in her life at that moment and she did not have it. The thick strap she'd unfastened had no buckle at either end. How could that be? How was that fair? Somehow, she would have to tie a knot in it.

And somehow, with teeth and fingers, she did. Now all she had to do was secure his dislocated arm under the rest of the webbing. A knot of torn shirt held it in place.

Poor Sam. Could she do anything for his burned face? For the moment it was too much to contemplate. The nerves throbbed in her arm. Again she had to retch and weep.

She dragged herself across his good leg and sat beside him. The grey-dusted ivy looked like the wall of a mausoleum but it gave when she leaned back and she relaxed into its strange cushion. The pain in her head had slackened to a hollowness that flooded through her, beggaring her senses, beguiling her to sleep. She would close her eyes for a moment, to ease the stinging...

She jolted herself awake again.

It was OK, he was still breathing. But she had to stay awake, had to think.

What had happened? The cars had been getting away. In desperation Sam had been pumping round after round into the barricade, in the hope of hitting something. And he had. Explosive incendiary rounds, she remembered. All the ammunition boxes, the grenades, Panzerfausts, perhaps mines or demolition charges, must have gone up as one.

But what about the sounds of battle? Those had come from the road beyond the ridge, possibly all the way down on the plateau. The escaping Nazis must have run into the Russian cordon. Theodor too. Well, there was nothing she could do about that.

And the Russians, where were they now? Waiting, she told herself. For the American paratroopers. With the Nazis out of the way, the ambush would still be on.

"Mila?"

She twisted around and found him looking at her. Bright scarlet eyes under the dust and camouflage paint.

Of course. The black paint. Not scorched, not burned.

She let out a laugh that was more like a sob.

"Hello," she said.

He managed to return the smile.

"Got knocked silly, I think." He groaned. "Ah, yeah – my leg. And shoulder. Ribs too, I guess. You?"

"My arm's broken. Haven't tried my legs but they feel all right. Been a bit busy."

He looked at the arm strapped against his side and the splints around his knee.

"Thanks."

"Any time, Sergeant Bradley."

She propped herself up on one knee. Making a sling for her arm from the shreds of the sweater Sam had loaned her was the easiest job so far. She stood up.

"Guess I took care of their rearguard, huh?"

"I guess you did," she said.

Although some of the plinths and balusters were still standing, all the coping and the statues had blown down and broken into fragments, one of which had ended up in Sam's shoulder. But that was far from the explosion's chief accomplishment. Peering through the rubble to the driveway, Mila saw that the place where the boxes had been stacked was now a crater, surrounded by scrap metal. She supposed the scrap was all that remained of the fountain, the old trucks and other vehicles – and the colonnade.

The entire front of the Radon Sanatorium had gone. In its place sagged a V-shape of rooms and floors that had collapsed inwards around the atrium. Only the west wing and turret still stood, and they were being consumed by a multitude of small fires. It looked as though the main blaze in the remnants of the east wing had been blown out.

Everything appeared to be coated in a fall of snow, but it was the plaster from the stucco façade. Glowing pink in the early light, a cloud of dust and smoke ascended in a slanting pillar toward the stars.

The stars. To the east they were isolated pimples in a blush of blue and gold. Tending to Sam had taken ages. It was getting lighter.

"We have to get down to the landing-field," she told him.

It took another age to get him upright, only to discover he could not support himself with his injured leg. By the time she had devised a way for him to use his rifle as a crutch, it was almost daybreak. A shambling, three-legged creature, they started along the road that led off the mountain.

Before they had reached the bend at the ridge, they made out the figure tottering towards them. Another strange creature fashioned from leftover limbs. As it ascended the slope into the light from the east, they saw it was Theodor. Wild-haired, limping, gasping for breath, in his arms he held the younger of the Jarsch daughters.

He had lost his spectacles and did not recognise them until they were upon him. Perhaps even then they were unrecognisable, or he wore that shocked expression permanently now. Only the girl, tucked into his chest, seemed to see them at all.

"All dead, all over," he was muttering between gasps.

Mila could find neither breath nor words. To see him like this, still alive, a child in his arms...

Strangers passing on the road.

Twice on the descent Sam's legs gave way and she hadn't

the strength to prevent his falling. After she had got him up the second time he looked and sounded delirious.

"Get the rescue..." he grunted, or perhaps *Forget*. "Blow... blow your cover..."

"Not to worry now, Sam, darling – think our cover's blown anyway."

"Anyway..." he muttered, clutching at her. "Get away."

Where the plateau opened out, they found the Mercedes and Kübelwagen. Even with the mountain between them and the sunrise they could see that one vehicle was blown apart and spread across the peat-bog, the other upside-down at the side of the road. The dark things around them would be the bodies. They were of all shapes and sizes.

Instead of going further they set out across the bog. Apart from the strange dolmens of stone and bogwood it seemed deserted. The Russians must have hidden in the long treeline. There might still be time to flash a warning to overshoot the ambush.

But there wasn't. From across the plateau came the screech of an amplified loudhailer.

"Slečna Slavík – Slečna Suková..." The metallic voice switched to English: *"Mister Brown – Sergeant Bradley..."*

"Well," she whispered to him. "You were right, our cover's blown."

"Stay where you are! If you move you will be shot."

"I guess that's it." As the words left her mouth a searchlight was switched on in the treeline. It played once across the plateau before fixing on them.

Dazzled, she turned to Sam and helped settle him to the ground. Now she saw how deathly pale he was under the streaks of camouflage and dust – blue-lipped, sweating, shivering. She saw the puncture-marks all over his face and torso, the dried blood at his ears and nostrils, the bloodshot eyes losing their light as the final wave of despair broke over them – and she supposed she must look very similar to him in that regard. Shielding her eyes, she shuffled around to put the

347

light behind her and let her arm fall to take his hand. Though his was weak and hers numb, she thought he returned the squeeze.

Without warning, the searchlight was extinguished. Mila cast about, uncomprehending, until she saw figures running here and there across the plateau and flares fizzling into life. Upwind, towards the south, a smaller, dimmer light came on. A torch, flashing. Dit-dah-dah-dit. Dit-dah-dah-dit. The letter P.

For PILGRIM.

"How could they know?" she whimpered.

Although the plateau had returned to silence, Sam's voice was barely audible now.

"Jones."

"Yes. I'm sorry, Sam."

With a gasp of pain he repeated: "Cover's blown."

Now there was something in the silence. She was aware of rushing air and thought it might be a squall rising through the treeline. Then out of the corner of her eye, tonelessly against the deep blue of mountains and sky, she saw shapes approaching.

Before she realised it, they were much bigger and already rushing over the field. The silence, still holding its breath, seemed stretched fit to burst when there came the thud and hollow rumble of the gliders setting down.

All at once it was a cacophony of crashing timbers, ripping fabric, thundering skids. And the sounds from the treeline – the whistles and shouts from the Russian units as they sprang into action. The searchlight snapped on again, and another, and another.

The silence returned, only to be shattered by the loudhailer.

"American paratroopers – you are surrounded by a superior force – your mission has been betrayed."

And how, Mila thought. Sam's hand had gone limp but she kept tight hold of it.

Either because they thought the assault team had got the message or because their leaders were indifferent to needless casualties, the Russians filtered out onto the peat. Scores of armed men approached the three floodlit gliders.

"American paratroopers – abandon your weapons and come out with your hands raised – you will not be harmed unless you resist. If you require medical treatment we can provide it – I repeat – you are surrounded – your mission has been betrayed..."

Mila blinked. She could have sworn an American called out: "Yeah? No shit, Ivan!"

Had the Russians heard? When the loudhailer came back on, the artificial voice sounded indignant, if that were possible.

"Surrender now or we will open fire."

This time there was no mistaking the reply.

"OK, you got us. We'll surrender – to your commander."

Some small noise or motion made her look down at Sam. He was still conscious after all and fumbling for the rifle.

*   *   *

At the head of a funnel of troops, cameramen and technicians, the two SMERSh officers approached the nearest glider. In the glare of the searchlights the plateau, the rock formations and the treeline beyond were still benighted, almost bled of colour. It made for a dramatic contrast with the view to the east, where the dark bulk of the mountaintop had taken on the look of a volcano, the immense column of smoke glowing orange and red against the sunrise.

Andreev glanced over his shoulder at the film director.

"Enough of a spectacle for you?"

The man began to bleat about light levels and film stock. Andreev ignored him. It was of no consequence. They would re-stage it later, with his men in the American uniforms. It was their uniforms that were important, together with their trial testimony.

As they got closer Andreev saw from the twin boom

design that the gliders were German Gothas, painted completely black or a dark, neutral colour. Clever of the Americans, and a pity too. But it was the men and their uniforms that mattered.

Gothas were towed aloft on wheels, which were jettisoned. Approaching this one from behind, they saw it had landed heavily in the soft ground, digging in its nose and breaking off a skid to tilt forwards and sideways on one wing. The rear section between the tail booms lifted with a wounded yowl and the figure of a soldier jumped down.

Andreev turned to his aide.

"Check they are filming this."

But Nemakhov might not have heard him. He was staring at the soldiers as they disembarked from the glider under the gaze of the searchlight and the guns.

Staring open-mouthed. At the Czechoslovak soldiers setting foot on their own territory.

Andreev became aware of the men around him muttering in dissent. Not looking at him, Nemakhov spoke too.

"Oh, you conceited *arsehole!*"

Andreev was stunned.

"They're Americans wearing Czech uniforms, idiot. How dare you!"

Nemakhov fell to his knees.

"And you call yourself a chess player! You deluded *peshka!*"

For the first time in as long as he could remember, Andreev felt a twist of fear. His hand twitched and the cane sank into the peat, causing him to lose his balance.

A moment later he wondered whether he would ever regain it.

The next figure to climb down from the gilder was wearing not Czechoslovak army uniform but Soviet. It was the GRU major he had encountered in that flyblown transit camp on the trail of Karel Sec.

Korolev. Wearing an evil smirk he hadn't managed to wipe

off his face, or couldn't be bothered to.

Now there was turmoil among the NKVD border troops, even among the SMERSh soldiers who were supposed to be supervising them. For a second, the film crew's lights shifted off the glider and shone in Andreev's face.

Korolev chose that moment to speak.

"Lieutenant-Colonel Andreev, I have here an arrest warrant made out in your name, together with that of Captain Nemakhov." He stepped into the lights and held out a folded sheet of paper, savouring his words. "You will recognise the signature of the Commissar General of State Security."

That was when Andreev knew he and Nemakhov were dead. Not even Colonel-General Rodin could help them now, if he was still above suspicion, or still alive. Beria himself, chief of the entire security apparatus and master of BORODINO, the top-secret atom bomb project, had disowned this variation on the game. Perhaps Stalin had changed the rules, as he had done countless times before. Perhaps the sacrifice had been part of a greater stratagem all along and he had been, as Nemakhov had called him, an unwitting *peshka* – just another pawn. Perhaps all and none of the above were true and Beria, having overreached himself, was rewriting the record of the game. If that were so, only two things remained certain within the smokescreen of fictions. The truth of what had happened would never come to light. But it would catch up with him in the end.

As Andreev handed the arrest warrant back to Korolev, their eyes met. Not a flinch or glimmer of sympathy, for all that Korolev must have understood he was a *peshka* too. The look of relish had faded, but it was no shade of regret that replaced it, rather an iconic serenity. It was as though a dead man had come briefly back to life and was resigned to return to its purgatory. It took a dead man to recognise it, perhaps.

Korolev might have upset their plans for Czechoslovakia and put another nail or two in the coffins of Beria and his cohorts, but he had surely hammered shut his own.

So what had the poor bastard got out of it?

Andreev broke free of the unsettling gaze to see a party of men coming through from the second glider. More Czechoslovak soldiers, led by the little man from their National Security Corps who had been Korolev's companion that day, Comrade Novák.

Separate gliders, just in case. He too had a copy of the arrest warrant.

"Colonel Andreev, I am authorised by my government, and your own Central Group of Forces, to request the immediate standing-down of your command. At this moment, a division of the Czechoslovak army is moving up from Jáchymov to relieve your units here. We are empowered to disarm them if necessary, but it would be preferable if you and your field commanders advised them to return to their assembly points…"

"Order," Andreev waited for Novák to look up. "A simple correction, Comrade, for your future dealings in Russian. One orders soldiers, one does not advise them."

But the fight was going out of him. He had spotted the group approaching from the third glider and began to understand how complete had been the betrayal.

An American, presumably the one who had called out, was being carried by two Czechoslovak soldiers. He could only be an American. With the ridiculous Panama and seersucker jacket, and because he was being carried so, he reminded Andreev of the former American President. A fellow cripple. Another dead man.

Alongside the American strutted a tall, broad figure in a trilby hat and raincoat. This one Andreev recognised.

Having noted his surprise, the little Czechoslovak politician said: "These are foreign diplomats who are here at my invitation as observers. It has been agreed this unfortunate situation should be resolved as openly and *transparently* as possible."

"Indeed." Andreev raised his voice. "Transparency has

been in short supply, I fear."

"*Razvedka*, Colonel," said the so-called British diplomat who had once been a Czech named Rastislav Zajíček and, somewhere in between, perhaps, a SMERSh informant. "Anything and everything, isn't that what you always said?"

Andreev turned his back. It was time for him to talk to his commanders. And Nemakhov, he would have to find a way to talk to him. On an impulse he turned again to Novák.

"I wish you and your government every success in these new times of openness, Comrade. But if you will permit me to offer a word of advice..."

"Yes, Colonel?"

"Keep away from your office windows."

*   *   *

By the time the patrol returned from the summit the sun was high over the mountain. Spotting the enormous Bath-chairs they had brought, Sloane began to cackle.

"Oh that's marvellous! Have you seen them, sport?"

Bradley let out a grunt.

"Travel in style, huh?"

"Play the cynic if you like. I for one am itching to go see what you left up there."

They waited for the soldiers to help them into the wheelchairs. When Bradley spoke again his voice was shaky.

"We left you Lossner, if that's what you mean. But we blew his apparatus and files to hell."

Sloane shook his head sympathetically.

"Blew yourselves to hell too. But that's not what I mean. The Scene of the Battle, sport! An Eye-Witness Account!"

"Yeah, well get yourself another witness."

"I would," Sloane said. "Only she has disappeared."

Bradley nodded towards the summit and grimaced as his shoulder protested. The Czech medics had fixed it up pretty good, plus his knee, Mila's arm, even Sloane's ankle, but he couldn't wait to get off the mountain and into a US Army hospital.

"She went up there after Jones."

"To remonstrate with her husband?" Sloane sounded pained, too. It was an awkward subject.

"She wanted to find out what had happened to some drawings that were important to her. No, I don't mean scientific shit."

"So she needed to talk to him, the husband, or whatever he is?"

"I guess."

"Hmm. It's a puzzle, I'll say that. You and her...?"

"Go to hell, Sloane."

"Well in that case I'll have to dine out on my own war stories. Wings into the Inferno – My Glider Assault into Certain Death, eh?"

"A certain rock, you mean," Bradley raised his good arm. "That one."

Sloane laughed.

"Got a smoke?" Bradley asked.

"Sure." Sloane propelled his chair forward and tossed a pack of cigarettes into Bradley's lap. A gold lighter followed. Bradley caught it and turned it over in his hand. The smooth panel for an inscription had been left blank, or effaced.

"Nice. Yours?"

Sloane shook his head. He too indicated the mountaintop.

"Hers."

"How the hell...?"

"I took it off Colonel Andreev, before you woke up, sport. She left it with the poor bastard who blew his brains out, apparently."

"Karel Sec. You know about that?"

Sloane rocked his head, pleased to be hiding something, waiting to reveal it.

"Bits and pieces. Andreev pocketed the lighter and replaced it with the matches you were meant to find. The ones that led you to the nightclub – and here, I guess. You can give it back to her now."

Bradley stared at him.

"Goddamn State Department!"

"Well, thereabouts." Sloane indicated the cigarettes in Bradley's lap. "Take one, they're yours. Literally."

Bradley frowned at the half-empty pack. Lucky Strike Green had indeed gone to war, and on the new-style white background that saved the precious copper, someone had scrawled a message.

Dear Sam. Thank-you, and Sorry! Renate S.

He blinked.

"She was working for you?"

"Not exactly," Sloane leaned closer, lowering his voice. "You left that pack with her in Prague. It was given to me for you by Major Korolev."

"You mean – the guy, just now?"

"The guy, yes. Just now...?" Sloane really was checking to make sure they weren't overheard. "No. He gave it to me in Frankfurt."

"The big visit you were preparing for?"

"The Soviet Repatriation Administration. I said they'd be GRU in disguise."

"They made contact with you."

"Through Korolev. He had picked up Fraulein Schelkmann. That's to say, she was... predisposed to talk to him anyhow. He's going to help track down her missing fiancé."

"She's OK?"

"I gather she's doing just fine, sport," Sloane smiled. Then he was back to teasing. "You and her...? Oh, I know, go to hell."

"So you – we – were working with the GRU on this?"

"Absolutely not. And if anyone suggests Korolev's boss lent us his airplane, you damn well point out to them that under the terms of the Lend-Lease agreement it was ours all along."

"And Jones is... what? Ours too?"

Sloane reached into his breast pocket for his sunglasses.

"You'll have to ask him about that. Smoke your cigarette, Bradley. You earned it."

He lit the cigarette. It ought to have been stale and wasn't, but Sloane had pulled off bigger sleights of hand than that. The airborne mission that Bradley had thought he was assisting with, for instance. Had it really been stood down at the last minute? Or did the planning for the Czech-GRU sting date all the way back to Mila's cryptic transmission, or even earlier? He wanted to ask, but he knew he would never receive a straight answer.

It was the perfect moment in the perfect morning for a smoke and yet he stubbed it out. Something was missing. When you had been through what they had been through and come out on the other side, no other company would do it for you, however entertaining. He didn't know how this would end but he knew it wasn't over yet. Until then, if he was going to share anything – cigarettes, war-stories – he was going to share them with her.

Maybe it was written across his face, or the other man had caught him glancing up there, but with a nod of understanding Sloane beckoned for the soldiers.

"Must say I'm eager to meet her properly. When we were getting seen to we kind of skipped the introductions."

Bradley was suffering. Only when they reached the smoother surface of the dirt road was he able to speak. All the while he kept his eyes off the two shot-up German vehicles and the bundles of Czech army-issue groundsheets that surrounded them.

"I don't know what deal you've done with the Czechs, but tell me this, Sloane, is she going to be all right with them? They may have let you help them save their country, but we're still behind the Curtain. Everybody calls that guy *Comrade* Novák..."

"Mmm. And it wouldn't blow me down to find our porters here spoke English."

"Screw that. Tell it to me straight."

"OK. The truth is I don't know what's going to happen to her, or her husband – her make-believe husband – but I wouldn't worry too much about that side of it. In my opinion they ought to give her a fucking medal!"

As the soldiers pushed them over the rise, he let out a low whistle. Bradley had to admit it was an impressive vista, although he'd cheerfully never have seen it again.

The Radon Sanatorium had all but disappeared. The two wings and their turrets had burned away to a blackened skeleton. The section left between them was a collapsed house of cards. Debris of all kinds radiated from the crater at the front and the gardens were a tornado-wreck of charred wood and plaster-dust. Even the summerhouse at the top of the terraces had fallen. And, everywhere, they made out the army-issue groundsheets covering bodies or parts of bodies.

"Jesus H. Christ! This was just the two of you?"

"And a man named Josef Voda. Me, I got here halfway through it all."

Picking up speed along the saddle, they saw that the soldiers who'd covered the bodies had gathered by the remains of the colonnade steps. With them were Jones, Novák and a man in Red Army uniform who must have been Korolev. One of the groundsheets lay at the foot of the steps. A soldier held the Jarsch girl in his arms.

There was no sign of Mila.

Jones was speaking Czech or Russian as they approached. He switched to English and his manner changed likewise.

"Mr Sloane, Mr Brown, how lovely to see you looking so much better."

"What's going on?" Bradley demanded.

"Ah, a terrible and unnecessary tragedy, I'm afraid," Jones and the others looked down at the bundle. "And after surviving all this – a simple accident."

Bradley couldn't breathe. He was struggling to rise and nearly passing out from the pain when Sloane laid a firm hand on his arm.

"That's Professor Lossner?" Sloane said.

Jones looked morose.

"Alas. Having survived the... fracas... he must have come back here and lost his footing on these steps. His neck is broken."

Bradley no longer cared about the others. Russians, Czechs, spies, communists – none of it mattered any more.

"Was it her?"

Jones seemed not to understand.

"Mr Brown? You can't mean this poor German orphan, surely?" He glanced at the little girl whose unblinking eyes had seen everything, but whose lips, judging by her vacant expression, would say nothing. "If it helps to clarify matters, I myself was first on the scene, and I can assure you Professor Lossner was already dead."

"But then where..."

Jones interrupted him again.

"Your confusion is understandable, but you have nothing more to fear. These trusty souls have searched high and low. Apart from the mortal remains of the Nazi renegades whom you battled so heroically – and whoever might have been in the surviving section of the building when it collapsed – there is no one left on this mountaintop except us."

Bradley nodded. A wave of something like sleep swept over him as he fumbled for the pack but he forced himself to light the cigarette and smoke it.

Now he understood.

EPILOGUE

Colour had returned to the Old Town Square with the late summer light. Although the square was bracketed east and west by the gothic steeples of the Týn church and the blackened tower of the Town Hall, in the expanse between it was as though the clouds of the past years had finally parted. The pastel pinks, blues and yellows of the facades, the gilded paintings on the stucco-work and carved portals, even the over-exuberant slogans on the streetcars and the gay print dresses of the girls seemed like the flags of a liberated nation. At last stripped of their *Winterhilfe* hoardings, the coppery green figures of the Jan Hus monument were thumbing their noses at Hitler's ghost.

A liberated nation? Well, maybe. Although one didn't have to look too hard to spot the uniforms dotted around the pavement cafés or strolling with the girls across the square. Czechoslovak, certainly, but also the Red Army and Komsomol, the many different battledresses of the UNRRA partners, even one or two Americans.

And standing on his own in front of the Town Hall, unmistakably, an Englishman, in an English uniform of blazer, flannels and cravat, sporting the Englishman's perennial sidearm, a brolly.

Limeys.

Bradley paid for his beer and struggled to his feet among the busy tables. With his walking stick tapping at the newly laid cobblestones, he made his way over to the English tourist.

Smith looked up at the sound.

"Sergeant Bradley. What a delightful surprise!"

Bradley took his hand, cracking a lop-sided grin.

"Are there any surprises in your line of work, Colonel?"

"One or two. Not that it's my line any more. I've retired. Thought I'd take a tour."

"Starting here."

"Mmm. Thought I ought to see what Mila was fighting for. While it's still here."

"She wasn't fighting for this."

"No? No, of course not. Mind you, I suppose that's none of my business now."

Bradley couldn't keep the bitterness out of his voice.

"Ain't nobody's business now."

They were crossing the square towards the monument. Bradley stopped.

"I failed you, Colonel Smith. I'm sorry."

"Failed me? Of course you didn't."

"I didn't bring her home."

Smith looked pained.

"That wasn't her home, we both know that. I just wanted her... out of danger?"

If it was a plea, Bradley chose to ignore it.

"She wasn't selling new identities to Nazis, was she?"

"One or two to friends, perhaps. The main cache of blank IDs came over here with Jones, after the surrender. You helped deliver them."

The suitcase at the handover. But why?

"They were marked," Smith said. "We've been picking up all sorts of interesting people who bought them from Buček's partisans."

"And the ones the Reds picked up led them back to Buček..."

"Well, not even Brian could hand the whole thing to SMERSh on a plate. Once he'd whetted their appetites, he could wait for them to ask him to fill in the blanks."

"So he didn't tell Buček to finish her off that day?"

Smith seemed genuinely horrified.

"Heavens no! He told Buček to spare her. Ordered him, more or less. Buček thought he was from SMERSh. So did Mila, of course."

Bradley remembered the men who had dragged her, wounded, frightened, from the grass. Their faces still inhabited his nightmares and always would. Jones might have persuaded their leader to spare her life but he had left her there with those men. A nice, professional touch. Did Smith know about that?

"You people," he said. "Reckon it was worth it?"

"To save this country? No." The harmless-looking gentleman gestured carelessly with his umbrella. Bradley suspected he could have described every Russian in the square in minute detail, along with their precise links to each particular arm of the secret police. "All we've done, I fear, is delay the inevitable. Regardless of men like Novák, the Moscow-lookers will take over one day. As the limitations of your cover story probably revealed to you, the Russian head of UNRRA here is working with the new Minister of Information to ensure the entire population believes the aid is coming from the east. Already they believe they were liberated exclusively by the Red Army."

"So what was it for? When it all flared up I thought it was about avoiding another confrontation. Then I get to the US hospital in Marienbad and it turns out Patton's been reassigned. His successors weren't about to start anything." Bradley shook his head in disgust. "For a while you even had me thinking Dresden was some kind of warning to the Reds, until I checked and found they were the ones who asked us to do it."

Smith sighed.

"You've been speaking to Sloane. I'd have thought you'd have gathered by now that he trades in a selective sort of honesty. Of course the Americans won't say Dresden was a warning to Stalin. That's what the second atom bomb on Nagasaki was for."

Bradley looked at him. The man wore the smile of a

tolerant uncle.

"There is going to be a war with the Soviets, Bradley, it's inevitable. But it's going to be a new sort of war. The bomb has changed everything. What you saw at Joachimsthal was the two sides establishing the rules. It was a negotiation – a trade-off."

"SMERSh for Lossner."

"If you like. We agreed to help them root out this dangerous element who weren't going to play to the new rules. In return they agreed to sacrifice Professor Lossner. We really couldn't let him go east."

So Jones had arranged an accident and the others had turned a blind eye. Bradley supposed he ought to be relieved it hadn't been Mila's doing. But it was hard to think like that.

"Your guy did a good job covering for your agent, up in the mountains."

"Upon the mountains," Smith repeated wistfully. "Yes. No one knew what the Czechs and Russians were going to make of her. Best for her to disappear. But she's not my agent anymore."

"She's nobody's agent anymore," Bradley reminded him. Feeling sorry for the older man, he added: "She's still your wife."

"Well..."

"Are you looking for her?"

Neither could meet the other's eye.

"Are you?"

What could he say? It would not have taken an intelligence chief to discover he had been sitting at that pavement café for a week now, ever since the Czechs had granted his request for convalescent leave from the hospital in Marienbad. And that was even supposing this encounter was a coincidence.

"Sure I am," he said. "Got something to return to her."

He took out the gold lighter and knew from the glint in Smith's eye that he'd recognised it. In surprise, he saw the glint was an actual tear.

"What did the inscription say?" he asked, handing it over. Smith smoothed a thumb across the blank panel.

"*For a pilgrim soul,*" he said. "I shouldn't have let her take it – British make and all. We settled on removing the inscription. Mila said that didn't matter, she'd always remember. May I ask where she lost it?"

"She left it with another pilgrim soul," Bradley said.

And for another pilgrim, he thought.

To give the old man some privacy he stepped aside, gazing back at the Town Hall. The sinking sun threw long shadows towards him, the shadows of the spire-less tower and the burned-out body of the hall. Rough luck to have burned, when so much of the square had survived the German assault on the barricades. Rougher still when you considered what had been in there.

Seven nights ago, still searching, he had returned to the nightclub Krypta and found someone who had known her in the old days. Kovály. A fat man in a bad wig with a heap of good connections. One of those connections had put him in touch with Josef Voda's son.

And so, on another night, in another cellar, he had finally chased down the real MERCURY circuit. Along with Vojtěch, there was an old guy who turned out to be Voda's comrade Ludvík. They had been held by the Russians then unaccountably released. Vojtěch's girlfriend was there also, looking about fourteen, and a pair of brothers, one with a fearsome stammer. In a mixture of his bad German and their bad English he was able to tell them how Josef Voda had died, killing Nazis, saving the Nightingale.

What he couldn't do was tell them what had happened to her. And he had wondered how much they weren't telling him.

But one question they had answered. He had no way of knowing if it was common knowledge or the product of their own investigations. The records of the *Lebensborn* programme in the Protectorate – if someone had filed the details of an adoption, where would that have been held?

They looked glum as they told him. Was it for real?

With all the other records, of course. Here in Prague, in the old Town Hall.

Smith's voice, behind him:

"I wanted to say a better good-bye."

Bradley wondered if he meant the inscription, then realised it was the answer to his question *are you looking for her?*

Me too, he thought. Better than whatever it was I said.

For the first time since the mountains, he found himself talking to her again.

Did you understand what I was saying to you then? About the cover. How I'd seen after the explosion that the fuse had ignited and the cover on the mineshaft must have blown? And if that was where you went when you followed Jones to the summit, did you manage to hide out down there until everyone had gone?

Did you manage it, Mila, with a broken arm and a dozen other injuries? Did you make it off the mountain?

Have you been here already, on your quest, your pilgrimage? Have you slipped through my fingers again?

Or are you coming – this evening – tonight?

Got room for another pilgrim?

AFTERWORD

I hope you enjoyed The Borodino Sacrifice! I would love to hear what you thought of it, so please do consider leaving a review on Amazon. You can also get in touch for news of Mila and Bradley's next adventure – or even an exclusive preview – at www.bypaulphillips.com/chasing-mercury.html

A NOTE ON HISTORICAL ACCURACY

The Borodino Sacrifice is a work of fiction that draws speculative links between documented events, such as MI6/SOE-assisted resistance operations in occupied Czechoslovakia, the Nazi atomic programme and the espionage-enabled BORODINO project in the Soviet Union.

In incorporating 'factual' context like this, my guiding principle has been to furnish my characters only with the knowledge that they might plausibly have had at the time, even if this does not correspond with what we currently understand to be the historical facts.

I am indebted to many texts and their authors and publishers for my research into the latter – too many to name here – as well as to the patience, generosity and support of all those who helped me discover my story, in England, France, Germany and the Czech Republic.

Printed in Great Britain
by Amazon